MASKS OF MORALITY

BY T.L. MUMLEY

Copyright © 2017 by Terri Lynn Sullivan

This novel is a heavily fictionalized story loosely based on the author's experiences. All characters, organizations, events and dialogue are either products of the author's imagination or are used fictitiously. Although some characters were inspired by real people, no characters are true representation of such. While the story and plot are rooted in the realm of reality, it is fiction based on the reality of the author's creation.

Cover Art Copyright © 2017 by Yocla Designs
Editor: Chansonette Buck

All rights reserved. No part of this book may be used or reproduced by any means, graphic, electronic, or mechanical, including photocopying, recording, taping or by any information storage retrieval system without the written permission of the publisher except in the case of brief quotations embodied in critical articles and reviews.

Published in the United States of America

The cataloging-in-publication data is on file with the Library of Congress. Registration Number: TXu 2-045-032.

ISBN: 9780692883020

AUTHOR'S NOTE

There are many books about a world presumed not yet existent, about a society that has become highly undesirable or fear-provoking by normalizing violence as a way of life. I see a connection with a message of social justice. The writer is often trying to illuminate a path we hope humanity does not take. Or reflect a path humanity has already taken.

I was inspired to write this book by a number of things. Bringing a beautiful child into a politically chaotic world my top motivator. When my son was three, I read Meg Wolitzer's *The Ten Year Nap* and was convinced I had to write about the contemporary dilemmas of upper middle-class women tempted to stop working after having children. At the time, I wondered if it could be me taking a ten-year hiatus from my lucrative high tech marketing career. Yet as I started to write while trying to find my place to contribute making this world a better place for my child's sake---that's exactly what happened.

MASKS OF MORALITY is a work of realistic fiction. Its setting is factual, and the characters, although invented by me, react in realistic ways to real-life situations. I pull on personal experience having worked for a multinational high-tech corporation in Silicon Valley. Although not anti-corporate, I am against corporate abusive practices. I connect what may appear as two opposing forces; corporatism and perpetual global war, which in actuality collide straight on.

Within my personal journey to enlightenment, I began to see modern America as the society I mention above. Those dystopian future novels and movies, reflected back as a mirror into our own culture today. I seek to portray the political sphere Generation Z, specifically those born close post 9/11, are imposed upon with each day.

If my story brings hours of entertainment, I am happy. If it also awakens the mind and soul, I will have achieved my purpose. If it pisses some people off, all the better. Positive change never came without divergent thoughts. Are you still wearing that social mask?

I hope you enjoy my political twister and find among the pages your own personal journey of social conscience.

Acknowledgements

To Chansonette Buck, my editor, thank you for all the time, expertise and advice. You really do rock, girl!

To my new friends at the Berkeley Writer's Circle. You know who you are! Thank you for your listening, wisdom and honest feedback. I only wish I had found such collective support before going nuts writing in isolation.

To all my friends who dared to bravely go where many would not: reading my manuscript and offering critiques. So happy we remain friends through that adventure!

To my family, Tommy and Ryan. Thank you for putting up with me. For believing in me. For seeing the story in my heart shout it's way to voice on paper. For that, I am forever grateful.

Quotation

"The terrible immoralities are the cunning ones hiding behind masks of morality, such as exploiting people while pretending to help them."

-Vermon Howard

Prologue

The Corporate Mask,
Before the Unveiling, April 1994

"Oh, shit!" Caryssa wailed, causing more than a few heads to turn. "My briefcase!"

Her emotions on fire with the biggest move of a lifetime, Caryssa Flynn had not slept a wink, then rushed off to the airport. She had worked in zombie mode for weeks of twelve-hour days on that presentation. And there it sat. In the front seat of her friend's car as it departed Logan Airport.

Standing in line, she studied the people. A scattering of families with young children. Professionals on business trips. Business people wearing *their* professionalism like good corporate citizens. No use of profanity, no forgetting their briefcases.

Caryssa reminded herself PowerPoints could be emailed. Her line began moving. She looked down to grab her carry-on. *Double shit!* She had on two different shoes. One black pump, one brown. A commercial clown.

She entered the first class cabin and stowed her carry-on, stretching out in the beautifully contoured two-tone butter-soft leather seat.

A forty-something woman sporting a Kate Spade bag and designer sunglasses sat next to her. She had a simple elegance and a polite smile. "Hello!"

Great. This lady wants to talk, and I want to sleep. Caryssa simply smiled.

They were served an award-winning pre-departure champagne, creamy smooth with almond and orange notes. *Maybe if I just put my earphones on,* Caryssa hoped, *my seatmate will get the message.*

"So... I'm Catherine. Where are you going, or coming from?"

Over the next hour their conversation touched on careers, family, belief in God, and much more. It was wonderful and exhausting, all starting with a simple question travelers ask each other. She did not mention her one-way ticket to San Jose.

Eventually, Caryssa fell asleep, too drained for further airplane talk. When she awoke, she was startled to find it was two hours later. Her champagne flute appeared on the table, looking as refreshed as she did after a much needed nap.

A news headline was flashing on the inflight entertainment screen. The words were a blur to her. Meaningless words. *"Operation Desert Storm"*—with its deep moral failures and long-term plan to destroy Middle Eastern nationalism—were worlds away. This flight was taking her to the main headquarters of the much-heralded super-information highway. There, she would help to create a global virtual reality.

She took another sip of the sparkling wine, placing the long stemmed flute back on the table. The jet was gliding like a swan on an unruffled lake. She chuckled at having been moved to first class on her employer's request. *Life is good!*

Suddenly the aircraft dipped, pitched, and dropped several feet, the champagne flute toppling onto her lap. *I'll never make it!* The thought quickly vanished as she remembered this was the norm flying over the Rockies. Nothing could quench her excitement anyway, despite the sensation she wet her pants as the bubbly soaked into her clothes.

As soon as the flight was calm, the attendant gave her a refill, and her excitement increased with the buzz of the bubbly. *Another promotion!* Her second in the three years she had been with Unabridged Networks.

This particular promotion was more than a step up, it was a job security move. She could still hear the warning in her manager's voice: *"You can either accept the transfer across the country, or be part of the layoffs in the reorganization."* His face contorted into a sneer.

Unabridged Networks was the fastest growing high tech company in America. And it was in a position to become the number one computer networking company in the world. If an employee were willing to be as flexible as possible—perhaps change everything about her current life, go completely out on a limb, give away her first born child—she just might make it to the top.

For Caryssa, it was worth it. She'd do whatever it took to be successful, including play the corporate game. This time she had been moved clear across the chess board—across the continent. An instant promotion to queen, working closely with the king, among the knights, bishops, and big rooks. And she was sure the game would go on with her moving into ever more strategic positions, checkmate after checkmate.

She sipped and basked in the glow of her promising future. Her career was the essence of who she was becoming. Her identity. And she liked it this way. "This is who I am," she reflected with deep satisfaction.

The excitement was mixed with trepidation. The job promotion was not what frightened her. What frightened her was the immense change involved. It would lift her out of her comfort zone. It would drop her three thousand miles from home, far from everyone and everything she knew and loved. It would drop her in Silicon Valley—home of the super-wealthy, land of technology toys, where she knew nobody. Techy geeks lurking behind palm trees.

Caryssa was terrified and excited at the same time. It felt like riding a rollercoaster. When two Cali managers flew into Boston to scope her out…it was flattering. It was stimulating. It was the scariest thing she had ever embarked on in all her thirty-four years.

Her employer made it all so inviting. A sexy red convertible to use while her car was being shipped to California. Flying her out first class. Big raise. Shipping all her belongings. Throwing in an extra five grand for incidentals. Putting her in a fancy hotel until her furniture and car arrived. All on corporate coin.

So there she sat in first class splendor, heading across America. Then, suddenly, another memory: *"We are not getting any younger Caryssa, remember your roots."* Her mom's words sent a chill through her. She did not even realize tears were spilling from her eyes.

Catherine leaned over, and spoke softly. "Is there something you hadn't shared with me? Did you just lose a loved one, dear? Or did the turbulence scare you?"

Caryssa realized she was visibly trembling. "Oh, neither, I got a job promotion and I'm moving my entire life out West with it."

Her seatmate looked into Caryssa's eyes knowingly. She nodded. "Well, that's sort of like losing many loved ones, isn't it, dear? That can cause internal turbulence! I know, been there, done that. My company has moved me across the globe a few times. But it works out in the end."

Encouraged by these words, Caryssa responded to her mother on the inside: I *need* to do this. It's *my* career! And it's *my* life! It's all good! She was climbing the corporate ladder. She was fighting her own personal fight. She was determined to succeed and her reward would be lots and lots of money. She was doing the right thing.

Reassured, Caryssa let her worries drain away. From that moment until they landed in San Jose, whenever the flight attendant brought her something, she took it. Every single salted nut. Every cookie. The throwaway slippers, the dark chocolates, the steaming washcloth. *I deserve this. I earned it. And there will be more where this came from.*

Her seatmate sensed Caryssa's new resolve, smiled, and lifted her own flute. "Well, here's a toast to your promotion and new adventure!"

As the plane began to descend and the captain came on the intercom with instructions to prepare for landing, the two women in first class clinked glasses, and sipped.

* * *

Caryssa instantly fell in love with the festive, foodie culture of the San Francisco Bay Area. Every day her passion for experiencing all things beautiful and pleasing was satisfied in some way.

One of the first things she observed about California was the therapeutic, cleansing, fresh scent of the eucalyptus trees. Silicon Valley culture combined high ambition with mellowness—something she had never encountered.

If she didn't stay in the office way past five, she would inevitably turn her laptop on at home. She kept her cell phone on at all times in case sales reps called her. *Technology is grand!* Enabling us to remain perpetually connected to where the coin comes from!

She thrived on this fast-paced energy--- It didn't take her long to be promoted again, and yet again--- to Senior Marketing Analyst. This was promotion number four within seven years with Unabridged Networks. And the money, prestige, and perks were well worth it.

Six years after moving to California, Caryssa left the big corporate world and tried out a few tech-startups. She moved to the East Bay and married her best friend and love, George.

Caryssa loved high tech despite the moral issues she was discovering as she opened herself to new ways of seeing. It was in her blood, this business of digital revolution. But she longed to incorporate a culture of care rather than a mere culture of coin.

When the third tech startup she worked for failed to get VC funding the entire marketing department was laid off. She and George traveled to London, South of France, and Paris. They went through Monaco to see Monte Carlo, to Antibes, and to Nice.

While in Paris, they conceived a child. Caryssa had no idea bringing a child into the world in her forties was about to change her life…forever.

But she would soon find out.

Chapter One

2008

If she had recognized what she sees now, would she have been so gung-ho to make it to the top?

Caryssa asked George "Would I have participated at all?"

"You are getting obsessed like a demon again, let it go already." George was staring robotically at the TV screen.

"Oh *come on*! I saw firsthand while working Boston's tech corridor and Silicon Valley how we sold our high tech souls to Israel and beyond! It's all about the money monster!" She glanced out her living room window.

The blood red sun streaked beams of orange across the sky, stretching from the city past Mount Tamalpais. The rays aligned over Alcatraz and combined with the reflection off the water, creating that quintessential bay area soft mystical twilight.

A fast approaching fog bank drifted across the Golden Gate Bridge, like fingers skipping over the water. The sun, hanging like a ball below a palm tree in the distance, was swallowed whole by fog, which moved fast, faster, and faster, as if alive.

Caryssa Flynn stood at her living room window. Within minutes, her entire view became a blanket of fog quickly moving toward the hills where she lived. Caryssa's life seemed to have moved in matching bizarre and swift fashion.

She had gone from cut-throat high tech marketing to frenetically devoted motherhood, from a workaholic gregarious party girl to a happy homebody. And home had clearly evolved to be California.

The San Francisco Bay Area with its cultural diversity and open, progressive-yet- pragmatic minds. It's rolling hills and relaxed attitudes. Then after the fog recedes, its ever present golden sunlight. The fresh air, like the flavor of fresh green beans picked from the garden, infused with eucalyptus and redwoods.

"You've been reading too many sci-fi's, dear." George's voice was soft and flowed to her ears, calming her spirits. She knew he shared her perspective in all this, and was just razzing her.

She laughed, throwing her arms up into the air. "Those *'sci-fi's'* are based on today's political reality! Now, a combo of robots and software are taking over my own marketing profession! How could I have foreseen this while choosing to stay home to raise my kid?"

Sipping a cup of Bengal Spice tea, waiting for the oven to signal it was preheated so she could slip some wild-caught salmon in to bake, she found herself almost shocked: had she really been living on the west coast for over fourteen years?

Funny, how one promotion can change a person's life. Computer technology was at the foundation of her move. Ironically, the same technology now threatening to destroy her prospects for work after having taken time off to raise Tyler.

The tech dinosaur syndrome was slowly kicking in. And her recent attempts to land a worthwhile job in her field indicated she just might be becoming a Brontosaurus.

George's eyes never left the TV screen, each hand working a remote "I'm sure glad for the internet. I mean…after all, internet technology brought you to the west coast, we never would have met without it!"

Visions of taking brutal measures to get that next promotion during her peak career days flashed before Caryssa's eyes. Silicon Valley! *What can she say?* It's deep in her heart. Yet she has learned so much since then.

"Yup, true, but what a shocker for me to learn the internet itself had been pioneered by certain corporate, government and academic agencies collaborating to further our nation's techno-military madness!" Her biggest fear in life.

She sighed as the oven timer dinged and she heard Tyler come laughing in the back door from pre-dinner soccer practice. What an amusing twist for a woman who now, at forty-eight, can't seem to get back to her professional career. With her deep devotion to her son, so rich and rewarding.

"Don't blame the internet! The life-altering event for you came with motherhood in your forties. Suddenly, you were obsessed with changing the world!" George's focus switched from TV screen to Caryssa's eyes.

"Blame the intern...*You just don't get it!* My beloved career in that high paying high tech world may have helped carve a path to endless war!" Caryssa set her cup on the kitchen island and reached for the tray of salmon. "Why didn't anybody warn me?" George remained silent.

"What's that, Mom?" Tyler asked from behind a laptop, now glued to his headset and some digital Avatars. "Were you talking to me?"

"See that! I helped bring this digital maze to yours truly, so your son can zone out in cyberspace! Society is drowning in technology!"

* * *

The next morning, after George had left for work and she had dropped Tyler off at school, Caryssa continued her musing, this time over a second cup of coffee. It's true she found it hard to imagine choosing any job over the opportunity to experience her own child's hopeful, open soul. Her favorite thing to do now on a Saturday night is curling up on the couch with her guys, chomping some popcorn with a good family movie. Simple love.

Sitting in her back garden in the morning sun, she gazed over the panoramic view from her home. She could see all the way from downtown Oakland to Mount Tamalpais, the Bay Bridge, San Francisco, Alcatraz, the Golden Gate Bridge, over the glorious blue-green bay. *Spectacular.*

She loved the beautiful house she had bought with George. A four bedroom, two bath retro gem tucked in the hills, with its lovely garden and spectacular scenery. All she ever needed to feel centered was to stop and glance out her window, or sit in her back yard facing the bay. Feel the breeze on her face, smell the fresh air and flowers.

Caryssa leaned into her pink jasmine of the vine, falling into its immense sweetness, drowning in its bright happiness. Listening to her wind chimes singing in the gentle breeze. She needed this so much right now. It was always a mistake to watch the news, and unfortunately she hadn't been able to avoid it at the gym. Moments like this were her refuge. Nature kept her more grounded in reality than the news ever could.

Those oppressive images stayed with her. Young soldiers indoctrinated into horrific actions. Made worse by her recognition that most of it is the product of collusion between global corporate America and power-hungry politicians.

Honestly, they might as well just make all their headlines read *"Breaking News! Dark Corners of Corporate Greed Causing Global Death and Destruction!"* That would pretty much cover everything she saw on the news or read in the papers. Repetitive fear-induced recordings.

She shuddered inside. The war-owned mass-media does so much to deceive the public. Her former self would *never* have believed it. But those eager beaver reporters wear the same deceitful masks of goodness politicians do, their words paid for by the same shady characters within the iron triangle.

She gazed out at her view, so therapeutic. It always kept her from getting too fixated on the downright evil in political and media culture. The dark evil that would just assume push an innocent immigrant child off the borders of this nation, merely due to being "undocumented."

How had someone once so self-absorbed and tech-obsessed become so philanthropic, open, and mindful? How had someone once so politically naïve, other than corporate politics--- become so clear about how our society was being run and for what global purposes?

Caryssa knew the answer. He was now nearly forty-eight inches tall weighing forty-seven pounds. Her boy, her joy, *her life.* Bringing that beautiful boy into the world later in life had pushed her to develop a social conscience, committed to volunteer community work on a weekly basis for more than half a decade.

The paradox was that Caryssa had always put her heart and soul into everything she did. As a technical marketing wizard on the rise before her marriage, she had held nothing back. And that was still true, but now she did it with parenting and volunteer work.

"You can't do anything half-assed, can you?" her girlfriend Samantha recently commented.

How Caryssa had grown to admire and love her friend. She met Sam and Jim Owens years ago when she had first arrived in California. They were part of her Tahoe ski pal group.

"Got that right, girlfriend" she replied. "But you know, during my ten-second career as VP Marketing for one tech start-up? I remember thinking *what the hell am I doing here. I want to start a family!* I guess it was a blessing in disguise when they didn't get their VC funding."

"I'll say. Wasn't that when you guys went on your amazing European trip and made a beautiful baby in the City of Lights?"

"Oh, yes!" Caryssa had laughed. "That was sheer bliss. The most stressful decisions we had were vin blanc or vin rouge today? This pâté or fromage? A baguette with my café au lait? Shall we stop at Le Couture Café or continue walking? Heaven. Just heaven!"

In the present moment, a reminder beeper went off in Caryssa's kitchen. She glanced at her watch. Only an hour and a half left and then she had to go pick Tyler up from school, and take him to baseball practice.

But really…what *had* happened to her career? Mommyhood took it over before she had even left it. The last professional marketing position she'd held had been over five years ago, while she was pregnant. She had still been a hot commodity then. They had hired her on the spot right after she got back from Europe.

She had purposely taken the position in a slower-paced industry at a fifty thousand dollar cut in salary, assuming it would be less stressful while she tried to start a family. She asked to work part time during the last two months of her term, petrified that because she was pregnant at forty-two she could go into pre-term labor. Human Resources said she would need a letter from her doctor confirming what her "hardship" was, and would still be expected to carry a full-time workload.

What a rude awakening.

"You've got to be kidding me!" a colleague she had befriended snorted when they talked about it over lunch. "Management ought to be utterly ashamed of their lack of empathy for new parents! There should be a law about this!"

Her OB-Gyn choked back disgust one day when Caryssa told her about the note and the workload her employer expected in her final trimester. "You know, Europe has family-friendly policies, unlike here in the States. For one thing, stay-at-home parents are paid for taking care of their children. It's recognized as having a high level of cultural and economic value to society."

"What!! They're *paid* for staying home with their kids?!" Caryssa slipped her feet into the stirrups and scooched forward so her doctor could examine her.

"Yup," Dr. Madell responded. "It may only be a small stipend, some two to three hundred dollars or so a month. But it's something! Good full-time parents raise their kids to be happy, well-adjusted citizens rather than the potentially lost souls that can result from lack of parental involvement. That's a huge accomplishment, and so beneficial to society. Do you know, I've read that if all that a stay-at-home parent does is added in terms of individual paid for jobs—acting as the kids' chauffeur to and from school, personal cooks, counselors, tutors, activity planners, soccer coaches and so on—they would make at least three hundred fifty to five hundred thousand a year?"

"Really!" Caryssa's eyes wide.

"Yup," Dr. Madell removed her gloves and washed her hands. "More than I make!"

Now, in the past five years since giving birth, Caryssa had not taken a job outside the home. Especially after the introduction she'd had to a system clearly failing one of its most critical resources—*mothers*. So often she would dress for an interview, wow them, be invited back for more interviews, and get an offer, only to discover the company was not willing to provide the flexibility needed to remain active in her son's life.

She found herself constantly torn between the pull to contribute to Tyler's future financially, and wanting to be there for him during these early years. To live in the moment, soak in every milestone of her precious child.

As a mom, Caryssa wanted to make the most of it while her son was young and still wanted to hug her and sit on her knee and snuggle. Or when he was an early teen, going through all those adolescent pains. She knew he needed her and would need her for some time to come.

At the same time, she'd go over their investments, what it cost to live even modestly in the bay area. What about when Tyler was ready for college? Costs were rising astronomically year by year. How would she and George be able to afford college tuition if she hadn't been working right along with him during Tyler's younger years? *Why did she give up her six-figure income of the 90's?*

But that was then, this is now. It came to what seemed like untenable options. She could always sell her house if she had to…or her soul.

Caryssa took several deep cleansing breaths of the eucalyptus- and jasmine-scented air. And then she stretched out for her daily jog.

While jogging, she passed by a neighbor who lived on the private golf course on her street. She was working in her garden. The house would undoubtedly sell for at least two or three million.

"Wow, what an incredible house and garden you have!" Caryssa called out to her in passing. She was happy, her blond ponytail waving in the California sunshine as her feet moved rhythmically to Sheryl Crow singing "All I wanna do…is have some fun…and I gotta feeling I'm not the only one…"

"Thank you," her neighbor replied. "I seem to have more time on my hands these days to pour into my yard work."

Caryssa began jogging in place. "Well, you must have a landscaper. I mean, you don't do all this yourself do you?" The yard had at least thirty different types of exotic flowers, succulents, and palms, plus waterfalls, rocks, and bird baths.

"Oh, by all means yes, we have someone do this." The neighbor swept her arm in an arc to reflect the impressive array of horticulture. "But I do regular weeding in between."

Caryssa stopped jogging in place, just stood there. She found herself in the moment. The sun on her face felt good. And talking with this woman, mysteriously profound. She had that feeling she gets when she is going to find herself inspired or guided by a loving unseen hand.

"You are an inspiration to us all!" Caryssa's eyes glazed over the vast garden. "I should make more time to do my gardening as a stay-at-home mom. But I get so busy with playdates, volunteer work at my son's school and sports teams, supervising homework, then dinner, bath, reading, getting the kid to bed…not to mention cooking, cleaning, shopping, bills.…"

She trailed off for a moment, aware that her neighbor was listening intently to her and nodding, her eyes full of empathy. "You know…the day just…gets away from me…Gosh, I work longer hours now than I did as a marketing professional in Silicon Valley!"

"How old are your children?" the perfect gardener with the perfect house asked.

"Oh, I have just one. He's five, in kindergarten."

"Ah…that's a fun age. And lots of work. My name is Alexandra Myers, by the way."

After Caryssa introduced herself, Alexandra put aside the spade, and looked straight into her eyes. "Actually, *you* are the one who is an inspiration to us all." Alexandra fretfully lifted the spade again. "All this?" she gestured behind her at her magnificent property. "All this is ultimately just a garden and a house. Material objects come and go. So does wealth. Trust me on that. *You* are the one making the most meaningful investment anyone could possibly make in a lifetime."

Alexandra paused for a moment looking at her feet. When she spoke again her voice was soft. "If I could do the crucial parenting years over again, I'd do things so differently." She gestured again at her mini-mansion. "This is what I have to show for all my hard work. A piece of property. We have several pieces of property for that matter."

She turned her gaze back to Caryssa. "Before I tell you what I'm about to tell you, I want you to know I realize there are cases where kids with devoted parents can still go astray. But…I believe that the chances are far less likely for that to happen with parents who take the time—I mean really take the time—to focus on their children, pay attention to their lives."

Caryssa nodded. She was all ears.

"My son is nineteen now," Alexandra continued. "And he's in rehab. Oh…we thought we were doing everything right. He was sporty and ambitious, accepted into Stanford and Harvard before he was done with his senior year of high school. Really shined in soccer and baseball. He was well liked, outgoing." She paused.

"The first thing that happened was he got burnt out on sports, didn't want to play anymore. He injured his arm pitching ball. Our family doctor prescribed pain killers. OxyContin. He was seventeen. At first he was fine. He just took it for pain. But you know how these things can go. Even a well-adjusted seventeen-year-old isn't a match for a drug like that. We were both so busy with work. We just…you know…didn't… notice. And then? Then it was too late. The drug had him."

Caryssa's heart went out to this mother who was sharing her deepest pain. She reached out and laid her hand on Alexandra's shoulder, found her gentle voice. "But it sounds like you were good parents. You gave him the best of everything."

"We gave him everything but the most critical thing a parent can give their child." Alexandra turned away to gather her composure, pulling a weed from a beautiful bird of paradise in full bloom. She whispered the next word softly. *"Time."*

After a few moments of silence, she straightened her shoulders, turned back to Caryssa more composed, and continued. "You see, adolescence is a lot like the toddler years. Remember when you were right there when your child learned to walk? He'd lose his balance and you'd be there to catch him and steady him so he could keep going? And if you didn't get to him in time sometimes he'd find a table or chair leg to steady himself with?"

Caryssa's eyes filled up with tears, her hands were shaking.

"Well, the same thing happens with teens. Teens need their parents' attention and guidance during their time of exploration. Without it they might find something else to hold onto, just like when they were toddlers. The difference is that teens think they know everything and they feel invulnerable. And they are at the age of experimentation. So what they find to hold onto might not be good for them."

Caryssa just nodded again, sensing this woman needed to talk.

"Oh…there were plenty of times Jake came to us to talk, but our response was always 'not now, we're in the middle of a huge case.' You see…we own a legal firm together, prosecuting attorneys for thirty years. When Jake was born we truly intended to put him first. But somewhere along the way we got caught in the momentum of our own success. We forgot that the most important tool to help our child grow is simply listening. We grew our wealth. But we failed our child."

Alexandra's quivering smile was accompanied by a tear slowly making its way down her cheek.

"Everything seemed fine. He had lots of friends, although I never took the time to get to know them. The boom fell when he got early admission to Harvard. He flew east to spend the summer getting acquainted with the area and participating in summer orientation programs. I guess he was still using OxyContin then. He had an active prescription for his shoulder. But some of the kids he met on campus introduced him to cocaine and heroin. That was it.

"He came back to see us before the semester started so we could have a big party with family and friends for him, and he was a stranger. We barely recognized him as the happy kid who had waved to us from the security line when we saw him off. He was hostile and angry. He blamed us for everything. He even said he hated how we made a living, and we had a lot to answer for. We were part of the problem, not the solution. He ended with claiming our law business helped America to put more people in prison than any other nation in the world!"

Caryssa kept her agreement with Jake regarding the American for-profit prison system to herself. Since prisons had been privatized, it had become "good business" to put innocent kids in cages for normal things like merely trying pot. Not to mention that the vastly high proportion of prisoners were young African American males, a source of slave labor for multinational corporations—where the inmates worked long hours for pennies an hour to make many of the consumer goods Americans bought every day without ever questioning where they came from.

Normally outspoken about such things, Caryssa bit her tongue. Hasn't this woman with the home that put House & Garden to shame been through enough tragedy? No need to fan the flames and give her more to beat herself about. She glanced at her watch. T-ball practice would start in half an hour. She had to get Tyler after jogging home. She wanted to stop and smell the roses, pick wildflowers along the way to place in her lovely kitchen.

Sensing Caryssa's shift in attention, Alexandra said "Oh, why am I telling you all this? Just keep on doing what you're doing, dear…and don't stop when he is a teenager. That's when they need you to listen, talk, know who their friends are, what they're doing on the internet, where they are—"

"Thanks for all the advice Alexandra!" Caryssa chimed in as she turned back down the hill towards her house. "I'm sure once your son gets out of rehab he will get right back on track."

Alexandra's reply stopped Caryssa dead in her tracks.

"No dear, I'm afraid not. You see, using those drugs even once can cause nerve damage. They're running more tests. We're hoping and praying for the best, but the bottom line is, he may never be the same."

Caryssa found herself crying uncontrollably as she finished her run. God. Life was just so fragile. Anything could happen.

She circled back to the comfort and beauty of her own garden, and stretched out her runner's calves. Then grabbed the coffee cup she left out, bringing it into the house before leaving to pick up her son. She heard Alexandra's message echoing in her heart.

"Take the time, not just on weekends, to focus on your child, to pay attention to his life."

* * *

That evening preparing supper, Caryssa remembered another moment, this one at Tyler's science fair. She had glanced at a mouse pad that read "100 years from now…it will not matter what your bank account was, what sort of house you live in, or what kind of car you drive. But the world may be a much better place because you were important in the life of a child." Like her neighbor with the perfect house and garden, that mouse pad had sent a deep and abiding message to her mother's soul.

Caryssa's thoughts came back to cooking and Tyler. "Off the computer now Tyler, and please wash your hands for dinner!"

And here was another irony for her to consider as she washed green beans in the sink and placed them in the colander to drain. For someone with a fast-track career history in computer technology helping to shape today's digital revolution, Caryssa had developed a contradictory attitude about what the digital age is imposing on kids.

She once had the industry hard-wired into her circuits, enthusiastically absorbed into the wired world of Silicon Valley. Now, her focus was on having less "toys" revolving around electronics. Too much technology. What alarmed her the most were the violent video games. First-shooter games had been developed by the military to desensitize people to killing. Now they were being sold to kids, and the end result was the same.

Today's tech-savvy generation was being steered away from the roots of humankind. They were continuously bombarded with stimuli outside of human companionship. Texting rather than talking. Facebooking rather than face talking. Out of touch with reality, obsessed with virtual reality. The young creating their own virtual habitat rather than playing in the woods.

Technology was advancing so fast and was such an integral part of our world. What would it be like when Tyler's a teen? It struck Caryssa as bittersweet, how she had so eagerly come to California to help bring this digital economy to the world. Now, she sees how the internet can hurt kids. Now, she worries about its effect on her own son.

Tyler, at age five, simply turns the computer on, types in his chosen address, and starts playing. At least at this point it's all non-violent, educational websites. But even this is brought on by our evolving digital craze. Our unhealthy reliance on so much technology ultimately gives technology control of our lives. Where will it lead? Where will it end?

Technology, once the key to her cut-throat drive for success, was now her way of disciplining her son. "I mean it, Tyler, off the computer now or no computer time for a week. If I have to count to three…one, two…!"

"But it's *educational* Mom! It's ABCmouse.com and ABCya.com! It's FunBrain!"

Focused now in her kitchen, Caryssa laid out Tyler's turkey corn dog, fresh raw green beans, pasta, and milk, all organic. Her motivation for having shifted from self-regarding to self-sacrificing came waltzing into the kitchen.

"Mmm smells like my favorite, corn dog!" he exclaimed.

Caryssa turned to the recipe for the dinner she had chosen for George and herself—prawns in garlic butter over pasta, with a pesche alla crema.

She poured herself a glass of Merlot. George was the chef in the family, and she did not share his gift though she loved benefiting from it. Whenever he cooked it was a taste sensation worthy of a five-star restaurant. He would be expecting her usual not-so-spectacular dinner menu. But tonight she would surprise him with something special. Her cooking class was paying off.

As the smell of sautéing garlic and onion filled her senses, Caryssa glanced out her kitchen to the view. The sun had set, but a dramatic orange beam stretched across the sky and Golden Gate Bridge, backlighting the rolling hills and palms.

I live in a sea of wealth, she thought. To her, prosperity was an overall state of well-being. In a society which values commercialism and materialism, appreciation for the simple things in life can fall to the wayside. Caryssa kept a Gratitude Journal on her nightstand to make sure she always remembered to give thanks. Again this evening, as she did every night before bed, she would take a few minutes to record the simple pleasures of her day.

She reflected back on when she had first discovered she was pregnant. Her world would never look the same. As her pregnancy progressed, her thoughts began to coalesce into a clear picture. By the time she held her newborn son in her arms, all her hopes, fears, dreams, and wishes had changed. Now, everything happening in the world took on new meaning.

It simply wasn't about *her* anymore.

The astounding beauty surrounding her shined through. She could see a blooming flower, hear the calm of the birds chirping. *Children laughing!* Yet she could also see the danger her precious child could be exposed to. Dangers far beyond the time she accidently dropped him in the bathtub as an infant.

Each evening before putting the baby in his crib, she would hold him, rock him gently, and pray God would protect him from harm. Not just him, not just her sweet boy, but all the children. That the world she was noticing would change for the better. Maybe she would have a part to play in that.

One night during that cherished birth year of 2003, she was holding her baby and rocking him to sleep while watching appalling events unfold on TV news. Including the unwarranted US invasion of Iraq, billions wasted to start "homeland security" rather than build schools and infrastructure, the rush of resultant financial turmoil and cynical surveillance. It *frightened* her to watch these injustices to our own people under mock protection, while holding her tiny child. Even back then, she could see they were major impositions onto future generations. The propagation of an immoral police state war economy.

Then a revelation. Why couldn't her next job use internet platforms to make a better world?

This memory was interrupted by the sound of the front door opening, and Tyler's shout of glee and giggles that Daddy is home. He ran to the living room to hide under the coffee table. Well used to this daily routine, George dropped his briefcase on the couch, kissed Caryssa quickly, and then walked through the kitchen and into the living room, calling "Where is he? Where's my boy? Honey, have you seen Tyler? Is he in the closet? No…not there. Is he in the bedroom? Noooo not there. Hmmmm. Where could he be?!" Then, sounds of little feet pitter-pattering over the hardwood floor, and laughter, and a little voice calling "Oh no! The Daddy Monster found me! *Save* me mommy! SAVE me!"

Caryssa loved these moments, the daddy-son bonding and the strong love her "boys" had for each other. She glanced at her child. A more beautiful child could not possibly exist, so happy and open.

"Wow!" she heard George shout from the kitchen as she was running Tyler's bath. "What did you do, get gourmet take out?"

She could not suppress a contented laugh. "Nope! I made that with my own sweet hands!"

"It's amazing!" George mumbled with his mouth full. "How was your day?"

"It was all good" She told him the details of her lovely yet emotional reflections and experience. "I will never tire of jogging around our gorgeous neighborhood!" Tyler raced by them buck naked with an armful of bath toys, squealing with delight. She turned to her husband. "And how was your day?"

"Oh…productive." She knew he preferred not to talk much about work when he arrives home. More carefree laughter came from the bathroom as Tyler tossed boats into the bubbles. How easily entertained he is!

Caryssa walked to the bathroom door, glancing in at her son's joyful splashing. Her gaze turned to George. "Imagine, if our business, political, and religious leaders could see the world through a *child's eyes!* We might have peace rather than war, acceptance rather than prejudices, equality rather than greed, purification rather than pollution."

"How do you manage to connect slap-happy bathtime with *that?* He shook his head. "Hear that, Tyler? While I work saving the bay, your mom is trying to save the world again!"

"You guys are silly"! Tyler dunked underwater again. Then poked his head up smiling right at them.

"I know, honey, I know," Caryssa used a cup to rinse soap out of Tyler's hair. "Nobody can make me laugh the way your daddy does. Now, heave-ho out of the tub!"

Chapter Two

As the weatherman promised, Monday was warm and bright. The playdate group met at their usual spot. Eucalyptus Park was nearly empty, so the spacious playground seemed all the more welcome. Caryssa had grown to love the weekly playdates in this beautiful hillside park with its open grass, lush flowers and palm trees. Today's group included "Mr. Mom."

Stan Gafferty, a balding, blue-eyed forty-year-old biomedical engineer, was a regular. A father of two sons, Tyler age five and Kieran age three, he had opted to be a stay-at-home father. Although this was an increasingly trendy choice, the others looked at Stan with awe and respect.

"I am amazed at you Stan…to have risen above the stereotype—even prejudice—that one of the most important jobs in the world can only be done by women." Caryssa tossed this declaration out there while plopping down on the park bench.

Stan looked adoringly at his sons, adding playfully. "The most important job in the world, ya say? *Ha!* Where's my fat paycheck then? "

It often seemed to Caryssa his happiness was tinged with frustration at given up his career. "I'm blessed to be watching my kids grow and learn, though." He never took his eyes off his boys as they raced to the swing set. "Watching them reach milestones where they sometimes change into a completely different person based on new abilities or perceptions of their world."

The moms nodded. They knew exactly what he was talking about. And they knew the hard choice it had been to forego a career. It was that way for them too.

Stan's youngest started running towards the street, and he ran faster to grab him. Little Kieran squealed with delight as his dad gave him a piggy-back ride back to the group.

"So what does your wife do for work?" Caryssa couldn't help notice what a clone Kieran was of his dad.

"Stacy works full-time in regulatory affairs for a biopharmaceutical company. We met while at Cal." Stan let Kieran down from his aching back. "We just have this fear, *who would raise our kids*? We want to be there for them. And we don't know how much time I have…so it makes sense for Stacy to be the breadwinner. I mean, after losing a kidney to renal cancer, I am counting my blessings each day with my kids…"

The others just waited…listening.

Stan gazed at the carefree children "The cancer was traced to chemicals I handled on the job---I don't think from the lab. It was likely during research mode. But I'm not taking that chance again. *My kids need me*. My Tyler was barely two when it happened, yet he was afraid of seeing his daddy that way. I'll figure it out when the time comes. But for now, I just…I just want to be there for my two sons as much as I can be."

Caryssa nodded and laid a supportive hand on Stan's shoulder. She admired him so much for his decision. Immersing himself in the world of nappies and parent-teacher associations, volunteering at his son's school, sacrificing the ego-buffer of his high-paying job. Taking time out for parenthood. *Real time*, not just weekends or the few rushed moments one gets upon returning from the office each night.

It is the bravest, most commendable thing she had *ever* heard of a man doing. She knew what it took. She almost opened her mouth to tell him so, but then stopped. Stan was a manly man. She didn't want to embarrass him in front of the others. Maybe she'd find a more private way to let him know at some point.

"That squashes the theory only blue collar workers are exposed to toxic chemicals," Caryssa mentioned to Stan. "The techies in Silicon Valley can be exposed as well."

A haze of pink buds softened the stark mid-winter branches of a few trees. Camellias, hellebores, and winter hazel swayed with the gentle breeze and slits of sunshine streamed through a palm. The children's laughter graced their ears as they ran up and down the hill, slid down slides, and played in the sand box.

It was mid-February, with temperatures reaching seventy degrees. "The drought situation is nearing what it was in the seventies," declared Brenda, mother of twins Rebecca and Rowan, one of whom was in Tyler's class.

"I heard they may make it illegal to water anything outside—no lawns, pools, or washing cars," Stan was glancing out at the beautiful bay.

"Hello global warming, welcome to California!" Caryssa gestured with hands famed out to her sides. "Next, comes the "Pineapple Express" of extreme rain. We should make mud-sliding a new Olympic sport!"

"Global Warming has been going on forever," Brenda retorted. "Otherwise, we would still be living in the ice age with critters like woolly mammoths, saber tooth tigers, and giant sloths ruling the world. It's no big deal. It's nothing new. Just nature's way. And...of course, we wouldn't have Ice Age movies either—"

"Well...No..." Caryssa responded. "*Maybe...* partly. But it's happening at a shocking level now, and directly related to over-commercialization and industrialization. Our children may never have a chance to have their own children. Life on Earth for humans could come to an end before then."

"I'm not a climate change denier, if that's what you think, Caryss" Brenda seemed a bit put off. "And I know it's partly caused by humans...but—"

A young man walking through the park barked over his shoulder "Oh man, your elitist liberal attitude is what's killing my dad's dry cleaning business."

Caryssa pictured the traditional dry cleaners building down in the flats spewing toxic perc, and wondered if that was his old man's business.

The group grumbled their displeasure. Another dogmatic mind rejecting reality. Stan inserted his cancer surviving self into the argument "those lethal chemicals in the air are among what's killing *people.*"

"*Fuck you!*" the young man screamed back as he moved on.

Caryssa pointed as two huge trucks lurched by leaving a trail of exhaust fumes in their wake. "Everyone is harmed by global warming and pollution," She gestured at the surrounding landscape, "including right here in this gorgeous hillside community by the bay."

They followed her gesture from the park to the breathtaking view of the Golden Gate Bridge, the blue-green bay, and the sailboats out on this glorious day. The smell of flowers drifted into the fresh air. And knew in their hearts she was right.

Since it's all connected, she threw out in the open "Not too far a stretch, to believe that Earth may become uninhabitable for humans. What with all the destructive technology—we already have a virtual network with drone strikes controlled by some zealot pilot believing he or she is fighting *'terrorism'*. And the CIA has faced indictment over evidence of bloody video games orchestrated by these zombie drone pilots."

"You are obsessed with Earth becoming like Venus, aren't you, Caryssa?" retorted Brenda. "And besides that, what the heck do drone pilots have to do with global warming?"

Caryssa dropped Tyler's toy truck into the sand box. "Our drones, clones, and war zones have *lots* to do with the destruction of Earth. Do your homework, girlfriend! The American Empire is the most brutal empire in history. As far as I'm concerned, it's past time to unmask our state-sponsored terrorism!"

"Well, crap, if you're going to put it that way," snapped Brenda. "What about the Persian Empire? That was a pretty big one."

"Yes, I will put it 'that way.' Caryssa was grateful the kids were too far to hear. "We live in an Apocalypse Now of financial and political turmoil brought on by a depopulation agenda! It's a new historical moment with unprecedented technological advances. The Persian Empire merely led the way to future empires after the Middle East had *its* chance to rule the world. The American Empire--- with its support of dictators, torture, preemptive wars, elimination of Habeas Corpus, police killing innocent citizens merely trying to protect clean water, wasted dollars from our pockets on drone strikes, the virtual elimination of privacy,... The list goes on and on. Not to mention we are the largest drug dealer in the world."

Brenda ducked into the mini-cooler to grab a bottle of Perrier, muttering under her breath "Trust me, I wish I hadn't…as usual…you needta get a life—"

"Didn't *The Wizard of Oz* teach us anything about bullying?" Stan interrupted, hoping to break the seriousness. "Bombs, bullets, and bullying, *oh my!*"

"*Ha,* let's follow the solar brick road, before our houses get blown away in a tornado and the wicked witch of the fossil fuel gang lights our straw hats on fire!" Caryssa was loving this.

"But really, how will we tackle global warming while still keeping the lights on and the music playing?" Stan added humorously.

"Well, those on planet Exxon are beyond the pull of reason," Caryssa joked back. "Want to truly be pro-american? Then recycle, compost, buy local, support green building and sustainable food, volunteer in schools, clean up the environment, care about the link between fair trade and human rights, *support peace!*"

"Oh, and try using solar lights for Christmas décor rather than showing off houses with a million conventional energy-hogging lights!" added Stan.

"Amen to that!" Brenda said playfully, recovering her sense of humor. "Really…do people need to blow out the electrical grid with a Las Vegas light display? Not to mention that dirty energy powers that grid in the first place!"

Too bad Brenda isn't totally onboard the planet *and* peace train. "Ah ha!" Caryssa crowed in triumph, laughing. "So can you admit our drones, clones and war zones do no good?"

"No…I don't reckon I am connectin your rather derailed dots on that one, Caryss. What do y'all think?" Brenda's slow mixed southernese drawl snuck in.

Caryssa knew from experience that Brenda, a well-educated baby boomer who has lived in the San Francisco Bay for over a decade, only falls into her southern accent now and then. When she is drunk, angry or talking about Bubba who lived next door in Raleigh. Seeing she is not drinking, and Bubba is dead, that means only one thing.

There was a collective silence among them. Caryssa wanted to drop the topic…but had to say one more thing. "It's seriously unacceptable, Brenda, that we are even *in* the Persian Gulf using ridiculous flipping false fear tactics of "Islamic totalitarian empire." While *our* empire becomes totalitarian in the process."

"Well, truth is" Stan cautiously placed his latte down on the ground near the park bench. "I'm not sure how many realize dirty energy, high tech, and the weaponry aspects of our economic culture are so inextricably linked. And yes, *causing* increased totalitarian government here through Pentagon fallacious panic tactics."

More silence.

"Oh look! Screeched one of the kids, "Is that a UFO in the sky?"

They glanced up at an object hovering over the park. "Looks sorta like a Blue Angel, but it's not that time of year" observed Brenda.

A hovercraft, looking for future "tributes" muttered Caryssa under her breath. A technological divide between rulers and the ruled.

"Maybe little green men who come in peace will beam down and our politicians and greedy CEO's will claim we need to bomb our 'alien enemies' joked Stan.

Caryssa's heart ached for her much loved Silicon Valley and its deep connections to the tyranny they mock. More so for their children's future. She tried to stir away from the never ending media-induced panic-mongering topic. "Anyway, I try to take proactive measures to reduce my footprint on the electrical grid, improving the intersection between profit, people, and the planet."

"Hafta admit, Caryss, you can have sucha way with words," Brenda complimented. "Girl, ya know you should be writing for some environmental or humanitarian activist group. *'The intersection between profit, people, and the planet'* that sounds like a tag line!"

"Well," said Caryssa, blushing a bit from the unexpected praise, "I was a Marketing VP, remember? In any case, I love my simple display of solar strings at the holidays. We plan to add a string or two each year. Why not look at it as an investment into helping our nation out of its dirty energy crisis?"

The parents watched their kids play. Caryssa let herself be lulled by the calm of the park's little duck pond and the tiers of soft cloud in the rich blue sky, appreciating the new life on the trees and the warmth of the air. The flowers seemed to be in shock at the unseasonably warm weather. In tune with the earthquakes and tropical hurricanes raging through parts of the East Coast, where once at this time of year the biggest concern had been blizzards. Was this Mother Nature, serving us a wakeup call?

She stopped to admire a tree covered in masses of pale pink-white blossoms and the slant of light from the afternoon sun. She could remember a time when she had not been this way, had not had patience or attention for the world's fierce beauty. Nature, beautiful calm nature. She heard the kids laughing in the background. A hummingbird danced and pranced nearby on a bougainvillea climbing a trellis. She wanted to pinch herself. How was it she lived in such peace?

Caryssa spoke into the beauty of nature, nearly whispering to her friends "When did I start seeing the world as a reflection of my child's future, unable to distance myself from images of violence, starvation, natural and man-made disasters, pollution?"

Brenda was filling a water bottle for one of her twins" Since his birth perhaps? That's what happened to me."

"Really…It's as if motherhood placed the fate of the world on our shoulders. Yet at the same time, I now see the beauty of the world around me so much more clearly! Motherhood has galvanized me. In both directions!"

Something happened after she had a child…Caryssa became filled up *with* her child. Her child filled every void, every hole. There was no overnight miracle, no sudden flash of revelation. It had crept up on her unannounced.

She glanced out at the beautiful view from the park again, momentarily watching the sailboats whiz by, making their way through a windy stretch between Alcatraz and the Marin coast.

She couldn't help but ask "I love my life and wonder…is that why I am able to take a healthy step back and view the nature of American society and politics in all its ugliness without shrinking away? Is it because I am not enthralled in any personal battle, have no internal demons to chase away? No anger issues?"

"Hmmm. Caryssa you fret about more than anyone I know, what you are getting at?" insisted Brenda.

"*No!* True, I am fearful about the direction my career may take. Concerned college will be too expensive or Tyler won't get the best, without me contributing to our family finances. But at least I'm not part of the robotic blind audience cheering youth on as they go from violent video games to drone warfare in the military—"

Tyler's voice interrupted her "Mom! I'm thirsty!" He dropped at her feet out of breath and panting. His cheeks were the color of roses, accentuating his sparkling blue-green eyes.

"Well, I don't do that either. Gotta admit I make it known I'm disgusted with how we always have money for stupid wars, not for education." Brenda had Rowan in her arms now southern drawl gone. "It's on purpose, to dumb down people *into* such violence."

"Looks like you kids are having fun!" Caryssa momentarily ignored Brenda. She is convinced our violent history was about monarch mind control as well, all dressed up in oppressive "honor." Reaching into her bag of provisions she grabbed Tyler's Klean Kanteen BPA-free water bottle.

The children ran off, giggling and playing stick monsters up and down the hill dotted with eucalyptus leaves and branches. She watched her precious boy, so carefree and happy. He was clutching one of his stuffed Puffles from the Club Penguin theme to his chest. That little stuffed smiley face went everywhere with him…and into the washing machine as often as his clothes did.

"Well, sure you *tell* us that Brenda. But then you *show* politically inspired posts over Facebook each Veterans Day of someone *"serving."* It's as harsh as the heartbreaking displays now, showcasing them like shiny trophies. Past bravado or present--- *stop glorifying hate and violence*! It's irritating… Give it a rest, Brenda! Learn to let go into the realm of reality!"

*"Argh…*Brenda walked away towards the restrooms up the hill.

Caryssa glanced at Stan "Our cultural lunacy. It creates worry warts over things that don't matter. Like gray hair and wrinkles, or imaginary *'enemies'.*

Stan merely shrugged his shoulders, switching the topic back to environmentalism "I was on an Internet blog earlier and saw a comment: 'listen to you tree-huggers! You've had a drink from the environmentalist Kool-Aid!! Putting the planet before the people!' That just makes no sense. If we kill the planet, we kill the people. Humans become extinct. Do people not understand that?"

"Tell them to look up the words 'biodiversity' or 'ecosystem'" Caryssa responded. "Ha! Maybe by the time Mother Earth heats to become like Mercury or Venus, we will have found intelligent life on another planet. And if we are still alive, we could always hop onto a space shuttle and move there!"

* * *

In the dingy park ladies room, Brenda was having her own thoughts. *God almighty! I get it Caryss! I agree today's patriotism is out of control, even inhumane!* She stepped out of the stall, and glanced at herself in the cracked blurred park mirror. *But why get so weirded out when I honor my dad during WWII? It's a different era…* She resolved to let it go. Caryssa was just too full of consciousness…frightened for our children's future.

Brenda took a deep breath, then hiked back down the hill from the restrooms. "Are we still saving the planet and people? I liked it better when you were talking about all the skiing, hiking and biking, you've been doing Caryss! You've become the accidental activist."

"Oh yeah! Caryss went from high tech to hippy!" Stan tossed his youngest son up over his head catching him over and over. His self-proclaimed parkside workout.

"I'll talk more about all the fluffy stuff again, don't worry!" Caryssa laughed. "I do see more and more people seeing we need to include environmentalism in every aspect of our culture. So there *is* hope!"

"Some seem suspicious of environmentalism. As if it's a form of ersatz religion" Brenda again regained her calm. "They see it as a creeping cultural elevation of animals that devalues humans. You know, as if we don't care about the people who need to make a living in ways that threaten people, nature and wildlife."

Caryssa was still on the idea of life on other planets. "What if there *was* intelligent life on Venus before its atmosphere became too deadly for humans? What if that intelligent life developed so much technology based on fossil fuels and explosions, turning its air into the mix of carbon dioxide and sulfuric acid we see on Venus now, and causing the extreme greenhouse effect?"

"*Mhum*" Stan uncrossed his arms, and leaned inward with a nod of his head. "While we're at it…how does anyone believe that we are a *free nation*? Don't people read, outside of what they are fed in a newspaper clipping? Public education is not even 'free' in America the way it is in other nations!"

This was not their typical park talk, which usually was all about the kids, jobs and their fun trips. *But it is about their kids…future.* "I sure am happy our kids all play so well independedly with no fights, so we can talk politics and the planet" Caryssa collected a few toys from the sand box, and watched as Tyler disappeared up the hill on a fun adventure.

Stan added "Politics, planet and the PTA. Look how it pays for all the basic supplies for the classrooms. Parent contributions fund pencils, paper, and photocopies—all the essential tools without which no teacher can perform their basic duties! Parents also pay for all field trips, computer lab, garden, and library…yet one military jet falsified in service of *'freedom'* costs taxpayers four hundred billion dollars. Jeez. That's more than enough to educate the entire state of California!"

"They think we are *'free'* because that's what they're being sold by the corporate media. That freedom is from mainly illusory monsters," Caryssa loved the shared point of view. "And people are being distracted from *real* issues. The propagandist make bigger deals out of freakish Lady Gaga in shiny metallic wigs singing the anthem in sports arenas than important events. People are more focused on what color toenails they have, fashion trends, or Reality TV."

An image of *Hunger Games* popped into Caryssa's mind…is the country as programmed as all that? In the end, she is sure we all want good healthcare, good education, clean air and water. *Peace.*

"Peace is not a profitable product, hence those in power don't want it." Caryssa was glancing at the swaying palm trees in the park, saying this out of context. Brenda and Stan both shot her a look, then smiled at each other and shrugged. She added "Power and freedom rarely, if ever, come together—"

"So…you don't think we *ever* fought for our freedom, Caryss? Brenda asked cautiously, ignoring her self-talk in the bathroom.

"No," was all Caryssa could say. She needs to remind herself of Brenda's upbringing enduring awkward Civil War reenactments as a child, and the deep conditioning that came with it. A bunch of half crazed middle aged men playing pretend glory of the massacre of so many of America's youth.

Yet, Brenda could be so perceptive. She smoothly added "Environmental defense should be a huge industry, not what passes for the *'defense'* we're sold today!"

Caryssa became energized, springing up from the park bench. "That's one area I am trying to get into! I want to do something around sustainability, whether environmental, education, or the food system!"

"That's great!" Stan had one of his boys on his shoulders now, the other hanging off his arm. "The things worth fighting for are non-violent fights for clean air and water, healthy communities, giving money back to our schools, and finding a cure for cancer."

Caryssa had chills, and then a premonition. Something *big* was going to happen. We can't go on this way as a society. Some big statement from the masses. Something about the rigged system of banks being bailed out to pay for needless wars for the 1%, people losing social services, seeing our country being sold to third worlds for oil profits, GMOs and chemicals that are banned elsewhere but not here, toxic profits, toxic assets… *greed*. Something is coming to challenge all that.

She could feel something in the air, the rolling boil of a pot about to spill over.

"Oh, dang! Look at the time!" Brenda interjected. "The twins have piano lessons! Before I go, though, on another subject altogether. I meant to tell you guys. I met an amazing woman last week! She's a mom, two young daughters. She owns a successful art gallery in Sausalito. She travels all over the world for her business. She's originally from Paris. You guys will just love her! Her name is Anna Beauvais, and I have invited her to come to our playdate next week."

As they watched Brenda and the twins gather their sand toys and rush off, Stan said "It will be interesting to meet this Anna."

"Do you know how old her girls are?" Caryssa asked.

"Oh, are you guys talking about Anna? I heard she had one little girl with her, about four years old," chimed in Laura, another mom with a son in Tyler's class who just arrived at the park. "From what I heard, she is divorced," she added.

"Maybe she has family in the area to allow her to travel the world like that," Stan said. "Although…she lives in Sausalito. She may have money for a full-time nanny."

"Well, I don't know about her personal life," Laura fastened her son Darren's helmet on for his scooter ride. "But Brenda mentioned she is a truly extraordinary person. And she is bringing some fancy foodies for a picnic next Monday, her treat. So that sure is inviting!"

Brenda's departure seemed to signal it was time to pack the rest of the kids, kites, and Klean Kanteens. Everyone seemed to leave at once. Another enlightening family day at the park.

Chapter Three

Between driving Tyler to and from school, working volunteer at the library and computer labs, coaching homework, helping with several community events, and supporting the environmental organization, Caryssa's week flew by. It was time to meet with the elementary playgroup again.

It was overcast and cool—a more seasonal day than usual for winter in the San Francisco Bay. Remembering Brenda's comment about the picnic planned with Anna Beauvais, Caryssa brought goodies to share, including grapes, crackers, cheese, and California rolls. She placed it all into her gourmet picnic backpack.

The same group met; Brenda with the twins, Stan with his boys, Caryssa with Tyler, and Laura with her son Darren. They were there for half an hour and still no Anna. Had the mystery mom blown them off? They decided to lay a few blankets out on the grass, open chairs, and start the picnic.

"Oh, here she comes!" exclaimed Brenda. Caryssa followed Brenda's eyes to the woman descending the hill towards them. She was holding a little girl's hand and carrying a food basket adorned with ivy vines.

There was only one word Caryssa could think of to describe Anna. *Stunning.* More like drop dead, knock out gorgeous. She was tall, with a willowy figure. Light chestnut hair with blond highlights fell to her shoulders. Huge, wide-set almond eyes and creamy ivory unlined skin.

"Veillex excuser mon retard---sorry I'm late! I ran into some traffic on the bridge." Anna's slightly crooked smile and French accent added to her charm. The little girl, dressed like a boy, clung shyly to her arm.

Brenda introduced Anna to the group.

"And what is this beautiful little girl's name?" asked Caryssa.

"This is… he's a little boy. Maybe your daddy should get those curls cut off soon!" responded Anna, as she playfully twisted Jared's long blond hair.

Anna sat on the edge of a blanket and began taking things out of her basket to add to the picnic spread. She had china, glasses, and a bottle of fine red wine, roasted chicken coated with spices, patè, collard greens, tomatoes and okra with garlic bread.

"Wow, the girl from Paris sure knows how to throw a picnic!" Brenda marveled.

"Ah *merde*!" Anna rummaged through her basket. "I forgot a corkscrew…and I am sure we have something to toast to! Like our new friendship. There's always something in life worth toasting."

"I happen to have a corkscrew!" chimed in Caryssa. She was happy she had decided to tote her heavy picnic backpack replete with plates, wine glasses and utensils.

"Best not make it a habit sipping wine during playdates," laughed Brenda. But today was special. It was a day to celebrate life. The soothing breezes of an early spring carried a message of hope and delight. Flowers were blooming, everywhere the smell of roses, lavender and pink jasmine. Everywhere the sounds of the children's laughter. The moment called out for celebration.

Tyler and two of the other boys came wandering over to the picnic blanket to grab something to eat and check out the new kid. Jared, no longer clinging to Anna's arm, wandered off with them to the sandbox to play with some trucks. It seemed as though he had known the other boys forever, already best friends.

"So you have…did we hear correctly that you have two daughters?" Stan asked Anna.

An awkward silence fell over the group. Brenda and Anna exchanged quick glances. Moments passed before anyone spoke. Caryssa saw something flash in Anna's gorgeous almond eyes. *Pain*. Seeing that pain, she suddenly wanted to clutch Tyler to her bosom and never ever let him go.

Anna glanced at Stan and then looked at the wine glass in her hand. "No…Well. Yes. But…no. Not now. They are both…gone."

And then staring off into the distance, her eyes pooling with quiet tears, she told the story of how she had lost both her daughters. One at twelve and one at sixteen.

"It was a cool, foggy, rainy winter afternoon. I had been working from my home studio in Sausalito. My youngest daughter Bianca had decided against my wishes to take her new skateboard out for a spin on our narrow, winding, sidewalk-less street."

Her voice choked with a sob. Brenda took her hand. "My rule for the skateboard was for Bianca to carry it across the street to the park. Especially in inclement weather, and never ride on our street. That day it was raining. Hard. Bianca…Bianca was known as a daredevil on her skateboard, prone to taking big risks."

Caryssa sipped her wine, recognizing her hand was shaking violently.

Anna continued, tears dropping onto her plate of hors d'oeuvres "Bianca was acting willfully defiant, after having been told it was not a good night for a sleepover. She needed to burn off some resentment. Best way to do that was to go out skateboarding. I was absorbed in my work, and didn't hear the front door slam."

Caryssa blamed herself for her cat getting hit by a car. Could she even imagine it being her *child?*

"The call came twenty minutes later. A neighbor had seen a car come around the corner and hit Bianca. The skateboard flew off into the street. She saw the car take off."

It was so quiet around the blanket, the carefree sounds of the children's laughter in the background rose chillingly around them.

"Bianca had been flung five feet from the curb. They found her deep in a cluster of juniper off the side of the road. She had died on impact." Anna paused, this time it was her hand visibly shaken while sipping her wine.

"The tragedy sent my family into a whirlwind of emotions—shock, grief, blame, guilt, anger. My first-born daughter, Cassidy, she….she…" another choked sob. "She was like a mother hen to her little sister, and took it the worst. She went from grief to depression. Her grades fell. She withdrew. She began staying out all night. Not telling me where she was going or who she was with. We were devastated by the loss of Bianca and just barely holding it together."

Caryssa winced. *God, life is fragile.* She glanced over at Tyler, skipping happily along the park path, blowing bubbles through a wand.

"Just before her sixteenth birthday, Cassidy announced to us that she was pregnant. Scared and heartbroken for her, we supported her all the way. She carried the child for thirty-two weeks, delivering a healthy but premature boy. She named him Jared." This time, Anna glanced lovingly over at her grandson.

The mom's collectively spurred Anna to continue, sensing she still needed to talk. Caryssa glanced around at the sheer beauty of the park, breathing in the scent of flowers.

"Her depression worsened. Now not only was she grieving her little sister, she was postpartum. Her hormones were crazy. She fell into despair. She would lie around the house. She spent a lot of time crying. She barely noticed Jared. She wouldn't eat. She couldn't sleep. She…she….."

Anna stopped talking and forced a smile. "Oh. My. Listen to me go on! We have barely touched our picnic!" She poured a second glass of wine for everyone… The silence that had fallen over the group remained, and the feeling of celebration was gone. Caryssa looked over at the kids and was glad to see that Tyler had successfully pulled Jared into their little social circle at the batting T, and was now letting Jared have a try at a hit.

Watching the kids play, Caryssa found she had tears wetting her cheeks for this woman she didn't know and for the daughters who had gone so soon. She regretted how she and the others had so quickly misjudged Anna, presuming that because she had a successful business she might be neglecting her kids.

How must the loss of her daughters have affected Anna's entire life?

These thoughts came to her in the cool, silent moments between the sadness and the sipping of superb wine. Between bites of the amazingly delicious food. Which seemed so at odds with Anna's story. Yet there was Anna, grieving unimaginable losses, and also willing to celebrate new friends and a beautiful day.

The mood of celebration broken, the parents began to clean up after the picnic. Anna and Jared were the first to leave. "Sorry to leave so soon, but we've got to get across that bloody bridge before traffic hits." Anna snatched up her empty basket. "Come on, Jared honey!"

Jared came running, out of breath and flushed from his rousing game of T-ball with his new friends. Hand in hand, they walked off.

Gathering her things, Caryssa tried to fill in the blanks where Anna had been too emotional to elaborate. As they all herded the kids to their cars, she asked Brenda "So…do you know what happened to Anna's oldest daughter?"

"Yes, I knew the entire sad story…but didn't want to be the one to tell you guys. I figured that if Anna wanted to talk about it, she would. Cassidy committed suicide when Jared was two months old. She had OD'd on some pills her doctor prescribed."

"Oh my God, how can one woman sustain such losses and still be so sane?" Caryssa had suspected suicide, but hadn't wanted to say it.

On the drive home, Caryssa remembered Anna's obvious joy at seeing the kids play, how she mentioned their sunshine souls. A mother, deprived of her daughters, now the grandmother of a child deprived of a mother.

"God bless those little souls" she said out loud to nobody in particular.

Tyler asked from his car seat in the back. "Who are you talking to, Mommy?"

"Oh…no one, honey. Myself, I guess. Or maybe I'm talking to my Guardian Angel. I'm not sure." What she was sure of was the finality of those girls lives made her think about God, and souls.

"Mommy, do you know the difference between a person and an angel?" Tyler asked, excited by this new turn in the conversation. "I do!!! An angel is mostly on the inside, and a person is mostly on the outside!"

"What…what do you mean by that, love?"

"Well, the angels, like they work with God, they are the good guys. They like, can see you in the middle like God does. They can love you in the middle, like God does. But like people, they can only you know, like see you on the outside. And the devil, well, they are the bad guys. They can hurt you on the outside. But they can't get you in the inside…in the middle…unless you let them in."

"That's insightful, little man. Who told you?"

"Oh, nobody told me. Nobody had to tell me. I already knew."

Caryssa's eyes filled with tears. For a moment she was so moved she couldn't speak. The little ones really do know stuff about Divinity that we adults have forgotten. And here was evidence of it, in her little boy.

She finally found her voice. "Tyler, Mommy and Daddy love you all the way to your heart and soul like God does."

But by that time Tyler was already off on a different topic, amusing himself with his toy truck.

Caryssa sometimes felt as if an angel tapped her on the head when she said or did something not entirely pleasing to God. It happened then, after her conversation with her beautiful little boy. It was as if the angel were saying "Yes, there is no deeper love on earth than the love of parent for child. Yet nobody on Earth can love like the Lord your God."

But more and more, Caryssa realized, she did not believe that. Believe in God? *Yes*. But believe in a love deeper than the love she has for Tyler? No. Never.

Chapter Four

Aside from all her community volunteering, Caryssa had been writing for an online magazine—*Serenity Media*. So far she had published twelve of her articles on various political, environmental, and social issues. Each article had taken weeks of research, interviewing people, and writing/editing/rewriting until spit-shined to make it ready for the digital publishing world.

The more she researched and wrote, the more radically her views of the current state of society changed. She became obsessed with the need to get the truth out there to contradict what was being presented in the media. *Presented and hidden.* She brought the same intensity to this work that she had to her work in the technical world.

That evening the busy day was behind her, dinner done and kitchen cleaned. Tyler was in bed falling asleep as George read him a final story. She sat at her desk to write yet another article. She opened her laptop. Can the click of a mouse help change the world?

Maybe not, but a quote from Alan Keyes in *The Hundredth Monkey* kept her going: "All it takes to bring about change is a change in the consciousness of a certain number of people, then it is adapted by everyone as the norm."

The problem with trying to change the world, she mused, is that anything less is certain to feel like a disappointment. And even though she might be doing more for society than when she made big bucks pushing more technology than the world can conceivably handle, that's not how the world saw it. She constantly got the message that unless she was making money and driving the competitive wheel for the manic race to nowhere, she was doing nothing. Not *working*.

It always struck Caryssa as ironic when people who witnessed her once workaholic ways asked "So what do you do with yourself during the days now?" As if she sat around eating bonbons. She should respond: "Oh, I have a lot of important things to do, like taking the knots out of my telephone cord."

So many kids lose their way, with parents succumbing to the economic and political decisions on the backs of their children society imposes. Unable to see what is transpiring in their world while they are so busy driving that competitive wheel to lala land, manipulated by unbridled capitalism.

"Whoa, gf," Caryssa whispered. "Have I gone soft? *Me*, the former cut-throat high technology marketer? Isn't capitalism what brought us this marvel called the internet? That super-information highway! All those cool technology gadgets zoning kids out today! It's helping me make a little money right now. Not much, but every penny counts."

During her corporate career, Caryssa had clawed and kicked her way up the ladder to senior level. It was all far behind her now. Faded in the distance. Another life in another world, nothing to do with the woman sitting here in her home office, doing a different type of work, for different reasons.

She had been cutting-edge analyst in the computer internetworking world. Now she was analyzing anything else she could, anything that might affect the future of our kids. Is she developing analysis paralysis, or did parenting wake her out of a corporate tunnel vision?

She clicked on a link to the first thing she would read for this next article. It will be good to get out of the house and into the city tomorrow. Maybe I'll gain some fresh perspective. Maybe I'm buried in my cozy bubble and when I meet my former colleagues I'll get a bigger view of all this.

Early the next afternoon she got on BART for her city adventure. She was excited to get out and spend time in San Francisco, see old work buddies. She left her house hours before the meeting. She had a pedicure, leisurely roamed the streets of Fisherman's Wharf, munched on chocolates in Ghirardelli Square, window shopped, sipped a latte, saw and smelled the sights. She even bought herself a knock-off Coach purse.

As it turned out, those hours playing tourist were the most enjoyable of the entire excursion. Oh, she loved seeing a few former business colleagues! They met at an elegant restaurant near Fisherman's Wharf, chatting over glazed oysters, risotto, and salmon on crisp bread rounds topped with caviar. They shared plates of fois gras, quail salad, ahi tuna with avocado. Between delicious bites of lobster served with basil and soybeans, sips of top wines the sommelier helped them choose with perfection…it really was fun.

But the conversations seemed a bit jaded. Like something was missing. It was as if they lived in a vacuum. From Caryssa's point of view anyway, there were big missing pieces to the jigsaw puzzle of their lives.

Wow. This is where I once was in life. It was great for the space I was in then. But at this age? Now? It seems—*empty.* Her old friends still had nothing to talk about other than business trips, work, or hanging with all the single people looking for other middle-aged single people.

Listening to them, Caryssa felt centered and grounded. Yet, also the opposite. As if she were locked out of the bakery with her nose pressed against the glass, looking in at all the treats she didn't have access to. Her former colleagues had an ease with each other that she couldn't match, despite her years of working in their shared world. After a while she found she was only half listening to them. *What fun things were Tyler and George doing at home?*

Had she become this simple? So easily content with the unpretentious beauty that is her life? Then a young male voice intruded on her reverie: "Why should I pay taxes into schools, I don't even have kids!"

After several PTA meetings with talks of yet more budget cuts across our schools—*budget cuts to our kids' futures*—hearing this was sharp reminder of our nation's poor fiscal priorities. And coming from the guy she saw pull to the curb in a new BMW worth at least fifty or sixty grand!

Caryssa's internal warning system told her to remain silent, to turn and walk out. She knew she could be overbearing on such subjects and she didn't want to ruin what had been a good time. She was about to mention she had an early morning getting her child to school, and say her goodbyes.

But then she realized she had yet to speak to her former work pals. This is what she had come into the city for.

After taking several deep and calming meditative breaths and appreciating the beauty all around her—the gorgeously fresh cut flowers in all the vases and vibrant mustard-yellow walls, amazing woodwork and modern, classic décor—Caryssa smiled. She looked straight into the eyes of Mr. Materialism, and asked with composure "So Sean. What do you like to do on weekends or when you're not working?"

"When I'm not working? Well, ah, I try to do this..." he gestured towards the group. "I come into the city and hang with friends, maybe go mountain biking."

"Oh that's great! Mountain biking is so thrilling! Where do you usually go?" Caryssa asked, maintaining the conversation. She could see Sean was a sincere person. Just young and self-absorbed with no care in the world for the next generation. *As she had once been.*

"Well, I haven't had the chance to go in a while, but I like Saratoga Gap," Sean took a sip of his Martini.

Caryssa nodded to the waiter as he brought a bottle of red wine around the table. "I've mountain biked there. It's beautiful, nature at its best. Do you ski? I find mountain bikers tend to love skiing too, we outdoor mountaineer types."

"Yes, I get to Tahoe when I can. It's hard as I work so late and am so exhausted by Friday I don't have the energy to pack my shit and go!"

"I understand exactly where you're coming from...been there, done that when I was at Unabridged Networks. What do you do for the company that keeps you so busy?"

At this Sean puffed out his chest with pride, a sparkle in his blue eyes. "I just got promoted to Worldwide Channel Manager for the Federal Division, working with channel accounts across the globe...areas in U.S. Army, U.S. Navy, and Homeland Security—"

*Oh God...*Caryssa's thoughts interrupted his spiel. *In other words... he facilitates our globalized tech war machine turning us into a violence-prone police state. Now how am I going to keep my big mouth shut?*

She had suspected from her research that we likely never needed Homeland Security beyond a means for a shadow government to suppress homeland dissent. And that had been buried in the rubble of needless fear and warmongering. What's it good for, other than stopping our own people from rebelling against tyrannical rule? Indeed, if we shut down the wasted $40 billion spent on this agency, we would be no less safe.

It reminded Caryssa how the philosophy of violence and paranoid need for so much security is woven into every fabric of our society. Including these networking systems connecting one thousand plus military bases across the globe. So deeply sewn into our financial, political, and moral core, directly contributing to social disorder and chaos. Sixty-nine cents of each of our tax dollar funding death and destruction.

While people complain about taxes to support our schools!

She glanced around the restaurant again, breathing in the intriguing scents of garlic, herbs and spices. Fresh cut flowers and lit candles adorned each table, complementing the classic elegance and décor. A palm tree swayed in the gentle breeze just outside the door.

She first responded with "Well congratulations to you on your promotion! You must have worked hard for that. Let me ask a personal question, if you don't mind?"

When Sean nodded, she asked "How do you feel about all those pointless military bases to begin with? Are you not concerned about the deep origins of imperialism and militarism tearing the U.S. apart today, leading it toward mediocrity and bankruptcy?"

"Well, I think there is a difference between being pro-war and pro-national defense. The military bases are there. We've already invested so much money in them. We need to be strategic. They need to communicate to each other."

Caryssa almost snorted at his cookie-cutter standard rationale. But then she noticed his nervousness. He *needed* to believe in this deceiving marketing spin to stay gainfully employed. But her concern for our communities and families took precedence…so she plunged on.

"You're contradicting yourself! Come on, you are a bright business man, you know that the only real reason the USA stays locked into the same insane thing over and over and expecting a different result is our immoral political system itself. Our acts of meddling in everyone's affairs around the world wherever *'freedom and democracy'* are claimed to be missing."

Sean flushed, and began stuttering. "I know…I know. But…but I feel like I'm pegged doing Fed contracts because I bring in so much business. It's…it's complicated." He threw up his hands in a gesture of surrender. "My company is now automating another navy terminal, and I'm project lead. That project is keeping a roof over my head. You see…we bought this high tech startup from Israel and—"

Caryssa interjected "And Israel has a *huge* presence on Wall Street, and is now Silicon Valley's biggest competitor!"

"I….I see the connection but it's…it's…*oh!* It's too big for this little fish here to fry," Sean muttered, turning away to signal to the waiter that he was ready for a second martini. "I'm only one person."

"If each of us little fish tried to fry the big fish, we could see positive change Sean!" Caryssa felt bad she had brought this up. She hadn't meant to hurt this guy. But…but…and here was the rub. Here was what drove her. She knew we mustn't remain complacent as a society. *For our kids sakes.*

The waiter arrived at the table to take Sean's order and ask if anyone would like anything else added to the immense spread of fine foods already served. Sean took that opportunity to play host for a moment, make suggestions, ask questions, and poll the others.

Caryssa was not ready to let the subject go. "Look Sean, I too felt pegged at one point in high tech corporate America. I wanted to get out from doing the hardcore competitive stuff I loved so dearly, because after a while it was a grind. I was driving so much revenue, management froze me on my chess square. I had no options. But you're young and smart, and they need you. Try to get past it, any way you can! Why should we have those barbaric training bases? We could be building schools, hospitals, and healthy infrastructure!" *Not oil pipelines* she wanted to add.

Caryssa's heart was beating so hard she was afraid it might burst and bounce out the doorway, land on the palm tree. Sean's only guilt was trying to survive unbridled capitalism.

The waiter came back with Sean's martini. He took a gulp before responding. "Phew! That's a lot to take in, Caryssa. And maybe more than I can handle. This is why I don't want to bring children into this fucked up world! But do you think political policy will change? I don't. Guns and war are far too deeply woven into American financial identity. From folk hero frontiersman Davy Crockett to vigilante Dirty Harry. I wish… I wish I could say that I will be changing my career path overnight But the truth is, I don't know if there's a position open for me in a new path."

"Oh, show me the money!" laughed Caryssa, as she slapped her share for fancy finger foods and wine on the table. "How many more mass shootings do we need to endure for people to see we need cultural change? How many times do we need to see our twisted propaganda claim the shooter was *'radicalized'*? Turns out Sean, the *world* is not so fucked up, it's a beautiful place if we let it be."

So deeply sewn into the business fabric of our society is this violence…right to this successful, educated man in his late twenties working the same sexy Silicon Valley circuit Caryssa had. And yet how hard was it to get school budgets that paid for disaster preparedness and safety mechanisms?

Even at Tyler's excellent school there was only one paid yard duty worker to hundreds of kids during recess. They were *begging* for parent volunteers. Caryssa did more than her share of school volunteering—Board of Directors, PTA, Library Duty, Computer Duty, School Site Council, driving to field trips, Book Fair Chairperson, PE volunteer, working at classroom parties, donating monthly to PTA budget to cover costs. She even helped kick-start a nonprofit foundation to raise money for the school, including pulling money directly from parental pockets.

Then there was the myriad of non-school-related stuff with sports she loves just as much. Coaching kids' tennis, team business manager for baseball. The list went on and on. So why was she feeling guilty?

"I…believe me I would rather work in a different space than the Federal division with this technology…but you know, these days you gotta go where the jobs are. I need to pay my rent," Sean sighed again. "The Pentagon is now trying to snuggle with Silicon Valley—but at least the tech folks I work with are wary of them."

She felt sorry for him, despite his big fat paycheck, his BMW, and his luxury apartment in the city. Sorry for him and others with no choice but to go with the flow. They seemed to believe there was no way out—they could either make money connected to our perpetual war games, or potentially walk the streets starving.

She excused herself and went to the ladies room, then came back out and sat with a bunch of her former business colleagues for a while. She chatted while enjoying more delicious glazed oysters. But the conversations were still focused so much on shop talk that she grew bored.

A guy who worked as a senior competitive analyst with her at Unabridged Networks sat next to her. "Hey Caryssa, overheard you talking to our top Fed guy, Sean. Are you really the Caryssa we knew and loved in Silicon Valley? Or have you been abducted by aliens and replaced by a super robot?"

Caryssa pushed the platter of ice, now empty of oysters, away from her, and pulled her white wine closer. She pointed the tiny fork at him "I'll accept the 'knew and loved' part as a compliment, thanks John. But *really*…as if thinking of dropping twenty six thousand bombs a year on poor countries for their resources as a criminal act is a spacy mindset? Nothing alien or far-out about that—"

"Next you'll be telling us that ET's are trying to create peace on Earth by stopping America from testing nukes." John placed the empty ice platter back on the mini raw bar for the waiter.

"Well, we do have an Apollo astronaut obsessed with aliens not tolerating military violence on earth or in space." She wondered if extraterrestrial intelligence may be more credible than the bloated top secret world of *'intelligence'* we created since 9/11. "All that nuke testing is how liberty dies…with thunderous bass and a techno beat!" she blurted out for good measure.

John threw his arms up in wonder, then headed towards the men's room.

The guy on the piano was now singing Billy Joel's "Piano Man." As if on key, the melancholy words floated through the restaurant. *"And he's talkin with Davy, who's still in the Navy, and probably will be for life."* She glanced around at the scene. *"And the waitress is practicing politics, as the businessmen slowly get stoned."*

She finally said her goodbyes to the group. On her walk towards the BART station, she felt grateful the sun was setting so late, and stopped to capture a photo with the sun's glow stretching across the bay. She walked again, briskly, to capture another sunset angle before the sun hid behind the bridge. Smiling into the sunset, in her happy place, her Kate Spade sunglasses flipped onto her head, she rushed towards home to see her wonderful child and hubby.

Caryssa hopped onto the BART train and situated herself in a cozy corner. The car was nearly empty at this hour of the night. She could sit back, read the book she had stuffed into her new purse, and veg out.

She did enjoy getting insight into the corporate world she had once lived in, but realized now why she felt so...*invisible*. None of them had bothered to ask her about her child, her life. Was being a mom not worthy of discussion?

Even though she didn't want to admit it, Caryssa had come to gauge people's character by how much they realize her child is the most important aspect of her life. And she had come to believe it's not a bad measure of friendship.

That night, on her way home from the city, Caryssa couldn't wait to see what amazing new mission her little boy may have built with his Legos or Lincoln Logs with his daddy. She was so excited!

"*You* made the choice to leave your corporate career." Samantha Owens's voice faded in and out with the spotty cell reception through the BART tunnel. Caryssa had called her on the way back from the city. "That's likely why you felt a bit of disconnect with your old corporate cronies."

"Yeah, but I felt inadequate around them," Caryssa admitted.

"But *you* made the choice to be that kind of mother. Nobody forced you! Lots of other women don't choose that path!"

"Oh sure...We've had a women's movement in America. There was Gloria Steinem with her aviator glasses and frosted hair. We had Betty Friedan who wrote 'The Feminine Mystique.' Women are powerful. And some can be superwoman, Sam, like you. But not me. I can't—"

"Not you, my ass! You are super-volunteer woman and mother of the year!" Sam retorted. "And Gloria Steinem has turned out to be a sexist, ageist, obsolete idiot!"

"Sure, Sam, some women are still working the fast-paced crazy techno circuit as moms, if they have either worked out some elaborate child care or have a husband who shares equally in the drop-offs, pick-ups, soccer practices and all. Perhaps he even lactated to feed the baby!"

Or they are like Linda...a mom of two at the school whose mother-in-law is at pick-up and drop-off five days a week, transports the kids to sports activities, does homework with them every day, volunteers her time at the school weekly.

"The women in our circle of friends who don't have kids have a different life...with lots of time and energy for an endless field of paid-for work. But some of us forty-something moms have come full circle…we *had* our powerful careers. We *want* to be powerful moms!"

"I'm listening" responded Sam. The cell reception was weakening as BART rolled ahead.

"I'm not always there for Tyler," Caryssa babbled on. "He goes to day care two days a week…next school year four days a week. He does most of his homework himself in daycare. I let him experience discipline or the growing pains of childhood pretty well. But I can't seem to let go enough yet to go back to a full-time job. He's still so young!"

"I understand!" intervened Sam. "I would quit my job in a flash if I realized Ben's needs were not being taken care of. But that's the sacrifice we older moms are willing to make if we can!"

…*crackle crackle*…The reception went dead as the BART train rolled through a tunnel, so Caryssa ended the call.

Once upon a time, Caryssa and Sam would never even have had this discussion. They had each waited a long time to have their kids. These women seem to dream up recipes, ideas for a better world. Then, sometimes lose them on the way to the grocery store, baseball practice, volunteering in school or while running a bath for the kids. They lost them on the way to greasing the path for their children to be successful in life.

It was a ripple effect, bringing a child into the world later in life, Caryssa realized. She didn't only care about herself now. She cared a lot more about the world her son lives in.

Caryssa considered the pros and cons of waiting to have a child. They owned their beautiful house, had money in the bank, held no credit card debt, and were able to have one parent devoted to their child full time. But she knew they could only do that because she had learned to be frugal. Her family finances were in many ways akin to a single mom's. One moderate income taking care of three people.

On the other hand, she worried that because they were older, either George or she wouldn't be around during the years when Tyler would still need their guidance. These thoughts haunted her. This time she shook her head and looked out the BART car window to chase away the fear of not being there for Tyler one day. She was here today, she reminded herself. We have today.

* * *

Caryssa pulled into her driveway two hours earlier than expected. After compiling a to-do list, she went about getting all Tyler's things ready for school the next day. Making sure his ducks were in a row to minimize the hassle of getting out the door on time and hence to her doctor's appointment on time. And then to do errands, if possible, before that 11:40 pick up from school and time for lunch and homework.

She rolled out of bed the next morning and shuffled into the kitchen to start a pot of coffee. It should be simple, getting the kid off to school. She'd prepared everything the night before. It should all go pretty smoothly. Wake him, he dresses himself *maybe,* feed him, give him a daily vitamin, get teeth brushed, face and hands washed, make sure sunscreen is applied, and transport him to that institute of learning.

It would be simple if the mere act of waking Tyler up was not akin to climbing Mount Everest. Especially the cold reception she got this morning, waking him from that perfect dream about some amazing Lego mission.

Tyler had burrowed more deeply beneath the covers each time she tried to rouse him out of bed, proving he could be as stubborn as his mother. Finally, she had attempted the tickle monster and jump onto mommy's aching forty-eight-year-old back routine. He started flipping and turning more ably than a greased octopus as she fought to wrest the covers from him.

Then, even though he had been dressing himself for at least two years, on this particular school morning the outfit Mommy picked out was all wrong. "Ok Tyler, go ahead and pick out your own outfit." Ten minutes later, it was down to Mom's threatening gestures that convinced him it might be prudent to postpone the fight over outfits to the next morning, and get dressed properly.

Is there a fashion contest thing going on as early as the kindergarten days? "Mom, why can't I wear ripped jeans to school? My friends do!" Tyler moaned. "It's the in thing!"

Next there was the task of getting her child to the table for breakfast. "I'm not hungry yet Mommy."

"You need your nourishment to use your brain at school, and we need to leave in ten minutes!" Caryssa responded. This morning the act of building a city with Legos looked more enticing to a five-year-old.

It came to a threat of the most diabolical, coldest, heartless and savage punishment: NO SCREEN TIME!

Finally, Caryssa had transported Tyler to school on time, parked in her usual spot, and then hauled him like a pull toy across the yellow crossing to school.

Her pull toy seemed to show a bit of resistance today, as if he needed his five-year-old battery changed, or had rusted wheels. Or was it that Caryssa, in the frantic pace of trying to get Tyler to school without needing a tardy slip, was walking a bit too fast for his legs to keep up?

Once she had finally dropped him off, a wave of calm washed over her. It was Mission Impossible accomplished.

Until tomorrow.

Chapter Five

Samantha Owens had given birth to her only child at age forty-two. Her husband Jim had been nearly fifty. Caryssa and Samantha shared similar joys, challenges, and fears.

It was a Saturday morning in the Owens home, and the now nearly six-year-old Ben was happily practicing his baseball hits off the back deck, barely missing a few plant vases and windows. Natalie Merchant's deep, gritty voice filled the living room as Sam dusted.

"Hey sweetie, I think we should get out to the park together and let our son practice his power hits without ruining our house and home," Jim shouted over the music, with a roll of his eyes. They worked too hard to own this house in the affluent Oakland foothills.

"Yeah, I hearya, honey. But I've volunteered to work at Ben's school today. It's E-Waste Day, remember? It's been on the calendar for months," Sam replied.

"You already worked the bake sale last month, and worked in the garden at the school. Not to mention all the time you spend at work. Don't you think we need some family time?"

"Yeah, of course. But I volunteered just two hours for E-Waste Day. I made a commitment. I can't back out now. We can still do something after that. Besides, we're going to the Science Museum with Caryssa and George and Tyler tomorrow, remember? Doesn't that count as family time?"

"I guess..." Jim said. "How about this. I'll take Ben to the park now and you do what you have to do. We'll figure out something for later on. Maybe order pizza and have movie night?"

"Oh honey…pizza night? It sounds great. But…should we be spending money on order in right now?"

"Maybe not, but look. We both work so hard. We have to take a break every once in a while. We'll scrimp somewhere else. Wouldn't you love to take a night off cooking?"

"You have a point! I'll be wiped out from the day by then and it will be nice not to cook. Okay. It's a date. You guys have fun and I'll see you later on."

The next day at the Children's Science Museum, Caryssa noticed that Sam didn't seem her usual cheerful self. "What's wrong?" she asked. "You seem preoccupied."

"Oh, I'm sorry. Yeah, I guess I am preoccupied. Money is so tight right now. Can you believe we had to think twice about having a pizza night last night? Jim is a supervisor at his organization, but he's tapped out salary wise. There's only so much money a social worker can make. Even if he earned a Master's degree, it's not clear he could further his career much. I don't know how we're going to get ahead."

Jim, who was standing near the women gazing at the giant replica of a dinosaur at the entrance of the Hall, said "Well dear, I am fifty-three years old with a five-year old son to spend time with. I will not be going back to school at all!"

"Oh, I am not saying you should…just it's so unfair how much you are paid for what you do for people!" Sam responded.

"I have more respect for you spending time with your son now Jim," Caryssa said. "Much more than if you went off to study for a Master's degree at this point in your life, just to have a chance at the proverbial brass ring. That can wait until he is older."

"Oh man, I can't study for anything when I'm sixty. I won't have any energy left!" joked Jim. "One college degree is enough for me!"

Sam interjected "You would not believe what he does. Some of the children he works with have been abandoned! Society expects the worst from them. Some have issues stemming from domestic abuse. It's so sad. There are homeless teens he helps…"

Sam trailed off, as the group caught up with the boys excitedly running towards the Kapla blocks.

"Do you think this place needs more scientific stuff?" asked Caryssa. "It seems there could be more."

"Yeah well, all these things cost money...you know the song and dance. The state cuts school district budgets during the Wall-Street-induced economic recession rather than other areas that make more sense, and it hurts places like these organizations for the kids," George sighed. As a scientist, he was insulted that we could ever consider cutting budgets around scientific research and education.

"Yeah...if we didn't spend so much on so-called defense," Caryssa added, making quotation marks with her fingers, "those school and scientific budget cuts would not be happening. What do you want, smart kids or smart bombs?"

"As if there is such thing as 'smart' bombs? They are senseless...we are such a techno-militarized economy. All that money wasted on destruction, rather than put into construction," Sam replied. "All that 'humanitarian' bombing. What does that even *mean*?! I wonder...how the heck did the USA, the nation we've been conditioned to think so 'civilized', get to this point?"

"Well, just as Hitler had his people indoctrinated, misinformed, inoculated, and dumbed-down to believe his lies, ditto with *our* dictatorship of leaders," Caryssa was loving the sounds of the little curious Georges running around. "Knowledge is power, and corrupt governments don't want the people in power."

Sam nodded. "Intellectual Holocaust! Cultural annihilation! The most developed nations are now the *least* civilized..."

Caryssa turned her attention again to the carefree, beautiful sounds of their children laughing in the background.

"Animals are not as bad as some humans!" Sam continued. "Why? Because animals aren't trained by society to deny their happy, loving nature in order to be a 'well behaved' animal within a badly behaved cultural norm. Well, maybe it happens at the circus, but that's not as bad as what we do to humans."

They were silent a moment, glancing at all the children enjoying the Science Museum, soaking up knowledge like little sponges.

Sam was on a roll. The conversation had touched a chord in her, and now she was the one who found it hard to stop talking.

"The Germans back in Nazi days were told that Hitler was sent by God to bring order to Germany, to give the country its autobahn and rescue them from the terror of the Jews. *Can you imagine?* And really, it's not much different here. What do you think 'one nation under God' means? That the U.S. has been commissioned by God to send multi-billions of aid to Israel on some radical mission to support 'his chosen ones'? This is how 'terrorism' is created. And the religious language is used to justify it. But it's been like that throughout history. Religion has a lot to answer for, if you ask me."

"We are a culture of irrelevant revenge. You know, it was Hitler himself who said 'What good fortune for those in power that people do not think.' And it sure seems to me most people in this country aren't thinking. It's scary," Caryssa sipped her latte.

"Yeah. Our culture itself has some type of personality disorder," Sam replied. *"Ingrained patterns of relating to other people, situations, and events with a rigid and maladaptive pattern of inner experience and behavior, dating back to previous history."*

"Seriously," Caryssa nodded. "If people loved each other as much as they seem to love our freaking flag, we would have peace! Hey...not to change the subject. But let's change the subject. I'm getting the heebie jeebies."

Sam giggled. "Yeah. Me too! What shall we talk about?"

"Well...how's your job going? Anything new and exciting?"

"Not much exciting. But it's helping to pay the bills. Don't get me wrong. I love what I do, love the legal profession. Some of the lawyers I work with can be ass-wipes, but that's par for the course!"

"Last I spoke to you, you were hoping to cut back your hours to spend more time with your son. What's with that? Any progress?" asked Caryssa.

"I did work it out with my boss to schedule in only 32 hours," Sam replied. "But honestly, I want to work less. The older Ben gets the more turmoil I feel, you know? He's in school now. So someone else is teaching him most of the day, but he still can't come home because of my work schedule and commute. So he goes to daycare to be parented by someone else. It's a good daycare, of course. But I worry that he's learning someone else's morals. And, besides that, jeez. I want more time with my kid! Time is going so fast and I can feel that the next thing I know he'll be off to college. There has to be another way!"

Caryssa reached out a comforting hand and gave Sam's shoulder a squeeze. She could see that her friend was almost in tears. "But obviously, you and Jim are balancing things out well with Ben. Look how well he's doing in school. And in life overall! He's a bright, happy kid."

Sam straightened her shoulders and reached into her purse for a tissue. It was clear she needed to change the subject. "How about you? You're so busy. All that volunteer work. I admire you, helping people in all the ways you do. I don't know how you manage, but I suspect I wouldn't be able to keep up with you if I were a stay-at-home Mom! And you still manage to stay so fit! How do you do it?"

"Well, fitness is important to me. Hey, I squeezed in some type of exercise almost every day when I was pulling seventy-hour work weeks. Why not now? I believe everyone has time to exercise, if they make it a priority. We have to stay alive a while, and stay as healthy as we can. We have kids!"

"Anyway, weren't you offered a job with the environmental organization you've been volunteering at?" asked Sam.

"Oh...yes!" Caryssa replied. "The founder talked to me about a position, very part time, helping with pesticide management and creating awareness with schools, pediatricians, and the parent community. Plus lobbying for stronger environmental laws. I got the offer letter yesterday."

"So this is the organization focused on the environmental effects on children?"

"Yes! It's called Mothers for Sustainability or MFS. This job pays *peanuts* unfortunately. I've finally accepted that I'm not likely to ever make the six figures I made ten years ago!" laughed Caryssa. "At least not anytime soon while I try to change the world for the better for our kids!"

"But this is what you want to do now...and maybe someday it will amount to more," Sam said. "It seems there is a push getting folks to see that one of the biggest issues facing our nation is environmental pollution."

"Yes. It's important work. I'm hoping the meetings will work with my schedule. That is a concern. How will I get to a meeting if Tyler isn't in school? It's almost summer break! I'll have to arrange something with a friend, and hope they'll be available when meetings come up. The schedule is kind of loose so I can't predict when I'll need somebody. Or I'll have to hope there is space in one of those over-priced summer camps for the day! The irony is that I will be spending my day's pay on child care if it comes to that. And then I'll have to ask myself why I'm even bothering to work. It's a catch-22."

Sam sighed. "I hearya. It's the double-edged sword we always come against. Hey, speaking of kids. Where are the boys?"

The two women walked around the corner, and there they were, their beautiful, sweet-natured boys, playing with the boats. Tyler, with legs up to his ears already, his twinkling deep-set blue-green eyes filled with laughter. She realized as she gazed at them, she is not trying to change the world. She already accepted this beautiful world as is. She is merely trying to find a fresh way to contribute in it.

"Don't you have daycare through your school?" asked Sam.

"Yes, and Tyler is signed up for two days a week. But there is no guarantee he can get in on whatever day the meeting would be scheduled. And it gets expensive!" Caryssa answered.

"Isn't it funny how before we were parents, we would lose our identity in our work, like it was the be-all and end-all of our existence?" Sam said. "Now, when we work outside of raising our children, breadwinner or not, it's almost like something we do on the side of our primary job. Something we try to squeeze in."

"Yup," said Caryssa. "Yet at the same time, I hear some employers say that the parents in their businesses are the most productive. They work more efficiently in many cases. They know they have time constraints in a way nonparents don't. So they buckle down and get done what needs to be done, no dilly dallying!"

"I think there is something fundamentally wrong with feeling like we need to integrate parenthood into our careers, rather than vice versa," Sam said. "They are *both* jobs, one taking care of the almighty dollar, the other the more important child. Of course, we need enough of the almighty dollar to take care of that more important part of life!"

"I know, right?!" Caryssa replied. "My mother will say to me now and then 'don't lose yourself in motherhood.' But wasn't I also advised not to lose my identity in a career? If we can't center our lives on our children, what is life about? Money?"

"I do see happier faces on the kids that have a parent volunteering time at school, or at least spending time with them each day," Sam responded.

"Speaking of which—I am so proud of you for making so many efforts to leave work and stop by Ben's school, or otherwise remain so involved," Caryssa said. "I know how hard that is."

"Thanks…I appreciate you saying that. It's not easy! So…when did you first decide not to go back to your career, Caryssa?"

"Oh, it's hard to say. Probably right away…I mean, I had sent my resume out and interviewed as early as when Tyler was seven months old, and again when he was nine months old. But neither job was anything that required my level of experience and education. I knew I didn't have time to work at my former level. And certainly not in the high tech industry…unless I cloned myself or paid for an expensive nanny!"

"Wow, I think I've heard something about the ghettoizing of a mother's career. I have *two* full-time jobs, motherhood and my paying one."

"I'm not superwoman like you," Caryssa responded. "I honestly don't know how you do it."

"Back atcha, girlfriend! I sometimes think that community would fall apart without you!" Sam said.

"Thanks. I don't know about that. But I do know that many of us have taken it upon ourselves to be everything to our children that our society refuses to be," Caryssa said quietly. "In any case, I guess the time I realized I would not go back to my career anytime soon was the first time I held Tyler in my arms. Both of us a little tremulous, the tiny bow-like mouth frantically searching for my breast. And I realized *he knew my voice!* I think that's what decided it."

"Yes…the ease, the awe, the fiery rush of love. Completeness!"

"Completeness! Yes! That's it exactly. My vision of motherhood, before the fact, never encompassed all that it is…a cultural, spiritual, bird's eye view of the world…no more tunnel vision about profession or self. No more seeing only what is significant in that one corner of the world."

"Yeah, I hear you! Oh, I can only imagine when you were writing all that high tech stuff," Sam said. "You are so passionate about everything you do!"

"I had megabits, gigabits, fiber optic, LAN, WAN, IP, routers and the weird wired world engrained in my brain. It's all I read about," Caryssa said.

"No wonder you got so burnt out!" Sam said.

"Yeah...like you said, I can't do anything half assed!" Caryssa laughed. "I put too much energy into everything I do. Now all that energy is being put into motherhood. And of course, this whole trying-to-change-the-world thingy."

As the women lapsed into thoughtful silence, the dads and boys came around the corner. "Hey ladies, we just finished the test your Lego buildings with earthquakes station. We're headed outside to the pond explorations area," George announced.

The little boys ran excitedly towards the fresh outdoors to new adventures, spirit, and fun, the dads following more slowly.

"Well, it looks like our kids sure aren't complaining about not having enough scientific things to explore," remarked Sam.

"Oh no...I guess there is plenty enough here to keep them entertained. In fact, we're surrounded with so much technology maybe I said there's not enough science too soon!" Caryssa replied. "I don't know about this nanotechnology stuff in that corner...kind of scary."

"What do you mean? Ben loved the nano zone stations! How to make things millions of times smaller! He especially loves the gecko on the wall...what could *possibly* be scary about this stuff? Are you getting weird on us again, Caryssa? Sometimes I think you over analyze things. You're not a career marketing analyst anymore, remember?"

For a moment, Caryssa felt a deep, familiar melancholy. The type of blow each time she realized how far her highly paid career was vanishing into the past. All the while she was learning about the environmental hazards we are all increasingly subjected to. Ironically, because of increasing technological innovations. And the driving force behind much of this technology? The toxics-rich semiconductor chip. The very technology that had brought her to Silicon Valley in the first place. She hadn't known then that semiconductor chips are highly toxic with glycol ether and linked to birth defects, miscarriages, and cancer. Would such knowledge have made a difference to her then? One of many questions Caryssa simply couldn't answer.

"Well Sam, yes." Caryssa looked around the museum. "I agree everything here at the Children's Hall of Science is great for the kids. I would never repeat what I am about to say in front of them. It's just that nanotechnology has too many questionable things about it. We have plunged ahead with putting nanoparticles into so many products out there. And several studies have indicated they might lead to a gamut of adverse health effects on humans and animals."

"Like?" inquired Sam, with a less than interested, rather bemused expression on her face. She loved Caryssa, but sometimes she was so...obsessed with all this stuff. It got hard to listen to.

"There are silver ion nanoparticles infused into things like antibacterial soaps, paints, lunchboxes, toothbrushes, plastic food storage bags— to reduce bacteria, mold, and fungus. But they have been scientifically proven to penetrate human organs, damaging liver, stem, and brain cells!" Caryssa replied. "Really, Hon. Don't buy Ben any of those soft lunch boxes saying 'microban' on them. Even Crocs have nano particles."

Sam hackles were rising. She was getting tired of being preached to. She knew her friend meant well, but really. "How the heck did we get from Mr. Gecko here to plastic food storage containers and fungus?" she barked. "Man, Caryssa, you are becoming possessed with the demon of DNA! I am half expecting your head to turn, and green shit to start spewing out your mouth! Satan will say 'Your mother sucks mold infested shrooms and will die of disease!' For crying out loud, can you give it a rest?! Can we enjoy our time here?! Jeez!"

"Sorry, guess I'm not promoting peace of mind, am I," sighed Caryssa. "All I know is that technology as a whole needs to be looked at further before we keep making these products. Too many health problems are linked to the clean rooms of chip manufacturers, the over-proliferation of cell towers, EMFs from so much wireless technology."

"Looking around here, I see lots of computers and other technology in one form or other. I guess we are all being bombarded with electromagnetic what-nots or nano-what-the-hecks every second of our lives. We're doomed!" laughed Sam, a little contrite that she had blown up at Caryssa. "But you know what? I can't get all caught up in this stuff like you do. It would drive me nuts!"

"I know…I know. It is driving *me* nuts! But it might be better to be an aware nutcase than an unaware cancer patient. These nanoparticles, which have not been fully tested by EPA, have been driven into mainstream stuff like socks! *Socks!* Hey consumers, get your toxic socks here, no more foot odor! I even saw nanotechnology listed as a material used in winter coats the other day!"

"OK, girlfriend, I'll be sure not to buy any nano-socks, nano-anything. I couldn't fit them into my budget anyhow if they are some trendy over-priced high tech clothing and gadget fad," Sam laughed. "If they are like those five-hundred-dollar smart phones people obsess about, nope!"

"Well, these technologies are being driven into every facet of life, including medical technology—you know, people are swallowing cameras and computers! It's great we can detect cancer early, but then it begs the question, might this technology itself be causing the cancer? People are swallowing this stuff, wires all hooked to them with electromagnetic waves passing through their intestines, their tissues," Caryssa shook her head. "Then they poop the toxins out! Talk about toxic fecal matter! Seriously. Its nuts!"

"Ha ha, that lady is talking about poop!" squealed a little boy running past them.

"Jeez…now you are getting gross on top of the weirdness," Sam said. "And you know, there seems to be nothing we can do about it…so much money thrown at these things that the science proving ill health is tossed aside like a wet rag, Look how long it took for people to finally realize cigarettes cause cancer, including second-hand smoke. And we *still* have the cancer sticks on the market! Anyhow, I think it's our food causing most of the cancer and other health problems. Our industrialized food system is the culprit."

"Now isn't that a soothing thought? We could at least decide not to buy half the electronics out there if we wanted to. But we can't starve ourselves. And most of us aren't in a position to grow our own food," Caryssa responded.

Sam took a sip of latte she had bought in the café, glancing around at all the little Einstein's at play, little Curious Georges running around soaking up the knowledge. Cute little monkeys only wishing to do well. Shouldn't we be looking at all this more optimistically?

"And there lies another of these 'great new technologies'…genetic engineering!" Caryssa continued.

"*Arrgggg!* Caryssa! Please stop! Enough is enough!"

"I'll stop, but seriously…google 'Monsanto' if you want a good scare!"

"Oh God, get me out of here please! If you won't stop, I'm going somewhere else!" Sam laughed, and ran off to join the boys and their dads, who had moved on to building some complex mission with the kapla blocks.

On the way home, Caryssa thought more about getting back to her marketing career. But this time in a socially and environmentally responsible corporation. A nonprofit or something. As Sam had demonstrated, she had the passion for the work. Plus she wanted a bigger audience. Hmmm…something to research. There had to be a company out there who fit the bill.

* * *

It had been a while since Tyler had brought up the angel and God theory. But that night, as Caryssa and Tyler said a prayer and she kissed him goodnight, Tyler threw her for a loop.

"Mommy, you know how the angels and God are on the inside?" His little arms went around her neck, while he looked dreamily into her eyes. She leaned over him. "Well, like, God should be *inside* people. That way, like…you don't have to want things on the outside so much, you don't need to fill up all the bad feelings inside you."

The bad feelings inside you? The empty holes? A nearly six-year-old's way of saying that if you let God—or whatever spiritual goodness you can identify with—in, you won't need so many material things?

"Tyler, that's so beautiful…can you tell me more?" Caryssa asked, feeling a huge tug at her heart.

"Well, like, you know, like…if God is in your middle, he fills it up. If he's not, there's nothing in there, so things….like people feel like they need stuff… sorta…put in their middle….like bigger houses, maybe even a super duper new shiny car!"

"Wow that is amazing. Where did you hear this, little man?"

"I don't remember, Mommy. Nowhere I guess. I kinda made it up. I feel like I've always known it. Or maybe I heard it in church," Tyler said.

Later that same night, as they were sitting together on the deck watching the lights on the bay, Caryssa told George what Tyler had said. "It amazes me...do you think he did hear this in church?"

"In church?" George responded. "Doubtful, since the Catholic Church has become big business. I wouldn't be surprised if he came to the conclusion on his own by observing us and how we live. He sees how frugal we are. He also sees how content we are."

George reached out and gently took Caryssa's hand, pulling it under his arm and clasping it tight to his chest, the way she loved. She scooted her chair a little closer so she could lean against him, her head on his shoulder. He kissed the top of her head. Then he continued.

"Our lifestyle is simple. But it's fulfilling. I mean, we live well. But we don't spend beyond our means. We don't have credit card debt. We don't live a life of conspicuous consumption. You could say we live a life of frugal and happy consumption."

Caryssa's mind danced in circles. *Has she become so frugal it shows?* She glanced out her living room window at the Golden Gate and Bay Bridges, the breathtaking view of the bay, and then looked around at her home. *I could not be that frugal if we bought this beautiful house together! We live the good life, skiing, hiking, biking, camping, dinners, traveling. We give Tyler a good life. And spend tons of time with him. It may not be quite the cherry blossomed childhood she remembers---huge house, two cottages, three boats, trip's to Disney. But who* does *have this today?*

"Did I tell you about the book we designed together for a school project?" she asked George. "It's called 'The World According to Tyler.' One thing it asked was for the child to name twelve people they love and why. One of the first five people he named was himself! He wrote *'I love me. Because I can do things by myself!'* Amazing."

"Wow. I am not being biased to say that *is* amazing...at his age, to already have the insight to know he has to love himself first....wow!"

Later that night, Caryssa reflected how she had made a practice of living moment by moment, frighteningly aware yet without sweating the small stuff. She hopped into bed and stretched, feeling the calm throughout her body. Then she snuggled up to George, who was finishing reading an article in one of his science journals. He pulled her close, took off his reading glasses, set them on the nightstand, and switched off the light.

As Caryssa drifted off to sleep, she thanked God for many things, including being at the "middle" of her child's heart, guiding her little prophet to happiness, such simple peace and joy of life.

That is all she needed to feel happy. Oh, and maybe one more thing.

"George honey?" she murmured before her eyes closed for the last time.

"Mmmmmhmmm…."

"Maybe we could get a wicker loveseat for the backyard patio, so we don't have to sit in separate chairs when we want to snuggle and watch the lights on the bay. Would that be conspicuous consumption?"

George laughed softly into her hair and gave her a squeeze.

"No, my darling crusader. It wouldn't be," he murmured. "It would be frugal, happy consumption. I'll take a look at the budget tomorrow and you start researching."

"Sounds like a plan," she whispered. "Sounds like…a…good…."

Chapter Six

On Sunday morning, Anna Beauvais rose, dressed, and went quietly out of her Sausalito loft to seek the spot where her thoughts were night and day. Her daughters' graves. She walked through the rose and bougainvillea gardens and into the field beyond. There, a footpath led to the churchyard.

A light rain sheathed the gardens in a frothy mist. Walkway lights burned in blurred images like the sun through thick clouds.

The air was mild as she entered the churchyard, and when she reached the two graves side by side, she caught the scent of two huge bouquets of flowers. She knew who had left at least one of those bouquets. There were only two people who visited often enough for such fresh petals. Her family, what was left of it, lived in France.

Her ex-husband Pierre. At least he visits his daughters, she thought sorrowfully. Pierre had written her off not long after that day. That dreadful day, when it had all started.

Letting images flow through her mind, Anna pictured the days when they were all so happy. She and Pierre married for over thirty years and still deeply in love. Two well adjusted, happy girls doing well in school, lots of wonderful friends. Cassidy, in particular, highly talented in art, had won numerous talent awards and had her work exhibited at several Sausalito Art Festivals.

Until that day, when her perfect world had fallen apart. Pierre never getting past the anger, the blame, pointing fingers. Was she that terrible a mother?

She had always spent time with her daughters, curtailed her dream of owning her own business, working out of the house only very part time until the end...*the end*.

Had Pierre done anything like sacrificing career time to help with day-to-day parenting? No, it had always been her. She had taken them to school, picked them up, and engaged them in all their activities, taken them to pediatrician appointments. So why did *she* feel all the guilt? And why did he blame her?

Anna bowed her head over the graves, as if she could see through the thick covering of earth to her daughters. Tears fell freely upon the granite stones. Nearly five years had passed since that day, when her world had spiraled out of control...and she was still racked with sobs at their gravesite.

She knew the anguish would never end. She knew she would continue to bury her sorrow by putting all of her life into her business. At least there was one thing left that belonged to her. Well two—her adorable grandson.

Anna loved her work. As much as any human being can possibly love what they do for a living. But she would trade it all in forever to have her daughters back. Her babies. Her life.

A deep voice broke her traumatic trance. "You should be crying."

Pierre stood there, in a long dark cloak, looking every bit as handsome as he had been when they were together. But he was still angry, after all these years.

"I wasn't expecting you to be here," was all Anna could think of to reply.

"I come to visit my daughters every day, sometimes twice a day," Pierre roared into the cold misty space between them. The wind howled, deepening the distance with anger. "I don't see *you* here much."

Twice a day? For someone who had spent more time working or on the golf course than with his daughters? And if so, why did she not bump into him more often, since she visits at least three times a week?

Rather than challenge him on technicalities she asked "Do you really still blame me for all that has happened? How much could you have loved me if you think that way? I loved our girls more than life itself! This is killing me!"

Pierre stood there, glaring at her. His jade green eyes, beautiful eyes, bored into her. How could this man be so beautiful on the outside but have such ice in his soul?

She knew how much she still loved him. She knew she always would. She gave him a sidelong, assessing glance. Over the past few years, his once thick, sandy blond hair had thinned and turned gray. His face was lined. His shoulders sagged. He had aged considerably. Obviously, this was killing him as well. But he was still devastatingly handsome.

And she knew, beneath the veneer of anger, the sensitive, loving man buried deep in his own sorrow.

"Oh Pierre, you are hurting too. Why can't you see that we desperately need each other?" Anna was shaking over her girl's gravestones.

He turned on his heel and strode away, not looking back. If silence speaks a thousand words, then Pierre had just told her one thousand times that yes, he still blames her for all their misery. She may as well have thrust a stake through their girls' hearts herself.

She was, after all, the mother. Mothers should feel guilty for whatever happens to their kids. It's a mother's prerogative to hold all the guilt. Part of their job description, at least here in America. But it was not like that in France.

The rush of responsibility, the tremendous ache in her heavy heart never went away. They had quarreled over their daughter's graves. How could they argue at such a sacred moment as this?

She turned toward the graves again and prayed. "I am so sorry girls… so very sorry." Then she too turned and walked away.

* * *

Both originally from Giverny, France, Anna and Pierre had graduated together in 1978 from the École des Beaux-Arts in Paris. Anna had studied painting and Pierre, sculpture. Both won awards with solo shows while students. They knew each other in Giverny, but something happened when they met again at student orientation in Paris. They fell instantly in love, became art-school sweethearts and married before they even graduated.

They moved to America in 1989, when Anna was nine months pregnant with their first-born, Cassidy. Pierre had accepted a position teaching sculpture at The Academy of Art University in San Francisco. Neither of them had initially wanted to move to the States, but it was where Pierre was offered a job in the world of art, so they did.

The happy couple bought a cozy condo-loft with a bright studio attached in the quaint little affluent town of Sausalito, and began to build a life together.

Their street—in a very narrow, winding, hilly area with no sidewalks—was always a point of contention for Anna. She wasn't able to stroll her kids or let them walk to friends' houses, and she didn't like that limitation. But she loved the artsy Bohemian community, the culture. It all reminded her a bit of the French Riviera.

Anna gave birth to Cassidy in September of 1989, exactly two weeks after moving into their new home. When Cassidy was three months old, Anna started teaching young children art classes out of her home studio. It wasn't a big money maker, but it gave her an outlet and the ability to stay in touch with her passion for painting.

Her students ranged in age from five to ten. They used markers, paints, pastels, papier machè, and Anna's favorite, collage. Cassidy had inherited the art gene, and by age two was clamoring to join in the classes.

Their second daughter, Bianca, came along in early 1994. Even with two children, Anna had continued working part time out of her loft. She taught art and design classes to children about ten hours a week.

To help her, Pierre had hired a part-time nanny to come to the house to care for Cassidy while Anna worked out of her studio, and this nanny continued on with them until Bianca was about four. A good eleven years with "Nanny Nancy" as she had become.

But the cumulative costs of a good nanny combined with the girls getting to an age where they could be present in the art class eventually prompted Anna and Pierre to give tearful goodbyes to Nanny Nancy.

They had toyed with the idea of having a French au pair live in to care for the kids while young. An au pair would be more affordable than a nanny, and would teach them to speak French. But their little cozy home did not have ample space for that.

Anna had planned to continue working the way she was until her girls each left for college. But Bianca's death changed her plans.

After the losses of her daughters and the subsequent break up of her marriage, Anna was too devastated and numb to do anything. Time was a blur to her. She did nothing but grieve. She fell into a deep depression. She could have handled losing her home, her business, all her assets, her spouse, and stayed strong. But losing a child is the most difficult loss anyone could ever experience. And Anna had lost two.

She managed to lift herself and go on. With all her nervous energy and the newfound time on her hands, she opened a gallery, "Exotic Exposure." There she created and sold her paintings. She also carried a small assortment of handmade art from around the world, particularly Indonesian, Indian, and Thai crafts.

Anna traveled to some of these exotic places at least twice a year to keep her inventory of arts and crafts fresh and new. She especially loved going to Thailand. It gave her a calm, peaceful feeling she never experienced in the States. Buddhism made sense to her. She figured if she couldn't see global peace happening in this crazy world, she may as well find as much inner peace as possible.

She still lived in the quaint little loft in Sausalito she and Pierre had bought together. After their divorce, Pierre had moved to the city to be closer to work, first renting a studio apartment and eventually buying a small Victorian home near Pacific Heights. She had no idea of his personal life, whether he was dating anyone, what he did. They no longer spoke.

* * *

Walking out of the churchyard after her encounter with Pierre, Anna thought about how one day things can be going along as usual, and the next day all one knows is changed…*forever.* She took a deep breath, let it out slowly, and made a conscious decision to put it all behind her as best she could. To draw on her inner strength as she had done for five years, and to keep moving forward.

She had come this far, hadn't she? Her business had grown to the point she could no longer run it out of her home studio, and she had moved it to a rental space in a very trendy location in Sausalito. Not just a key location, the best, drawing international artists from across the globe.

And the emotional tones that had been coloring her daily life over the past few years had gone from black, to a somber dark gray, to what might look like a light pink. Not rosy…but pink nonetheless. Things were looking up.

She had her grandson Jared, sweet, beautiful Jared. He was all she had left, a bittersweet reminder of happier times and of tragic losses. Anna had not been able to look at photos of her girls for a long time.

When she returned to the loft, she brewed a pot of chamomile tea, cut some sourdough bread and spread the slices with sweet cream butter and raspberry jam. "It's time," whispering to herself. "You can do this. It's time."

She put her snack on one of her carved Indonesian trays and carried it into the living room. She set the tray next to the cedar chest that doubled as a coffee table in front of her yellow leather couch. Then she dropped to her knees and, hands shaking, carefully cleared off the art magazines and lifted off the top.

Suddenly, she wasn't hungry anymore. The smell of the bread and jam made her feel sick. Her hands trembled. Her vision blurred. She felt the sensation of an ice pick in her solar plexus. There was the shoebox. There was the scrapbook. All she had to do was reach and lift them out, one by one, and set them on the floor in front of her. All she had to do was nestle into the soft plush carpet and lift the lid off the shoebox.

She sat there for a long time. The tea got cold. When she realized that her knees were cramping and her feet were asleep, she returned to the moment. The noonday sun was burning through the slats of her open vertical blinds, sending rays across the room. How could that be? She had only been at the gravesite for an hour or so. It must have been 8 o'clock when she'd arrived home. She had planned to open the gallery after breakfast and…

She finally reached in and drew them out, first the shoebox, then the scrapbook carefully, as if handling precious china. She placed them on the carpet. She took a deep breath. She lifted the lid off the shoebox. And there, miraculously, were her girls. Masses of pictures of her girls.

Tears flooding her face, smiling and crying at the same time, Anna dumped the photos onto the carpet and began spreading them about so she could see them. Her girls. All pale blond with big green eyes, smiling at her from the photos in her hand, on the floor, her tears spilling onto them. Her girls, alive and well, laughing into the camera. Bianca, a real ham, with her "sexy" pose: hip out, hand on hip, opposite arm flung into the air, sassy smirk on her face.

And then she saw it. Sweet Lord! How had she never noticed it before? Perhaps she had been buried in too much pain and grief to see it. But there it was. Jared's jade green eyes, his mother's eyes staring back at her from the photo.

"Jared is a complete replica of Cassidy! "Anna murmured. Cassidy, who looked so much like Anna's dad. Generations of love in those jade green eyes, destroyed in a moment's time.

She could only look at the photos for a few minutes. Then she had to put them away. The last photo she dropped back into the chest was of her parents. She chased away the pain of knowing they never had the chance to see their granddaughters. It had taken nearly five years to be able to open the chest of cherished moments. She could wait a little longer. One day she would find joy in them. But today hurt too much.

Looking at those photos brought a flood of memories. Anna leaned against the couch. She put her head back and closed her eyes. She knew she would be opening the gallery late today, if at all. She let the memories come...

Cassidy, at age two, in Anna's studio...reaching up to the palette and covering herself in paint. She remembered being so annoyed. *"Those supplies cost an arm and a leg, and we can barely afford this place!"* she had yelled.

The stab of guilt washed away in an instant. Cassidy, she had realized, was already demonstrating amazing artistic abilities at age two. Most children that young could barely make a smiley face or stick person. But Cassidy had created a sidewalk mural with chalk, knew names of world famous sculptors and painters, and made amazing things out of clay molds. She had crafted a dog with clay that actually looked like a real dog.

And she was always such a happy baby, a happy toddler, and a happy teenager. *Until...*her baby sister was killed riding a skateboard...

Bianca, with her lithe, gymnastics body and graceful dancing. At the same time, she could be such the tomboy, at the skate park riding better than any of the boys; she ruled the half pipe. When Bianca came along, the boys would move out of her way as she bombed the hills, and watch her in awe. They begged her for tips on how to do tricks.

Bianca had asked her mom and dad continuously if they could help her open her own skateboarding teaching business when she was old enough.

That skateboard. Anna had fretted over whether or not to get her daughter a skateboard at all, never mind the new pro-grade, electric one she got that Christmas. *That Christmas*, not even a month before the day she was killed.

Anna had paid a thousand dollars for that gift…the gift that got her daughter killed. Oh my god, *I* had bought her that!

"Please Mom, I got nearly all A's on my report card…please, it's all I ask for, nothing else. It goes 18 mph!"

Her eyes shifted to her small entertainment center, where another photo stared back at her. A photo she deemed worthy of framing then. A photo she will forever cherish now. Pierre, holding baby Bianca in his arms, while kissing four year old Cassidy on the cheek.

"It's her favorite hobby, and she is damn good at it," defended Pierre at the time. *"Let her have her fun. She needs an outlet. We can't go on protecting them forever, they will just want it more if we do. Let them learn to take risks in life!"*

Kind of ironic, the one defending the decision to buy the skateboard in the first place, the one to point fingers of blame in the end: *It's your fault, you were not paying attention to her!*

* * *

The next morning, Anna woke bright and early. The emotions of the previous day had slowly subsided and she was determined not to get caught in that quagmire again. Today she would celebrate her life. She would move forward as she had determined to do. She pulled on her exercise clothes and running shoes for a jog in the breathtakingly beautiful hills of Sausalito. On the way out her door, she passed yet another favorite photo. Of her as a toddler on her daddy's shoulders. *Her daddy…*

Jogging through the quaint streets of Sausalito, Anna took in the views, sights and smells she loved so much. She passed the San Francisco

Bay Model exhibit and kept going through town for a while, then up a short but steep hill on Alexandra Avenue. She slowed to a walk.

Stopping at the top of the hill, she turned her gaze to the magnificent view below. She could see the north side of the Golden Gate Bridge. There were scattered sailboats all about, and the city was shining beyond them.

She had been doing this circle back to her loft since moving to Sausalito twenty years ago, and knew it well. Sometimes, if she had the time and extra energy, she would keep going through town and then across the Golden Gate Bridge. Usually she would stop at the Visitors Center, other times go farther up Lincoln Blvd, past the WWII monument. But those fifteen mile runs are now few and far between.

Besides…each time she had done that reminded her of those last bitter, nerve-racking years with her dad. These monuments, she felt, glorify involvement in wars deceivingly deemed "inevitable." Yet, even with WWII, the proverbial "good war"—Wall Street filled ranks of government procurement offices and armament boards and arranged for their cronies to cash in. And every decade since has been managed by bankers from Wall Street advising Congress and the president on what is "good for the country." Then we wonder how we come to electing dictators with no morals.

She would rather remember the happy years, riding on Daddy's shoulders to the beach, how he taught her to ride a bike, his daily *"Who do I love more than anything in the world?"* How she would giggle, and point to her heart and say *"Moi! Papa, Moi!"* And he would pull her into a bear hug.

Albert de Gaulle. How a man once so happy-go-lucky, healthy, and devoted to his wife and only child could have become so harsh and detached was mind boggling. Full of revenge and hatred. He had become addicted to heroin in Vietnam and had quit cold turkey with each trip home.

Yet, she knew why. Every time her father came home during that period at war, she overheard terrifying stories her parents never meant for her young ears to hear. Including how he was taken prisoner. His narrow escape, along with two American soldiers working as allies. But not until after months of brutal treatment, and watching in horror as his friends were tortured and killed one by one.

She remembered...*God she remembered*...how emaciated daddy looked. She hated how war had changed him. That was what had killed her mom, she was sure. Cassandra de Gaulle had never been the same after her husband went off to fight. In the end, she died of heartbreak.

As she ran through the streets of Sausalito, moving into runner's high, listening to the sound of her breathing and her footfalls on the pavement, Anna remembered the last time her parents argued.

She remembered hearing Maman scream: "Alby, tu ne devrais pas y retourner. La plupart des soldats français sont déjà partis... les américains peuvent les remplacer Alby! Ça suffit pour toi, tu es presque mort! Ta fille a besoin de toi! J'ai besoin de toi!"

"Alby, you should not go back. Most all the French soldiers have left already...let the Americans take over, Alby! You've had enough, you are nearly dead now! Your daughter needs you! I need you!"

She had heard him scream back: "Je me réveille en sueur avec des images de mes amis de guerre entrain de mourir, brûler à vif devant mes yeux Cassie."

"I wake up in cold sweats with images of my friends at war being killed, after seeing them burn to death before my eyes Cassie."

That was his last tour. In May of 1968, at nearly the same time that fierce demonstrations broke out against President de Gaulle's government, Anna's daddy died in a massive explosion in South Vietnam.

Anna will never forget as a preteen, sneaking down the stairs when the two death messengers were whispering to her uncle. The men had quarreled about the war. Anna's little face pressed between the staircase railings, she had overheard her uncle whisper harshly in a French accent *"my baby brother died in a war waged with master illusions of threats of communism put forth by shady CIA. A control of resources feeding the industries of imperial centers. Don't fucking tell me otherwise!"*

With all her losses---her parents, both at such a young age. Her daughters, her marriage, which was like yet another death. Hard times make a stronger person, right? Well then, she should be able to handle whatever life blows her way going forward.

Which brought her back to business. Her art business had been thriving for a while. Even in the current nasty economic climate, people in Sausalito and surrounding Marin locales seemed to be buying art. However, lately even this was slowing. Her target market—which tended toward middle-upper and upper-upper income—was apparently forced into downsizing its lifestyle as well. Some were even moving out of the area.

Anna had been toying with the idea of closing shop and going back to teaching kid's art classes. She loved her business, but wasn't sure whether it made sense to invest more to make more in a downturned economy. Closing would enable her to spend more time with her grandson.

But could she afford that? Her business, even with downturn, made more for her than teaching art would. And she already had to watch every dime.

Anna's inventory was getting low, which meant more trips overseas, more investing in quality works, and overall more work for her. Lately, she had seen a few would-be art purchasers walk into her studio and then walk right out after asking when she would be carrying more oriental arts and crafts.

She made the last turn that signaled she was now heading back to her loft. *Running is good for the body and the soul, but it's also good for business.* Something about all that oxygen to the brain. *It helps me think things through,* she thought.

And profit margins seem to be feeling the squeeze. Is it time to raise prices? Lower prices?

Regardless, to sustain any success, or even keep her business open for that matter, would be dependent on making sure her collection is of exceptional quality. At the same time, priced to market well in a crappy economy. *Merde!*

And then there was her own work. She wanted to make sculptural art books, in which she would combine painting, collage, photography and light in multi-layered wall pieces. All this would take time, and money for supplies. And speaking of money, the building owner had recently lost a few rentals from business closings. So he had raised her rent.

Anna slowed to a walk for the last couple of blocks. She would stretch out on the floor in the living room. It had been a good run. She'd make notes after her stretch-out and shower. But here was the most important factor of all, in all these considerations: She wanted to spend more and more time with her grandson. Anna was at her happiest when she was with Jared.

She also wanted to help Jared's dad out as much as possible too. Josh Bowen was one of the nicest boys she had ever met. And he was, really, still a boy. A boy-man, at age nineteen, with a four-year-old son. Her heart ached with Josh's recent words to her. "I do what I can, and love my son Jared unconditionally. But it's kinda really hard for me." Anna sees this, both financially and emotionally.

Anna started up the stairs to her loft, holding onto the redwood handrail, a little out of breath still. After losing so much, she knew one thing. She would never sweat the small stuff again.

She would survive, whether her business did or not. What's money, but just another brushstroke in this painting called life?

Chapter Seven

In the end, Anna resolved to spend as much time with Jared during his early years as she could. What kept her awake at nights more than her business was worry over her grandson's future and the sacrifices Josh had to make. All the "what-ifs."

At a time when Josh should have been enjoying college, he worked hard trying to support his son. At nineteen, he had already taken work with contractors needing help with roofing, painting, remodeling, and other jobs.

Anna had taken the time to try to get to know Josh's parents after losing her girls. They were, after all, her grandchild's grandparents. But Marsha Bowen was the private type, and Josh seemingly went with anything she said. Which was not much.

From what Anna could gather, Josh Jr.—as his parents called him—came from a decent family. Hard working, they owned an antique shop in their hometown of San Anselmo. After Josh Jr. had become a dad at the tender age of sixteen, things had gotten a bit tense in the Bowen home.

Early one morning Josh dropped Jared off at Anna's. He'd gotten a call to help a roofing contractor that day. Anna offered to make him breakfast, which he gratefully accepted. He slid into the bench seat in her sunny breakfast nook. Jared wandered off to the cubby Anna had created where he could stash his toys.

"Crepes okay, mon fils? And eggs and bacon? And fried potatoes?" Anna asked, opening the fridge. "Oh la la and fresh squeezed orange juice! Do you have time?"

"Sure," Josh said, and although his eyes looked tired he was smiling. "That would be awesome. I don't know when I'm going to get lunch. It's a tight deadline. The roofer's way behind and the homeowner is totally pissed. Gonna be an interesting day. I need all the food I can get right now!"

"Coming right up!" Anna paused and took off her eyeglasses. "Hey, how are things at home?"

"Oh…well…that. Okay I guess. You wanna hear something horrible my dad said to me last night?"

"Sure, cheri," Anna answered, feeling the sides of her eyes start to quiver. "If you'd like to share, I'd love to hear."

"Get this. Out of nowhere. Sitting at the dinner table. He turned to me and said 'Why didn't that girlfriend of yours have an abortion after she got herself pregnant?' You know, like it was something she did to herself? Like he wasn't talking about *our baby*?! After all these years?! Like he didn't even know his own grandkid?! Like Cassidy didn't even have a name?! Jeez."

Glancing over at Jared, who was playing happily with puzzles in his special corner, Anna was infinitely grateful they had not made that choice. If they had, she would not have her sweet grandson. And Josh would not have his son. She also knew that Cassidy's pregnancy was not the reason she took her own life. Her daughter had been severely depressed after losing her sister.

Anna's eye quiver became stronger, and she was afraid she'd start sobbing. "What did you say to your father Josh?"

Josh cradled his head in shaking hands and then looked at Anna. "I can't…I still can't believe he said that. I told him Cassidy did not 'get herself pregnant'." I had as much to do with it as she did, for cryin' out loud. I told him 'He's my kid, Dad! And he's your grandchild!' And then…I dunno…I just couldn't be there. I couldn't eat with him. I couldn't look at him. I ran out the door. And I walked for a long time before I finally went home again. I dunno, Anna. I think I need to get my own place. If I could afford it. Sometimes I feel like I don't even know my own parents."

By now tears were rolling down Josh's cheeks, threatening Anna's resolve not to break down herself. This was a time to listen. "But you know, Anna? What if she didn't have the baby? What if she committed suicide before Jared was born? She could have. I know how depressed she was. She was in bad shape. But if she had…? I would never have had the chance to hold my son…"

Anna wiped her hands on her apron, stepped closer, and put her arms around him from behind, kissing the top of his head in a motherly way. "It's okay, mon cheri, cry. You need to cry. In France men cry. It is not considered unmanly. You cry."

Josh put his head on his arms and sobbed. Quietly. Like a man. So his little boy wouldn't hear him and think he was the cause of any pain.

*　*　*

It comes back to all the what-ifs, doesn't it? Anna thought. What if I had not been so close yet unavailable to Bianca that day? What if I had foreseen how distressed Cassidy had become? How had I not seen it?

Anna needed to let go, and live in the now. And now, she wanted to do whatever she could to help Jared and Josh.

According to Josh, after the baby was born his mom had taken one look at that little face and said she would take her grandson in and enable Josh and Cassidy to finish high school. After Cassidy's suicide, and for the next nearly three years, Jared had spent most of his time with both grandmothers, going back and forth between Anna and Marsha. Anna's marriage had collapsed in the interim, and Anna had been starting her business as well. It had been the craziest time of Anna's life.

When Josh graduated from high school, his parents had given no more direction to him. They had insisted he be on his own. "On his own" included no financial assistance. It was as if they expected their kid to go from childhood to full self-sufficiency, just because of a piece of paper. In a way, they dropped him off a cliff. Anna didn't like to judge, but she found it curiously cold hearted, knowing what Josh had gone through.

Anna decided she would help finance Josh's night courses in landscape architecture. Even though the small college fund she and Pierre had set aside had been exhausted by home and business expenses, she would pinch her pennies and scrape up the money to help him out.

*　*　*

The next day, when Anna walked up her driveway after completing her evening jog, her phone was ringing. By the time she got the door unlocked and entered her kitchen, the answering machine went off. While she was taking off her running shoes, she heard a vaguely familiar voice leaving a message.

Anna turned and started approaching her bedroom door, her hand hovering over the doorknob. She didn't know why she was hesitating, and then it hit her.

She froze, her heart beating fast. The vaguely familiar voice was clear to her now. Oh my Lord! Why is he calling now, after all these years!

State Plaintiff Attorney Phil van Wagner was finishing his message as she walked over to the answering machine. She did not pick up…she was still shaking, her heart beating in her ears. After he stopped speaking, Anna pressed the flashing button to hear his message again.

"Hello Mrs. Beauvais. It's been a while. This is Phil van Wagner. I handled the vehicular homicide case when your daughter Bianca was hit, back in 2004. We received an unusual call today from the local police department. It appears your neighbor, the one who had originally called in the hit and run, recently attended a yard sale a few blocks away. She saw the car…well she allegedly saw the car that struck your daughter. Listen, I can talk better in person so please call us back ASAP. The bottom line is, we have sufficient information to reopen the case."

Reopen the case?

Anna felt as if someone had sucked the wind out of her. Feeling shivers through her spine, she whipped off her clothes and jumped into a hot steaming shower.

But the heat of the shower did not control the cold shakes. A sense of impending doom washing over her. Anna crumpled. She slid onto the bathtub floor, racked with sobs. She stayed like that for a good ten minutes, the water running over her.

After she had gotten into her pajamas and calmed her sprits she knew she had to call her lawyer back. Hands shaking, she dialed his office number. He answered on the second ring. What she heard next crushed her healing heart further.

"Thanks for calling back so quickly Anna. Lois Wright, the neighbor that had originally called in about the hit and run on your daughter called the local police today. She was apparently attending a yard sale, and saw a blue Honda Civic parked in a garage. She recognized the license plate as the one on the car that hit Bianca."

"After all these years, she suddenly remembers a license plate?" Anna realized she sounded shrill, but she couldn't contain her disbelief. Then "Why didn't you call the police first?"

"You mean instead of calling you first? In a vehicular homicide case, we never take police reports for granted. Remember now...the official police version of the event differed markedly from what the physical evidence shows happened, and the local homicide folks know that. In fact, both parties were contacted before calling you to reconvene, not just myself, but Delaney as well."

Melanie Delaney, the accident reconstruction specialist, had been as thorough as possible when she led the investigation nearly five years ago, together with the Sausalito police detective bureau.

But with no license plate recognized or recorded and hence no defendant, the case had been dropped. Filed as a cold case. And there it had stayed all these years.

"Why, after five years, is Lois Wright suddenly saying she remembers the license plate of the car that struck my daughter?" Anna asked. As if from a long distance away, she could hear how piercing her voice was. She found herself going into her kitchen to make a cup of herbal tea to help calm her nerves, but when she got there she reached for a bottle of wine instead. A very good, very old, very expensive bottle of red wine.

"From what I gather, she suffers from memory loss. Plus, we think she may be a bit of a drinker," van Wagner replied.

A drinker. Anna laughed inside, as she rummaged around in a drawer for a corkscrew. "Short-term memory loss? That was five years ago! So she isn't a very valuable witness then?"

"Actually, the police went ahead and ran the license plate number she gave, which is a vanity plate---KAT2VIC. Lois said she specifically remembers the KAT, as she is a cat lover. It's as if she was shocked into remembering when she saw the car and license plate again. Anyway, the police traced the license plate to a Bill Garth, who lives two streets from you. They have contacted him as well. And, here's the thing...he has confessed to hitting a skateboarder on your street in January 2004!"

Anna went to the cabinet and selected a piece of her finest stemware. She set it on the table, which was covered with a treasured table cloth she had designed and created with rare and expensive fabrics from all over the world. She began to pour, but her hand was shaking so badly she knocked the glass over. She watched as the wine spread through the fabric, turning everything blood red.

"Merde!" she screamed. "God DAMN it!!!!"

"I know this is a shock, just when you might have regained some inner peace. But Anna, this is finally your chance to bring the defendant to justice! Let your daughter's soul rest in peace!"

Oh my dear Lord. He has no fucking clue how much this hurts!

"I...I don't understand. Why open the case again. He has confessed, right?!" she asked.

"Ahhh, a confession doesn't equate to a guilty verdict. All defendants are innocent by law until proven guilty. Plus...well frankly, things don't add up here."

Anna took a deep breath. She tried again with the wine. This time she set the stem glass on the marble-topped kitchen island, and steadied it at the base with one hand. She poured carefully. She poured until the whole round-bellied glass was full to the brim. Then she lifted the glass, looked at the wine's color in the light, swirled it around to aerate it a bit. Finally she brought the glass to her face, the bottom rim at her upper lip, the top at her forehead, and took a deep, soothing inhale.

Oh. Yes. Oh yes indeed. *Très bien.* This wine was going to do the trick. Already its aroma was calming her nerves. One of the many benefits of having been born French. She knew her wines. And she never scrimped. And her wines never failed her.

Soothed now, Anna turned back to the conversation. "What do you mean things don't add up? Surely people don't go around saying they are guilty of vehicular homicide if they aren't!"

"Well...yeah...you have a point there," Phil said. "But here's the thing. Bill Garth is among the folks that lucked out and hit it big with the dot-com bubble before it burst. He retired early and lives in a million plus dollar home near you. He drives an old model Lamborghini, and has never been seen driving the Honda. That said, he does own it. It's registered in his name. But the only time any neighbors have seen that Honda taken out of that garage is when Garth's son comes home from college. And before he went off to college, it was only the son driving it. His dad bought him the car as a gift after he got his license. By the way, the son is now a medical student at UCLA."

"A son." Anna's mind was racing. "Was he the one driving the car?"

"We don't know yet. But Garth is likely protecting his son. It's his only son. We'll be investigating this further, but whoever was behind that wheel, father or son, should be held civilly and criminally responsible for Bianca's death."

"But. Wait. This all happened five years ago. If it was the son, he would have been a juvenile. He would have been maybe sixteen years old!" Anna was feeling a little sick. She reached for the wine bottle and topped off her glass.

"True. But you have to take into consideration the legal facts of the case. It's serious. It's homicide. Vehicular manslaughter. Murder in the second degree. The victim, your daughter, was only twelve years old."

"I know," Anna said. "I know. But…"

"No buts, Anna. The law treats defendants in juvenile manslaughter cases as adults. Besides, he is twenty-one now. He's not a juvenile. He's an adult. Quite competent to stand trial. And don't forget. He left the scene of the crime. He hit your daughter, killed her, and ran. And we need to bring the person responsible for your daughter's untimely death to justice."

Anna reached for a chair and sank into it. She took another sip of wine. What her lawyer was saying rang true. How could she not want to move on with this trial, to have justice served? Didn't Bianca deserve that?! And yet…and yet…this young man wanted to be a doctor. He wanted to do good for people. *Save lives.* And the whole dot-com thing? Who knew how that family was doing now? Who knew if their investments had disappeared, as so many others' had? Who knew if they could still make payments on their Sausalito home? Times had changed. Nothing is ever what it seems.

"Listen Anna…I know this must be so hard for you. But I have a question. Do you still have the skateboard Bianca was riding? I'm asking because the police got a search warrant and took a look at the car. There's no sign of damage, but of course that could have been repaired. It's been five years, after all. In any case, we want to try to determine a matching paint transfer."

"I…I don't know. I have not wanted to even *think* about that thing. I guess I can take a look around my basement and garage."

"OK, great. We appreciate it. If you find it please let me know. And take care. I'll be in touch."

Anna took the bottle and her glass and moved into the living room. She set the bottle on the floor and sank onto the couch, leaning her head back into the soft leather, wine glass clutched to her chest. She felt utterly crushed. Empty, almost. After a while she leaned into her wine glass and took a huge gulp. It warmed her as it went down her throat.

"That's more like it.".. She took another slug.

She had tried so hard to forget that day. Now, her memory went back to one conversation in particular with Ms. Delaney, the accident reconstruction specialist on the case.

"The weather was rainy and foggy that day, visibility questionable," she had said. "Your road is narrow, winding and there are no sidewalks. Not a good place for a child to be skateboarding. And, without having done a breathalyzer on the driver, we can't even say if the person was drunk. We have no reliable witnesses to say the driver was speeding. The defense will have a strong case here. They could easily win on reasonable doubt."

And what about Bianca's daredevil skateboarding adventures? She would fly higher than any of the boys on the pipe at the skate park, no fear. She was mad at her mom that day, defiantly taking the board on the street. There were too many questions. Could she have been so distraught she rode into the street? Bounced off a rock?

She got up, and decided to do what she hadn't been able to do for five years. She decided to take a look in Bianca's closet.

She made her way to Bianca's bedroom. A little wobbly now, from too much wine and no food. She went to the sliding mirrored doors of her daughter's closet and opened them. She tried hard to focus her eyes. Damn. Should have eaten. But there it was. In the right hand corner, unmistakable under a pile of other stuff, one wheel popping out of a tear in the bag it was in. *Bianca's skateboard.*

Anna pawed through all the stuff covering the skateboard, throwing it all to one side—scarves, sweaters, coats, vests. What a mess. Once the skateboard was clear, she pulled it out of the closet. She sat hard on the floor and lost her balance for a moment. Whoa. Too much wine.

Straightening herself with both arms, she set the skateboard between her knees. It was still inside a zip locked evidence bag. She had not touched it since the police had handed it back to her. She had placed it carefully in Bianca's closet, covered it with a bunch of Bianca's clothes, and shut the closet doors. Hiding the evidence, she supposed now. In any case, she had not looked back.

It was now time to look back. Anna didn't want to. But she realized now she had no choice. Time had caught up with her. Taking the skateboard over to the light from the window, she searched it for clues through the bag. There it was. On the left tip of the skateboard, a blue mark, a faint scratching of what must have been auto paint.

Had the cops not seen this after the accident? Well of course they must have…but without a car to match the paint, what good would that have done?

Suddenly, the fire of revenge burned inside her. Her rage sobered her instantly. Forget about her previous high-minded thinking. Forget about the driver's future. Forget about all that. Her twelve-year-old daughter had been killed. Here was some evidence to convict the killer. She would follow up with this, no matter whether the culprit was thirty-five or sixteen, drunk driving or not. Somebody had to pay. Why not the culprit?

She picked up the phone and dialed. Her lawyer's assistant patched her through to his direct line. "Phil van Wagner."

"Phil. Phil. It's Anna. I have the skateboard, the…there is a blue paint scratch on it. Let's move ahead with this. What's next?"

"Great! So glad you came to your senses Anna! Your daughter deserves this. Drop the skateboard off at the Sausalito police department, and have it delivered to Homicide. They work closely with the forensics team. Have you touched the skateboard since the accident, or has it been in use? Typically such evidence would have stayed zip locked at the scene of crime."

"No, are you kidding me?! It's been in her closet for five years. Trust me. I never wanted to see this thing again!"

As soon as she hung up, Anna grabbed the skateboard, her car keys and purse, and flew out the door. She heard her home phone ringing as she swung open her car door, but ignored it.

She drove straight to the police department. She was like a woman possessed. She grabbed the skateboard, waved away the receptionist's attempts to stop her and find out what her needs were, and walked straight into the chief's office. As it happened, a detective was sitting across from Chief Carl, discussing a case. When Anna barged in, both men looked over in surprise.

"I…I…excuse me. I'm Anna Beauvais. My daughter…Bianca…she was…well…she was…and I have the…"

Anna couldn't go on. She looked at the skateboard in her hands. She raised it so the two men could see it.

"Oh. Oh yes," said the detective. "I remember you, Mrs. Beauvais." He stood and offered her his chair. "Please. Have a seat. I was the detective on Bianca's case. Detective Anza. Do you remember me? Would you like a cup of coffee or something? I was just leaving. Would you like to talk with the Chief?"

Anna looked at them, one by one, and at the seat that was being offered. Suddenly she didn't remember why she was even there. "No. Thanks. I need to get going…"Um…here." She thrust the skateboard into Detective Anza's hands. "This is…my daughter Bianca…it's her…it's her…"

Detective Anza took the skateboard from Anna gently. "I know. I know. Thank you. We will use this evidence to catch the person who killed her. Thank you, Anna, for coming in today. Can we…can we offer you a ride home? Anything you need?"

"Oh…uh…no…no thanks," Anna said. "No thanks…me…I drove here…" And then she turned on her heel and went back the way she had come.

When Anna got home, her cell phone was ringing. After she finally dug it out of her purse, she pressed the voicemail icon and heard a young man's voice. "Hi… this is Brandon Garth. Please call me. I need to talk to you about the case. Something…well please call me so we can talk."

Something *what?* Anna was too tired and stressed out to call him back just now. She desperately needed to take care of herself and that was what she was going to do. She would call him…in due time.

What she did not know was that the "something" he wanted to talk about would change the direction of the case. And her life.

Forever.

Chapter Eight

Before parenthood, "happy hour" on Friday nights at Caryssa and George's had been a rocking, rolling, until three-in-the-morning kinda bash. Anywhere from five to twenty-five close friends stopped by weekly to rock the house away.

But parenthood had *grounded* them in happiness. They seemed to have their own private happy every day. "We've become a couple of happy, middle-aged homebodies!" Caryssa said to George one evening.

The tradition continued, but now more family-style. Families with children Tyler's age stopping by became the norm. His friends' parents became their new current group of friends.

This Friday, the group included Sam and Jim and their son Ben, and Stan and Stacy and their sons Tyler and Kiernan.

Caryssa loved preparing for these gatherings. She always wanted her home to be especially lovely, soothing, and inviting for her friends. She made each Friday happy hour evening special that way. This time, before her friends arrived, she ran around the house cleaning, putting fresh cut flowers in the kitchen, living room, and family room, and lighting scented candles all around.

She had popped into the quaint shop at the bottom of the hill known for its soaps, candles, and teas, and bought quality decorative scented soaps for each bathroom. She arranged her special decorative washcloths and hand towels on the racks as she had seen done in bed and breakfasts. Finally, she selected a mix of delightful music to display on her ten-CD table, starting the evening off with some relaxing Chopin.

It was a beautiful night, with the sun setting over their tranquil home and garden. Caryssa felt great. She had just stepped out of a beauty parlor, and made a quick pit stop at Marshalls. Her blond hair was freshly highlighted and cut, she had on a lovely new sundress with sunflowers all over it, and classy strappy sandals to match.

She had opened a bottle of chilled Pinot Grigio for those who preferred white and a bottle of Zinfandel for those who preferred red, and was setting out stemware when Sam, Jim, and Ben arrived. Stan and Stacy and the boys were following close behind.

"Knock knock!" Sam said, coming through the door into the kitchen. "I brought dessert! Tiramisu! No...I didn't make it myself. You know I don't have time to be a domestic goddess...but they make it at this fabulous bakery near us. It's so yum."

"Oh thanks!" Caryssa reached for the box Sam was holding out towards her. "This is great! I haven't had time to even *think* about dessert. I put together the finger food, and as usual George is working his magic on the grill. But we forgot about dessert. You're the best!"

The three boys gathered around Caryssa. "Hey Mrs. Flynn," said Ben, who was speaking for the group. "May we go find Tyler?"

Caryssa smiled. "Sure, honey. Make yourselves at home. I think he might be near the patio bistro helping his dad get the salmon and veggies ready for grilling."

The boys ran out to the patio, yelling for Tyler. Caryssa turned to Sam. "He's such a little gentleman!"

"Sometimes," Sam winked. "Oh man. We so love coming to your house. You guys live the way we do. When friends come over, our kids aren't relegated to some back room playing videos or watching a kid movie to keep them quiet. As if sitting quiet with their head glued to a screen without saying a word is behaving more than running around, laughing, making noise, and playing!"

"Or communicating with *us*!" added Stacy, joining the two women at the island, picking up a wine glass and tracing the gold lines that wound through the stem and bowl to create a glowing rim. "Wow, Caryssa, you're using your good stemware tonight?"

"Yup." Caryssa lifted up one of the fancy blown and etched wine glasses from Romania. "It's just us, and you guys are worth it to me. These were wedding presents. I bring them out whenever I can, because it makes more sense to use them than to stash them away in some china cabinet until we're dead and gone!"

"Love it," said Stacy, reaching for the bottle and pouring herself a glass of the perfectly chilled white. "Sam? May I pour some for you?"

"Sure!" Sam proffering her glass. "Thanks!"

"Welcome! Now…what were we talking about? Oh yeah. Kids. They need to learn to socialize with adults too! But be themselves and have fun at the same time." Caryssa gestured towards the boys, who had made their way from the patio to the living room. "See? What a jovial scene."

"Yeah…others would rather see them socialize with some digital Pokémon than with real people or make noise" answered Sam.

As the kids ran around in circles, entertaining themselves with the easy, carefree way only children are capable of doing, the adult conversation continued to flow easy like the instrumental classical music in the background. "I feel like I've lost relationships with other adults since not working outside the home," Stan said, while staring straight up at the ceiling. "This is so delightful, kicking back with a glass of wine and having some much needed adult conversation."

"Yeah…copy that!" Caryssa laughed, reaching her glass out to Stan's for a clink. "Welcome to our world, Stan baby! Moms have been saying that since the beginning of time!"

"So how's the school librarian work thingy going Caryssa?" asked Samantha. "And all those other volunteer jobs you do for Tyler's school?"

"Oh, it's so nice of you to ask about *those* jobs!" Caryssa responded. "Nobody seems to ask about those non-paid jobs! As if they don't qualify as work! It's all going well. I love the kids coming in and asking 'Tyler's mom' questions about the books…and Tyler loves my involvement. May as well do it now, before he gets to an age it would be embarrassing to have mommy around at school."

"Hah!" Stan laughed. "Tyler's Mom! That sounds familiar. Funny how we no longer have real first names. We are our kids' mom and dad —our new identity in life!"

Eventually they moved all the food and wine to Caryssa's backyard, and lit the fire pit. Caryssa also lit a few tiki torches for added ambience. Her wind chimes were singing their magic songs.

The sunset now presented itself as a striking streak of fiery orange-red across the sky, turning the still water of the bay the same color. Caryssa took deep breaths of the jasmine-scented air, loving and living the moment. The tiki torch flames against the fiery sunset over the bay lit her senses, while the warmth from the fire touched her soul. The red wine she had bought from the little Italian shop paired perfectly with the simple finger foods she had chosen for starters, and with the salmon George had grilled to perfection. Everything was simple yet elegant.

She felt blessed that both the quaint little soap and candle shop and the Italian grocery were less than a mile away. She let her eyes drink in the fire lit sky and bay, violet, amber, and rose.

"What are you thinking about, girlfriend?" Samantha asked. "You have that faraway look in your eyes."

Caryssa shook her head as if to shake out the meditative thoughts, and focused again on her guests. "Oh, sorry you guys. I was basking in all this beauty. I guess I zoned out! What are you guys talking about? I thought I heard the word *sex?*"

"Oh, sex, what's *that?*" Stan laughed. "You *did* hear the word! We were talking about how it is seemingly nonexistent in our lives now, being married with young kids and all…"

"What?! Stan Gafferty talking about sex?!? I never thought I'd see the day!" joked Caryssa.

Stan was very private, more of an introvert than Caryssa was seeing in him tonight. "Give me a few glasses of vino, and anything goes! One more and I might let down my guard and tell you my life story!" he joked back.

"Really, though, who has energy left for sex?" he continued. The others nodded and murmured assent. "Seriously, I used to complain about an occasional sixty-hour work week. That sounds like half-time now, compared to taking care of two little ones! There seems to be no end of the week as a parent. We're on call 24/7."

"I know Stan has the toughest job between the two of us," Stacy insisted. "I get to go sit in an office all day, and can even pretend I am getting something done while hiding behind my computer. I honestly don't know how he does it, and I don't know if I could, in his place. Toughest job in the world."

Stan laughed and reached out to stroke his wife's shoulder. "Honey. Get a grip. You 'hiding behind your computer' is what pays the bills and keeps the roof over our heads. We're in this together. And if the roles were reversed? The conversation wouldn't even arise."

"Well, when I go 'back to work' there will be prerequisites in order for me to accept the offer," Caryssa chimed in. "The organization would have to be very flexible and understand that my child comes first. I am pretty sure not too many high tech businesses fits that mold, at least not the ones I've worked for! I loved working in corporate, but I don't want to go back to the bottom-line atmosphere any time soon…and when I do it will be with a company that has a socially responsible bottom line!"

"Darlin'!" Stacy interjected. "You should look into nonprofits. They tend to be more family friendly. And you'd be giving back to society in a positive way."

"I have," Caryssa responded. "They do seem more family oriented… but so far the few I've spoken to need more hours than I am available to give, or most of the work can't be done from home."

"What about the option of getting back to the high tech sector, so you can make the big bucks you made, but working it out to do it from home, with a nanny?" Stacy asked. "You have over twenty years' experience and are highly educated!"

"I do have a couple of friends I worked with at Unabridged Networks that do that…but they haven't taken years off like I have. They stayed with it. So they are not viewed as obsolete dinosaurs of technology like I am!" Caryssa glanced over at her rather large Dell laptop. No tiny tablet for her. "Plus…it's not where my passion is anymore. And…you know what? Truth is? Here's the thing I can't get past when I start to think about going back to work, even if it would help our family's finances. I don't want some overpriced nanny taking care of my child. I don't want her being the one to see all his milestones, while I lock my soul away in some home office all day. The bottom line that I can't seem to move past? My time with my son. Time that will never, ever come back if I waste it now. "

"Yup. I know how you feel," Stan responded. "And you know what? That high tech industry we keep yearning for and regretting leaving? It isn't exactly the hot pot it once was anyhow, from what I hear."

"Omg!" Sam chortled, taking a sip of her wine. "Wait! Girlfriend! Remember that cover letter you once typed for that high tech company? It was so freaking funny! And most politically incorrect! Like you would *ever* get a job saying that to corporate!"

"Oh right!" Caryssa said. "We were having a glass of wine that happy hour evening. I showed you a printout of that job listing I found on the web. What was it? Oh yeah…Marketing Director for a high tech startup. What a joke."

They had laughed at the ridiculous list of unrealistic expectations regardless of background and work experience.

It didn't matter if the candidate had twenty years of experience and an MBA, or was just starting out. Positions paying fifty thousand dollars less than she had made over a decade ago, required ten flavors of redundant software and platform 'expertise' that had emerged into the market overnight. "Where's your *'online presence'* they ask.

She wanted to answer with a humorous "I moved to Silicon Valley over a decade ago to bring you any *'online presence'*.

That was the moment Caryssa realized the industry had moved on and it wouldn't matter how much of a powerhouse she had been before the birth of her son. She hadn't kept up. Couldn't have. She was no longer "qualified."

Even so, she knew from the job description that she had no desire to work there. So she and Sam collaborated on a mock cover letter. With each glass of wine they had gotten more and more creative, more and more in-your-face. It had been tons of fun. They set the tone exactly as if it had been written by a prospective employer. They reversed the power relations—the letter articulated the qualifications the company would need in order for her to work there.

After selling herself as to how she could single-handedly move the business forward with all her amazing proven results-driven marketing talents, she had listed the qualifications for any company she would join:

"Company must be highly family friendly, must provide flex-time, must understand mentality of 'work to live, not live to work,' must be flexible enough to allow employee to work from home around children's school schedule when needed. If you do not meet these qualifications, please do not respond, as I get inundated with calls from prospective employers."

Sam loved it, but she was also a little nervous. After all, her friend's career was at stake. "Caryssa. This is brilliant. And true. But are you sure you want to send this? You're well known in the tech world. You've been gone for a while, but you still have a great reputation. Are you sure you want to risk that? What if someone in this company knows you?"

"Well, then I commit career suicide!" Caryssa had responded. "Honestly, girlfriend, right about now? I don't care. Who knows, maybe my email will provide some much needed humor in somebody's day. I'd like to think I left them with a message: *'Hey there is life beyond these corporate walls!'* Ready? Cuz I'm gonna push Send."

"Well, if you're sure. Yeah. Okay," Sam looked leery. "Just Do it!"

Caryssa pushed Send.

"Whatever happened with that?" Sam asked now, reaching for the newly opened bottle of white to pour herself a refill. "I forget. Did you ever hear from them?"

Caryssa snorted. "Are you kidding?! What do you think?!"

"Oh...yeah..." Sam replied, taking a sip from her fresh glass and looking out over the bay. "Duh, right?! My bad..."

"Why do jobs that help society more often generate less income?" Stacy asked. "Teachers, nurses, people like Jim who help children and other people through troubled times, and the environmental folks building sustainable community should be the ones making the huge six figures, double six figures!"

"I agree," Stan replied. "Humanity would be in a much better position if we paid the big bucks to the community organizers for social campaigns that hold corporations and politicians accountable for obstructing the change needed in the way we create energy and deal with pollution. Not those making destructive technology."

"Oh, you mean like the so-called peacemakers? The ones making technology to help keep the rest of the world *'in line'*?" Caryssa shuddered inside just thinking of it.

"Whoa," Stacy said. "Is this coming from the gal who worked in the high tech world for so long? What you came to California for?"

"The technology I promoted wasn't all destructive," Caryssa retorted. "Disruptive maybe, which is not necessarily a bad thing. Silicon Valley is bringing innovation into education and leveling the playing field. Apple just gave an underserved school in our kid's school district 300 iPads. It's the destructive use of technology I object to."

"I dunno…" Stan said. "I think maybe all technology should be questioned. Is it helping? For instance, now we have technology layered on top of the kids' tests. They're getting burned out. They're just kids, after all. But now their grades become data points on a website. And any digital error could turn a hard-earned A into an erroneous D. It's scary, really."

"Well," Caryssa slowly answered. "I kinda agree. Maybe it's a matter of degrees and management. It's true we need technology. I mean, it *has* shaped our lives, and in many ways made our lives better. For instance, thanks to modern medical technology, illnesses we once thought untreatable are easily cured. And the internet itself has been a technology marvel. All that information at our fingertips now." It was like she felt compelled to defend what brought her to California.

"Do I detect a questioning tone of voice? Like…perhaps we've allowed technology to get a tad bit out of control?" Stan raised a single eyebrow in question.

"You have a point there, Stan…I mean, doe's anyone really need a refrigerator with a built-in LCD TV? Our cell phones do everything for us but burp and fart!" laughed Caryssa. "Texting causes more car accidents than drunk driving, never mind kids zoning out while texting and crossing busy streets and getting hit!"

"Folks!" Sam interjected. "I thought we were here for a light evening of socializing. Must we always solve the world's unsolvable problems? Come on. Hey, Caryssa…didn't you say you had special drinks planned for after dinner?"

"Oh! Yeah, I almost forgot! Usually these would be pre-dinner cocktails but we got so distracted with political satire. I've got lavender vodka martinis, with Ketel One. It's in the freezer. Who wants one?"

Everybody raised their hands. They knew how wonderful the lavender was from Caryssa's garden. The lavender, blending so calmly with the wind chimes.

"We might need to sleep over, though!" Stacy joked.

"No worries, honey, you know we have plenty of room, and the boys would LOVE a sleepover!" Caryssa responded. "What do you think, George?"

"Go for it," George was doing a little dance in place, swaying to the music that switched from classical to rock. "How often do we do this?

It's a special night. Don't hold back! But, you know what honey? How about if we take a break from solving the world's problems?"

Caryssa leaned over him from the back, folded her arms around his chest, and kissed his neck. "Of course, sweetie. Everybody has worked hard this week. We've earned a break. We're not going to fix everything tonight."

Stan was having his own private thoughts. He felt inadequate with the guys when topics of careers came up. It was always an inevitable *"So…you used to be a molecular engineer, right"?* He was onto the tech talk, actually wanted to move the topic onto his own vision of saving the world from certain biochemicals he was subjected to. But the chance didn't arise.

When she returned with a tray of lavender martinis, and handed them out to her guests, Caryssa saw that the energy in the group was softer than ever. There was the scent of lavender filling the air. The ambience of glow from the fire pit and the tiki torches. The lights on the bay. She always talked about letting go, *into* the big heart of humanity. But realized there needs a collective acceptance of what truly is for everyone to do this.

Why not let it go for now, and be in the moment with her friends.

And that is what she did.

Chapter Nine

After the call from the plaintiff attorney, Anna threw herself into her business with utter abandon. Working often from dawn to dusk, she got more done than she had in months. She babysat Jared in the afternoons while her neighbor Carol came over with her three-year-old daughter. Jared and Jordan would play together and Carol would watch over them while Anna worked.

During this time she had three messages from Phil van Wagner about the case, and two messages from the local police. And, curiously enough, there was one from her ex-husband Pierre.

She had not called any of them back. Why was she faltering?

She had dreams of Josh going through the same nightmare as Brandon, crying to the police that he didn't mean to do it, wasn't drunk, the roads were bad, he couldn't see the child…then the authorities dragging him off to prison. Josh screaming, "My child Jared needs me! Please don't take me to prison!"

Then that would phase out, and her daughters would appear, alive and well. Big arms reaching for them, some kind of monster taking her girls away from her. She woke each night dripping in sweat.

"Are you sure the night sweats aren't from menopause?" Carol joked, trying to lighten the mood when Anna told her about the dreams.

Finally, one evening after dinner and a couple of glasses of wine to bolster her courage, she conquered her fears, listened to her voicemails, picked up the phone, and dialed Phil's number. It was after hours so she was hoping to get his voicemail. Ease into it. Maybe buy some time before she actually had to talk to him. No such luck. He picked up on the first ring. Apparently plaintiffs' lawyers are never off duty for long.

"Hi Anna, I'm glad you called. I was about to try you again. You're a hard person to reach!"

"I know," Anna sighed. "Sorry Phil. It's been…crazy busy the last week or so…you know…"

"Sure. No worries. It happens. Hey, listen. Good news on the case. Forensics found the paint transfer on the skateboard to be an exact match with the Garths' 2001 blue Honda Civic. The police have also been busy, talking to several witnesses, including your neighbor Lois again. The defense has a chance of winning this on reasonable doubt… but we are shaping up to have a damn strong case too."

"Several witnesses? Who else do you have other than my neighbor?" Anna asked.

Phil hesitated, then spoke slowly. "Well…your ex-husband has been working with the police. He wants to get this guy. He's pushing for finding the defendant guilty of an entire spiraling effect on your family. Not just the vehicular homicide, but also subsequently tearing your marriage apart and causing your oldest daughter to take her life. We…he brought forth witne—"

"*What?*" Anna interrupted "How can anyone prove Garth guilty of all that? My marriage fell apart because Pierre and I could not sustain the stress, anger, and emotions of losing our daughters! My oldest daughter committed suicide because she fell into a deep depression over losing her sister, added to the stress of early motherhood!"

"Exactly…think about what you just said. Listen, the defendant fled the scene of crime after committing what amounts to vehicular manslaughter. California Vehicle Code 20001 imposes five years of prison *in addition* to the penalties arising out of vehicular homicide itself. So that could be nine years in prison. Plus the laws about wrongful death are designed to hold a person who caused it responsible in many ways. The responsible party could pay for burial expenses, funeral expenses, loss of companionship of child, loss of value of child's life. The punitive damages could be in the millions. It's looking like at least ten million could be awarded to you."

Anna felt like mentioning holding politicians and connected business magnates accountable for the wrongful death of millions of our youth at war, but she held that back.

"Ten million!? That's...that's...how could a medical student pay that?! And wait...you said something about witnesses? That my husband brought forth witnesses? What witnesses?"

"Oh, I was getting to that. Pierre provided three witnesses...friends of yours, who can testify that your marriage was as strong as any marriage can be before this tragic accident. And the police found two witnesses from Cassidy's school—her best friends, who can testify that Cassidy was a happy, socially outgoing, award-winning artist at the top of her class before the accident."

"How did you get Cassidy's friends involved? This is not even about Cassidy! It's about Bianca's death!"

"It's about your entire family Anna. Pierre's right. Your entire family has been torn apart. The police went to Cassidy's old school. They looked at the yearbook for her grade, as well as spoke to her former teachers. They found out who her closest friends were and interviewed them. This all happened within four days of the case being reopened. The police went to both girls' schools. They have strong testimony about Cassidy that will help our case, and also that Bianca was a fabulous skateboarder, very controlled, and always wore a helmet."

But also a complete and utter daredevil always out to prove something. Would she be betraying her dead daughter's spirit if she mentioned this? Isn't she expected to defend her daughter in the name of justice?

"Anna? You still there?"

"Yes. I'm here. I'm...I don't know. I'm finding it hard to take this all in."

"You said yourself you were eager to get on with this. Why such hesitation now?"

Oh nothing, Anna thought. I can't wait to drag the Garth family through this ordeal. I can't wait to ruin a young medical student's life over this. To cause so much pain and stress to his parents. How fun this will be, millions of dollars, like winning the lottery!

She was torn between the guilt of not wishing to punish the boy who had struck her daughter and the pain of losing her family. Was she not expected to want retribution? It seemed to be the American way.

"I know I'm not making it easy for you to do your job, Phil. I apologize. Let me know what comes next."

"Well, Bill Garth is still maintaining he is guilty. But he and his wife were very nervous when the police went to check out the car, and Mr. Garth is covering something up. Homicide has someone scheduled to go to UCLA and talk with the son."

"Are they going without any forewarning? He's just a kid!" Anna cried, suddenly remembering the message from Brandon. The message she had ignored.

Phil tried to reason with her. "I know. I know. But that's the best way to get a real reaction from him. The element of surprise can make the difference between a rehearsed answer and the truth. There's a lot a detective can determine from body language, facial expression, etc. And anyway we need to get to the bottom of this now."

After they hung up, Anna sat and thought about how hard this was. Almost all her closest friends had been her daughters' friends' parents. Losing her daughters had entailed losing this circle of friends. Her support system was gone. Her work buddies were art friends, and none of them were parents. They didn't get it.

The friends she had made through her daughters had continued to contact her for a while after the deaths. They would invite her to events or outings, try to encourage her to join them. But Anna had been reluctant to get together with them. It was too painful. Their biggest common interests—their children—had been removed. She couldn't join them in the stories of their kids' foibles and accomplishments, and they all seemed so hesitant to talk about her loss. But she needed someone to talk with. She needed not to stuff the emotions. And on the rare occasions when those friends did mention her loss, it was all about getting revenge.

Anna understood their anger. They had suffered the loss too. But the desire for revenge disturbed her. And she didn't want to be influenced by that kind of thinking. So she had gradually let those relationships slip away.

That was why lately she had been trying to connect with the new playgroup, after meeting Brenda at the Discovery Museum that day with Jared. These were new friends, far removed from her own tragedies, so they didn't avoid the subject out of fear of upsetting their kids.

Right now, one woman in particular she felt a connection with. The woman with the only child, a son. She seemed so linked with him, as if they were tuned into each other's needs. The deep love between them so vitally transparent. What a rare connection they had. And her love, passion, and devotion were so amazing.

And...there was something else. Something else she had noticed. What was it? Oh. Yes. She seemed to have a visionary quality about her. As if she saw things, knew things other people didn't catch. *Caryssa.*

Brandon, too, is an only child. Caryssa would be able to identify with him, with his parents, and with Anna's reluctance to pursue the horrific course of action everybody else involved with the case seemed to want. She'd have a more open, heartfelt viewpoint into the Garths' situation than anyone else. And into Anna's own.

She made up her mind. She would call Caryssa today. She needed support. She needed someone who could, without bias, help her clear her thoughts. Help her find the right path. The middle ground. And not just someone in the legal profession with nothing but financial profit and "justice" in mind, or someone with daughters who may over-identify or hold to the notion that daughters need protection from other peoples' reckless sons.

Anna called Josh to arrange to pick Jared up in the morning. She knew she had plenty of work to do, even though her recent workaholic momentum had propelled her ahead in every facet of her business. She still needed to devise a business plan for the next year and consult her assistant regarding potential investments. But that could wait. She wanted to make sure she spent time with her little grandson every day. That was her top priority.

Next, she dialed Caryssa Flynn's land line and cell numbers, and got voice mail both times. She left messages, and then realized that since she would be spending tomorrow with her grandson, she'd better get some more work done after all. God, her mind was so scattered, her head too busy with the trial…

Rather than drive to her office and gallery in the village, she went into her home office to get some paperwork done. Sitting at her desk, she found she had far too much nervous energy to even focus on business. Glancing around the tiny office, she realized why each time she came in here she had an uneasy feeling.

This was exactly where she had been sitting that fatal moment when a car struck her daughter. It was as if the worst type of omen existed in this very spot. Anna had not moved anything since then. Her desk was in same spot; everything remained as it had been. Including Bianca's picture, which pierced her soul every time she glanced at it.

This is no good. Something has to change. She stood and starting moving things around. Where her strength came from to move the heavy desk and all the file cabinets was beyond her. She felt like a woman possessed. She moved everything. Changed everything she could about her office. She even took piles of papers and tossed them into the recycle bin. If she hadn't read through them by now, she never will.

Next, she got out furniture polish and dusted every piece of furniture. As she was dusting the top of her desk, she accidentally knocked the picture of Bianca off. It landed on the floor. She instantly felt such a pang of guilt. Was this some kind of message? Was it a reflection of her failure as a mother? Then she glanced at the wall above the desk. There! Both her girls, smiling straight at her. She burst into tears.

I have to get out of this house. I have to get out now, or I'm going to lose it.

She dropped her dusting cloth and rushed to her bedroom to grab a jacket. On the way, she passed the girls' bedroom door. They had shared this room all their lives, since their tiny house had only two bedrooms. Something stopped her. She paused at the door. Except to retrieve Bianca's skateboard for the investigation, she had not been inside this room for...how long? She couldn't even remember.

She leaned against the doorpost. She looked in at the twin beds. The carpet. The little throw rugs. The lamps. The corkboards with all the pictures of lives just beginning. Her heart sank. Nope. No. She still couldn't go in. She kept walking. She grabbed a fleece jacket from her closet and put it on as she made her way back out to the front door, and the pavement, and the street.

Enough. Enough memories. Time to walk. Or run. It didn't matter. Time to get away. It would all still be waiting for her when she got back.

***

The next day Caryssa took Tyler to the park. The minute they got out of the car Tyler took off towards the play structure. Caryssa was surprised to see that this time he didn't stop there. He kept going, to "hike" the little hill behind it.

In the past, she had been nervous to let him venture off alone like that. But lately she had been letting him have free range. After all, he wasn't a toddler any more. And she always kept him within eyesight. But still she worried. Was she getting careless?

She laid her picnic blanket out on the grass, and began to set out plates, cutlery, snacks, and drinks. Brenda and the twins were there, and they had promised the kids a picnic. As she set out the last snack dish and surveyed her work, she remembered that her cell phone had been ringing earlier, but she had been driving and hadn't picked up. When she checked her voice mail, she found a message from Anna requesting a playdate today.

Oh, how nice. Perfect timing. I hope she can join us now. She called Anna back, and could hear what sounded like a sigh of relief when she picked up the phone. "Hey Anna! Great to hear from you! I have been thinking about you and Jared. Are you all right?"

"Oh yeah, sure, I'm okay," Anna lied. "It's just that…well…I realized I need time outside my house and work. I'm about to pick Jared up for the day. Any chance we could meet for a playdate?"

"Today?"

"Yes. I need a friend right now and I have to get out of Sausalito. I need a break. I could meet you in the East Bay if that helps."

"Perfect! Amazing timing. I'm at Eucalyptus Park with Tyler right now."

"Great! It may be close to an hour from now…is that okay? By the time I get Jared and drive over the bridge…"

"No problem. It's beautiful out and I have a book with me. Brenda and the twins are here and we're about to have a picnic, if I can get Tyler off the hill he's hiking. They'll be leaving for dance and gymnastics soon, so you might miss them. But we're here. Can't wait to see you both!"

While waiting for Anna and Jared, Caryssa went to find Tyler. "Tyler, Jared is meeting us here soon, wanted to let you know." She peered into the trees but couldn't see him.

"Okay Mom, but right now I'm too far up a tree to come down very fast."

Then she saw him, more than half way up a large redwood. How the heck did he get so high up there? There are barely any branches! "Be careful! No higher up than that Spider Man! And don't climb onto any branches that don't look safe!" she called.

Yikes. When to let go, when to pull in the reins? She did not feel like spending the afternoon in the emergency room with a child with a broken collarbone or unconscious from a head injury. On the other hand, she loved how Tyler enjoyed nature. He hiked, biked, rode his scooter, skied, climbed trees, and caught little critters. He loved the outdoors.

She and Brenda had been talking about just that while their kids were playing.

"Funny how we come to the park and bring all these playthings, plus have the play structures here, yet our kids prefer the trees, hills, sticks, and rocks!" Brenda had joked.

"Yeah, I like it. I remember my siblings and I would play outside all the time. We would play in the woods, skate on the pond, run the street after the ice cream truck, build forts, ride our bikes everywhere," Caryssa agreed. "We even witnessed our kittens getting killed by their daddy cat."

"Ohhh, the last part sounds a bit tragic!" Brenda said.

"It was...but it was also a good life lesson. I feel that through nature we learned early on about life and the inevitability of death. I think it made us stronger. We were in touch with nature. Not perpetually connected to some electronic object like so many of today's kids. It seems so...so unhealthy."

"Yeah, seems more and more people are starting to see that! In fact, I am starting to regret our decision to succumb to the Wii. It is hard enough to get them away from TV, the internet, their DVD players... what were we thinking? I am beginning to think this overload of technology is a grand mistake, and an expensive one at that!"

Caryssa was once an avid technology evangelist. Hard to imagine now that she was among those same early Internet adopters now backing away from the technology craze. Trying to get back to living in the real world.

She realized Brenda was still talking. "I do think my kids are inside too much, between all the homework they get and the electronic distractions. It seems like between getting ready for all that testing in schools and regular homework, kids don't have time for exploring the outdoors. Something wrong with that picture, don't you think?"

"Taking nature and outdoor play away from children is like taking away oxygen. I believe in the theory that ADHD is more a problem with our society itself, than with the child. In many instances, I can't help but wonder if children are mistakenly labeled because of the effects of the artificial environments we impose upon our kids. And doctors are so quick to throw meds at these kids. Scary, really."

After a few moments of silent reflection, Brenda added "I guess you could say when we were kids the woods were our Ritalin!"

"Yeah, I think you're right. It seems all the more important to talk to our kids every day, what with all the pressures on them. To let them know we're here. To listen to what they say. They're under way more stress than they should be. I make a concerted effort every day when I pick Tyler up from school. But I worry too…when he's a teenager will he talk to me the way he does now? When I *really* need to know what is going on?"

"Well geesh, be grateful that he talks to you now about school… trying to pry information out of my kids is like trying to yank thistles from the vegetable garden!"

They were sitting on the blanket, eating grapes, crackers, cheese, patè, olives, hummus, and homemade chicken salad. Looking towards the trees and hills where the children were playing, Caryssa marveled at the fresh beauty and the sound of children's laughter all around her.

Not long afterwards, Brenda and the twins left. Caryssa sat reading her book. Soon Tyler came running out of the woods. She was relieved to see that no bones were broken. He waved at her and then headed to the play structure.

Anna and Jared showed. By now, Caryssa had been at the park for over two hours, and was silently hoping for a very quick second playdate. Her list of things to do was mind boggling and she hadn't planned on an extended time at the park. Even as she smiled and waved to Anna, she was mentally ticking off the tasks she'd need to find a way to put off till tomorrow. Which, of course, would make tomorrow's workload overwhelming too.

"Breathe, girlfriend," she sighed. "Don't send yourself to an early grave stressing out over details. What needs to be done will get done." She wished she could believe that.

Anna and Jared approached hand-in-hand, as they had the first time she'd met them. My what a beautiful grandma and what a beautiful boy. Caryssa felt a surge of love for them both. She didn't know why, but these people were special to her. As she watched them approach, she almost saw a glow surrounding them.

"Hey Tyler," she yelled. "Here comes Jared! Why don't you come and say hi? Play a while with him while I talk to Anna, okay?"

Tyler took the slide to get down from the play structure and ran over to the blanket. By the time he got there, Anna and Jared were there too. "Hi Jared wanna play?"

"Um…" Jared shyly looked into Anna's face.

"It's okay honey. Go play with your new friend. I'll be watching," Anna reassured him.

Jared smiled at his grandma. Then he turned to Tyler. "OK! Let's go! What do you like to do in this park?"

Tyler grinned back at him. He liked being the teacher for the younger kids. "Oh. Tons of things! Come on…I'll show you the play structure!" And the boys ran off together as if they had always been best friends.

For the next forty-five minutes or so Caryssa gave her attention to Anna. She listened intently. She didn't interject with her own stories or problems. She sensed that was what Anna needed…someone objective to hear her. Someone to really *hear* her.

Anna sat on the blanket with her legs crossed, and the minute she opened her mouth she simply could not stop. She told Caryssa everything. She held nothing back. Every once in a while she would notice how much she was talking and feel awkward, but she couldn't help it. She had to share this. And she trusted Caryssa.

She told her new friend all about what was going on with the case—the witnesses the police and Pierre had whipped up, how Pierre was aiming to bury Brandon Garth with the weight of what had happened to their family, the possible ten million quoted as her "right." Bill Garth still taking the heat for his son.

"I...I sense that you don't agree with all this? It sounds to me like you would love to walk away," Caryssa said when Anna finally fell silent.

"Yes! Thank you for *getting* that!" Anna responded. "I don't want to hurt Brandon and his family. It happened so long ago. And it was clearly an accident! Nobody is at fault. It all seems like...I don't know...like negative energy. I know firsthand what it's like to have your life come crashing down. Why cause such calamity for yet another family? I don't want to be responsible for something like that. And you know what? Yes...justice...blah blah. But really. How is ten million dollars in my bank account going to make any of this better? I don't know what Pierre is thinking. What we long for is to have our daughters restored to us. And you know what? That's not going to happen this side of heaven. So the rest of it?" She put her head in her hands. After a long silence she said "The rest of it? I wish it would go away."

The two women sat there in silence for a while. Then Caryssa broke the silence. "Do you want some unsolicited advice?" she asked, laying her hand on Anna's arm.

"I guess so..." Anna said. "No. Really. I do. That's why I came to see you. I'm just...lost in all this. So if you have some words of wisdom, Caryssa, I'd be so grateful to hear them."

"You need to do what your gut tells you. Easier said than done, I know, once you get caught up in our legal system. It tends to work against the good side of our humanity. But Anna, do what your heart, soul, and conscience tell you to do. Follow your best self on this. At least...that's what I would want to do if I were in your position."

"My heart, soul, and conscience are telling me not to repay a kid evil for something that was not evil. It was an *accident*... and even if it weren't? I don't believe in revenge. I learned that the hard way when my dad lost his life in the Vietnam War. He was eaten up with the desire for revenge, and it killed him. I don't even believe in repaying anyone evil for *real* evil...it would need to be *true* self defense!"

How refreshing to hear someone *finally* share her point of view---in a society imposing negative social fiber to our kids. With the horror of war as "service" and death penalty as "justice." *Horrific injustices to our own people*. No wonder such corruption in our legal system.

"I agree with you, Anna," Caryssa kept her voice soft. "I think you know what to do. And I'm here to support you. You call me any time you need backup, okay?"

"Okay," Anna said, wiping the tears that had begun to pool in her eyes. "Okay. Thank you, dear friend. I will do what you advise."

As she and Tyler left the park, Caryssa realized that she recognized in Anna the same peaceful and harmonious nature she herself strived for over the past decade. A formidable task having grown up in the Northeast, with its harsh culture of blunt confrontation. She had learned that true mindfulness cannot be practiced while holding onto harsh cultural training. She had made lots of progress, but she knew she would be working on this for the rest of her life. She was happy to have found a soul mate in Anna, who seemed to be traveling the same path.

As she pulled into her driveway, Caryssa vowed to make an effort to see these two as much as their busy schedules allowed. Anna's easygoing selflessness was just the antidote needed in this crazy world. *Positive energy.* Despite the tragedy she had been through—worse than anything Caryssa had experienced—this woman seemed to have only love, compassion, and understanding for others.

If there were more Anna's in the world, what peace we would have! She was a calming balm and bounty to the soul. She felt light-headed. Almost giddy. To have discovered this wonderful new friend.

"Come on, little man, race you to the front door!"

"No fair, Mommy! I'm strapped in!"

Caryssa laughed as she slid out of the driver's seat, closed the door, and opened the door to the back where her boy was sitting in his car seat. "I know, honey! Aren't we all! But I have a feeling we're going to keep getting freer, the more we wake up and pay attention!"

Tyler laughed. "You're crazy Mommy! Now get me out of here. And then when we're both on the ground? Then the race will begin. And you *know* I'll beat you!"

"Indeed! Caryssa reached in to unhook him. "We'll both be on the ground. That is exactly where we need to be."

* * *

Tired from a long week at school and an extended playdate, Tyler was easy to get down that evening. After one book, his eyelids drooped and his angelic face softened into sleep.

Caryssa stood over his bed, looking at her sleeping beauty, and prayed. She always prayed for her child to be safe, happy, and healthy, and she prayed for the world, her family, her Dad, her friends. And, when she remembered, added something for herself. Even that prayer always came back to her child. She only prayed that she would stay around long enough to be there for him, never for anything for herself. What else did she need?

When did I stop praying for myself? Right around the time I became more concerned with my child and his world as a whole than for anything I need?

Life takes on new meaning. If she were to die tomorrow, it would not be herself she would worry about on her deathbed. It would be her child, who needs her guidance and love.

She gently touched his fine hair, as she so often did when he was sleeping. George appeared at her side and together they stood looking at him, this beautiful child who had changed both their lives.

She heard the familiar sounds of trains and sirens far off in the background while they lived tucked up in the serene, safe haven of the hills. Earlier, walking through her living room, she had glanced out at the big city across the bay. She could see all the magnificent lights shining brightly beyond the calm dark water.

Once upon a time, she had not been able to get enough of the big city. San Francisco, with its beautiful rolling hills, wonderful restaurants, cultural diversity. Now "The City"—as locals called it—seemed too busy and too dangerous. She realized she needed this safe distance, this gap in time and space. To manufacture for herself some perimeter that would protect her family from what she heard about each day.

Caryssa supposed that was another reason she was always happy to see Tyler's stuffed SpongeBob assume his place at the foot of his bed at night. She took comfort in SpongeBob's vigilance. As well as Tyler's Bear, a squeaky teddy bear head attached to the corner of a soft blanket. It had been his "lovey" since infancy. And if he still has it at age ten, twelve, thirty, just as well.

She looked at him, clutching Bear in his right hand, close to his heart. She kissed his forehead again, then glanced at the Band-Aid on his elbow. He had taken a fall on his bike earlier in the day, and she had nursed his boo-boo until he stopped crying. She gently kissed his boo-boo now, then turned and went into her own bedroom for the night.

While getting ready for bed, she glanced out the bedroom window at the vast view of the San Francisco skyline and the bay. The same amazing view she saw from their living room, family room, backyard and kitchen. *Life in the clouds sure feels surreal. Do I live in a fantasy world, a fortress in the air, apart from reality?*

She had once asked George this question. She felt so far removed from any physical harm yet her mind took her places too hard to handle at times, like a moth to a flame. Never scared for herself, but so concerned for her child's future…all the children's futures due to her nation's appalling political actions.

George had said "No Caryssa, you are *too* in touch with reality. That's the scary part for you. Those remaining apathetic may appear calmer. But remember, you can't change what you can't control. You need to let go for your own sake sometimes. Do something for yourself. You care more about others than anyone I've ever known."

After tucking herself in and turning off the light, Caryssa fell into a deep sleep. She dreamed of being on vacation with her family. They were all there, George and Tyler, her parents and her five siblings. And others. Grandma and Grandpa Chevalier, George's sisters, her cousins, her large and varied circles of friends, a whole cluster of people she loved.

They were sailing across the ocean, the steward serving cool tropical drinks. The sun was shining in a clear blue sky and the fragrance of exotic flowers wafted across the water. Beside her lay her enchanting child, his blue-green eyes gazing at her. Her child, happy and contented, radiating sweetness.

He jumped into the ship's salt water pool, squeals of laughter floating through the tropical breeze. They passed islands, deserted, haunting, and beautiful. The air pure. Across the slip of ocean was America…seemingly a world away. The islands and sea through this stretch of the voyage still pristine because humankind had not yet had time to destroy the beauty.

Suddenly, the ship struck a mine and started to sink. Her comfortable couch was now the metal deck of a barge. She grabbed Tyler to protect him. Her pillow became a coil of tarred rope, the sweet smell of flowers became fumes from a nearby coal factory working overtime. What had been a golden sun in the clear blue sky was now a pale shadow barely visible through the poisonous sulfurous clouds from the chimneystacks. Nobody could breathe.

Caryssa awoke with a start. These dreams had become common since she had become a mom and aware of how humankind was destroying the planet.

But what good does losing sleep over it do, she thought, turning over and closing her eyes. George is right. She can't change the world by worrying about it.

She fell back to sleep quickly, with one last prayer: "Forgive them Lord, for they do not know what they are doing."

Chapter Ten

The Golden Gate Grind is a trendy café nestled near the bottom of the hill a short distance from Caryssa's house—offering astounding views of the great orange bridge and contrasting hills, ocean, and sky. On rainy or cool days, the playdate parents started meeting there as a reprieve from the park or the inevitable mess that could accumulate at their houses.

Today was one of those cool spring days. This time they met while the kids were at school, a way of making the most of the three hours or less they might have to themselves during the course of a day.

"Do you know what's wrong with you true born and bred Californians?" Caryssa asked, stirring her latte.

"Yeah, we make you Bostonians feel inferior, because we're self-aware and mellow," Stan joked.

Brenda snorted. "Omg Stan, I have to admit you have a point there. I've been to Boston. I've seen those people get all bent out of shape about nothing. It's weird. One time during a business trip to Boston? A guy backed into the airport parking lot and slammed into my rental car. Good thing I bought the insurance. He got out and screamed at me. I was all…'dude. Chill. *You* backed into *me*'. Seriously. I took half the responsibility, no problem, but there are calmer ways of handling life's little accidents. I wanted to teach him to meditate or something. I felt bad for the man. Dude was off the charts stressed!"

"Wait a minute…why did you take *any* responsibility? He hit *you*, right?" asked Stan.

"Well yeah, but my rental…I was in a tiny Euro-style car stopped too close behind his Hummer. I was waiting for a spot on the other side. I'm pretty sure he couldn't see my car when he turned around to back up. So yeah. It was both of us to blame. I had no problem at all taking partial responsibility. It's the *way* he handled it. Practically grabbed my purse out of my hand. 'Whea yore fuckin' money?! Look at the damage to my Humma! I have two kids ta sen ta college! I can't afford good insurance! I'm gunna be out two thousand dollahs just fuh the deductible!' Poor guy. I learned more about his personal life within twenty minutes than I have about Boston's violent history in my entire life!" laughed Brenda.

"That's why God invented alcohol," Caryssa laughed. "It seems their antidote to every calamity."

"We Californians do our fair share of drinking our concerns away too. We have wine country!" Stan retorted.

"Well I'm doomed then, as both an original Bostonian and now a Californian. Anyway. Back to what I was saying," Caryssa said. "Perhaps all the earthquakes, mudslides, and fires made you native Californians a bit soft. I mean its *sixty degrees* out and you say it's too cold to go to the park!"

"Our kids are at school right now, isn't that why we go to the park to play?" reasoned Brenda. "Besides, this is one trendy little café! It's a nice break from our routine, don't you think?"

"Well, yeah, I agree, Brenda. But we do have little Kieran here, and my girlfriend Donna is going to show with her little one too. This place could get pretty boring for two three-year olds," Caryssa said. "Plus… sixty degrees? What a buncha wusses!"

As if on cue, Donna Hodges walked in with her three-year-old son Miles. Her daughter, now in kindergarten, was at school. She sat, with Miles in her lap. Looking around she caught the server's eye and waved him over.

"Mocha for me, please. Miles honey…would you like some orange juice?"

Miles nodded. "And some orange juice, in a plastic glass, with a straw."

The server wrote her order on his pad and looked around at the rest of the group. "Anything else for you folks?"

"How about a plate of biscotti for the table? On me," Stan suggested. "Any takers?"

Everybody nodded, among murmurs of "yum" and "that would be so nice."

"Okay," Stan said. "A plate of biscotti please?"

"Sure thing, sir," the server said. "Coming right up."

Brenda leaned in close to Caryssa's ear. "What do you think he *really* does?" she asked. "Grad student? Artist? Actor?"

"I know…" Caryssa responded. "It's so hard for these young people to make their way in this world right now. I wouldn't be surprised if he's a grad student living in his parents' basement. We should ask him."

Brenda frowned. "Nah…too personal. Unless you want to ask him. I wouldn't put it past you. And I bet you'd inspire him too."

Caryssa leaned hard against Brenda's shoulder. "Goofball!" she laughed. "Maybe. We'll see."

After brief introductions around the table, Donna fell into the conversation with the simple ease so typical of Caryssa's community of parents.

"So Donna. How do you and Caryssa know each other?" Brenda asked.

"Well, I guess from skiing, right Caryssa?" Donna responded.

"Oh, yeah," Caryssa said. "I've known Donna's husband Ned for… what…fourteen years? We met him first at the ski house in Tahoe. And then we met Donna through him. Those guys are part of our 'Squawlywood' friends."

The waiter returned to the group and set a platter of fresh-baked biscotti in the center of the table. "Enjoy! And then turned to Donna. "Oh, and ma'am…your latte and orange juice will be out soon."

Donna smiled her appreciation to him, reaching for a biscotti. "Yeah we love going to the ski house. What a great community. Dunno if any of you are skiers, but you would be so welcome. Anyway…wow it's so nice to pull myself away from my computer and come out here to enjoy the conversation, a latte, and this delicious banana pecan biscotti."

"Are you one of those archetypal supermoms that combine the career thing with parenting?" asked Brenda. "I tried that route before…it didn't work with trying to take care of my twins."

"Oh, no. I totally get you. No, with two young kids? I can't see going out to work. I don't know how I'd do it. I help manage my husband's properties from home. It's not a paid job. But it fulfills my need to feel productive, and I can be my own boss, make my own schedule. And of course it does help with the family finances, because I'm doing the grunt work he doesn't have time to do. And doesn't have to pay a contractor. Big wheeler and dealer, right Caryssa?" She winked at Caryssa.

"Oh yeah…" Caryssa laughed. "Your guy is a total wheeler and dealer. And not too shabby on the expert slopes either."

"I know!" Donna laughed" But truth is? He couldn't do it without me. Or keep up with *me* on the ski slopes!"

Caryssa and Donna high-fived across the table.

"Truth!" Caryssa said. "And we need them, too. It's a total team thing."

"Yup," Donna said. "It so is."

Miles began squirming in Donna's lap. "Mama…down!"

"Okay sweetie, down we go. Let's go explore." She turned an apologetic face to the group. "Sorry you guys. He can't stay still for too long." Everyone smiled. They knew exactly what she was talking about.

"Go on," Stan said. "Take your time! We'll still be here when the young man is ready to come back to the table. But I can't promise the biscotti will be!"

Kieran and Miles, the two toddlers, were playing quietly at the next table, fixated on Kieran's transformer toy that changed from a truck into some supernatural being of great power.

"Well I guess I was wrong that two three-year-old boys can't sit and play quietly," Caryssa observed.

Brenda brought the conversation back to careers and motherhood. "I recall years of us fighting for gender equality, and winning. The equal pay for equal job thing. Now, it seems like there is once again a shift in women's roles, going back to the realization that maintaining a high-powered career while taking care of young children can be impossible. At least without costs to the family, to the children."

Caryssa took a sip of her vanilla latte, enjoying the classical music in the background. She glanced out the window at the Golden Gate Bridge, its orangey-red glow flickering off the bright greenish-blue bay beyond Alcatraz Island. Palm trees swayed in the cool breeze, and a light fog was rolling in over the Marin headlands. The therapeutic scent of eucalyptus trees wafted in the open window on the breeze, fresh with recent rains. The bay was full of sailboats and windsurfers. Hard to believe

Tahoe was only three hours away, with snow and skiing. She could not imagine living anywhere else could be as wonderful.

"I remember a woman at Unabridged Networks made a comment to me after I got yet another promotion," Caryssa took her eyes off the bay. "She said something like 'You are lucky you have so much extra time to devote to your career, Caryssa. I have to leave here at five sharp every day to pick up my children from after-school activities, be sure they do homework, stay in touch with their daily lives, work out the usual pre-teen and teen years growing pains, cook them dinner and all.' At the time I couldn't relate to her at all."

"Well, she was right! So what did you say to that comment?" Stan asked.

"Well…I realize now my response to her comment was rather oblivious. I didn't have kids. I had no idea what her life was like. How could I? I told her I earned the promotion from working damn hard. I put in an average 60-80 hours a week."

"Well, you did work hard! Don't you feel that you earned those promotions?" Brenda argued. "I mean damn if someone *doesn't* get promoted through hard work! It's the least the company could have done for you. You were a top performer!"

"Oh sure, I don't think management would have doled out a couple fifteen thousand dollar raises, had I not been so productive. But I realize I was working so many hours, simply because—*I could!* I had no higher level of responsibility waiting for me at home in the name of a flesh and blood child. I had more time on my hands. And I guess…well…it seems now that merely working those hours is not a reason for management to promote one person over the other…workaholic habits should not be rewarded so much."

"Now you realize that woman was working the 24/7 primary job of Manager of Motherhood, plus doing that full time job at the internetworking company?" added Stan.

"Maybe so," Brenda argued further. "But regardless, I don't agree that if someone puts in so much effort they should not be rewarded. Especially if those big hours bring big results."

"Of course!" Caryssa countered. "I agree, Brenda. Yet we can't let corporate America turn people into corporate robots!"

"I don't think Caryssa is negating the need to be rewarded for a job well done…she's saying that not all employees are ruled by school schedules, ball games, keeping their kids alive, etc." Donna reasoned. "We shouldn't lose sight of what is really important in life."

"Think of those people that do both…the nine to five every day *plus* the craziness of their kids' schedules!" Stan said. "I couldn't do it…which is why I don't."

"I hearya, Stan. And I'm convinced nobody can," Donna said. "Not well, anyway. Something has to give, and usually it's at the expense of the kids. Now that's what I can't do."

"Well, that's what I mean. Anyone with small kids can choose to be in an office forty-fifty plus hours a week. Just throw them into daycare all day or put them with a grandparent or nanny. But would we *want* to…would we want our kids raised with other people's values, morals, and methods of discipline?" Stan responded.

"Seriously, I wonder now how the hell she did it," Caryssa said. "She was at senior analyst level with me. *Omg* that position was a tough grind! And come to think of it, she was very efficient at it, more so than I. She had been a systems engineer before that, so she didn't have to meet with all the product managers to understand the technicalities. She understood it, because she had helped design it. Anyway, I had the prissy attitude 'well you only work nine to five each day.' But now, as a parent? I know she worked way harder and way longer than I did. She had two jobs!"

"Well, I don't think anyone realizes what it takes to be a parent, until or unless they become one," Donna said. "Even if they have ten nieces and nephews and take them ten hours a day every day, they have no idea!"

"Hey, not to change the subject, but did you guys hear that Anna Beauvais's case was reopened?" Brenda asked.

"I didn't know anything about a case to begin with," Stan said. Two seconds later, recognition dawned. "Oh, are you talking about her daughter Bianca's hit and run?"

"Yeah," Brenda responded. "It was a cold case for years. All they had to go on was a blue Honda Civic, no license plate. There are quite a few of those around. Anyway, I guess the neighbor suddenly seems to remember the license plate, after seeing the car again."

"What I wonder is how someone just... suddenly *'remembers'* a license plate, when the incident was something like five years ago?" Caryssa asked.

"I guess the woman suffers from some type of memory loss, and rumor has it she is a bit of a drinker," Brenda said. "Anyway, she was at a yard sale and she saw a blue Honda Civic parked in a garage. The license plate flashed into her memory of that night...it had some kind of symbolic meaning to her. The police ran the plate she gave them, and they have contacted the owner. He confessed!"

"How does that work, if he confessed? Will there be a trial?" Stan asked.

"Yes," Brenda responded. "According to Anna, they want to go forward with a trial. But what is not certain is if this guy even hit Bianca, despite his confession. There is reason to believe his son was driving the car, and he is covering for him. You know, Caryssa, Anna mentioned she is planning to call you again for a playdate. She has been taking Jared more often these days."

"Actually she already did...and maybe I'll beat her to it and call her first this time around," Caryssa said, remembering her vow to squeeze in time with Anna and Jared whenever possible.

"You guys have *way* too exciting a life for me!" Donna said. "This sounds like something from CSI, not real mothers' lives. A hit and run, little girl killed, mysterious closed case reopened, cops now going after the fugitive defendant."

"Brenda, what about the son, have they questioned him yet?" Caryssa asked. "I just saw Anna last week. She told me a lot but not all these details."

"I guess he is at UCLA. The police have plans to go there and talk to him," Brenda responded. "Get this...Anna told me that her lawyer is talking punitive damages of possibly ten million dollars! He says that this fatal accident caused the whole spiraling effect on Anna's family, and wants to go after the defendant in a big way."

"If he is at UCLA, he must be quite young. He would have been *really* young when the accident happened," Donna glanced at her own son.

"I know, sad. Have you seen the papers today? This case is front-page news. Made big headlines, as the kid's dad is high profile in the community. At one point he founded a highly successful dotcom. He has been likened to a Steve Jobs type dude. The kid is reported to be a great student, well-behaved, well liked, in med school, top ten percent of his class," Brenda said. "There was mention he might be a trust fund kid."

"When I saw her last week she distinctly told me she does not want to press charges, she does not want this kid to even go to trial!" Caryssa said.

Stan, who had been either silent or chasing Kieran away from the front door during the discussion, suddenly piped up. "Wow, I almost find myself hoping this kid does gets off…I mean he must have been at most sixteen at the time. He has his whole life in front of him, an inspiring one at that."

"I know," Brenda interjected more loudly than she had intended, face red with sudden anger. "But this is Anna's daughter we ya'll talking about…her whole family was torn apart! I reckon we can't let people get away with reckless driving just because they are teenagers! Our five-year-olds know right from wrong!"

Oh no, southern drawl slipping in, which means Brenda is mad. Caryssa took a deep breath and glanced out at the Golden Gate Bridge, always a source of serenity.

Heads turned in the café. Miles and Kieran, playing with small trucks nearby, started crashing into each other playfully "Oh no, I am driving too fast, I'm gonna crash into you…Oh no, watch where you are going, don't drive so fast, you are a bad guy and I'll get you, I'll kill you!"

"Oh my," Stan reasoned. "I didn't mean to push your buttons, Brenda. Maybe we need to calm down a bit here. It is a hot-button issue and it touches all of us right where we live. Both the victim and the driver could have been ours. Either way, tragedy. So let's take a step back. The problem with the case seems to be there would be too many unknowns at this point…we don't even *know* if the kid was speeding or drunk, or even driving recklessly at all."

"But he fled the scene of the accident!" Brenda argued, leaning forward across the table as if to accentuate her words. "Its five years later and he hides out at school with no remorse for his actions? Come on Stan! I don't think we can let that one go, no matter what!"

Why was Caryssa shaking? Her hands were trembling underneath the table. Then it hit her.

She thinks about this all the time…one day, Tyler will be a teenager driving…

Chapter Eleven

Somebody in the corner near them asked the group if they could keep their voices and kids quiet. Some people were trying to watch the Warriors game.

Of course, America's sports distractions are more critical than a family's life. But the group understood – they were in a public place. They toned it down.

"Well, I think we need to change the subject, Warriors game or not. We're all getting a bit hot under the collar."

"I agree, Stan," Caryssa said. She turned to Brenda and laid a calming hand on her forearm. "I know how you feel, girlfriend. I feel the same way. But remember. One day your kids will be sixteen and driving. This was not an adult that hit the child and fled the scene. And we don't know if this kid was driving above the speed limit. We've all seen bikers and skateboarders take crazy risks out there. As Stan said a while ago, there's too much we don't know yet. So we can't judge. Let it go."

After the group finished their coffee and conversation, they went to get the kids from school, run errands, and do whatever other projects they had going on the side.

Caryssa had twenty minutes before the 11:40 pick-up at school, so she stopped into her house on the way, to take care of a few things. Walking through her kitchen, she noticed her message machine was blinking.

She pressed the button, and Anna's soft, poised voice with its distinguished French accent came over the machine. "Caryssa, this is Anna. I am going to be in your area again tomorrow, and wanted to know if you would like to meet for a playdate again. Jared has been asking for Tyler, and I thought maybe you'd like them to play together."

Caryssa had the feeling there was more to Anna's request, some unspoken need to talk. She felt some type of mysterious connection with Anna. They seemed to share some innate understanding of the unknown, still to be discovered. She loved being around Anna's positive energy. In a world of self-serving greed and anger, it was so refreshing to hear this woman talk. To experience her loving perspective.

She made a mental note to call Anna back, finished her tasks, and rushed out the door.

At pick-up, the usual bunch of parents were hanging together by the fence while the children played for a bit. From across the street came Stan's cheerful voice. "Hey you guys, it's another beautiful day in sunny California! Anyone interested in meeting us at the rock climbing structure at the park?"

Caryssa had been planning on spending the next two hours helping Tyler with his homework, but what a beautiful day. There's always later…Parks make life better!

"Count me in," she yelled. "See you guys there!"

At the park, Tyler wanted to ride his scooter. So Caryssa took his scooter and helmet out of the back of her SUV. He rode for a few minutes, then joined the other children climbing the rock wall. As usual, Tyler passed all the others and got to the highest point of the structure within seconds. For a kid who can be shy, he had no fear when it came to climbing!

"Oh my gosh Caryssa, look how high up Tyler is!" Stan exclaimed.

Caryssa was purposely trying to look the other way, perpetually tormented over when to let Tyler go. If anyone ever tried to say she was overprotective, let them see her allow her child to do this.

"I know, boy do I know. He has been a climber since before he turned one. This is nothing compared to what he does with his dad going rock climbing. According to George, he is up there some fifty feet climbing cliffs! Honestly. I don't even dare look. Even on the play structures. He's such a daredevil."

"Ah…according to George…so I take it you don't go with them?"

"Are you kidding?! Oh no, I purposely don't go, on account of trying to save myself an early demise from heart attack! Their rock climbing adventures are when I use up some nervous energy going out for a hike or bike while praying he remains safe."

"Well, it's a good thing he has a helmet on…did you put a ground rule down?" asked Laura.

"I wish I could say I did. He happened to have it on while riding his scooter around. But yeah, he needs a helmet when he's climbing high. Thanks for the reminder, Laura," Caryssa responded.

A man who looked to be in his early thirties was trying to get his little girl to leave the park. "Come on pumpkin, Daddy has to get to work now! Mommy will pick you up in a little while from the day care."

"No Daddy! I don't want to go to day care! Nobody loves me there! I want to stay and play with you!" she cried.

"But pumpkin, Daddy has to go to work. I can't hang around the park all day with you!"

The other parents cringed slightly as well, as he picked up his cute little girl and carried her screaming to the car, all the while yelling at her to stop crying. "Kids are still at the park playing Daddy, I want to stay and play!" the little girl screamed over her father's angry voice.

"Daddy has a job to go to! Some people have no job to go to! You should be glad I can put a roof over our heads! Now *get* in the car! Now!"

"Wow," Stan joked. "We have no 'job' to go to, we must be a pack of park bums!"

"Oh no, not park bums! We better all throw our children into daycare every day and let someone else get paid to do the job of watching over them, while we get a real job already," Caryssa laughed.

"Yeah, he made sure we would hear it, seeing his little girl wanted to play with our kids in the sand," Laura said. "What's next for her, boarding school?"

"Well," Caryssa said, interjecting a note of balance into the conversation. "I know how he feels. It is a conflict. And you know, like with Bianca's accidental death, we don't know what is going on in this dad's mind today, or his life. For all we know he could be this close to missing a mortgage payment. So let's not judge on appearances."

The others nodded. "And anyway," Caryssa continued, "I do miss earning a paycheck. I'm happy I might be working part time soon, even though it will amount to petty cash on the side once in a while. I want to contribute to my family's financial security. I just don't want to do it working for corporations destroying our society and environment, or in a way making my family suffer, or deprive Tyler of his Mommy. And at least for now I am super grateful I don't have to make such choice. Lots of people in this world don't have the luxury. And it's not their fault. It's the fault of the system."

"Especially since we don't have free college tuition or healthcare like many other nations," Stan chimed. "Our nation's investments are all screwed up."

Caryssa suddenly remembered she had been planning on reviewing her portfolio and making sure all her investments were both building cash for Tyler's college and supporting green and conscious businesses. She made a mental note to check in with her financial advisor when she got home.

When she and Tyler got home from the park, Caryssa got him started on the part of his homework he could do himself, and went straight to her home office, dialed her financial advisor's number, and left him a message to please call her back. Then she gathered her financial reports and went back out to the kitchen. She sat with Tyler as he worked on the sheets his kindergarten teacher had sent home with him, copying the alphabet and numbers with his jumbo pencil.

After a few minutes her phone rang.

"Hello, this is Caryssa."

"Hi Caryssa, this is Jed Blankenship. From Blankenship Investment Services. You left me a voice mail? How can I help you?"

"Oh. Hi Jed. Thanks for getting back to me so soon!"

"Of course. You are an important client and we want to be sure we are meeting your needs. How can I help you today?"

Caryssa spread her financial reports out in front of her. "I know my tiny portfolio is doing well. But…well…I'm invested in a lot of companies I simply don't believe in. I left it up to you to choose, because you are the financial analyst and the expert on the market. But now I'm looking at my reports and I'm appalled. I'm investing in oil? *Dirty* energy! I want to invest in clean energy. And I'm seeing Monsanto, Yum Brands, and Halliburton on the list. These are socially and environmentally corrupt giants. I don't want my money supporting them. They make their money from human suffering."

Jed took a deep breath. Another upset progressive client to placate. This seemed to be happening to him more and more every day. How do these morally conscious people expect to survive?

"I understand Mrs. Flynn. Believe me I do. These are the tradeoffs we have to make in order to make money for our clients…and right now? Those stocks are where the money is. I'm investing wisely for you, so you can send your boy to college and so you will have enough money for your golden years. Maybe someday the money will be in socially responsible companies. But for right now? You told us your goal was to grow your portfolio. Your portfolio is growing. Would you like me to change your investments? If so I can't guarantee you'll get the results you've been getting with us. But of course, it's your decision."

Caryssa looked more closely at her statement. She saw her portfolio had nearly doubled over the past year. "Okay, Jed. I see your point. You have grown our portfolio and it looks super healthy. But my values have changed. I also want to promote sustainable living. Please remove the stocks I mentioned. And replace them with the best green stocks you can find worth investing in. I don't care about the ROI. Well. Wait. Of course I do care about the ROI. But I'm not willing to sell out my son's future or my soul to get it. I need to be able to sleep at night."

"Sure. I'll do some research, make some changes, and update your data. You'll be able to see it within twenty-four hours. Will that work for you, Mrs. Flynn?"

"It will. And thanks, Jed, for your cooperation."

"How are you doing on your homework?" she asked Tyler after hanging up the phone. "Need any help?"

"Nope, Mom, thanks anyway! I GOT this! But sit with me, okay?"

"Always, my dear sweet little man. Whatever you need. But Mommy needs to make another phone call. Let me know if it breaks your concentration and I'll go out on the patio."

Tyler was so involved with his penmanship lesson he didn't even answer. He was going to get this right. He leaned on one elbow with his head in his hand, focused on the paper and on the fat pencil in his little fingers. He could do this. He knew he could.

Caryssa left him to his work and dialed Anna's number. She answered on the second ring.

"Oh Caryssa, thank you so much for calling back. I know you might think it strange I am calling since we just met last week. But I…well… Jared has asked for Tyler, but I also wanted to talk to you. Could we meet for a playdate tomorrow? I can come to your place if that works. Or the park? Your choice."

"That would work great…why don't you come to my place? We can have tea and chat. I'll make sure Tyler gets all his homework done today so he can play with Jared tomorrow."

Anna came over the next afternoon. Tyler quickly took the younger Jared under his wing, showing him around his room and exhibiting his vast array of toys.

Over a cup of jasmine tea with home-made scones, Anna poured her heart out to Caryssa. "I feel like I need to tell you about my father. I feel it has much to do with my ambiguity over how to handle Bianca's case," she began.

Caryssa listened without saying a word as Anna spoke of her father's horror in the war, how she and her mom had begged him not to go back the last time he came home, how he went back for imposed upon illusive retribution and was killed.

Caryssa took Anna's hand. "Don't torture yourself about revenge because your dad's heritage demands it. Whatever tradition of vengeance they had in the old days, it should be long ago and far away. You can hold yourself to a higher standard."

"I am not so sure about that…my lawyer, all the newspapers, my ex-husband…everyone seems to say justice must be served. I'm expected to want the death of my precious little girl avenged. As if it will preserve her memory better."

Caryssa remained silent. She had the feeling Anna did not expect an answer. She needed loving attention, somebody to listen.

Anna glanced at her in appreciation and continued. "But it wouldn't be justice, would it? It would be…revenge. A vengeful concept of justice at best. A young man would be sent to prison rather than finishing medical school. And yet another good family would be torn apart. None of it would bring my little girl back."

Caryssa opened her mouth to speak, but no words came out. She felt the presence of her angel. The message was clear. *"Silence!"*

But the silence remained for a longer period than Caryssa felt comfortable with. Was this her queue to speak? Offer some profound advice on a topic she has no experience with? Where was the angel when she needed her?

Anna saved her just in time. "Thank you so much for listening to me Caryssa. Exactly what I needed. So many others tell me how I should feel, what I should do. They come up with some type of solution, as if they know. But this is something with no easy resolution."

"I could not even *imagine* what you are going through Anna. So I wouldn't presume to offer you any more advice," Caryssa said, leaning forward and laying her hand on her friend's arm. "And I'm truly honored you're sharing this with me."

"You know, I wonder…I thought of you because, well, because you have only one child, one son. Like Bill and Nancy Garth. They just have Brandon. They are very protective of him, and should be as good and loving parents…"

Caryssa instantly felt a newfound respect for the Garths. Doing whatever they could to protect their son. Not succumbing to the crushing pressure of a flawed justice system.

While Caryssa was having her private thoughts, Anna was having her own. Why do I feel so close to this woman, when I could never feel close to friends growing up?

Then it occurred to her. While she had been so busy trying to assuage her mother's grief, she had closed off all friendships. A pattern still continued through her adult life. Even though she had a large circle of friends growing up and all through university in Paris, she had never learned to be close to anyone. She was too afraid of losing love.

"I'd like to ask you a hypothetical question" Anna paused, taking a sip of tea and a deep breath. "I know this will be hard to answer…but I want you to put yourself in the Garths' place. Same situation, but imagine Tyler was sixteen, and he was driving."

"I…wait a minute…are they now saying they know for sure it was the son driving, not the father?"

Anna didn't say a word for several minutes, which seemed like an eternity to Caryssa. Finally Anna responded, her voice faltering.

"Actually, I haven't told the police this yet…or my lawyer. But it *was* the son."

"What…what happened?"

"I had a call from Brandon Garth. He told me his dad is covering for him, he was the one driving the Honda that day. He cried on the phone, wants to meet with me. He is at this moment on an airplane from LAX to SFO, arriving at six tonight."

"Oh Lord! Have you agreed to meet with him?"

"Why of course! Caryssa, I believe him. I believe this kid!" Anna burst into tears. Caryssa reached over the table and gathered her in an awkward but heartfelt hug. Anna cried until she had no more tears left, and then straightened up, wiped her face with her napkin, blew her nose, and regained her composure.

Caryssa waited until she could see Anna was ready to talk some more. Then she offered what she thought was a supportive comment. "Well, if he said he was driving, I am sure he was."

This set Anna off again. "No! That's not what I mean!" she cried. "I asked him why he didn't stop. He said he did stop, and he saw nothing but a skateboard. He had looked along the side of the road to see if he had hit somebody. There was nobody there. And the sound had seemed more like a pop than thud. So he thought he must have just hit a skateboard on the side of the street. So he left."

Anna's story at the park flashed through Caryssa's mind. *Bianca's body was found five feet from the curb, on the other side of a juniper bush.*

Anna went on. "Brandon told me after he read the paper, he realized he must have hit the girl. But he was frightened. He was only sixteen. He said he was not driving above the speed limit, in fact was going much slower because it was foggy and drizzling. He also said the papers had the story all wrong…they said a witness saw the car drive away fast without stopping."

Anna did not mention what the police and coroner reports had said after the accident. That a car going as slow as five miles per hour can cause internal bleeding and kill a person on impact. Bianca had a skull fracture and internal bleeding to the brain. It was not known whether this was from hitting the ground or the car's impact. What was known was the skateboard hit the car and sent Bianca flying five feet to land beyond a juniper bush, near several jagged rocks. Traces of blood had been found on one of the rocks.

"Do you still want me to answer the hypothetical question, now that I know about his call?" asked Caryssa.

"Absolutely! If you wouldn't mind."

"If this happened to Tyler, and he was now a top medical student at UCLA, great kid, whole life ahead of him, never a menace to society? I would do whatever it took to protect his innocent soul. This is not a case of an adult drinking, driving recklessly, and hitting a child. This is a *child* hitting a *child*."

The two women sat silent with their thoughts for a few moments.

Finally Anna spoke. "Brandon said the cops were at his school the day he called me. That must be what prompted him to get in touch. Can you imagine the cops sneaking up on the kid at his school, no forewarning, interrogating him!?"

"Unbelievable. Would make me livid. What's going on with the case now?"

"They have been working on jury selection, which could take forever. They've already seen over two hundred potential jurors and they still don't have a complete jury. They want the perfect representation. Both prosecution and defense want plenty of parents in there so they can hit their hearts with their spin."

"Did I hear correctly this might even be televised?"

"Yes, this guy Garth is high profile. Have you not read any of the articles in the papers this week?"

"Afraid not. I read so many environmental journals, internet research, nonfiction about politics, Tyler's school papers I have no time left over. And when I do, trust me, its novels over the newspaper. As a matter of fact, I'm trying my hand at writing one. In any case, I can't stand reading those twisted lies in the news."

"Exactly. I can't believe half the stuff they say about me. Your novel, even if it's entirely made up, will have more truth in it than anything you see in the paper. In one piece they said I am a struggling art studio owner looking for a quick cash fix at expense of an aspiring young med student. In another I am referred to as a rich Sausalito art entrepreneur. And what they say about Brandon is worse. Poor little rich boy finally getting what's coming to him. I honestly don't know where they get this stuff.

It's as if instead of actually reporting, they sit at their desks and create fictions. But the readers don't know that."

Caryssa nodded. "Yup, that's why I pretty much ignore it. It isn't news. It's what you said, exactly. It's fiction. And you're right, there's going to be a lot of truth in my novel, I have this vision of telling a story nobody can stop reading till the end. But, you know, getting back to the case? I don't understand how the prosecution can have sufficient witnesses…wasn't there just the one woman with Alzheimer's?"

"Yes. Lois Wright. She doesn't have Alzheimer's. She's just a bit flighty. Drinks too much. Artsy type. I plan to visit her and get a feel for her myself. I've not yet met her in person. It's been too painful hearing details she may have seen. But anyway, they have plenty of witnesses, both Bianca's and Cassidy's friends."

"Cassidy's? Why? The case isn't about her."

"I agree. But according to the plaintiff team, the case is about my entire family. They are pushing for huge payout against the Garth boy for the bigger loss. All the repercussions of Bianca's death. It's a bit absurd. But I have to tell you, Phil van Wagner is a shark. That man has not lost a case in over ten years. They say he's magic with the jurors, which frightens me on behalf of that young man Brandon Garth and his parents."

The more Caryssa got to know Anna, the more she liked her. To be grieving so deeply for the loss of her family, yet compassionate enough to feel for the boy responsible for the accident that had killed her daughter. Human decency, unheard of in the world, *in America*.

Was he responsible? Caryssa remembered Anna's words in the park when she told them the sad story. *Bianca was a known dare-devil on her skateboard, always taking big risks.*

"You know how much a parent loves a child, that gut-wrenching, jump in front of a truck to save your little one, constant worry over their safety, health and wellbeing, sacrificing every fiber of your being love?" Anna was saying.

Tyler, Caryssa thought. What could she say? He'd once been a part of her. She'd heard his heart beating inside her at twelve weeks, she'd felt his movements within her the last five months of her pregnancy. After his birth, she had taken one look at him and couldn't believe anything more beautiful could exist in the world.

That feeling hadn't changed, although she wasn't a perfect mother. Nobody could take on such a challenge and be perfect. Parenthood is not as painless as working for a business or even running one, as difficult as that can be. Or merely having responsibility for a pet. It's *far* deeper, far more risks involved, with far more to win and lose.

Anna's voice brought her back from her reverie to the conversation. "I feel like a ping pong ball. I get bounced over to one side of the table, and I feel like, okay, I am going to get revenge on the person responsible for hitting my daughter with his car. She would still be here today if he had not driven my street that day. My entire family would still be intact."

Caryssa waited for Anna to continue.

"But then I get bounced onto the other side of the table and feel like, wait a minute, couldn't *anyone* have hit her in such poor visibility on my narrow winding street? If not Brandon, then the next car to come along? This is Bianca we're talking about. More guts on a skateboard than anyone and willfully defiant that day. I can't discredit my own daughter's quirks in this. There are too many questions still open."

Caryssa nodded. "I'm sure the prosecution team will have a field day with the fact Brandon didn't call the whole thing in to the police when it happened. Not to mention five years went by with him still not saying anything."

"But, Caryssa, a moment ago you said you'd do whatever it took to protect your son's innocent soul, if something like this ever happened to him when he is old enough to drive."

"I did…and I would. I'm playing devil's advocate here for a moment, thinking through both sides of the case. I'm an analyst, right to the core. When I get a gnarly problem to solve, I go after it until I've looked at all angles and create a picture representing the whole problem. You have to get the problem nailed first. And not shy away from the details," Caryssa explained. Then she smiled. "It's what made me so good at my tech job back in the day. That's why they paid me the big bucks."

"Oh…no," Anna reassured her. "I didn't mean to imply you're being insensitive. Far from it. You are the only person I've felt comfortable sharing the ins and outs of all this with. I love how you listen to me, and let me cry, and don't try to fix it, or worse, tell me how I should feel. Every time I try to make sense of it all I break down. And my mind goes blank. I need you to apply your analytical skills to this!

"And anyway, if anyone is being insensitive it's me. How can I be so hardened, to not want to go after the person responsible for my daughter's death? I am more worried over tearing the Garth family apart than I am about my own family torn apart. Has my heart turned to steel over the past five years?"

"No. Not even close. Quite the opposite. You're being open and compassionate, and I have to say I respect you a lot for that. It couldn't be easy to put aside the anger about what happened. Woman, you suffered the most difficult losses anyone could possibly suffer, and you're still thinking of the other person! To me that's downright amazing."

"Thank you. It's sweet of you to say, and I'll do my best to take it in. Sometimes I am so hard on myself. I've been trying to learn to point my compassion inward, but it seems harder than to give it to others.

"But the truth is I do have anger. Funny thing is, it is not directed toward the Garth boy. For the longest time I was consumed with anger and with wanting to get the responsible person in trouble. I didn't have the facts. So I had visions of some drunken asshole hitting my daughter and then taking off at full speed. But time passed. And I adjusted. Life went on. Not a moment passes that I don't think of both my girls and miss them.

My anger has changed. Now it's directed at…well…I don't know… the reporters wanting a story, and my lawyer's team wanting to put the screws to the Garths. Everybody wants to make a buck out of people's tragedy. It infuriates me. Before it all came back into play, I had this under control. I was starting to feel like the wounds were starting to heal. And now it's as if…"

Anna couldn't finish. Her hands were cupped around her now cold tea, and they were trembling.

Caryssa finished her sentence for her. "It's as if someone is tearing the wounds open and pouring salt in."

"Yes."

Caryssa put her tea cup down and gave Anna another hug. Neither woman said anything for a long time.

Anna found herself watching Jared and Tyler play in the living room. Suddenly it all fell into place for her. Suddenly she knew where she stood. In a way she would not be manipulated out of. It was a clarity that had been a long time coming, but once she had it she knew it was unshakable.

She stood up.

"Thank you, Caryssa," she said warmly. "I feel so much better. You really helped. Let me corral my grandson and we'll leave you to get on with your day."

After Anna and Jared had left, Caryssa was picking up the kitchen a bit and starting to get dinner on. The newspapers had been thrown onto a chair at the back of the table that morning. As she picked them up, her eyes swept the headlines.

Then she saw it.

"Money-hungry artist looking for quick cash fix? Did victim's parents fail to direct dare-devil skateboarder away from danger zone? Neighbor's sudden memories bring five-year-old cold case back to life. Fugitive defendant guilty of felony hit and run?"

How can such callous pieces be published in our newspapers? Caryssa tossed the paper onto the table, skimming the headlines. Reporters, hungry for a story, turning family tragedy into a soap opera. Not concerned at all what their lies do to people's lives. Dear Lord, how did this amazing woman stay so calm and compassionate?

Earlier, at the Golden Gate Grind, Brenda had suggested the gang meet there again in a couple of weeks to watch the opening statements. Caryssa hadn't been sure that was such a good idea, but after Anna's visit and seeing those news stories, she decided she would go.

If the case even went to trial. After what she had learned about Anna's beautiful soul, she had a strong feeling it just might not.

Chapter Twelve

It was a hot spring day in late May. Tyler emerged from his bedroom with his baseball outfit on, glove in hand. "Hi Mommy! Where's Dad? It's time to go play some ball and celebrate the end of the league season!"

Caryssa looked up from the dishwasher, where she had been trying to find places to put the breakfast dishes before running a load. "I don't know, honey. Last time I saw him he was heading out to the yard to pull weeds and put in the new plants he bought me for Mother's Day. But you're right. We need to get going soon! You go find him. I'm gonna get changed. It's already hot out! Where's the fog when you really need it?!"

Tyler laughed. "You're silly, Mommy. You know we all like it hot. *Fog fog go away! Don't come again some other day!*" He ran over and gave her a hug, and then headed out the door yelling "Dad! DAD? Daddy!!! Where are you?" Somewhere below at the far end of their property George called back "Right here, son!!"

Smiling to herself, Caryssa went into her bedroom, slipped out of her robe, pulled a bright turquoise tank top out of her dresser and a jean skirt off a hanger in her closet. As she put them on, she rummaged through a basket of baseball caps. She was looking for just the right one. Ah there it was…emblazoned with the name of Tyler's T-ball team. Perfect.

She grabbed a hair tie off the dresser and scooped her thick blond hair into a high ponytail, then put the cap on at a jaunty angle and pulled her ponytail through the space at the back. She grabbed a lip gloss and swiped her lips. Surveying herself in her dresser mirror she thought

"Yup. Good enough for a day at the park. Besides, who needs Ann Taylor when I have my beautiful boys?"

Back in the kitchen, Caryssa saw George had packed a picnic lunch and Tyler was dancing around him in excitement. She put her arms around George from behind as he stood at the counter about to close the basket. "Nice idea, honey. But you do know it's the celebration party today, right? Which means lots of food already there?"

George turned around, pulled her into a bear hug and kissed her. "I do indeed… But I packed some special stuff just for you. I know how hard you worked on the celebration committee, to make the party perfect. You deserve a reward."

"Really?" Caryssa playfully tried to reach her arms around George to open the basket. "What's in it?"

"Ohhhh no you don't!" he laughed, pinning her arm to his side. "No peeking. It's a surprise!"

She gave up the struggle and gave George another kiss. "You take such good care of me! How did I land such a prince?!"

George smiled. He pulled her into a deeper hug and nuzzled her neck, murmuring "Only the best for my best girl."

Meanwhile, Tyler was already heading out the door. "Hurry up, you guys! Hurry UP!!! No more mushy stuff! I don't want to be late! It's the last game of the season!"

Laughing, they said in unison "Okay little man! Here we come!" George grabbed the picnic basket off the counter and closed it, and then he and Caryssa followed their excited son out to the car.

When they arrived at the baseball field, the usual fun community faces were there. Caryssa had grown to love the families since the season had started. She always looked forward to these special times. They would gather around with their chairs, coolers, and conversations. She felt especially drawn to one family in particular. Bryan and Charlotte Garrity had twin five-year-old sons, Kevin and Keenan, both on Tyler's team.

Bryan Garrity volunteered as an assistant coach for the team. An Irish-Italian Catholic originally from Connecticut, he had moved to San Francisco in the early nineties. There he had met Charlotte, they had married, and soon welcomed their twin boys into the world. After the twins were born, the family had moved to the East Bay.

As part of her mandatory parent volunteer hours, Caryssa had organized the end of season party with Charlotte. When they arrived at the field, Tyler took off to join his team and George followed Caryssa, carrying the folding chairs, picnic basket, and blanket. Charlotte saw them and waved to them to come over and join her.

"Hey Caryssa!" Charlotte was setting up her own chairs and umbrella. "Great to see you guys! Looks like we have the turnout we hoped for!"

George set their stuff down, nodded to Charlotte in greeting, and then turned to Caryssa. "Honey, I'm going to go—"

"I know," Caryssa said smiling at him, "take some videos."

He laughed. "You know me too well."

As George walked off towards the field, Caryssa pulled out her lawn chair, set it up, and sank into it with a sigh. "You're right" She surveyed the scene. "Great turnout. I'm still exhausted."

Charlotte laughed. "Me too. But it's *so* worth it."

"Yup," Caryssa laid the picnic basket between them. "And my sweetie packed me a special basket as a reward. I'm sharing it with you."

Charlotte started to respond but then noticed the game was starting. "Ooooo…" she said, pointing towards the field. "To be continued!"

The two women watched intently in silence for a while. George was walking around the periphery of the field with the camcorder, seemingly talking to himself while taping one of life's most precious memories.

After the first inning, Caryssa opened the picnic basket. "Wow, Check it out!" As they began pulling the delicacies out for a well-earned feast, Caryssa asked "So explain what you do for work again? I know it has to do with the environment. I am so interested. I'm trying to move in that direction professionally."

"I work in ecology. I'm sure you know what it entails." Charlotte had her eyes on the delicious spread George packed for them.

"Sure," Caryssa said. "Isn't it the scientific study of relationships between organisms and their environment?"

"Exactly," Charlotte placed a couple spring rolls on her plate. "I focus on environmental issues starting at the minutest level, and reaching to the human. For instance, why frogs are mutating and disappearing. Three guesses why, and I'll give you a hint: toxic waste! The studies I do show scientific proof of the detrimental effect modern civilization has on the environment, and how it is hurting humans as well. Over and over I see if we don't improve the environment, human life on this planet might become unsustainable. And it's frightening how most people don't get it."

"Geesh, humans becoming extinct like the dinosaurs once did!" joked a parent sitting nearby overhearing the conversation. "Makes me fear for our next generation!"

"Fascinating and frightening! Particularly alarming are the environmental effects on children," Caryssa interjected. "Since becoming a parent, I have become so concerned about the future of our planet, our kids! I worked in the high tech arena for years and made good money. But if I can find work in this field, some way to contribute? I'd start at peanuts if it meant making a difference!"

Charlotte said "That's a great attitude, Caryssa. And I believe the environmental sector will be the hot pot in the very near future. Good things are to come. And you have lots to offer, with your analytic and marketing background. Tons. I say go for it!"

"Oh…good hit Tyler! Run to first base! Run! RUN!" Caryssa shouted. "Oops sorry, Charlotte. I'm listening. But wow what a great hit! Especially for *my* kid, the master of striking out."

Charlotte laughed. "Totally get it, girlfriend." "Tyler is on fire today!"

"Thanks for understanding," Caryssa pulled out the sparkling water, then poured two cups. "And, back on point. Our politicians talk as if they are concerned with the environment, but the next thing they do is approve offshore oil drilling, some senseless pipeline or 'clean coal,' which anybody paying attention knows simply doesn't exist!"

"Oh, but we're drilling for America's future! Our jobbier future! All we have to do is ravage our National Parks," Charlotte joked. "Until the shadowy criminal cabal known as 'campers' try to hoard those precious resources!"

"Hah! Tell me about it!" Caryssa laughed. "But seriously. On a more personal subject. You work full time, right? How the heck do you do it? I am always amazed when parents can work, but still remain involved daily with their kids. What's your secret?"

"Well," Charlotte responded. "I work from home, which isn't as great as it sounds. I work thirty-five hours a week. We have an au pair. She's great. But it is very expensive, and truth be told, I feel like I just work to pay her. By the time taxes are taken out and all. But it keeps me in the game, my mind working, and helps me stay sane in an otherwise insane world."

"I can see. Staying sane is a good thing. Sometimes I feel like I am losing it. I'm so focused in on the great martyrdom of mommyhood. But then I get anxious thinking what the upcoming job, as part time as it will be, will do to my time with Tyler. I don't want to lose that." Caryssa sighed. "Believe it or not, I want to do an even better job at motherhood than I already am. Such mixed emotions!"

"Emotional turmoil seems to be a main ingredient of motherhood," Charlotte replied. "I feel so anguished over having to work, not spending enough time with my boys. It kills me, especially knowing what we could have had from Bryan's side of the family. Well, Wait. Bryan's happiness is more important than getting entangled in family drama just for the money. But still, it would be so great to be able to save for college, and to spend more time with our boys."

"So…what does Bryan do for work?" Caryssa inquired cautiously, curious about his family background but not wanting to step on any toes.

"Oh, he's a landscape architect. He has his own business. He was doing well for a while there. But it's very slow right now. Nobody wants to risk spending money. As a result, I have to work full time so we can make ends meet. We didn't plan it this way. We wanted one of us to be home. But this is how it fell out. And, you know…" Charlotte hesitated. Then she took a deep breath and continued. "I shouldn't tell you this, but I always wonder how my family would have fared if my husband had not had a falling out with his father."

"Really!" Caryssa said. "I'm intrigued! What happened?"

"Bryan is from a highly affluent family in Connecticut. Let me first tell you, I love Bryan with my whole heart and soul, and am happy he is not following in the footsteps of his pompous ass of a father. Anyhow, he dropped out of Harvard after two years of law studies, then left the East Coast and his rich family. When he first arrived in California, he had no job and no skills.

"He pretty much bummed and thumbed his way across country on American Express and Carte Blanche. He even got arrested once for possession of pot. It seemed like he was on the fast track to nowhere. But after a while, he found himself. He figured out what he loved and what he wanted to do with his life, outside of the family expectations. He went to Cal Poly, almost as a protest, and studied landscape design. He was good at it. So after college he was able to make a good career. He did beautiful work for his clients. They loved him. The referrals poured in. By the time we were married with kids, everything looked like it was going to be one of those 'happily ever after stories.'

Charlotte hesitated "And then the bottom fell out of the housing market."

Caryssa groaned. "Yeah, I hearya. Seems to have affected everybody. But wow! What a great story! Like something out of the movies or a good book. Keep going! Although I just hafta say. Getting arrested for possession of pot is one area we can see how the USA has never been as free as we've been taught to believe. There are far worse crimes than merely carrying around an herb--- legal in some states and shown to have amazing medical benefits."

"Oh, believe me, I am not teaching my sons to be so naïve as to think our country has all the freedom we rave about. I'm with you on that one! Anyhow, Bryan is so sweet…all he ever wanted was a comfortable, happy, simple life. He didn't want to have his career path handed to him on a silver platter. Especially if such a life and career path, no matter how rich he would be, meant any of the shady things he witnessed firsthand as a little boy. His dad's political career was…hmmm…how I shall put this—"

"You don't have to," Caryssa interjected. "I can imagine. And wow, how sad. No wonder he lost his way for a while."

"Yeah. But it gets worse. His dad was emotionally abusive. And both parents neglected him horribly."

Suddenly, Caryssa put two and two together. Charlotte answered her question without her needing to ask.

"His uncle was the one assassinated, remember? You wouldn't believe! His uncle was once the lead candidate for US President, but was assassinated by a sniper before the general elections"

"No kidding!? I *do* remember, and that was Bryan's Uncle! You go girl, married into such history!"

"Ha! History, of *violence*! His father, a US Senator from Connecticut, had been shot and nearly crippled during a primary campaign. As you can see, his family was so well liked people couldn't wait to shoot them!"

"OMG, I just can't believe this story. You could write a book! Caryssa had her eyes on the baseball field realizing they were not really watching much of the game closely. "I can't believe his Uncle ran for President!"

"I know, right? Anyhow, rather than these tragedies bringing the family closer together, they drove Bryan away. He felt compelled to escape from the political mythology seemingly making the Garritys more than ordinary men or women. Like demigods, or demigoddesses, embodiments of virtue, goodwill, sacrifice. It was too pretentious for him. And he knew it was built on lies."

"I'm getting a feeling for the direction this took," Caryssa said. "Let's see. Bryan's father wanted him to follow in his footsteps. Bryan didn't. So they had a falling out. Am I close?"

"Oh… it gets even uglier. His father *disowned* his only son! Cut him off! He would have gained control of a thirty-five-million-plus trust fund. But he would have had to play the game and toe the line. The dirty game of politics depressed him too much. He had to choose happiness over the family legend. He decided he'd rather be happy with a moderate income he earned himself than filthy rich, miserable, and spoon fed by the Feds."

"You know," Caryssa responded, "I respect Bryan more. Most people think money is the most important thing in the world, to the point where they don't care about or even want to recognize any detrimental effects their jobs may have on society or other people."

Charlotte laughed. "I don't know. We're struggling in these tough economic times. At one point Bryan had ninety people working for him in the landscaping business. He's had to cut to twenty, and still needs to cut back. Apart from creating enemies—nobody likes to be laid off—the financial burden is taking a toll on our family. We're not broke. We've curtailed spending to match our income. But I have two sons to send to college and we can't afford to save a dime even with both of us working."

"Yup…us too. And especially with all the budget cuts in schools, we parents have more to worry about with respect to our children's future."

"Exactly. Education should be the last place the budget is cut in a recession. What future does our nation have without educating its young? You know frankly, I don't want my in-laws' thirty-five million of dirty money. I don't want to feed from the fat cats sitting in Senate seats and taking money from pollution and war industries. Kind of goes against the grain of everything I stand for, in my career and as a mom. But..."

Caryssa completed her sentence. "But it would be nice to get a little financial support from the fat cat side of the family for your children's sakes, in a nation making outlandish decisions to cut back at the expense of the children."

"I could not have said it better myself. Sure, take some damn cash from the fat cats. Maybe I'll be able to spend precious time with my kids then. Either way, it just kills me!"

"So tell me more about Bryan's background. This is so fascinating," Caryssa offered Charlotte some curried chicken salad from her picnic basket.

"Well, his adventures to California, as well as his overseas travels, put him on the front pages of newspapers on every continent for a while. That's what happens with high-profile families. Anything the media can use to make a story. All the hoopla made him turn even further from family. He started taking big risks before heading to Cal Poly."

"Risks? What kinds of risks?"

"Well, let's see. Shooting rapids on the Colorado River. He capsized and nearly drowned. A full-on confrontation with a bull in one of Madrid's rings. And my personal favorite, going on an African safari in an open jeep, and getting out, which was against rules mind you, then getting attacked by a rhinoceros!"

"Hey, I think I saw him in Jurassic Park!" Caryssa joked.

"Ha ha, let me tell you, his escape and radical departure from his political family was the stuff of endless magazine covers from *People* to *Playboy* and *Vanity Fair*. He became a national obsession, this simple, self-made man of mine. No wonder he got a bit off track for a short period of his life."

"Yeah, there's something to be said for being a wallflower. I'm partial to my privacy." Caryssa sipped her Perrier while watching the boys play ball.

"The articles in the magazines and the twisted propaganda in the newspapers made him out to be a total loser who lacks ambition just because he didn't wish to take his place in the political elite of his heritage. Funny, but those articles seemed to drive him to have less ambition for a while. Politics the way he witnessed it as a child infected him with a cynicism making him question the value of any achievement or attainment, inside or outside the political arena."

That last statement hit Caryssa hard. Had the political environment of the high tech corporate environment—as well as what she sees in our corrupt politic overall, caused an equivalent feeling in her? She made a mental note to revisit the idea.

"Well it sounds like he found his calling, and look at him out there always smiling," she observed. Caryssa nervously pushed her hair behind her ear. Politics, which impacts our daily lives, unnerves her. She laughs when people say they don't care about politics. They basically are saying they don't care about their life.

The two women took a moment to glance toward Bryan, coaching the young team at center field.

"Bryan loves spending time with his boys, takes great pride in coaching ball and playing with them in the backyard," Charlotte agreed. "I just hope his calling in landscape architecture sees better times economically sometime in our kids' lifetimes. He was making great money before the housing market crash. His landscape business is connected with that. And the housing crash has been going on since our kids were born!"

"You know," Caryssa ventured after a pause, "it's none of my business of course, but I think it would be good for Bryan and his dad to reconnect. Not just for the potential financial angle, but…you know…life is short! Those family relationships are important. And especially to your boys. I hate to see money and career choice cause rifts in families."

"Well, it's funny you should mention it, "Charlotte said. "Bryan and his dad have started speaking to each other again. Of course, it is still regarding money and not a touchy feely thing. Bryan's business focuses on environmentally sustainable design. He is investing in all sustainable materials for his projects, how he differentiates himself on the market. People in the bay area love it. But to keep making it happen, he needs capital, lots of it…and…"

"And his dad helped him out?"

"Well, yeah. The Garrity family foundation made an eight-hundred-fifty-thousand-dollar grant to Bryan's business to help get it back up and running the way he envisions it. A far cry from the thirty million trust fund…but it sure helped! There are still challenges with obtaining all sustainable sources. Especially in the area of renewable, clean energy. If our economic policy overall would stop the boom and bust cycles and stop continued asset stripping of our earth's dwindling resources…"

"Yeah, dwindling *dirty* resources!" Caryssa interjected.

Out of the blue, Charlotte changed the subject. "Do you ever worry about how it would affect Tyler if you lose your husband?"

"Sure…it's a huge concern. He needs the influence and love of his dad. And he especially will as a teenager, so I hope George lives that long! But truth be told, I fear as much—possibly *more*—the effect on Tyler if he lost me."

"Mommy's little boy?" Charlotte smiled.

"It depends what day of the week. He can be Daddy's little boy too. But I am the nurturing one, the one who takes him to school and picks him up every day, oversees his homework, picks him up from daycare, organizes playdates, gets him on sports teams, makes sure he gets his bath or shower, helps him brush his teeth, takes him to the pediatrician, takes him to the dentist, does most of the nighttime reading, gets him to bed…well, you get the picture!"

"Oh, I know. I'm not sure if Bryan even knows where the boys' pediatrician or dentist offices are!" laughed Charlotte. "And the one day I asked him to drop the boys off before work, he didn't even know where to drop them!"

"Exactly! I'm frightened if something happened to me tomorrow, Tyler would not even get his basic needs met. Homework would fall to the wayside. Paperwork to sign up for sports, volunteer stuff for the school, or he'd be allowed to spend exorbitant amounts of time on the internet!"

"Well, don't forget they are going to grow up and start doing so much on their own. Sooner or later, Caryssa, you might have to let go a little. Especially all the community volunteer work you do!"

"I don't agree we should ever let go. I'm frightened of losing touch with Tyler's world when he's a teenager. Charlotte, our boys will need us as much when they're in high school as they do now. I mean, not for getting to and from places, doing their laundry, taking care of their personal and hygiene needs. But to step in where needed to be sure they don't fall prey to the warped society we live in."

"Oh believe me, you're preaching to the choir. I don't mean letting go that way, but finding something even part time, to feel you are contributing to Tyler's future financially as well as emotionally. Anyhow, you have your family back East, right? I know it makes a big difference. At least I have my mother here. She helps me a lot with the kids."

"Yes, it does make it more difficult not having family here. I love California and love living here. So beautiful. But none of it can take the place of my family. And my dad has been terminally ill for a while. I wish I could get back there more often to be there for him"

Charlotte didn't respond with words, but leaned over, gave Caryssa's shoulder a squeeze, and looked into her eyes for a moment to show she understood and empathized. Then, as if to lift both their spirits and redirect the afternoon to more positive things, she said "Oh look, Caryssa! Tyler is up at bat again!"

Chapter Thirteen

The game was coming to a climatic end, with a few parents on the sidelines going a bit too wild, as if winning meant their child's college scholarship. Or demise in life.

George rejoined Bryan at the edge of the field for the last play of the game, still shooting his video. After the play, excited kids ran past them, ready to join their families and get on with the party. The two men exchanged high-fives, as their boys came running over.

"Great job, guys! Well played! Give me thirty!!!" Bryan lifted both his hands so the boys could all high-five him at once.

Then the boys ran ahead to where Caryssa and Charlotte were waiting, and Bryan and George followed more slowly, dissecting the highs and lows of the final game of the season.

While the two families walked to the park area for the festivities, Caryssa listened as Bryan joked about how at this age, coaching the kids means a lot of telling them to watch for the ball while out on the field rather than the airplanes or birds flying by.

"True, but some of those kids can hit," Charlotte said.

"Oh yeah they can! And catch! And I'm pleased with how well Tyler and the other kids learned the game of baseball in this league. It's amazing how fast they learned the rules and positions!" Caryssa chimed in.

Bryan Garrity, tall, brown hair, sparkling blue eyes, with a slightly crooked Irish grin, pulled one of his twin boys, Kevin, onto his shoulders while the other boys ran ahead, down the hill to the park.

After hearing bits and pieces about Bryan's ordeal with his family back East, Caryssa realized she and George should count their blessings.

Things weren't perfect, but she could not *imagine* having a parent disown a child. Both their extended families couldn't seem to embrace viewpoints outside of harsh political cultural 'norms' they grew up with. Yet nobody has ever done anything so harsh, so cold...

True, the natural rhythms of their life were thrown off when they traveled east to visit family. There was a total lack of structure. Yet, they were always surprised at some family members' subtle strange reactions to their harmonious lifestyle.

In a world where stress has become so endemic, worn like a badge of courage, should this be such a surprise? Busyness is put on a pedestal, and it was probably a shock for relatives to encounter a side of the family not valuing it. She loves her family and George's...every single one of them. So it was something she had learned to live with.

As if reading her mind, Bryan said "George mentioned you guys go back East every year to visit family. You're so lucky to have those relationships. I haven't seen my family in years, and my parents have yet to meet my sons."

Caryssa couldn't speak for a few minutes, she was so taken aback. Then, cautiously commented "Wow, I could not imagine. It is so important to have Tyler see his grandparents and our family. Is there any way you could bridge the gap for your kids' sakes?"

Bryan started tossing a baseball in the air and catching it. "It's more complicated than you know. There's too much repressed resentment going on in my family to bring my boys into. They fight about money like it's the end of the world, even though they are extremely wealthy. What hurts is I really should get a piece of the pie to help put my boys through school, pay bills, and deal with life's economic challenges." He reached out and ruffled Charlotte's hair as she walked beside him. "Perhaps even let this great mommy spend more time with the boys."

Good Lord, thought Caryssa. This nice man can't even get a piece of the elitist 1% pie from his own Dad. "I'm for that!" she laughed. "But first, here's our spot! Help me spread out this blanket and set out the lawn chairs again, so we can continue this conversation in comfort."

After the group had set up their new space on the grass near the play structure, Charlotte turned to Caryssa. "Things have become so expensive, especially where we live, no matter how we crunch the numbers it ends up the same. We both have to work full time. How do you do it?" she asked.

"How? I don't know, by not spending more than is sustainable to the planet or our wallet I guess. Keeping it simple."

Charlotte high-fived a baseball-happy kid. "But I've seen your house Caryssa. When we stopped by to give you Oakland A's tickets. Your house is amazing…and the view!"

"Geesh…we simplify too, but maybe we aren't doing enough," Bryan said. "Our boys have every damn toy on the market, including the Wii. But it's so expensive here in the bay area. Even without spending a little more than perhaps we need to, I don't know if I could keep up with the mortgage with my business slowing the way it has been."

"Tell me about it!" Caryssa said. "We haven't started any type of college fund for Tyler yet, and I worry. We need to figure out how to do it. But meanwhile, we're taking this thing called life one day at a time."

"Honey, Caryssa does have a point though," Charlotte said, taking Bryan's hand. "It would be a good idea to be sure your dad finally sees his youngest grandchildren sometime before they turn seven. Who knows, maybe you can tap into some of his greed pile so we can keep a roof over our heads while spending more time with our children!"

Bryan remained silent for some time after Charlotte's comment. He was looking towards the children playing on the structure, in particular at his own twin boys.

"I don't want them to end up like me," he said finally, very softly, almost as if he intended nobody else to hear him.

Charlotte heard it, though, and she answered him passionately. It seemed clear to Caryssa this point came up between them regularly. "Wait a minute, mister! What do you mean, *end up like you!?* You ended up just fine, more than fine! You have your own business; you're well educated; you're a great dad; you have tons of friends who love you. And I love you and the boys love you. You seriously need to stop thinking this way!"

George, never the one to feel comfortable around other couples' intense conversation about family matters, got up and walked over to the play structure, where he began encouraging Tyler to try his skills on the steepest climbing wall.

Bryan patted her hand. "I know, honey. I know. I just mean…how I was as a teenager and young adult. I don't want my boys angry, lost, not wanting to be anything like their dad…blaming themselves their dad spends no time with them."

"But Bryan…*that's just it!* You are nothing like your dad! You are a caring, sweet, levelheaded man who adores his sons, is there for them every day. Your dad was never concerned about anything but what people thought of him, his social class, how much money he has. It's not the same animal at all!"

Charlotte was nearly shouting. A few heads turned. But this didn't stop her. She was on a roll. The subject had hit a hot button for her and it was time for her to say her piece, public place or not.

"Did he ever play ball with you? Could you even imagine a guy like him taking the time to coach his son's team? And where was your mom while you were growing up? Too busy having her hair and Botox done! Ugh! It makes me crazy to hear you compare yourself to them as if you are like that at all!"

"I know it does, honey. And I'm sorry. I'm doing my best. I think we need to change the subject now," Bryan said quietly. "But eventually my sons will need to know and understand my darker moments. Let's drop it, and try to have some fun today, okay?"

Caryssa stood up. "I'm gonna let you guys have a little privacy." Charlotte looked up at her, grateful for the empathy and understanding, and nodded her assent. Caryssa wandered down to join George, who was now helping Tyler cross the monkey bars. Watching George with Tyler, she realized for the millionth time what a great daddy George was, and how much Tyler adored him. There's no possible price tag on that. At moments like this, she was willing to overlook that George could get more involved with the daily routines.

She stood there, people around her talking, and watched. Tyler had a good, loving relationship with all four of his Grandparents. So critical. So essential to a child's window into his parents' early lives. And for his own sense of family history and identity. Grandparents bring such an enriching dimension to a child's world. Parents can't provide what grandparents can. They are too busy with the nitty gritty of raising the child.

She had wanted to say this to Bryan, but knew it was not her place. She also realized it's exactly what Bryan was trying to protect. He wanted to protect his boys from the ugliness they might see in their family background, despite it being worth multi-millions of dollars.

"*Bryan's dad disowned him by age eighteen, just because he chose not to follow in his footsteps. He kicked him out of this own house with barely a penny in his pocket, while he himself lived on as a rich bastard,*" she remembered Charlotte saying. "*Oh, he was paying for his college education when Bryan was studying law at Harvard, but when he quit, trying to figure out what he wanted in life, that was it.*"

Her thoughts were abruptly returned to the baseball game when she saw one of the mothers approaching her. "Hey Caryssa, thanks so much for organizing this end of year party!"

"No problem, it was fun planning it. I love being involved wherever possible. Thank *you* for letting so many of the elementary school parents know about this awesome league! What a fun season!" Caryssa responded. Looking back at the picnic spot, she could see Charlotte and Bryan had come to peace and were now talking and laughing, so she went back to join them.

Eventually the party ended. After all the trophies had been handed out to the children and everyone had chipped in to clean up, the two families walked to the parking area together and parted ways.

***

In the Garrity car, the twins were busy squealing with delight recounting a play during the game or something that happened in the park. Bryan and Charlotte remained silent for quite a while. Suddenly, Bryan grabbed his cell phone from his pocket, plugged in his hands free Bluetooth device, and pressed a speed dial number seldom if ever used.

After a minute, he spoke. "Uh...hi... Dad? It's me...Bryan."

Charlotte could hear Clarence J. Garrity's voice through Bryan's phone, but could not make out what was being said. Her heart was racing, and her palms had suddenly become sweaty.

In the back, the boys got more excited. Keenan leaned forward in his car seat and patted her on the shoulder. "Hey Mom, is Dad talking to Grandpa?"

Kevin said "Don't be silly, Keenan! Grandpa? We don't even know Grandpa. Dad never talks to his dad."

Then Bryan said "Great, great Dad, we are all doing excellent. The boys just finished their baseball season and are doing well in school. Charlotte and I both love our work."

It was strangely silent in the car while Bryan listened to his father. Charlotte noticed he did not have the speaker phone on as he usually did. He was afraid of what Clarence might say and what the boys might overhear.

"Well, yeah. She works, Dad. She sort of has to. I mean my business is great and all, I've done well, but with the economy…"

More listening. Charlotte suddenly noticed the boys were unusually quiet in the back seat. She turned to look at them. She found them both still leaning towards the front seat with their heads cocked in Bryan's direction, trying to hear what their Grandpa was saying. It broke her heart. They hadn't even met their grandparents on Bryan's side, yet yearned to hear their Grandpa's voice.

"Sure Dad, hold on a minute." Bryan reached behind him and offered the cell to the boys. "Make sure you use my Bluetooth, boys. Don't hold the phone to your ears. You can take turns saying hi to your grandfather."

Kevin spoke first. "Hi Grampa," he said shyly. After his responses to Clarence's questions were curt: "Yup. Yup. Mmmhmmm. Good. Recess and math. Baseball and soccer. OK. Uh-huh. OK. Me too. Bye." Then he handed the phone to Keenan, and much the same clipped conversation ensued.

After Keenan was finished, he handed the phone back to Bryan. By this time, they were parked in their driveway. Bryan said "Hi. Dad? I'm back." But the line was dead. "Dad? I think maybe I lost you. I can't hear you. Dad? You there?"

"No Dad, he's not there anymore," Keenan declared. "He hung up. He said goodbye and hung up."

Charlotte felt her heart was pounding, she was so angry. She felt like taking the cell phone and whipping it out the window. *He hung up on his grandsons? After we finally make effort to connect with him? Without even speaking further with his own son?*

Bryan calmly asked the boys what their Grandpa had said to them.

"Oh, he asked me things like do I like school, am I learning a lot, said he wants to see me, how is my mom doing, what's my favorite part about school, what sports do I like…that kind of stuff," Kevin said.

"Yeah, he asked me all that kind of stuff too!" Keenan added. "He wants us to go visit him!"

"Yeah! That's what he said to me too. He wants us to go to Connecticut, and he wants to come to California to see our house and watch us play ball and stuff!" Kevin said excitedly.

He wants to see my boys, Bryan thought. He wants a glimpse into our lives. He's even willing to come here!

"Yeah Daddy, he said to tell you to make plans real soon to bring us to Connecticut to see him and Grandma. Then he said some mushy stuff, like, he said…well like he said he loves us."

Bryan and Charlotte both felt like crying. My dad has never, not once, not that I can remember anyhow, told me he loves me, Bryan thought.

Bryan turned to Charlotte, and was not surprised to see the tears rolling down her face. She kept her face turned towards the house, not facing the boys. But the tears kept rolling.

Silence.

"Hey Mom and Dad, what are we waiting for, can't we go inside the house now and play?" Keenan asked.

The question set the adults in motion. Charlotte sat for a moment longer. Bryan got out, opened the back door, unlatched each boy from his safety seat, and said "Okay, off you go! Who wants to see if he can make the house key work?" This was a favorite game for the twins, as the lock was sometimes sticky. Keenan grabbed the keys from Bryan's outstretched hand and they both pelted the walk to the front door.

Bryan went around to Charlotte's door and opened it for her. Her face was tearstained and she seemed to be lost in thought.

"You okay, honey?"

"Oh. Yeah. I'm okay. It's just…a lot for one afternoon!"

Bryan smiled and offered her his hand. She took it, smiled up at him, and got out of the car. By the time they reached the front door it was open, with the keys still in the lock, and the boys were already in their playroom. Bryan went to the fridge and pulled out a bottle of juice. He twisted the cap and began drinking. Then he offered it to Charlotte. She took it and helped herself. Then she spoke.

"Well honey, that's good. Really good. Your Dad seems to want to mend fences. I'd say the ball's in your court now."

More silence.

Charlotte continued. "I think maybe the ball has always been in your court, Bryan. Even though he is the one who broke the relationship, your Dad is too stubborn to make the first move. Who knows how long he's been wanting to connect but couldn't?"

But I was not the one to walk away from his own son, Bryan thought. His resentment still burned deep.

After years of marriage, Charlotte could usually read her husband's mind. "But *he* thinks of it differently, Bryan. His mind is twisted from decades of alcoholism, workaholism, egoism, self-centeredness. He sees it as your fault. You walked away from *his* dynasty. He thinks you disrespect his work and his status in the world."

"And so…your point being?"

"And so….he's your father. He is wrong, yes. We both know that. But can't you let it go? Hasn't it been long enough? What if we could changes things going forward? Let's think about the boys. They need their grandparents. Not just my folks. Your folks too. I'm talking about forgiveness. Before it's too late. You said earlier in the park you don't want your boys to grow up to be like you, and I argued you down, because you are a wonderful person. And you were so courageous to reach out to your Dad."

She put her arms around his waist and squeezed him tight. "It's one of the many reasons I love you so much. But now your dad has responded. You set the wheels in motion. If you stop it now? If you take this opportunity away from the boys? They may never forgive you. Oh, sure, in time they'll forget this moment. But somewhere down the line, it will come back to haunt you, believe me. And that's not even starting to address how much *you* need this honey. *You* need it too. Give him a chance. Maybe it's too soon to forgive. But just give him, yourself, and the boys a chance."

"Shhh," Bryan said, glancing toward the playroom, placing his fingers to his lips. "Well, I don't know, Charlotte. I don't know. If you're right, I could have started the game a long time ago." Then he turned and walked away.

As Charlotte began taking her potluck dishes out of the bag and setting them on the kitchen counter to be washed, she heard him ask the boys "Who wants to go to Connecticut and see where your Daddy grew up?"

"I do! I do!" they answered in unison.

Charlotte arrived at the doorway in time to see them both run to Bryan. He got on all fours and they jump onto his back, after which they rode their Daddy Horse around the room.

"Hey Daddy, how come we've never seen your mommy and daddy, like we always see Mom's mommy and daddy?" Kevin asked.

"Yeah, how come that? How come we don't see your parents?" repeated Keenan. "Your daddy said he loves us. Didn't you know he loves us? But if he loves us, how come we've never seen him?"

What to say?

Bryan gently sat up and the boys slid off and stood in front of him, looking into his face and waiting for his answer. He placed a hand on each beloved face and said "It has nothing to do with either of you. Your grandparents love you and can't wait to see you. It's my fault. You know how…well…sometimes people get mad at each other and don't want to talk to each other for a while? Well, I guess I let that go on for too long."

The boys thought for a while. Then Keenan said "Well, that's sort of like what happened yesterday at school. This kid Sammy took my backpack and wouldn't give it back to me. And then when I told the teacher and she got it for me, he teased me. He said I was a scaredy-cat and teacher's pet. I'm not! I just wanted my backpack and he was too big and too fast for me. Anyway, I didn't want to talk to him for the whole rest of the day."

Oh man, I would hate to see these boys lose their innocence, Bryan thought. Maybe it never has to happen, if I'm always there for them. Always there for them even though my dad was not there for me. I will always be there for my boys, in every way. No matter what.

Chapter Fourteen

Caryssa had been working four months at Moms for Sustainability (MFS). At first she had been excited. But the longer she was with the organization, she saw making a difference would be more difficult than anticipated. She started to feel compelled to shake and shock the plodding bureaucrats in the heavily carpeted county office buildings into awareness of the disastrous environmental hazards they were exposing people to, *especially children.*

The county level meetings Caryssa attended bi-monthly were heated discussions that got her Irish blood boiling. The county staff would sit there, first telling how they would do some of their job manually, and then, with lack of staff and financials as the excuses, handle the remainder with 'treatments.' Treatments referred to the spraying of toxic chemicals—some of which had been linked to cancer, birth defects, and other fatal health issues—in and around schools, parks, hiking trails. Then they would nonchalantly mention they may not be able to post warning signs because it cost too much and they would finish by whining about people losing their jobs.

All in the name of some weeds! The system protected corporate greed more than people.

At first she thought she might be able to change everything by speaking out. But she soon learned the layers of beaurocracy run too deep to change anything with mere words! There were times in those meetings she felt like stopping all her efforts, not lifting a finger for what might be a lost cause.

"Let's present the financial analysis showing how the health costs from illness caused by such practices far outweigh the cost of the products, permits, and posting" Caryssa suggested to Sarah.

"I've done that already…it went over like a smelly fart in church." Sarah, who was Founder of MFS had a Master's in Public Health, and explained how these chemicals were all either known carcinogens, highly toxic neurotoxins, or endocrine disruptors, how they affect children, the most vulnerable.

"I even displayed heart-wrenching pictures of kids with fatal health issues linked to toxic pesticides, including a little girl with leukemia. She was a soccer player, doctors found large traces of synthetic weed killer in her bloodstream. The pesticides were systematically sprayed on her soccer field one day before games." Caryssa flinched at this news, picturing her own child rolling around on his soccer field.

"It had no effect on the county staff, except to trigger more whining. They complained how precious their time was" Sarah tossed a stack of papers on the table before them, while they waited for country staff to arrive.

"And here we are, about to sit through yet another meeting paying out of pocket trying to help the county's IPM program to protect community citizens. *As if a bunch of weeds would hurt anyone---*beyond being a bit of an eyesore!" Caryssa was breezing through Sarah's stack for any clues of what to say. She was about to speak to a large audience, and had no chance to prepare anything. Time to wing it…

They both had given up their high incomes after bringing their children into the world, to care for them while caring for community. They attended these meetings on a volunteer basis, sharing similar passion.

"I started this organization, after witnessing shocking chemicals used at my son's preschool in Lafayette! "She told Caryssa. "Young children are five times more vulnerable to toxics than adults."

One of the first things Sarah had asked Caryssa to do was to craft a letter targeting support groups for mothers as well as health and environmental groups in the county. The objective was to get more voices against the spraying of toxic pesticides and to educate homeowners being misguided by manufacturer's false advertising of product "safety," such as Monsanto's Roundup.

Caryssa wrote the initial draft of the letter in a fit of characteristic passion. The tiny bellicose Irishwoman residing in her genes and subconscious urged her on, whispering to her a great injustice was being perpetrated, and it was up to her to expose this ugly truth to all the mothers on the planet.

Right then, she mentioned to Sarah "I feel disheartened some may think my letter mere words on paper. Inconsequential, disposable pages to be used for starting barbecues."

"No!" said Sarah. "Don't get discouraged. *Think of our kids!* Use that as your guiding light when you write. And speak, including momentarily in this room!"

Caryssa remembered the glow of accomplishment she felt when a new competitive analysis or article she wrote was distributed throughout the computer networking industry. At least fifty of her articles successfully published across *Wireless Review, PC World, Certification Magazine, Network World,* and a host of other leading trade rags.

The incredible rush she got when a magazine with her articles in it came back from the printer, and she would hold up the pages for the first time, seeing *her name* in print! Lining all these magazines up in towers on the floor of the condo she rented in chic Saratoga. There they were, *her words,* manifested as a physical thing, ready to go out and make an impact on the networked world.

And now, reflecting on her letter to Mom's support groups, she realized she wanted to ignite social change over those wires. To bring her written words and Internetworking background together to make a positive impact. Write content with a conscience.

She recognized at once the intensity and purpose with the agenda during the peak of her career—days of public speaking in front of thousands in that global capital of the tech world. *Silicon Valley.* God how she had loved it

The same intensity and purpose reared its head at its current audience, as the country staff and community citizens started pouring into the conference room. According to tradition, she knew she was expected to speak at these meetings in a quiet honeyed voice, shuffling, and humble.

But mothers can at times have no sense of restraint when it comes to their children. Especially when it comes to sitting there listening in the stolid immovability of a broken system. Listening to someone who gets paid six figures to do nothing but approve the spraying of toxic, cancer-causing chemicals in places her child and other innocents may unknowingly hike, bike, and play in creeks.

So at this meeting of over a hundred people, including twenty committee advisory members, Caryssa finally let them have it. She played out her hero, Erin Brockovich:

Her voice was strong yet calm "You have been presiding over an environmental desert. This county district requires sweeping reform. It demands you forget, for a moment, about money, budgets, and balanced books. Forget about your lack of staff, building plans, ordering more products or equipment. Think instead of children, people. *Human beings*. Never mind other living creatures like your pets. Feel for once what IPM stands for. It is about protecting and enhancing public health. But county staff is failing to practice that in the name of getting the job done quicker, pressure from chemical companies, or out of fear of job security."

Caryssa paused a few seconds collecting her thoughts; for once nobody cut her off, so she resumed.

"Yes, we all need to make a living. But not at the expense of humanity and life itself." Caryssa took a moment and made eye contact with each person letting her words sink in. "You've all heard the statistics on what threats these actions pose, especially for children. You've seen the pictures of the damage already done. Perhaps you don't have kids, or they've grown up so you think they are no longer vulnerable. Whatever the reason, whether it's a dream of power, a narrowness of soul, or you've built a wall of hardness to humanity, you're leaving no room for *the person*."

Other than someone clearing their throat, there was not a sound, no one interrupted, even though the allotted time for speaking was only three minutes and Caryssa had gone well past it.

"Let's quickly go through some data, shall we? How is our nation's health trend? Esophageal cancer has tripled in past thirty years; children's chronic lung disease such as asthma up two hundred percent in past twenty years; learning disabilities have nearly tripled; children's cancers are up thirty percent in past forty years; women's emerging illnesses such as fibromyalgia are increasing. Meanwhile, the US creates the second highest CO^2 emissions *in the world*, while ranking about dead last in health care out of any developed nation. It all adds up to a recipe for disaster, and the ingredients you are adding to the recipe are the poison icing on the cake."

Caryssa shoved ten of these frightening data points down their throats, in an effort to crush them with a mountain of fear, hoping they would gag and choke on the knowledge. She wanted to bury them under the weight mindful parents today hold on their shoulders in a system creating pollution, prisons, and war for profit more than protection or the good of society.

Did she sound like a lecturer? She was sure some were thinking she needed to get laid.

But she didn't care what they thought, only what they *did*. Her lips trembled as her speech came to an end, the great secret she had nursed in her soul having thundered out into the open room. Before she sat again, she shot them one last zinger: "If you are not disturbed by this, then perhaps you should not be on this committee or working for the people."

The county staff and other committee members sat like Buddha's, with their hands resting on ponderous pot bellies, their mouths agape with disbelief or incredulity. *How could she?* But not one person countered her statements.

Next she passed out the slides to Sarah's presentation, which had all the ugly facts and figures of America's health trend as it relates to harmful chemicals, including heart-wrenching pictures of children with cancer scientifically linked to spraying pesticides. Many living in the most upscale areas of America.

One member made a snide remark about Caryssa being recalcitrant or not going through the chain of command, but it was not even worthy of having the secretary add the comments to the meeting minutes. In fact, Caryssa was sure not one word of what she had said would be recorded.

But she had said her piece. And if she was able to create even a small amount of social consciousness among the committee to help the world be a safer place, it's all that mattered.

As the meeting adjourned and Sarah and Caryssa packed up to leave, Caryssa asked "So…how did it sound, Sarah?"

"Well, it sure as hell got the message across. I saw every single person in the audience jolted by the statistics you fed them. They took notes. But Caryssa, I've been doing this for a long time. Truth is, there is no way to overcome the inevitable insult when one creates awareness around the way someone's means of making a paycheck hurts citizens. And you know what? *Tough shit!* You did well. Who knows, maybe there will be a ripple effect."

Sarah had been involved in speaking out at countless public meetings, including one where a multinational corporation used a cancer-causing chemical agent in building materials for Pacific Elementary School in California. *Poisoning children for profits.* The builder used toxic waste in the cement to cut corners. Chromium VI, the same chemical inspiring the movie *Erin Brokovich.* One of the company's workers had even threatened Sarah's life because she might hurt the corporate bottom line.

During the next county meeting, they did a joint presentation to county staff. Sarah served up the pitches, Caryssa swung from the heels. More staggering facts about our nation's health trends and birth defects, much proven to be caused by pesticides. They finished off with a photo of a little boy with burns all over his body from these toxic chemicals being sprayed on the baseball field.

As the job went on, however, it became more and more humdrum for Caryssa. And it was very time-consuming. Not just the meetings, but doing outreach and advocacy out of her home, conference calls, refining a presentation for the right audience, proofing documents, assisting in writing grants.

Was she making a difference? Helping to restore people's health? Awakening a social conscious at some level? She doubted it. They didn't seem to be making any progress at all.

Those who had known her in the high tech corporate world spoke of her as highly driven. Now, she was divinely driven with this hidden motivation, committed from the foundation of her soul to humanity's fundamental right to wellbeing. She loved what she was doing, but because it was contract work for a low-budget nonprofit, she was getting no software training, and making peanuts. Just enough to buy her some makeup now and then or get a latte.

How wonderful all that stuff Caryssa talked about during her high-powered data networking career can be. But a double-edged sword. Data mining was now able to find out everything about a person, down to her choice of bra and panties. All that data about you used to target you in direct marketing. Even children were entered into all those machines, right from birth. The data knew all secrets, including if a child had some type of learning disability. The lists sold to businesses for target email marketing and sales forecasting.

As soon as we input our name, address, credit card details, phone numbers into any online site…there goes the data, and it's then sold or rented to businesses. With it goes our right to privacy.

Caryssa sighed. *Technology.* We can't live with it, and we can't live without it due to the overly industrialized globally competitive world we live in.

"You've become the former technologist warning the world about technology," George had laughed one day after she had shared these insights with him.

"We humans are all just another number in the data world. We've become so inhumane with all this technology social networking sites ask us to prove we are human by unscrambling words most human eyes could never conceivably even unscramble!" she responded.

"But you are slipping back into the Stone Age, Wilma Flintstone!"

"True, where I once talked technology so much I had gigabit breath, now I have yet to go from my stupid phone to a smart phone," Caryssa giggled. "And now, it's hard not to want to think more about my son's real life outside the computer-stale air of an office. And it doesn't matter as much if I never make the big bucks I made in the high tech corporate world. It matters more to know I am giving back to society."

"I know, honey. You've changed so much since we first met. I was proud of you then, and I'm proud of you now. You never stop growing. But sometimes you try to do too much community stuff"

Caryssa sighed. "Isn't that the truth? And you know what? Here I am in beautiful, sunny California. A state among the most environmentally, socially, and technologically aware in the country. But guess what I'm doing on Saturday? Yup. I'm volunteering to pick up trash along the shore. Seriously, I can only imagine how bad it might be in many other parts of America."

George laughed. "Former high tech business professional turned trash collector! Good thing you have a sense of humor!"

One day when Caryssa was volunteering with the green team helping pick up trash on the side of the road, a couple stopped their car beside her, with such pity in their eyes. The woman rolled down her window, and held out a wad of dollar bills for Caryssa. It dawned on her, they thought she was homeless!

She was relieved to meet many others out there helping clean up the shores, people with advanced degrees, business owners, a CEO of a major non-profit. It was so refreshing to see!

"American society seems as desensitized to toxic pollution as to our culture of violence." Caryssa eyes turned to the book she just finished reading, *Parts per Million*, while she pointed to it---"Case in point, Beverly Hills High School's 2003 landmark toxic tort suit against big oil when more than a thousand people were diagnosed with cancer and other terminal illnesses—proven to be directly linked to the oil derricks pumping up and down the school's athletic fields."

If this happened in wealthy Beverly Hills, it could happen anywhere else in America. The environmental organization she worked for was based in an upscale area of the East Bay. *And it had been started due to alarming use of cancer causing pesticides in its preschools!*

"Industry pundits are still trying to spin it as if Erin Brockovich was some sort of white trash out for money," joked Caryssa one day at a local town meeting with the Environmental Services team.

"And who cares if she *did* net tons of money from the ordeal! She should have, for such a great cause!" responded a green team co-volunteer. "What makes people think anyone has a right to make money off toxic chemicals, which are hurting rather than helping society? Yet if someone does something positive for society, it's looked at as hurting profits in some industry…and suddenly they are accused of being only in it for the money! Talk about crazy making!"

The following weekend, Caryssa and eleven of her girlfriends went to wine country for a spa day. When the topic of what she wanted to do for work came up and she shared her dream, one of them said "What do you mean you want to do something to make this a better world for your child. How could Tyler *possibly* have a better world? He lives in a beautiful house with a killer view, in the most amazing community of people anyone can ask for, skis in Tahoe, flies back and forth across the continent twice a year, goes on trips galore, has fabulous involved parents."

"It's not his life now, or mine I am talking about. I could not be happier! It's the future of our kids I'm talking about!" Caryssa responded. "You don't understand as you don't have kids!"

They were having mud baths while chatting, and her friend gave her a shoulder massage.

"You care way too much, Caryssa. Nobody cares as much as you do. But you need to care about *yourself* more."

As she soaked, Caryssa realized her reason for not wanting to continue with MFS ran deeper than pay and not learning new-fangled digital marketing skills. Although the increase in awareness was an eye opener, and she loved helping communities, she was growing weary of seeing things with reality colored glasses all the time. Oh to see things through deceptive rose-colored glasses again!

At times she felt so disheartened by the truth, as if someone had thrown darts at her balloon. She was sickened and saddened by the way her country's leaders were handling things. Equally by how otherwise good people remained in deep denial about it all.

She had been insanely driven in her corporate days. But her ambition then was to make a lot of money and serve the corporate infrastructure. Her ambition now seemed so much higher. So much more balanced with spiritual and social awareness. She had thrown away all of her masks, and put on her soul. But she needed a balance, and her friends were right. She needed to learn to take care of *herself* as well.

If I can't change the world, she resolved, sinking deeper into the soothing mud bath, I want to at least better society in some small way, engage in something governed by ethics. But I also want to get *paid* for saving the world!

And I need to do it in a way that also nurtures me. I need to make some time for Caryssa.

Chapter Fifteen

Later the following week, as she was sitting at her desk making yet another to-do list, Caryssa's Skype line rang. She hit Video Call and there was Sarah smiling back at her. "Hi Caryssa. How are you doing?"

Caryssa took the hair tie out of her mouth, pulled her hair back off her face and into a ponytail. "Great. Great, Sarah. A little frazzled. Lots going on this weekend and I'm behind. You?"

"Oh. Great too. Busy too. Hey. Do ya know about the "Save the Parks" event this coming Saturday?"

Caryssa nodded. "Hmmm…I seem to remember something on the group calendar. Why?"

"Well…we're a little short-staffed this weekend. I know you said you'd have to sit this one out. But we're hoping you'll rethink it and be there to work the booth? Sorry it's so last minute. We had some cancellations yesterday and we're tearing our hair out. You know how important this event is to our cause."

Whee! More saving the world for free! Only this time? I'm not taking the bait. I'm putting my mud bath insights into practice, starting now!

"Sorry, Sarah, as I told you before, we have soccer on Saturday at noon. That conflicts with the event. This is a busy weekend—soccer on Saturday, sleepover Saturday night, and birthday party on Sunday. Plus friends are coming over Saturday evening. I'm just jammed. I hope you find somebody."

After Sarah signed off, Caryssa patted herself on the back. Good job finally learning to say "no" to so much community volunteer stuff!

And what a relaxing, superb Saturday night it turned out to be! Sam and Jim Owens came over with their son Ben again. Little red-haired, outgoing, confident Ben came running in the door ahead of his parents, his usual backpack in one hand—full of this weeks' show and tell, toys, jammies, a change of clothes, and toiletries for his night's stay—and his favorite pillow in the other.

He greeted Caryssa as he ran past her, through the living room, and into Tyler's bedroom to deposit his stuff. Caryssa heard the two boys, who had been friends since infancy, excitedly run down the list of what they wanted to do on their overnight, and where to start. "First we should build our tent!" she heard Ben say, and Tyler counter with "No, first we should go outside and I'll show you my new fun house!!!"

Next thing she knew, Sam and Jim were standing in the kitchen offering her the bottles of wine they had brought to share. It was one of those fresh-smelling, clear San Francisco Bay Area nights. The kind that only happen after the winter rains hit hard all week and then suddenly it warms up for a day. The therapeutic scent of eucalyptus, juniper, and flowers were wafting through the air again.

Caryssa had been in a great mood all day from the sudden delightful weather, and after having had a fabulous weekend skiing in Tahoe. She had decided to go all out with the food. She had made everything herself. Since she knew her guests were fish lovers, she had made a seafood cioppino, but without mussels as she couldn't find those on sale. For hors d'oeuvres, she laid out homemade shrimp egg rolls, wingettes, her favorite goat cheese with rosemary pita slices, and crab Rangoon.

The boys, now in first grade, played happily outside. Tyler's new fun house, lovingly built by George, offered them a little hide-a-way in which they could talk about all the important stuff happening in their nearly seven-year-old lives. Like the coolest and latest Lego sets, the play they made in soccer or baseball, the massive dinosaurs in their books.

The parents sat around the fire pit in Caryssa's backyard paradise overlooking the San Francisco Bay. The sunset over the Golden Gate Bridge was stunning. It cast a mystical glow over the tranquility of the evening.

"I am finally happy!" Sam said, taking a sip of her Chardonnay.

"What do you mean, Ms. Happy Feet? You're always happy!" Caryssa responded, laughing.

"Oh, but I mean really happy, not just life in general, but my job too. I finally cut back to twenty-eight hours. I don't feel so guilty anymore. I spend more time with Ben. Maybe I'll even go all out and bake real cookies to bring into class rather than store bought!" Sam said.

"Heck, who needs to be a 'working mom' to not have time or motivation to bake versus buy! We feel guilty too, isn't that part of motherhood? Can't say I've ever baked anything for Tyler's class," Caryssa admitted.

"Yes you have Mommy! Remember the gingerbread cookies we made together?" Tyler chimed in on his way past in search of more toys to take into his fun house.

"But of course! The little gingerbread boys we made together for your class Christmas party! Hey, I am a Betty Crocker mom after all!" Caryssa laughed. "No but seriously. I'm so happy to hear how happy you are Sam!"

"Thanks, girlfriend. Truth is, I'll be even happier if I quit! I mean, it's great to be working a shorter week, but still the commute from Oakland to Alameda takes too long with all the traffic. My day is shot with all the driving!"

"Would you really quit?" Caryssa's mouth half full of spring roll.

"Heck yeah, might even quit without a new job lined up!" Sam said after taking another sip of her wine.

"But…I thought you were happy!"

"Oh, but I am happy, because I am making Ben much happier with my time! It's not the job, it's that awful commute that will kill me! I can't work from home anymore. They decided I need face time with the lawyers in the office."

"So…they agree to cut your hours but then take away telecommute privileges?"

Before Sam could respond, George yelled from the kitchen "Hey Caryssa, why did you cook dinner before our guests arrived? It's getting cold!"

George, the discerning chef. Always giving Caryssa cooking and serving tips, even when she didn't want them.

"Don't worry dear, I guarantee it will still be delicious if we heat it up quickly in the microwave," Caryssa called back, rolling her eyes at Sam, who giggled and gave her a thumbs up. "I didn't want to be in the kitchen cooking when our friends got here. I wanted to chat!"

"You can't chat while cooking?" George asked, by this time standing behind Caryssa's chair and giving her a peck on the cheek

"Not with this recipe, sweetie. I needed all the concentration I could get. Only *you* have that special talent of cooking and talking at the same time! Did you check out my seafood cioppino, by the way?"

"Sure did, looks pretty good." George sounded hungry.

"Just pretty good? Dude! Show a little respect! I slaved over that dish!" Caryssa laughed, reaching back to poke him with her elbow. "By the way. If you're hungry, feel free to heat some up! Anybody else ready for the main course?"

By now the light was fading and the fog was starting to show up on the horizon, promising a chill to the air. But it was still warm near the fire pit and so lovely with the tiki torches, they decided to take dinner outside. Once they were all seated again, this time with their food, George poured more wine into uplifted wine glasses in vibrant colors.

"Girlfriend, I love these glasses! They're so pretty. You'd never know they're plastic!" Sam said. "Where'd you get them?"

"Thanks," smiled Caryssa. "I love them too. They go with everything, and great for outdoors. They were on sale at Pier 1. A real steal."

The conversation flowed easily, with soft background sounds of clanking silverware and dishes. Discussions about the boys' school activities, family trips planned for the year. And, as usual, work.

Caryssa glanced over at her beautiful garden again, marveling at the multitude of flowers. She saw color, succulent stems, and glistening leaves. There were pink and white low borders enclosing Spanish and Greek lavender, rose beds, cactuses, Mexican sage, and other various plants she could not even name.

Then she noticed something even more beautiful, and sat riveted, watching.

Tyler stood among the scented, now misty garden, his striking blue-green eyes gazing happily up towards his fun house, calling for Ben to come see some amazing little critter lurking in the borders. *Good God, did this beautiful boy come from me?*

She watched her son as he jumped up and down squealing with delight over a butterfly fluttering from flower bed to flower bed. "Where do I want to land, here? No there!" he giggled, mocking the butterfly's flight in search of nectar.

He did not know that to his mom he was the most beautiful thing in that garden. *This world.* Drowsy birds peered at him. Bees blew about him and one landed on his chestnut hair for a moment before lifting off again. A white butterfly, probably the same one that had just delighted him, came to rest on his shoulder, raising and dropping its wings.

Caryssa had never felt a love so deep. A compassion so enormous that it could make her almost physically ill and wretched. She loved each moment with her Tyler, living life one day at a time. Was it through this deep, abiding feeling she had learned compassion for all of humanity? She had come to view every person out there—the good, the bad, and the ugly— as someone's son or daughter.

Sam interrupted her reverie. "So how is the gig going with MFS?" she asked.

Caryssa filled Sam in on her contract job, how she felt about not gaining any of the new digital marketing skills, how she was growing weary to the bone hearing all the factoids about pollution and its direct link to increases in cancer and other diseases, and how we can't do anything about any of it because somebody on some committee always has a roadblock to offer.

"Truth be told? I love the *concep*t of what I'm doing—creating awareness of the environmental hazards we're imposing, specifically on children, and coming down hard on politicians and corporations causing it. But it's…I don't know…it's distressing. Not only distressing, but I'm beginning to feel it's all an uphill battle against political corruption."

"And besides," Jim interjected. "You environmentalists may be helping to cause our economic downturn. Don't forget we make the biggest profits off all those terrible things!"

"That's the corruption I'm talking about," Caryssa countered. "Money buys pollution and war. It's the money spent on mindless military that's causing economic disaster. Not environmentalism."

Sarah had introduced her to documentary after documentary exposing the ugly truths about industrial pollution and poisoning, as well as our obsession with materialism and what it is doing to our world. *Who Killed the Electric Car, The World According to Monsanto, Food Inc., Garbage, Crude, GasLand, Your Milk on Drugs—Just Say No!, The Story of Stuff,* and others.

Now Caryssa had to stop herself from becoming furious while driving down the street and seeing the fumes and oil creeping out from exhaust pipes, knowing what it is doing to human and animal health. Knowing that with all this technology we have, we could surely have many more alternative cars out there.

She had never even thought about this stuff before having a child. And now, with all she'd learned working with Sarah, it was almost all she *could* think of.

As if reading her mind, Sam said "It's scary how many people are getting cancer."

Caryssa nodded. "I know, right?! And from all indications it appears that compared to other industrialized nations many government and medical organizations are behind the eight ball with respect to regulations vs. credible scientific research. So why should it surprise any of us?"

"But to get back to our original topic," she continued. "I like working from home as far as the flexibility is concerned, but it's hard. I have to get my work done while Tyler is in school. Otherwise I'd be sitting at my home computer telling him to go out and get fresh air, not to get on the computer or watch TV. Inevitably he sneaks downstairs to the family room and turns the TV on. Then I feel guilty that I'm not spending time with him. But then, on the other hand, when he's at school is also the only time to run errands, exercise, and take care of this thing called life. It's like I still have to be in two places at once, and I don't feel like I'm getting anywhere."

Working from home had also created other tradeoffs. Because George had grown used to her staying home, certain primal gender specific assumptions had been activated. He went to work. She did pretty much everything else.

In her attempt to adopt a routine, she had unconsciously stepped into some kind of 1950s June Cleaver stereotype. Even so, when was the last time her kitchen floor had been mopped? Months ago? There weren't enough hours in the day.

She could not imagine doing even more…for instance, like Stan Gafferty. He was *everywhere*. On the Board of Directors for the baseball league AND school, coaching his sons' team, PTA President, VP of fundraising before that, volunteer extraordinaire for both the elementary school and his younger son's preschool, all drop-offs and pick-ups for both his kids, taught chess, and more. And still, he found the time to bake cakes for school events.

"But he doesn't work!" George would respond when Caryssa brought up the topic.

"I can assure you, George that what Stan does is *work*," Caryssa would insist. "He just doesn't get *paid f*or any of his hard work. We would have to live in Europe to have that benefit for this job! Stan doesn't work in one job, he does at least ten jobs! The guy is utterly amazing, a hero."

There she was each morning, dragging Tyler like a pull toy to school. No makeup, no power suit, no pressed pants. No manicured nails. No expensive shoes. No status jewelry. Just her happy, humbled honesty. And the community of people at the school were never looking at the face, the features, or the body anyway. They were looking inside—at the soul. All those wonderful dedicated souls seeing to their children's needs.

Caryssa had never complained. She loves her mommy job. She so looked forward to picking Tyler up and asking him how his day went. Hearing the excitement in his voice about some cool art project or getting another of his many "Student of the Day" awards. These years were too precious to put aside.

It's that she found it so difficult to ever think about herself too. She had made a commitment in her mud bath spa day to get better about that. But it was hard to find the time to do things she loved to do. Golf, for instance.

"Hey Caryssa and George, you guys going up skiing again next week?" Jim asked.

"Yup! We'll be in Tahoe all through President's Day week. Renting a condo right at the base of the mountain again. Can't wait!" Caryssa answered, forgetting all about golf in her excitement about ski week. They had nine glorious days ahead of them, skiing every day, hot tubbing every night, walking through the quaint village, window shopping, seeing friends, and enjoying the night life at the ski resort. "Who cares if it's colder than a witch's tit right now…"

"Well, I hate to break up the party," Sam winked, "but I have some partying of my own to do with this man of mine now that we have the night to ourselves. Thank you guys so much for dinner. As always, give us a call if anything goes wrong. And the next overnight is at our house."

Caryssa laughed. "You guys get going! And don't worry, nothing ever goes wrong between those two. They're thick as thieves. We'll give you a call in the morning after breakfast."

"Great, thanks!" Jim said. "We can see ourselves out. You two stay here and bask in the ambience."

After hugs all around, Sam and Jim made their way out to the street. As their car started, Caryssa could hear the boys giggling in Tyler's room. She sank back into her seat and sighed a contented sigh, reaching out a hand for George.

"Life is sweet, isn't it honey?"

He squeezed her hand. "It sure is."

* * *

Presidents Day week came in a flash, and before Caryssa knew it, she was skiing her favorite trail. They had rented the same little condo they usually got, at the Norwegian-style inn just off the slopes, and could see two of the hot tubs and chairlifts from their balcony.

They saw many of their ski pals, and had a great time. Tyler attended the ski school program a few of the days and skied with Caryssa and George the other days.

Even though it was as magical as ever and she was happy to be there, Caryssa felt a sense of impending doom. She couldn't shake it. She would check off all the things she normally worried about and see that nothing was there she hadn't already taken care of. So why was she feeling this way? She couldn't attach the feeling to anything, but it was as if God were trying to tell her something.

After a couple of days she realized the feelings were about her father. So every chance she got she would call her parents' home.

Each time she called, her Dad answered with the robotic voice he had after having the laryngectomy. Using his electro larynx, he would try to tell Caryssa something, but she could never get what he was saying. Eventually he would hang up in frustration. And she would be living in a moment of helplessness…

One afternoon after one such difficult conversation, Caryssa headed out of the condo towards the mountain to get a few more runs in for the day. While carrying her skis over her shoulder, trucking through the heavy snow, she had a sudden and overwhelming déjà vu. She was a little girl, her Daddy beside her. He was carrying her skis over his shoulder as they walked through the snow towards the ski slopes.

She didn't realize that she had tears streaming her face until she bumped into one of her friends on the chairlift.

"Are you okay Caryssa? You looked like you were crying as we boarded the chair," Joe asked. She told Joe about her Dad, and about her déjà vu. They were both quiet all the way up the mountain. She knew Joe understood, and Joe knew words wouldn't be helpful right now, but companionship would be. So he just sat with Caryssa as the lift moved them up the slope.

Caryssa looked behind her to appreciate the view unfolding as they rose. The spectacular blue of Lake Tahoe, the snowcapped mountain peaks all around, the valley below them. The air so fresh and clear. Such a beautiful world. Skiing was so pleasant. Skiing and golf, two things her dad had loved for years, and had taught her to love, and would never be able to enjoy again.

The lift approached the top, and she soon faced the downslope. She most always skied the expert slopes and this was one of the toughest. Joe was next to her.

"You going?" he asked.

"In a minute," she answered. "You go ahead."

As Joe pushed off and floated down the bumps, Caryssa looked out at all the beauty of the receding layers of mountains in front of her, rose-tinged in the glow of afternoon winter light. She took a deep breath and let out a sigh. Tears streamed from her eyes and froze on her cheeks. She barely noticed.

"This run is for you, Dad. This run is for you," she whispered.

And then she pushed off.

* * *

Shortly after this emotional ski run dedicated to her dad, the cancer took him to heaven.

There were so many things she needed to say to him, things that had been trapped in her heart through the years. She said them before he slipped away, gently and lovingly, while holding his hand---hoping it would ease his pain.

She got those words out, those hand touches, those hugs, into the crucial last moments. *Words.* Loving words—transferred from her heart and soul to his heart and soul. So her dad could take all those good words with him into that afterlife place. And no doubt, that loving spirit went to any heaven that might exist.

To help her push through the grief during the weeks that followed, she made sure to enjoy a bit of her favorite things: the sunshine on her face, swooshing down the ski slopes with friends, loving life and remembering the man who had instilled in her the love of life and skiing. Skiing was the best antidote for her heavy heart.

Caryssa loved après ski as much as skiing; sitting in the sunshine sipping wine, chatting with friends, smelling the barbeques, and watching all the shiny, happy people.

I've never seen an unhappy person walk around the ski slopes. Caryssa joked to passersby "You'd think we are all snorting cocaine or on ecstasy, everyone so cheery." But no…skiing tends to bring out the best in people, naturally.

One day, she sank down onto their bed, head in her hands. It was too much. Too many loved ones dying of cancer! They had also lost George's Dad and some close friends.

"I feel like I'm dying of heartbreak," she told George.

George tried to be helpful. "Honey, why don't you do one of those causes? You know, the 'walk your ass off for a cure' thing or something?"

"Because we've had *enough* of looking for cures! We've had cures, pushed aside on purpose! We need prevention! Oh don't *even* get me started!" she shouted.

"Sorry honey," George said, throwing up his hands. "I wasn't looking for a lecture. I was just trying to help. I'm suffering too, ya know. It's not all about you."

A profound realization hit Caryssa. An oddly strange, peaceful feeling that pushed past the anger. *He was right!* She held him close. "Oh honey, I'm so sorry!"

An enlightening engulfed her. Some moral lessons from death of loved ones teaching her about life itself. A transformation, awareness. A consciousness. Absorption. A stillness, and connection. Of just…*being*. In the moment of every moment life has to offer.

And that enlightening motivated her…

* * *

Caryssa did end up doing an exercise your ass off thingy to fight cancer: "Swim Across America" a charitable organization dedicated to raising funds and awareness for cancer research, prevention, and treatment through swimming across our nations beautiful open waters and pools. Unlike some other such causes, proceeds go directly to the beneficiaries.

When she told Tyler what she was going to train for, he said "Oh great! Just like Dory says in *Finding Nemo*, when life gets you down, just keep on swimming, keep on swimming!"

No matter what it took, she forced herself to drive down to the shoreline a few times every week for months, don wetsuit, bathing cap, and goggles, walk into the waves, and immerse herself in the deep, cold water. Out, out, out she swam, so that when she stopped and treaded water to gauge how far she had gone, the people on the beach looked tiny.

She swam back and forth along the shoreline, past all the people and past the rocks and back. Over the course of three months' training, she felt herself getting stronger and stronger physically and emotionally. The water was absorbing her grief. Battling the waves was challenging her muscles. *She was healing.*

On the day of the event, the swimmers tossed flowers dedicated to their loved ones into the water before jumping off the ferry into the bay. Caryssa wasn't in any competition. She was swimming for the cause. She blew past her fundraising goal and swam the mile and a half from the Golden Gate Bridge to Chrissy Field Beach.

When she found herself standing on the beach, exhilarated and out of breath, she stopped to soak in the incredible beauty around her—the majestic bridge, this time in the distance rather than looming over her as she swam, Sausalito, Alcatraz, the sailboats on the bay, the blue sky, the seabirds.

George was at the finish line, camera in hand. He knew exactly what she would want, and they headed over to the party on the beach, the delicious cooking on the grills, the people laughing. It was a warm, beautiful day, with a clear view far past Alcatraz. Music was playing, booths were set up with all sorts of food, and somebody handed her a bag of goodies specially put together for the swimmers.

Caryssa made her way to the changing area, stripped off her wetsuit and changed into the dry clothes George had packed for her. When she found George again, he was talking with one of his coworkers who had also done the event, Elaina.

Elaina, a PhD as well as an MD, works as a toxicology specialist. She had spent the first fifteen years of her career as a surgeon, treating children with cancer. Now she was working in environmental protection, like many of the other swimmers, in order to find and eradicate causes.

"So Caryssa, how did your first swim go?" she asked.

Caryssa laughed. "As well as could be expected, I guess. At least I finished! I thought I would never finish, I was so exhausted I was ready to give up. But then I remembered how so many had battled cancer, so I kept going. And I'm so glad I did! It was so wonderful in every way—emotionally, physically, spiritually!"

Caryssa was laughing as she spoke, and nearly in tears. She felt so good, punch drunk.

"It is such an amazing experience, isn't it?" Elaina said. "This is my third time doing it, and I resolve to do it each year. I have to say, though, I've stopped using the word 'battled' to refer to healing from the disease, or even 'fighting.' Have you listened to what they're saying over on that stage?"

She pointed off to a corner stage, where Caryssa spotted a woman speaking about the many scientifically and clinically recognized environmental links to cancer. Most of it focused on food. *Ah-ha...No wonder all the foods on the tables were identified as non GMO or organically grown.*

Elaina continued. "I treated so many little cancer patients when I was a practicing surgeon. At Children's Hospital in Oakland. And I learned a lot about how our approach to the disease can make a difference. I truly believe that if a person feels they are battling something inside them it only makes them sicker. *Attitude is everything.* Cancer is not an alien object or something apart from our bodies to kill off. We are all born with a potential cancer gene. More people than we realize are born with a genetic mutation—a 'predisposition.' But there needs to be a number of cells before it becomes cancer. Without going too far into details, I can tell you that eighty percent of cancers come from environmental toxins. Meanwhile, our whole society and medical system wrongly look at cancer as some sort of 'us versus them' fight."

"That makes a lot of sense to me," Caryssa said. "I wonder about the cancer clusters forming around my home town and surrounding areas on the East Coast. So many people are dropping like flies. It's scary to watch. And there are toxic superfunds all over that area. People don't recycle, and they use more pesticides. When I mention this to my family, they claim I'm an alarmist, or going all negative."

"I know exactly what you mean," Elaina responded. "I have relatives near Buzzards Bay. It was found to be one of the most toxic bodies of water in North America, with hundreds of pounds of PCBs dumped in it. It's a Federal superfund site—highly contaminated, or was before actions were taken to clean it up. How many people could have been protected from the cancer caused by just that one site?!"

Music played in the background and the air smelled of barbeques and sunscreen. People were dancing off to the side, laughter and life abounded.

Elaina continued. "This 'fight cancer' attitude gives cancer *itself* more power. It instills fear. And this fear only gives the disease more power over people. Cancer treatment is an *industry*, a four hundred billion dollar industry. Conventional medicine and its 'battle' against cancer kills both good and bad cells through chemo. We try to burn it out, radiate it out, and cut it out."

She recognized the look of dread on Caryssa's face. *No more awareness, please!* I'm trying to live in the moment!

"Oh…don't get me wrong, there are times these may seem like the only choice, but more because it's too late than for any other reason. The amount of cancer that could have been entirely prevented is astounding. I believe wholeheartedly that out of the hundreds of children I worked on, few had any genetic predisposition. It was most always some form of toxin that caused that tumor, whether in or around the household or in the surrounding environment. It nearly killed me. Once I knew about the environmental causes, I had to put my surgical practice aside and get to work on prevention."

Caryssa was growing weary of this conversation. It brought up such a sense of sadness and helplessness. She wanted to get back to the party and that heady feeling of celebration that had faded for her as she listened to Elaina. But she also wanted to take advantage of this woman's expertise while she had access to it, to get some questions answered. "Is it true what I've read, that the medical profession has seen more than one potential cure emerge, only to have the science purposely pushed aside?" she asked.

"Oh sure. Lots, in fact. Cancer is very profitable industry. And not just for the highly paid oncologists. All those diagnostic machines. The pharmaceuticals. It's huge. *Fight or battle?* We need to fight for clean science. It seems our entire political/economic system has a serious allergy to the truth. So here I am working in toxicology, making less money but feeling far better in my heart and soul. I just hope our next generation of doctors are conscious enough to push for including the environmental aspects in both medicine and prevention. It's a critical element missing right now."

At that moment a live band started to play. Caryssa and Elaina looked at each other and smiled. Enough of this, let's go celebrate!

Suddenly they were all dancing, laughing, drinking, and eating all the healthy delicacies set up on the various tables. Caryssa felt so calm, happy. She glanced out at the San Francisco Bay, past the palm trees, the beach, and all the people celebrating life. Celebrating the finish line of the Swim Across America, celebrating the "fight" or "battle" or "healing," whatever they wished to call it—against cancer. Loving and living their life to the fullest.

She looked around for George. There he was, next to one of the food tables, talking with a colleague. Always the intellectual, was her George. Always getting sucked into heated discussions about important issues. She snuck up behind him, put her arms around his chest, and nuzzled his back. He turned his head to acknowledge her.

"Come on, honey. Let's get back to dancing. Enough serious talk for one night!"

"Shut up and dance with me?" chimed in the colleague.

George laughed and set his wine glass on the table. "Shut up and dance with you? It's what I live for, gorgeous."

As they moved a little closer to the band and began to move in rhythm to the music, Caryssa leaned in to whisper into her husband's ear.

"You were right, that day we fought. This was a good thing to do. And I'm so glad I did. Thank you, honey. And know what? Elaina brought up *exactly* what I was angry about. Despite that issue being *true*…I feel at inner peace! I'm learning to let go!"

George winked at her and pulled her into a wild swing that lifted her off her feet.

"Any time, beautiful. Any time! Now try to keep up! Show me your best moves!"

Chapter Sixteen

While George and Caryssa were dancing on the beach, Anna Beauvais was sitting in her cozy loft living area nursing a glass of Malbec and watching the Sausalito sunset warm every inch of her space.

The past year had gone quickly, with a nightmarish quality. She had never been able to shake the feeling that she was walking through a storm and could be hit by lightning any minute. But at the same time, nothing seemed real. How could this be her life?

The case had been drawn out to what seemed an eternity. So often she had been on the verge of calling Phil and saying "Drop it all, it's only causing more hurt." But something always stopped her. Some compulsion to protect her child's spirit. *Both* her girls' spirits.

As she sipped her wine, she remembered Brandon Garth's visit, the same day she had met with Caryssa and had such a life-changing flash of insight. What an impression he had made on her. And ever since, she had lost as much sleep over the prospect of ruining this young man's life as she had over the loss of her own girls.

Brandon had walked into the foyer of her house, all six-foot-two of him. He had a lean, athletic build, and classic good looks. Short, blondish hair accompanied piercing blue eyes. And when he smiled, he had the dimples of a child. And really, at only twenty-one, he *was* still a kid.

Her first thought when she saw him was *"I've had the opportunity to live free for fifty plus years, shouldn't he?"*

Those amazing blue eyes had looked straight into Anna's, and before he even spoke, she could see it. *Feel it.* Those eyes spoke volumes—innocence, a gentle nature, intelligence, kindness, love, integrity. His eyes were a window into his soul.

And what she saw was a purity, so clean, unblemished. An innocence that must be protected. This was the Garth's only child. Did she wish to inflict pain on his parents along with him? For what? Millions of dollars? Wasn't there enough exploitation of innocent souls by the political and legal system?

They stood in silence for a moment, just looking at each other. Tears formed in his eyes when he finally reached his hand out to her and spoke. "Hello Mrs. Beauvais, I'm Brandon Garth. I hope I don't shock you by being here. I just...I needed to tell you to your face that I am so sorry for what happened that... day."

Then he had started crying. Hard. Years of pent-up anguish washed out of his system. "You don't know how many sleepless nights I've had... um...how awful I've felt about my car being the one that your daughter was hit by. I...I know I should have stepped up after realizing...realizing that...uh...I hit someone. *A child.* Your child. But I...um...I...was scared of going to prison. I wasn't driving recklessly...in...in fact, I was going below the speed limit since I couldn't see through the fog. Oh God, Mrs. Beauvais, I am so sorry!"

A million memories flashed through Anna's mind. The prosecutor's past words--- *"The defense team has a good chance of winning this case, on reasonable doubt alone. But my office has not lost a case in ten years. We will get this bad guy. You will have your retribution, and millions of dollars for the reckless wrong doing..."*

Then sounds of her beautiful, carefree daughter's laughter as she took dangerous turns with her board filtered through her thoughts. She knew Brandon was still speaking, but so many images and memories were flashing before her eyes.

Words of wisdom from a parent at the skateboard park further blinded Anna from Brandon's voice. *"Your daughter is more daring than any of those boys out there. But she might get herself in trouble one day with all those reckless risks she takes."*

"Reckless risks." Suddenly Anna was sure what would be more of a reckless wrong-doing...her going along with winning this case. It had been an accident. Not this young man's fault any more than it was her daughter's. There was too much reasonable doubt in her mind to live with.

Anna looked at Brandon with the most sympathetic, caring look she could muster up through all her turmoil.

"What am I doing?! "Come further in, Brandon." She gestured towards the kitchen table. She had mindlessly just left him hanging in the front foyer. "Can I get you anything?."

Brandon sank into the chair she had pulled out for him, visibly more relaxed. "Thank you Mrs. Beauvais, I'm fine. A glass of water would be nice."

Anna reached into the cupboard and pulled out two glasses and filled them each with water.

Brandon took a sip and resumed his story, this time he spoke more steadily.

"I swear on God's name I wasn't drinking. *I was only sixteen!* I hadn't even *had* a drink yet at that point in my life. Some friends tried drinking by then, but that didn't appeal to me. Especially seeing how stupid they were when they were drunk. She came out of nowhere fast. I didn't even see her. It was almost as if the skateboard hit my car, not the other way around. I lost control because it scared me. *It all happened so fast!* Oh God…"

At this Brandon broke down again. Tears drowned his face. He slumped onto the table, shoulders wracked with sobs.

Anna knew right then she would not bury her daughters with the destruction of this boy's life. The media frenzy about "elite white boy privilege" was ridiculous.

How could this be, her letting go after so many years of wanting to put the culpable driver away? She was no longer masked by anger. Her mother's heart took over.

"And I *did* stop," Brandon continued, straightening up and wiping his face with a paper napkin. "It wasn't like the news claimed. I stopped. I didn't see anybody. I got out of my car, looked around, even walked around a little, and there was no person, no dog, no nothing. Just a… um…well, a skateboard at the edge of the street. I got scared, maybe there was someone, somewhere. But then wouldn't there be a…um… a…" He couldn't bring himself to say the word.

A body. Anna cringed. *Her body was found hidden behind the juniper.*

Anna sat there silent, ready to listen some more. Something inside was telling her to hug this kid, but she held back.

After a few minutes, Brandon went on. "My dad…everyone says he is so rich because of his house and how he made it big in the stock market. But truth be told, this would bankrupt him, spiritually if not financially. No disrespect to your daughter ma'am….uh Mrs. Beauvais. But I would hate what this would do to my parents. They are so good. I could handle prison if I had to as an innocent man. It's *them* I am scared for. My mother would die of heartbreak. I mean it really would kill her. She couldn't survive this."

Brandon was crying uncontrollably. Anna has survived losing her daughters. Now authority wants to make this young man's life a tragedy off her tragedy. Hand him a sentence worse than death.

The next thing she knew, she was holding out her arms, embracing and consoling him. Her soft, gentle words came out without preamble. "Brandon, I want you to know I believe you. I believe what you are saying. I am so sorry you had to go through this. I will not subject you…your family…to a trial."

She ever so gently took his wet face in her hands. "Brandon, I promise you that. I will *not* subject you or your family to a trial. I am dropping the charges. I don't know how these things work. But if it's up to me? There will be no trial, not one dime out of your parents' pockets, and even more important, not one day in jail for you. There is no reason for that. You've already suffered enough, especially because of the media circus."

They had sat like that for a while, without saying a further word. When Brandon looked up again, his sparkling blue eyes rimmed red and such distress in them, Anna had reiterated "I do *not* blame you. I am going to drop all charges against you Brandon. Please understand that. I could not harden my heart enough to do that, not for all the money in the world. Your life is *far* more important than the damn millions our unjust judicial system is promising me."

After Brandon left, Anna had gone over to Lois Wright's home, the neighbor who had allegedly seen the whole thing happen and had called it in. She was finally ready to hear her story.

With a glass of wine in one hand and a paintbrush in the other, Lois was crafting a dark and dreary landscape. She sat at a drafting table painting the scene with watercolors, hoping to peddle it at the summer art and wine festival.

"I saw the blue Honda coming down your street and heard something strange…like the sound of metal popping," Lois told her, not looking up from her work. "I didn't have my glasses on, but could make out the figure of young Bianca. I saw her body go flying into the air."

Anna winced at how casually Lois said those words. As if her daughter's body were a piece of debris, nonchalantly tossed to the side. But she mustered up the courage to ask "You say you saw the car coming down the street. About how fast would you say he was driving?"

"Honestly, I couldn't tell from that distance, but he appeared to be sort of creeping along …until he took off. What do you call it…peel out?"

Anna's voice almost failed her when she asked the next question. "Did…did you see Bianca skateboarding as the car was coming down the street, before she was hit?"

Lois put her paintbrush down and stared at her work for a while. "That girl was a sight to see on that skateboard, doing those popping things. With her long blond hair and wiry little body flying down the road, popping up like that."

Doing those popping things! *Mom, look at me on my skateboard, look how high I can jump. Great honey, just make sure you are always in a park doing that…not near the streets.* She was a good mom, wasn't she? She always told her daughter not to skateboard near the streets. How would she know Bianca would do that? Anna felt sick to her stomach, guilt-ridden.

"One more question. Did you see her do that…that day… the…the popping thing?" she asked.

"Oh, for sure. She was doing that thing, bend her knees, bang and jump, the skateboard pinging up in the air like a dolphin, her arms in the air. I didn't need my glasses to recognize the tricks of the trade. Seen my grandson doing those pop ups in the park."

"It was almost as if the skateboard hit my car first, and I lost control for a second because it scared me."

Anna's heart was pounding so hard, she was afraid Lois might hear it. "I know I promised only one more question…but this is the last one. Did you see Brandon back up, stop to take a look?"

"No…but you see, I had run to my bedroom to find my glasses and call 911 after I realized she was hit. But something strange…the car was past the stop sign and turning into the main street before I ran to my room. When I returned, it was just approaching the stop sign, then did a right turn peel out thing. It was almost as if someone reversed the film in a movie."

"I did back up, and got out of my car. I looked all around and only saw a skateboard. So I thought I just hit a skateboard on the road. There was no person! I was frightened!"

The phone rang, startling Anna out of her memories of her visit with Lois. She stood, set her glass on the memory chest that served as a coffee table, and walked over to the phone. She glanced at her caller ID. It was Pierre. She picked up the phone.

"Anna, I have reporters swarming my apartment. It's driving me nuts!"

"I had two outside the house earlier. It looks like more vultures are starting to accumulate. Isn't this fun? It's only going to get worse if we allow this dog and pony show to proceed," Anna replied.

"What do you mean *if*?! It's not like we have the right to drop the case," he argued. "Dog and fucking pony show? You bitch, my girls were no dog or pony!"

"Oh, don't we? We are the victim's parents! The proverbial plaintiffs! It's gone on long enough. Like I told you after that visit from Brandon. *He* is also a victim. An innocent top notch college student with not even one speeding ticket to his name. It was an accident. I'm done flip-flopping and wavering. I'm dropping the case first thing in the morning. *He* is no fucking dog or pony either!"

Silence.

After what seemed an eternity, Pierre finally spoke. "Anna, listen. A lot of work has gone into this trial, the defense and prosecution teams working long hours selecting the jury, piling up witnesses to testify. A lot of money has been poured into it already. I know we will win Anna; the prosecution and wrongful death lawyers are sharks. We deserve this. And that young man, dog or not, has to pay for what he did."

"That's precisely why I want to drop the case! Sending a boy-man—who was just a teen when it happened—to prison? Throwing millions of dollars at us? That won't bring our family back! Nothing can do that. *It's gone.* I want to be able to sleep at nights. And honestly, Pierre. What happened to you? This is not the man I married. This is not our way, the way we were raised to act. Sometimes I think the worst thing we could have done is come to this bloodthirsty country. It's changed you. I'm not going to let it change me."

More silence. Then Pierre blew up more.

"You fucking bitch, you never *were* a good mother! This never would have happened if you hadn't let her go skateboarding in the fucking goddamn street! You should be ashamed! And don't put it on me. I'm right to want to avenge our daughters. And our family."

Then the phone went dead. Anna stood there for a second, phone still at her ear listening to the dial tone. Finally she placed the phone on its receiver.

I miss you and love you too Pierre.

Those words had stayed in her heart and mind, never making their way to her lips since their divorce. Since Pierre had left her, accusing her of being at fault for both daughters' deaths.

Anna was climbing the winding wrought-iron staircase to her bedroom when the phone rang again. Sure that it was a reporter or Phil, she kept climbing. But then Pierre's shaky, pleading voice came over the answering machine. As soon as she heard him she descended the staircase and rushed to the phone, her hand poised over the handset as she listened.

"Anna, I know you're there. Listen, Cherie. Ècoute moi. I'm sorry I hung up. Je suis desolèe. I'm so sorry I hurt you. I'm sorry I used profanity. I'm sorry for my anger. I'm… ah mon dieu…I'm not perfect. And, well, I'm hurting too! I…I miss my girls. I miss you. I miss…*us*. Anna please! Pick up! I need to talk with you. Anna? Please, please for the love of God, pick up. I want to drop the case too. And *fuck* the ten million dollars! *Fuck* revenge. You're right, it won't bring back our girls. I don't know what possessed me to ever think it would. Anna…!"

He was crying. She could hear it in his voice. He had never cried in the twenty-plus years she had stood by him.

When his voice trailed off she picked up. "Did…did you say you want to drop the case too?" she asked, breathless.

"Yes, absolutely." Then, in the next breath "And I love you. I love you Anna. I never stopped loving you. And I need you. And I want to hold you right this minute. My life has sucked the past six years without you.

Nothing means anything. I've been walking around like a ghost and a man possessed. Oh Anna, I am so sorry. I just did not handle losing my baby girls well. I wanted to stay angry at the world, at God, at you, at *him*."

Anna cringed, remembering their former rage against Brandon. An innocent, beautiful boy the unjust American justice system would have manipulated them into ruining.

Pierre continued "I needed to blame someone, and that ended up being the one person I love more than life itself. But I can't stand to lose you too. And you are all I have left of them. Please forgive me, cherie. I beg you. Can you forgive me? Can we walk through this together now?"

Anna couldn't speak. Tears tickled her cheeks. She grabbed a tissue and started frantically blowing her nose. Could this be happening? After six years? Had she heard him correctly? After she had gathered her composure she finally spoke.

"Pierre. My love. Of course I forgive you. Can you come over? Or should I come there?"

"I'll come there, my darling. It's the least I could do after what I've put you…*us*…through. I'll come the back way to avoid the reporters."

"Good. I'll leave the back door unlocked. And bring your toothbrush."

"Okay. I will. I can't bear to hang up. You hang up first."

"No. You hang up first."

"I can't. You hang up first."

They both laughed "OK," they said in unison, "I'm hanging up now."

When her phone was back in the receiver at last, Anna flung her arms around herself and danced about the loft, as she had all those years ago in Paris when she first knew that she and Pierre would be lovers.

She was still dancing half an hour later when she heard a soft tap at the back door, and a whispered "Cherie. C'est moi."

Chapter Seventeen

The next morning, Anna and Pierre drove to the courthouse together, Pierre at the wheel of his beat-up BMW. His fingers clutched the steering wheel. Along the way, Anna thought of losses: her daughters, six years of her marriage, her parents, and her youth.

The Plaintiff Attorney's words flashed through her head: *"The punitive damages of wrongful death…the spiraling effect on your family could net you at least ten million dollars."*

They no longer had their own kids to feed, clothe, and send through college. Why enable the media frenzy exploit everybody's suffering?

"We have each other Pierre," she heard herself saying in the quiet of the car. Neither of them had spoken during the past twenty minutes while sitting in traffic. "That's all I will ever need now. You and our sweet Jared."

Pierre remained quiet, a solemn nod of his chin his response. The Golden Gate Bridge under their tires provided solace in an otherwise glum moment.

"I keep thinking," stammered Anna…"what would happen to this bright college kid's life if the jury found him guilty under a warped legal system, which offered "Liberty and Justice *for some*?" A convicted *child killer*, how would he be treated in prison?"

She knew she could never get over the anguish of destroying the Garth family, a young man's life. There are enough youth's lives destroyed in this world by cruel acts of revenge and 'justice.'

Anna quickly chased those thoughts away, her mind refreshed from the first good night of sleep in months, maybe even six years. She and

Pierre had made tender love last night, and fallen asleep in each other's arms after crying for an eternity. All that pent-up tension was now gone. Amazing that on the day of the trial that now wouldn't be, she felt like herself again.

They had no idea of protocol, or if this tactic would even work. Is the political dishonesty of the justice system powerful enough to override....*oh, she needed to stop thinking!*

Finally, they were in the Mission District, turning off Seventh Street near the courthouse. They found parking easily, which had to be a good omen. Pierre got out of the car, went around to Anna's side, opened her door, and handed her out to the sidewalk. She was once again his queen, and he her king.

Holding hands, heads held high, they approached the courthouse. Passersby stopped to stare. Faint whispers of "are they together again?" barely registered in Anna's ringing ears. Reporters flocked around them in droves within feet of the BMW, so it was hard to move. Cameras flashed in their faces. Shouted questions came at them from all directions.

"Mr. and Mrs. Beauvais, have you reconciled your differences?" barked one reporter.

Neither Anna nor Pierre dignified the reporter with a response, not even the expected "no comment." Together they pushed through the crowds. Determined. Confident. Excited about their decision. They didn't answer one question thrown their way.

*　*　*

Meanwhile, at the Golden Gate Grind Café just across the bay, three parents from the elementary school gathered around a table, ready for the opening day of Beauvais vs. Garth to be aired live on the huge flat screen TV. The place was packed, all eyes on the screen.

"Is this being aired everywhere? Or just locally?" one of the patrons asked.

"Nationwide...heck, it's like the OJ case or something, what with Mr. Big Bucks vs. Gorgeous Money Reaper there," his friend replied.

Caryssa, Brenda, and Stan glanced at each other, cringing at the crude remark about Anna. "That guy is in for a surprise," Caryssa muttered under her breath to the other parents.

"Yep…fresh entertainment for the masses," whispered Stan.

"A true reality TV show, feeding on real people's misery." Caryssa needed a glass of wine, and started wishing they met at a bar instead of the coffee shop. "*Step right up folks, get your popcorn, the show is about to start!*" she practically laughed the words out.

On the big screen, Defense Attorney John Mills walked into the courthouse, cameras flashing around him. He was on the small side, with a neat compact build, kindly eyes behind frameless glasses, and a pleasant, intelligent face. Stan thought; *too soft a look?* He took a gulp of his latte. *Shit, he'll be clobbered!*

The reporters went wild. They thronged him, shoving mikes into his face, elbowing each other to get closer. "Do you believe the allegations that Pierre and Anna Beauvais were at fault for letting their daughter skateboard on dangerous ground on a foggy day?"

Caryssa cringed at the callousness of this remark. "*Let* her skateboard?" *Are these reporters parents themselves? Have they no clue about the willful defiance of a preteen?*

"No comment," Mills replied.

Another reporter "Is it not true that a twelve-year-old should know better than to be skateboarding on a narrow, winding road in inclement weather?"

The journalists swarmed the case like vultures, jostling for attention. More unnecessary fuel to the fire "The kind of weather that fogs windshields and makes it difficult for a driver to see?"

"No comment."

"Mr. Mills, isn't it true that your key witness is now ready to testify that indeed the then sixteen year old teenager was *not* driving to endanger…"

This time Mills didn't respond verbally but gave an irritated wave of his hand, as if he were pushing away a swarm of flies.

The camera switched to a commotion off to the right, as the TV reporters continued gathering like predators fighting over footage.

Unlike Mills, lead prosecutor Phil van Wagner looked flashy and charismatic. Tall, dark, and handsome. *People Magazine* had named him one of the sexiest men alive. Sexy. And ruthless.

"I heard van Wagner is a brilliant prosecutor. He outsmarts the defense in every case," remarked a heavyset brunette woman at the next table. "Eats the defense team live, like a shark."

"*Shit!*" Caryssa wailed.

Brenda glanced at Caryssa with an odd look. "What, don't you wanta get justice for Anna's daughter? What kind of loyal friend is that? What do y'all think?"

"Yeah," the woman's companion replied. "I read in the paper he's relentless, never rests. Both of them are Harvard Law grads…but their courtroom styles might be quite the contrast for the jury. I heard Mills is the diplomatic soft-spoken type."

A shiver went down Caryssa's spine, listening to this conversation. She felt frightened for Brandon. The images of his young face splashed all over front pages of the newspapers haunted her.

More camera flashes, pushing and crowding for coverage, then "Mr. van Wagner, is it true the victim's parents are now going after more than ten million in punitive damages?"

"No comment," replied van Wagner.

"Mr. van Wagner, what are the consequences of the defendant failing to step up until five years after the event?"

Caryssa thought she detected him slurring under his breath, *"a prison sentence"* as he walked away. Wow, what ever happened to constraints a lawyer can say?

Phil van Wagner looked dangerously impressive, a powerful figure. Very controlled, an arrogance radiating from him even through the veneer of silence.

The reporters swarmed around something happening ahead. There was a huge commotion directly in front of the courthouse. Now the camera was on Anna Beauvais, in a lime green cable-knit sweater, with her butterscotch hair blowing free.

Caryssa was struck by how beautiful Anna looked on the café's big screen, all gleaming blond streaks and huge almond eyes. Eyes that for the first time in a long time looked bright and full of confidence.

"Mr. and Mrs. Beauvais, are you prepared to finally seek justice in the name of your daughter—actually your *daughters* since the second took her own life because of this needless tragedy?"

What Caryssa secretly hoped for came next.

Pierre responded with a subtle shake of the head, remaining silent.

Anna stopped, turned, and looked straight into the camera. "Why yes. We *are* prepared to seek justice. *But not revenge.* There will be no trial. My husband and I are pleased to announce that we are dropping the case against the defendant, Brandon Garth. Likewise, we seek *no* punitive damages."

"*Yay*!" Caryssa screamed the word, nearly falling out of her chair.

"The dog-and-pony show ends here!" Stan announced happily as he carried a fresh round of lattes to each parent.

"Seriously! Added Caryssa. "This media and legal circus has made enough money exploiting family tragedies!" She pointed directly to the TV screen airing the cast of amoral circus show characters. "Let them go back to their desks and think about what they're doing. Surely this isn't what they dreamed of during journalism or law school."

Pandemonium broke loose. "Mr. and Mrs. Beauvais, surely you are not walking away from what could amount to a *ten million* dollar lawsuit of wrongful death for your young daughter against the defendant?!"

The two attorneys, who had already entered the courthouse, must have seen Anna's response on the TV monitors from inside the lobby.

Phil van Wagner came back out, looking at Anna disbelievingly, and mouthing *"No! Not another word!"*

"Yes!" Stan yelled from his café seat at the Golden Gate Grind.

Reporters swarmed around Anna and Pierre, cameras flashed wildly. So many questions were being asked, it was difficult to comprehend any of them. Through all the commotion, the viewers could hear Phil van Wagner's incredulous "Do you know how much time and money have been spent on this case since re-opening it over the past year and a half?"

A commercial came on, and the group of parents from the elementary school sat there stunned. Finally, Brenda broke the silence.

"Wow, that's not what I was expecting!"

From across the café came laughter, then "Someone paid that good looking gal off to drop the case…*come on!* Like someone would drop the chance at ten million freakin' dollars!" This from a male wearing a do-rag, pirate-like bandana along his forehead, tied at the nape of his heavily tattooed neck.

"Yeah…like the rich fucking father…he has been wanting to protect his precious criminal son…this is vehicular homicide of a little girl!" screeched a red-haired woman with a ponytail poking up from the top of her head, like Pebbles from the Flintstones. "If it was my daughter, I'd want him fried!"

A little girl not all that much younger than the sixteen year old defendant at the time of the accident. Caryssa glared at the woman stuck in the harsh Stone Age.

Stan exclaimed in a voice loud enough for others in the café to hear "Personally, I'm *glad* the case is being dropped…there's too much pointing towards this outstanding young man being not at fault."

Caryssa also purposely responded loud enough for others to hear. "Yeah, plus no amount of money will bring her daughters back. It would do nothing but crush yet another family."

The unruly gang at the other table shot back dirty looks. "Shit man, give me the fuckin' ten million, dumb ass, if ya gunna just drop the case!" one of them said, glancing back at the TV screen.

Just then, the live report came back on. Spectators and reporters were still swarming around the courthouse. A reporter spoke into the microphone.

"This is Jamie Evans reporting live on KTVU, from San Francisco. We have just received word that the much-publicized case of Garth vs. Beauvais has been adjourned until further notice. There is no further report at this time. Thank you for tuning in. Now back to our regular programs. Local news coming up at five, and then at six national news."

"There's *no way* she dropped the case. Someone paid her off." Repeated bandana dude.

The TV screen flashed back to the case, and all eyes in the café glanced up again. The camera was now inside the courtroom.

Defense attorney John Mills whispered something to Judge Yale. The judge took his gavel and gave it a good bang. "Court is recessed until further notice."

"Oh my God, it hasn't even *started* yet!" someone in the café yelled.

The camera was now focused on an intense interchange between van Wagner and Anna. The plaintiff's lawyer was fixing Anna with an angry baffled look. The microphone picked up bits of their conversation.

"How could you give up this opportunity?" van Wagner hissed.

"*Opportunity*? An opportunity to ruin yet another family? How could I not?" Anna replied calmly.

In the café, Stan proclaimed "Anna is ethical and classy to the bone. Even hard-core idiots like this attorney can sense the virtue radiating from her."

"So true," Caryssa joined in. "Anna is so beautiful inside and out. A *real* humanitarian."

The camera did one last sweep before another cut to commercials. The lawyers at the prosecution table were squirming. A ten million dollar verdict and visions of percentages in their pockets fading away fast.

Caryssa and the rest of the parents decided they had had enough. The crowd inside was merciless. It was a gorgeous day, so they decided to take their lattes to the bistro tables out front. A huge palm tree waved in the sunshine, and the view of the Golden Gate Bridge was magnificent. Sailboats were everywhere, and the bay shone an exquisite turquoise blue.

The three of them sat in silence for a few minutes, Brenda almost sulking.

"Are you *really* upset Anna dropped the case? Caryssa admonished.

"Well…no, not really. I'm just amazed," Brenda said.

"I'm not," Caryssa responded. "I would have been amazed if she hadn't dropped the charges. *Disgusted* actually!"

"I'm relieved at the outcome," Stan glanced at each of them. "I don't want Brandon, the alleged defendant, having to swear his innocence to a non-compassionate judge and biased jury."

"And the prosecution team playing up the aggressive male driver story," Caryssa added. "I could not have sat and watched that inhumane, unfair crap."

"Oh my God, Caryssa! *She was a twelve-year-old girl!*" Brenda exclaimed.

"Yes! And *he* was only a sixteen-year-old boy!" Caryssa argued. "You sound like pitiless Pebbles back in the café, wanting her revengeful bam-bam."

Brenda did not seem to connect the remark with the crude patron that wanted the kid *"fried."*

She continued "He is still so young, a twenty-one-year-old college kid. His entire life is in front of him! Get over it, Brenda!"

"Well, I still wonder if this whole terrible tragedy could have been avoided," Brenda crushed her latte cup in the palm of her hand "I sure hope he wasn't driving fast or drunk. No matter, the whole thing just sucks."

"Just look at his record now," Caryssa intoned. "He's a straight A medical student, highly respected by his professors and peers, by all reports does no drugs, only drinks socially, and that very lightly. He has never even gotten a *speeding ticket*. That hardly sounds like a menace to society. And I'm just disgusted with a system that is so revengeful and cruel it would define 'justice' as Anna getting multi-millions of the fucking almighty dollar while this beautiful kid gets bullied and beaten up or worse in prison!"

"True. Our nation's statistics with so many in prison is embarrassing enough," Stan spread his arms upward, revealing his palms. "And what scares me is that could be one of *our* kids someday. Just got their license, driving very cautiously due to fog and poor visibility. Then the daredevil, risk-taking skateboarder flies into street out of nowhere—a daredevil skateboarder pissed off at her mom I might add—and next thing you know, innocent child accused of killing another innocent child. "

"Or it could be one of our kids on the *skateboard*," Brenda countered. "Let's face it, our kids will defy our orders. Didn't we go against what our parents suggested at times ourselves?"

"No way, no skateboards will be allowed in my family!" Caryssa exclaimed. "Well, at least not anywhere on the streets…Inner Park only."

"That was Anna's rule," Brenda reminded her quietly.

"OK, then no skateboards *at all*. Those things are too dangerous. I tell Tyler that it isn't wise for anyone to even ride bikes in the streets, including adults. Why take chances around cars, never mind breathe all those toxic fumes."

"Oh, come on Caryssa! You've ridden your bikes with Tyler over the Golden Gate Bridge into Sausalito and Tiburon several times…which means you've ridden on the streets. *Winding* streets. Just like the ones this little girl rode her skateboard on against her mother's instructions.

And we see Tyler on a scooter all the time. He skis steep mountains and climbs tall jagged rocks. So say Tyler got rolled over by the grooming machine at a ski resort. Would you not want to have a trial against the driver?"

"If the driver was at fault, maybe. But you're forgetting that there is too much indication that Brandon was not at fault. It's possible Bianca was at fault. We can't be sending innocent kids to prison or putting a delicate family through that. It solves nothing. And yeah, we've ridden on the streets. It's hard not to. But I prefer not to ride on streets at all with Tyler. Nine out of ten rides we take are off-road."

Stan chimed in. "And no matter what, even if a child is willfully defiant to her parents like they all would be at some time, even if she is innocent of anything but that willful defiance...*nothing* can justify taking revenge for her life. Not when we have so much reasonable doubt. We as a society, put innocent people—*kids*—in prison way too much, while the real criminals walk."

A small, uncomfortable silence fell over the group. Brenda changed the subject.

"Hey Stan, where's your little guy Kieran today?" she asked.

"Stacy's working from home, so we decided to have him play at home while I watch the trial. Speaking of which, I should go relieve her so she can get some work done! He must be bugging the crap out of her!"

After Stan left, Caryssa decided to ask Brenda what she had wanted to ask for the past hour. She leaned towards her friend. "OK, let it out, something is bothering you girlfriend. What's up?"

Brenda looked momentarily startled. "Is it that obvious?" Then she hesitated.

"Yeah, it is. You way overreacted to this whole trial thing." Caryssa looked straight into Brenda's eyes, keeping her head neutral. "I can tell something else is going on. And it's okay if you don't want to talk about it. I won't push. But I'm here if you need an ear. Is it about the trial?"

Brenda sighed and looked at Caryssa gratefully. "You know me so well. It's nothing to do with Anna or the trial. I haven't spoken to anyone about what's bothering me. I'm too embarrassed, or maybe too guilt-ridden."

"*Guilt-ridden*? You couldn't have done anything too bad...you are the epitome of motherhood, a female Einstein, a beautiful goddess, splendid in nature, representing all things good and pure...which is why I was flabbergasted that you would even think Brandon Garth should be put away!"

Although, Brenda does fall off the 'good and pure' train, at times drowning in the syrup of patriotic sentimentality with the rhetorical sloppiness and authoritarian shallowness of our cultural insistence of *"hero* "worship of violence. That, we can do without.

"I cheated on Ron," Brenda blurted. "So that's how 'good' I am!" Within seconds, the tears were streaming down her cheeks. "Do you know how I feel? It's not just Ron's trust I violated, which is bad enough. I feel like I've cheated my children! I've rocked their world, deflated their perfect little float, and crapped on their daddy!"

Caryssa was stunned into silence. "Wait, you told the kids?"

"Of course not! Nor Ron. But my soul knows!"

"Brenda, honey. Okay, so you made a mistake. It sounds like you'd never do it again."

"It's not that easy! I mean, no I won't let it happen again, no matter what. But every time I look into my kids eyes, I see Ron. I've violated my family, my children, and their world!"

A couple came out of the café to the bistro area where Brenda and Caryssa were sitting by themselves.

Caryssa smiled at Brenda. "Do you want to take a walk, where it's more private?" she whispered.

"Yeah," Brenda replied, gathering her things. "Good idea. Let's go sit in my car."

Once they were settled in the car, Caryssa just listened as Brenda continued. "No matter what, I won't tell them. But no matter what, it will be on my conscience. They won't know, I can't let that hurt into their lives. Any of them. But I know!" and here she broke down sobbing. "I know, Caryssa! How am I supposed to live with that?"

"Oh Brenda, I know it must be so hard," Caryssa pulled her friend into a warm hug. "I think...I think anything that happens to us or our family, we tend to think of our children first. Like I think about if I lost George...it would not be just me I would be grieving for. I would be grieving far more for Tyler."

The two women sat in silence for a moment. Then Brenda continued. "I can't, I just can't let the kids know, or Ron. But it's the kids I worry about it affecting the most. I hope my own hurt doesn't seep through to them. You know how family secrets can end up hurting kids just because they are secrets? How kids pick up on what isn't being said? The proverbial family elephant in every room? I'm so afraid my secret is going to do that to them somehow. And if it did? I'd never forgive myself."

"Don't keep blaming yourself," Caryssa straightened her body, spreading her palms in front of her. "I mean, if it happened, there has to be a *reason* Brenda. Everything happens for a reason. And in marriages? It takes two to keep the passion alive. You and Ron are in this together, and if you were drawn to cheat, Ron has a part to play as well. So what is missing in your life, your marriage? You don't have to tell me, but just think about it."

"Well, it's weird. The guy I was with…I'm not even really *attracted* to him. I love Ron so much. I guess…well, between the day-to-day martyrdom of motherhood, Ron working long hours, and…I swear with two kids and both of us working so hard, we can go five or six months without sex. It's not Ron's fault any more than mine. I'm too damn tired!"

Caryssa chuckled "Yup that's the story of more than half the moms I know, including me…too damn tired. We can easily go months without intimacy, even in the best of marriages!" But truthfully, for Caryssa, she is happier being a Mom than when sex was so within reach. She *feels* the love.

Brenda continued, her head down towards her lap. "And…I don't know…his attention made me feel like an attractive woman again…one thing led to another…"

"Well Brenda, I guess in time you'll feel better, the guilt will dissipate. You said it won't happen again. Just look at it as a mistake, learn from it, and move on. And remember…it's not all your fault. It takes two to keep the spark lit."

Meanwhile, in a certain Sausalito loft, two lovers who had been married and then divorced and who had just beaten the justice system were rediscovering just what it meant to keep the spark alive.

And sparks were flying.

Chapter Eighteen

By the time Bryan was able to work around family schedules and plan their trip, it was late September.

For the first time in Kevin and Keenan's six year-old lives, they were flying across the country to meet Grandma and Grandpa Garrity. It had taken Charlotte nearly two weeks to pack, even though they would be there for only a week. She kept putting things in, taking things out.

"Sweetheart, why are you bringing so much for the boys?" Bryan was eyeing the overstuffed suitcases. "You do realize they can't weigh more than fifty pounds?"

"This is New England we're visiting, you never know what the weather could be. The boys need to be prepared." Charlotte tossed in another sweatshirt they may ever wear. "Besides, your Dad may take us out on one of his yachts. Even if it's comfortable inland, they'll need warm clothes."

Their flight out of San Francisco was delayed due to heavy fog. Between the delay, overblown post-9/11 security theatre act and leaving two hours early to be subjected to such---it was ten hours later when they started to descend towards La Guardia airport.

To Bryan, Charlotte appeared a bit nervous while disembarking. Then it hit him. *This will be the first time she's ever met my family. The first time she's ever had a glimpse into my fucked-up childhood.* How will I feel? Angry at how I was treated as a child? *How will his boys be treated?*

Clarence Garrity met them at the airport, insisting they not rent a car. He was frail, and in a motorized wheelchair. Bryan was shocked to see him this way. Other than the period of time his Dad was recovering from a sniper shot while serving as a US Senator, his memories of him was of a strong, burly man.

The introductions were strained. Bryan and Clarence were awkward with each other. Stumbling for words. And the boys acted as if their flesh-and-blood grandfather was a complete stranger. Not surprising. Because he was.

But when Bryan looked closer, his Dad's vulnerability and deep sadness were transparent to him. This formerly stoic, cold-hearted, ruthless political bastard was human after all. The way his father looked at his sons broke his heart.

And by God, he could see himself in him. His Keenan looked just like him too. The aqua-blue eyes, dimples, crooked Irish grin.

He had not expected to be moved this way. His family's turmoil, its past pains points, dropped deep into his gut. His mixed feelings blended together in a rush of heavy resentment. He challenged his Dad's change with a mistrust he wished he could push aside. For hid kid's sake.

"Hello, father."

"Hello, son."

Silence. The boys clung to their father's sides. Charlotte nervously placed the novel she was reading into the side pouch of her bag.

Finally Bryan bent to hug his dad. What started as a man-to-son pat turned into a deadlock. Both of them turning it into a body crushing entanglement bordering on a fear of letting go. And when he looked at his once emotionally detached Dad afterwards, he had a tear sliding towards his mouth.

It was as if the reservoir of guilt had been released. The dam broke loose. As if he could finally acknowledge: *This is my only son whom I not only let down in the worst way, but have neglected for years.*

He turned and glanced at the boys. They both looked scared and confused. "Can I get a big hug from you boys too, hmmm? Come and give your old Grandpa a big hug please," Clarence nearly begged the twins, holding out his long, thin, shaking arms.

They just stood there with blank stares. Neither moved.

"Go ahead boys," Charlotte reassured them. "It's okay. Go…hug your grandfather. He is your *daddy's* daddy! He really needs a hug."

The boys remained frozen. Standing. Still. Staring. *Why were they so hesitant?*

Bryan took Charlotte aside where others couldn't hear. He whispered…"Honey, I think they remember the argument we had after the last baseball game. We had shouted back and forth, with the twins in the back seat—about how badly my parents treated me, how they disowned me, threw me out to fend for myself at age eighteen. Kids listen."

To the twins, their own grandpa was the "*bad guy.*"

"Well, maybe later," Clarence said, smiling through his sorrow. "You don't know your grand-daddy, do you now? We'll just have to make up for lost time. No rush. Come on now to the car. Do you have all your luggage, Bry Guy?"

Bryan was gazing at his sons, willing them to hug his Dad. While understanding in his heart why they wouldn't. He too, was angry at him.

The last of their suitcases had shown up at baggage claim, and Bryan had them all piled up onto a cart. They followed Clarence in his "wicked" wheelchair as the boys referred to it out to an elevator and down one floor to the parking garage.

The "car" was a wheelchair accessible luxury limo with an attendant to lift Clarence out of his chair. The boys were excited, and jumped into the back section.

"Oh check it out! There's a whole bucket of juice boxes! And some chocolates!" Kevin exclaimed.

"Look Mommy, something for you and Daddy!" Keenan shouted.

Charlotte looked over and saw a bottle of champagne on ice. Not just any champagne, but Cristal, which Charlotte knew cost hundreds of dollars a bottle. Also, there was a platter of very fancy looking hors d'oeuvres, things Charlotte had no idea how to pronounce, even if she had any clue what they were. And fine china. And silver to serve and eat with.

Clarence smiled, seeing Charlotte's reaction. "Are the accommodations to your liking, my lady?"

Charlotte couldn't even answer. She was speechless. She just nodded.

"Permit me," He lifted the Cristal out of the ice bucket, then loosened the muselet, holding the bottle at a forty-five degree angle. He struggled while rotating the base of the bottle when his hands and arms started shaking so much, he couldn't hold onto the bottle. Bryan tried to help him, inadvertently removing the cage so that the cork prematurely popped. Champagne exploded all over the place.

"Now that was more than the standard fssszzzz" laughed Charlotte. She was drenched in sparkling wine.

"Oh darn!" Clarence looked almost embarrassed. He was looking more vulnerably human than ever, and Bryan actually felt bad for him. Clarence recovered and said "Heck, a little Champagne shower never hurt anyone!"

He reached for a champagne flute, expertly pouring her a glass, despite his still shaking hands. "We don't want to waste any more of this, now do we?"

He handed the flute to her. His twinkling blue eyes flashing a moment of deep remorse about the past, as he gave her a playful wink.

"Dad!" Are you flirting with my wife?!" Bryan was actually having fun with his Dad. He can't remember this ever happening. How he can joke through his anger and pain was beyond him.

Clarence chuckled. "It's a father-in-law's prerogative, son of mine. And I have a lot of time to make up for."

"Okay then pour me some bubbly too," Bryan tried to see his once cold, distant father anew. But mostly what he was remembering was his womanizing. He chased the memories away, and attempted some light humor "You always were a ladies man, Dad."

"It ain't over till it's over" His father switched on some soft music at the same time the boys discovered the Nintendo Wii game system, drowning the tunes out. "I may be an old man in a wheelchair and on my last legs, but I recognize a beautiful classy woman when I see one!"

Bryan reached across to take the flute from his father, images of the beautiful young women he paraded past him as a little boy a repressed memory. He wondered what his boys might think of his Dad overly admiring their Mom. Or if it was a way for him to finally say *"son, you really have made a good choice in life."*

The boys were so busy finding buttons to push and discovering what happened when they pushed them that they hadn't even noticed the rather tipsy emotional Irish family reunion.

Charlotte blushed, "Oh stop it, Clarence. You're embarrassing me!"

Clarence pulled the bottle out of the ice one more time and topped off everybody's glasses. "I'm so glad you're here…Thank you for making the trip. He raised his glass to toast. "To…long awaited family meetings." He clicked his glass against Charlotte's, then Bryan's.

They rode in high-class splendor out of LaGuardia into New Canaan where the Garritys owned a stunning colonial with a mini golf course and two swimming pools, each with a hot tub.

Once off the highway and into New Canaan, Charlotte started watching the scenery that unfolded outside the window. It was like a Norman Rockwell painting. A sophisticated, simple, but classic village with lots of quaint charm.

They passed fine boutiques, coffee shops, antique stores, bistros, and spas. Scenic, winding roads would eventually bring them to the sprawling mansion where Bryan had grown up.

It was late September, and the autumn foliage was good enough to make a postcard photographer drool. "How gorgeous New England is in the fall!" Charlotte was twisting and turning to view all angles from the limo. "How far are you from Manhattan?"

"Oh, forty miles or so. Not far. Why, would you like to plan a trip into the city one day while you're here? I can make the limo available for you."

"I'd love to see it if we have a chance. I've never even been to New York City," Charlotte said.

Clarence raised his eyebrows. "Never? The greatest city in the world? Then you must, my dear. And we will make it happen this trip—"

"You'd think by the sounds of things my wife has been living under a rock," Bryan interjected. "She's been to almost every continent in the world, just not everywhere in the States."

Bryan recognized at once he was defending her because he doesn't want her to seem low class to his dad. But judging from Clarence's behavior so far, he seemed truly overjoyed to have them there in his world.

"So...apart from a trip to Manhattan, I have a few plans I hope you'll like." Clarence went on. "First off, at least one day out in my newest yacht. It depends on the weather of course, but so far Wednesday is looking to be perfect. I'm docked up at the Yacht Club not too far from our house. And anyone up for some golf? We have my course to ourselves. And my chef will do a few great barbeques out by our pools. We could get in some beach days, too. There's a beautiful beach just six miles away. The boys will love it. There's so much to do. I wish you were staying longer. But first, you all must be hungry."

Bryan could not believe how passionate and family-oriented his father was being…so caring and responsive. He had gone to the beach with his dad as a kid maybe once or twice that he could remember. Clarence Garrity had always been too busy for him. And his mother? *Well, his mother…*

"I sure am hungry," he said. "Thanks for asking, Dad. How about you boys? You didn't eat much on the airplane."

"Well, what do they feed anyone these days anyway, except some peanuts and a purchased FrankenFood snack box?" Charlotte stomach growled. "I'm hungry too."

The twins said "Me too! I'm hungry!" at the same time.

"Well," laughed Clarence. "I guess that settles it. Just in case, I made reservations at one of Barbara's favorite little French restaurants. She was sorry not to be able to meet you at the airport, but she had her regular spa and beauty parlor appointments. She never misses those. She'll meet us there. It's family-friendly enough for these two young gentlemen. I know the owners and the chef personally and they are holding the place open for your arrival."

The limo made its way into the village and parked just outside the bistro. The chauffeur got out and went around to open the doors and hand them all out onto the sidewalk. Bryan was surprised to see his Dad walk on his own, with no need for the wheelchair. As he walked beside his ailing father, he said "So… Pops, you're not crippled after all!"

"Oh, I can walk a bit. Just not for long." It seemed like his Dad had something else to tell him, but thought twice about it.

* * *

This was not the type of restaurant she and Bryan had ever taken the boys to. Extremely elegant, its bright mustard yellow walls, white table cloths, earthy artwork, and floral arrangements screamed "Caution! No young kids allowed!"

"Geesh Clarence, are you sure this place is okay for our boys?" Charlotte wondered if they would even consider giving the kids crayons and coloring sheets. Or if they would expect them to sit like statues. "I mean, they're well behaved, but they are, after all, six. They'll need to be able to get up and play."

"Oh, no problem," Clarence assured her. "We'll be the only ones here. And Ken, the owner, has a surprise for us!"

The bistro made Charlotte feel instantly cozy and warm on this cool New England autumn night. The intricate French décor made her feel as if she were in the heart of Provence. It was the kind of place you instantly knew the food and wine would be spectacular. The kind of place she and Bryan had cut from their budget since the boys had come along.

Barbara Garrity walked in just before Clarence ordered the wine. Although she had never met her mother-in-law, Charlotte knew even before she walked over to join them that this modish woman was Bryan's mom. Barbara was not attractive in the classic sense. But she carried herself with a certain grace, a sense of confidence.

"Hello, sorry I'm late" Barbara's hand flew to her just styled hairdo. "I'm Barbara...I'm...She glanced at the twins fretfully. "I'm your Grandma! She sat. No kiss for anyone.

Charlotte found her to be cold, but wondered if it might be because she was nervous to finally meet her only daughter-in-law and her grandchildren. After all, it had been seventeen years since she and Bryan had married.

What struck Charlotte the most was realizing that Bryan's parents did not know him—*at all*. They still saw him as the little boy who had lived in their mansion. That little boy the au pair took care of. *That runaway teenager.*

They did not know the man their son had become. Nothing about his dreams, what he liked to eat, his business, what made him happy.

But they seemed to make a concerted effort to get to know their only son during this elegant meal at this chic bistro. Over the course of two hours, they learned that Bryan preferred rice over potatoes, fish and chicken over red meat, a latte over tea, classical and jazz over rock and roll. And that he cherished his humble work as a landscape architect and Cal Poly education—regardless of his ultra-rich upbringing.

Charlotte had the tomato tart, then the filet with frites. Bryan had some delicious looking cassoulet dish. There was patè de la masson, steamed asparagus, foie gras, and mousse au chocolate. It was a meal fit for royalty.

"Thank God the limo is taking us to your castle in the clouds! I've lost track of how many glasses of wine we've each had." The wine and exhaustion from travel gave her a feeling of floating. Clarence or Ken just kept pouring into their glasses each time they glanced away.

About midway through the dinner, Ken came out with a giant Lego set of the Eiffel Tower. It was already put together, so the boys just stared at it in awe. It took three people to help carry it out.

"Hey Mommy, that's the Lego set I wanted, but you said it had too many pieces!" Keenan exclaimed.

"More like far too expensive, at a few hundred bucks" mentioned Bryan.

"Oh my, look at that thing!" Charlotte gasped. "I can't believe how realistic it is…the flag, the elevators, the colors, every little detail!"

"It's built to scale, 1:300 from the original blueprints," Ken said.

"Wow!" Kevin shouted.

"Go ahead boys…you can play with it, tear it down if you'd like, make a mess even. I have only your family here tonight, in honor of your visit," Ken gestured towards the giant set.

The two boys pounded on the Eiffel Tower, which stood as tall as them. Pieces landed all over the floor, and they started building smaller missions around it.

"Hey, did you boys finish your dinner?" Charlotte asked. She knew that now that this masterpiece was out, there was no way of getting them back to their burgers and frites, which she realized must have been prepared specially for them. She hadn't seen a kids menu. No surprise, in a restaurant this fancy.

"I can wrap up the boys' dinner if you'd like," the waiter offered. "I guess our timing was less than perfect. It looks like they're too excited to eat now."

"Oh, that would be fabulous, thanks," Charlotte responded. "No worries. They're little. It happens all the time at our house. Sometimes getting them to eat is a bite-by-bite challenge."

The waiter smiled at her and bowed slightly as he removed the twins' dishes.

Later, riding in the limo towards the mansion, Bryan asked "Why did I not see the check for the meal back there? I was ready to contribute, but I never even saw a check. Was I zoning out or something?"

"Oh, it was taken care of in advance, son," Clarence said. "Ken has me on a perpetual tab. He knows he will get paid at the end of every month. This was our treat."

It wasn't long before the limo stopped at a magnificent iron gate, which reminded Charlotte a bit of the gate at Buckingham Palace. She saw Clarence press a remote control on his seat's arm-rest, and the iron gates opened up to a long, winding, tree-lined stone driveway. She could see that Barbara, who drove back separately, was pulling in just ahead in a new Lexus that seemed almost frugal amidst the opulence surrounding them.

As they moved slowly towards the front entrance of the mansion, Charlotte glanced at her husband, the professional landscape architect, and saw that his jaw had dropped. The impeccable, park-like grounds of the property looked as grand as any spa resort Charlotte had ever been to in her life. Trickling waterfalls, at least five of them, magnificent gardens, a carriage barn, even a private duck pond.

"Is this a fancy resort kind of place Mommy? I thought we were going to Grandma and Grandpa's house?" Kevin asked.

"Oh sweetie, but this *is* Grandma and Grandpa's house," Charlotte was enchanted.

"Hah!" Keenan shouted. "Wow, it looks like a palace! Oh I know, a king and queen must live here!"

Charlotte laughed, and reached over to tousle her son's hair. "It sure does, honey. And soon you and your brother will get to explore it."

When the limo came to a stop and all the passengers had disembarked, the boys ran towards the duck pond, yelling "quack quack quack!"

"Mommy, I have my leftover bread from dinner, may I feed the ducks please?" Keenan yelled back.

Charlotte glanced at Clarence for an answer. The attendant was helping him out of the limo.

"What did he ask, dear?" Clarence had been deposited back into his motorized wheelchair to ride the long walkway. "To feed the quackaroos? Well, we don't usually let...oh dammit, go ahead. Tell them yes! I just won't let our groundskeeper know. David claims they poop all over the lawn whenever they're not fed their usual diet."

"Okay, boys," Charlotte called. "But stay out of the water, and don't go anywhere else!"

While the boys ran to feed the ducks, laughing about grandpa's poop comment, Charlotte went into the house, trailing just behind Barbara. She heard Bryan and Clarence talking behind her on their way in.

"Things have changed, Dad, since I've seen the house. It looks so different now…even nicer than ever."

The way the words "the house" fell off Bryan's lips made Charlotte shiver with the impersonal tone of it all. "She wanted to shout. "*This* house! This *home*! The one you grew up in!" But she kept it to herself. Time enough to let Bryan and his dad work out their history. She decided to let father and son alone a bit. "Hey guys, I'm going back out to check on the boys" She was not sure how safe her little guys were feeding the ducks by themselves.

Clarence was able to walk around the house, slowly. "It's been a while since you've seen it, hey? Sure, it's gone through significant renovations and additions. The house is now considered a certified energy star home. It's a "Smart Home."

That stopped Bryan in his tracks. *What?* He should have recognized the green design himself. He had been too immersed in the utter beauty of the property itself. Or was it a wine-induced delusion? The landscape architect in him had to admit, his parents' home had an exceptional design, unrivaled architectural detail.

"Since when have you ever been environmentally correct?" he asked. "I don't recall you guys ever giving a hoot about going green."

"Oh, these days we all have to try our hand at the green thing, otherwise the pain in the ass conservationist knock down our plans," Clarence complained. "Come on, I'll give you a personal tour."

Bryan went on with his father, walking through the house. There were eight bedrooms, all decorated splendidly with separate intricate themes. Eight-and-a-half bathrooms. Every one of them gorgeous, marble-tiled, showers, fancy baths.

There were four floors. For those who did not want to climb the splendid spiraling staircase, an elevator was available. Following Clarence around as he pointed out all the features, Bryan thought that despite how magnificent this house was, it was also impersonal. More like a hotel than a home. *Had he really grown up here?*

Then he realized with a start that the elevator was likely put in for his Dad, so he didn't have to try to walk up all those stairs.

Custom walnut woodwork and moldings were all through the house, as well as shiny hardwood floors. A two-story vaulted great room with beamed ceiling, a chef's kitchen with all the best appliances and a breakfast nook, and a huge wood-paneled library.

They walked out to the four-car heated garage. Then out to the large back patio where Bryan could see the in-ground heated swimming pools he remembered swimming in throughout his childhood. The tennis courts were off to the right. Behind the tennis courts, only partially in view, was his father's mini golf course.

"Hey dad, you must get out and play, what with your own little golf course and all?" he asked. Then it dawned on him his Dad could barely walk.

"Oh, that. You remember my golf course? It's just a practice course. Do you play?"

"I've gotten out there pretty often in the past…but with the kids and my business and all, it's hard to find the time. I never got all that good at it anyway," Bryan was sorry he had asked. "I mean, I've scored par on some holes, even got a hole in one by accident one day, but really I kind of suck at it."

"What's your handicap?"

"My handicap? Couldn't say. Perhaps it's my swing!"

But the joke was either lost on Clarence, or his mind was too preoccupied. "Well, then it will be good for you to get out there and practice on my course. It's an easy par three, but very well-manicured. It's better taken care of than the course I've belonged to for a few decades down the street. I should cancel my membership. But you know, country club expectations and all…"

Bryan chose to ignore the country club comment. "So…you…can you play, Pops?"

"Well, I don't walk the course any more. But I can pretty much stand there and swing as well as I could in my early days."

The property was on a ridge overlooking pastoral landscapes. The fall colors right now, surreal looking. It took Bryan's breath away, even now after all these years. *I grew up here.* Yet he couldn't remember this beauty. He only remembered the pain. Much of it blocked out.

They went back into the house, and could hear Charlotte and the boys talking excitedly about something. He followed the sound up two flights of stairs and found them in the playroom.

Charlotte met him at the doorway, her eyes alight with excitement. "Oh honey, the boys will just *love* playing in this room. God, just imagine having a playroom like this at home! Come in and check it out!"

When Bryan entered the spacious playroom, which was filled with as many toys as one would find at a toy store, he felt…*hurt?* At the very least, hurt for the inner child in him…but happy for his boys at the same time. Had his parents done this just for them?

When he was a child, his mom had called it the "romper room." This was where Bryan would be sent with his au pair to get him out of the way for guests during all those elaborate parties his parents threw. Drunken bashes with politicians, captains of industry, movie stars, and other elites. His father's philandering…

The only attention Bryan got in those days came from his German au pair—a beautiful exchange student with long blond hair and tits like mountains. And that was precious little attention. She'd sit and watch TV. He had to amuse himself. If he asked her for something, she always made it clear that he was a pest and she had better things to do.

There weren't many toys back then, just a TV, a few trucks and balls, even though it was a filthy rich household. *Now look at it!*

Done up in several hues of blues, the room had shelves upon shelves of organized drawers chock full of things. A huge selection of quality toys including crafts, games, science and building kits, and Legos galore. An entire wall had an organized selection of educational and developmental toys.

In one corner was a giant blue Sully from *Monsters Inc*. It smiled happily at the boys. Bryan was half expecting it to come to life and say "Boo." In another corner, SpongeBob, as big as an adult, invited them into his goofy arms.

The boys were going crazy. "Wow Mom and Dad, can we get a store like this at our house please?"

"Oh sure, we'll just need to hit the lottery first dear," Charlotte replied, staring at the huge stuffies in disbelief.

"What Mommy? Did you say yes?" Kevin's eyes opened wide.

"Oh sweetie, of course not. We don't even have the space for all these toys. I was making a joke," Charlotte walked in a circle in awe.

"Well we can just get a bigger house, and then get a store like this!" Keenan chimed in.

"Money doesn't grow on trees," Charlotte began, but then nearly tripped over something. "Oh my gosh boys, look at this!"

It was an entire section of Legos, mostly put together, some half done —Indiana Jones, Harry Potter, Toy Story, Star Wars, Space Police, and more. *Who was doing this?* She wondered.

She looked up and saw Clarence standing in the doorway. "Oh my," he said, as if knowing her question. "Our pool boy came in and worked on these over the past week or so. He's a good kid. Sixteen. Still loves his Legos, big Star Wars buff. So when I told him I had some Lego-crazy grandsons coming he was all over it."

"Wow! I wish toys grew on trees!" Keenan giggled. "You have lots and lots of money Grandpa! Does that mean you're a bad guy?"

Clarence looked bewildered.

"Now Keenan," Charlotte quickly chimed in. "You need to forget that phrase in the book I read to you, saying money is the root of all evil."

"Money gets a bad rap, son." Bryan patted Keenan's curly head. "Money is not evil. And neither is the love of money, if money is produced from love. I say, if handled right? Money *is* love. And that's the change we're making in the world."

Then he turned to Clarence. "Dad, did you have all this done for our boys?" he asked, awestruck.

"For my grand boys here, sure!" Clarence replied, although his look implied more. "And uh…well…trying to make up for your lost childhood, son."

Bryan tried to sound composed, but he was so shocked to hear his dad say this he felt like coming unglued. "Trying to give back to my inner child, Pops?"

He wanted to cry, to say *"*Dad, it was never anything with a price tag associated with it that I lost as a kid. It was *your love!"* But the words never escaped his lips. Just as they were never spoken when he was growing up.

Will true words of love be spoken now? Or is this visit merely a money-chasing game?

Chapter Nineteen

The look on Clarence's face when he heard Bryan's words was heartbreaking. Bryan suddenly got it. He had to let it go. The whole childhood thing. Making a fairy-tale playroom for his twins was the only way his dad knew how to make up for what had happened. He was a man of action. Not a man of words or emotion. And it was up to Bryan to grasp the apology and to accept it.

"Thanks Dad, we really appreciate all this," he said. "Hey boys, go tell your Grandpa how considerate this all is. How happy you are with what he did to please you. Thank him. Go on, give him that hug he didn't get at the airport!"

Neither boy made any indication that they had heard Bryan. They were intent on putting together more of the Lego sets.

* * *

Charlotte almost felt like crying, looking at Clarence. He was wearing his heart on his sleeve, the obstinate jowls softened, eyes focused lovingly on his grandsons. *Come on, boys,* she thought. *Come on!*

OMG her heart couldn't take it anymore. She spoke up. "Boys…did you hear your Daddy? C'mon, go over and give your Grandpa a great big hug and kiss! Look what he did for you!"

The boys got up and walked slowly, awkwardly, towards Clarence, and put their arms around him. Instinctively, Bryan and Charlotte moved towards them. Then all five of them were hugging. The adults hugging and crying.

"Mommy and Daddy, why are you crying like that?" asked Keenan.

"Oh, these are good tears son, no worries!" Bryan responded.

Barbara appeared in the doorway, clearing her throat nervously and addressing Charlotte. "Ahh…I…I've set up the boys' room with all their things, and would like to show you and Bryan to your room," She remained at the door's edge and kept her distance from the family hug. "It has a spa with an open view of the golf course, and a fireplace. It's just one of those 'eco-friendly' fake fireplaces. But the maid lit it for you. We hope you will feel comfortable."

"Barbara doesn't like my new bio-ethanol design for all our fireplaces," Clarence added.

"That's not entirely true!" Barbara snapped. "I just miss the smell of burning. To me it's part of the ambience. Why can't we have real fireplaces? I just don't get it."

Bryan remembered the marriage never being happy. It was a marriage of convenience. This tension felt so familiar. It usually preceded a full-on blow up. He hoped there would be no awful fights like the ones he had been subjected to growing up. He wanted to spare his boys that experience.

*　*　*

As it turned out, there were no fights between Bryan's parents. They barely spent any time together. Barbara mostly kept to herself, going out to the yacht club, meeting her friends for lunch, spending a lot of time pampering herself for herself at the spas.

Charlotte was beginning to see why Bryan's dad had been able to mistreat him so badly growing up. His mother was too self-absorbed to stop it.

Nonetheless, over the next week Charlotte, Bryan, and the boys had a wonderful time with Clarence. They went out a couple of times on his magnificent yachts and played golf, even if it amounted to a miniature golf style putting around the greens.

They spent a wonderful full day at the Nature Center, which the kids loved, especially the new solar greenhouse. They went to the Children's Museum. They hung around the house, which had more to offer than most of the village hot spots.

It ended up being a bit too cool for the beach, which was ok with the kids. They had so much fun swimming in Grandpa and Grandma's heated pool they never missed the beach. And they never made it into NYC, which was fine, as Charlotte realized the glimpse into her husband's childhood arena was more important.

One night near the end of their vacation, Barbara came into the boys' room when Charlotte was sitting with them, reading them stories.

"Charlotte dear," she asked. "Would you and Bryan like to have a night out to yourselves? I fear I've neglected to spend as much time as I'd have liked with the boys…and it's dawned on me the week is nearly over."

Charlotte's mind raced.

How would Barbara treat the boys if she left them with her? Would she even make sure they ate dinner, brushed their teeth? Would she read a bedtime story to them, tuck them in, and kiss them goodnight?

As if sensing Charlotte's hesitation, Barbara said "Oh, Clarence will be here as well, after his time at the yacht club. I just thought perhaps you two would like a night out. Go to dinner or a show? The boys would be in good hands. I'm not the wicked witch of the east, you know."

And with that she showed her teeth. Her mouth was smiling but her eyes were cold.

Charlotte detected the phony smile, but she softened a bit. This is what a politician's wife has to do. It was so ingrained by now, after decades, that she didn't know how to smile a real smile. Poor thing. And really, what could it hurt, leaving her boys with Grandma? Why did she feel so protective? She had to admit it was because Barbara had mistreated her own son, had been too weak to stop her from abandoning him as a teen.

But that was then. This is now.

"Well, that is kind of you Barbara" Charlotte felt hesitant to commit alone. "Let me talk to Bryan. Maybe we'll take you up on your offer."

***

When Charlotte brought it up with Bryan, he got angry.

"Why would you even question it? Of course we should go out! Why would you not trust my mother?" His arms crossed, and he clenched his fists.

Charlotte's eyelids narrowed, and her lips tightened. "Oh, I don't know, maybe the fact she has not seen you for what…twenty years or so? And her part in allowing *her own* eighteen-year-old kid to be thrown out of their rich household with not a dime in his pocket? Sorry Bry, but she is not exactly overly friendly with the boys. And she doesn't even go out of her way to talk to you, her only son. I don't know, there are a lot of reasons not to trust her."

Bryan remained silent, his nostrils flared.

Charlotte continued. "She has not once, during this entire week, done *anything* with us. We went everywhere with your father, helping him in and out of his wheelchair. Which, by the way, had to be exhausting for him. Where was she? At the spa?"

He paced back and forth. "My mother has never been the one to be involved in *anything*…that's just her. It's how she is. She's fiercely independent," Bryan stopped pacing, and took a deep breath. "We can't change who she was then. But she can now. And now she's trying. And we *can* leave her with our kids—she's their grandmother!"

Charlotte's eyebrows pulled downward, as she shook her head. "So how 'independent' was she when your Dad insisted you leave the house and never come back just because you chose not to follow his fucking career footsteps, huh? Seriously. Where was your 'independent' mom during all that? I could not imagine treating my boys like that when they turn eighteen!"

"She's my *mother!*" Bryan shouted. "Back. The fuck. Off!"

Charlotte looked over in horror to see the boys now in the doorway. They were both standing there, toys in hand, frozen in place.

Kevin began to cry first, then Keenan. "I don't want to stay here with Grandma! I want to go out with you!" Kevin wailed.

"Now look what you've started!" Bryan yelled. "Great, just great! You've turned my sons against my mom! Great job Charlotte! So she isn't perfect, *who is?* This was her way of reaching out to us, *to them!*" Bryan's face was red with anger as his arms reached out towards his sons.

"Shh…quiet Bryan," Charlotte said, her voice lowered. "Your parents must be wondering about us. Oh…oh come here boys, I'm sorry. It's all right, everything's all right. I didn't mean to say those mean things about Grandma. Your dad and I were just…just…Oh! It's not your fault."

"I don't want Grandma to watch us! We want to go out with you guys!" Kevin cried. Keenan just stood there crying softly, his favorite stuffed Teddy, which went everywhere with him, clutched to his heart. His brother was the warrior. He was the peacemaker. "Me too," he sniffled.

"Charlotte," Bryan spoke very softly, lovingly now. "Listen honey. Listen boys. I know that Grandma and Grandpa have not gotten real close to you guys. And that was my fault, not theirs. But now she… they…*want* to. Oh come here, all of you!"

Bryan hugged his boys, and Charlotte squeezed into the family hug. They were all crying again, especially Bryan.

"Listen boys, why don't you two play with these Legos and things, while Mommy and Daddy go talk to your grandparents? It would be nice for you to hang out with Grandma tonight. It's Grandpa's night out to play cards with his friends…and Grandma is going to make it super fun for you guys."

Charlotte and Bryan ended up going out to dinner at a delightful wine bar and restaurant, which was just around the corner from the French bistro they had gone to as a family their first night in Connecticut. The best thing was, they didn't have to drive. The limo driver dropped them off, and said he would wait in front of the restaurant for as long as they needed.

When they had finished their lovely meal, Bryan waved to the waiter, who came right over. "Check please?" Bryan said.

"Oh, no Sir," the waiter shook his head. "You're all set. Your father called ahead."

Bryan and Charlotte exchanged grateful glances. "Well," Bryan said, smiling, "that was very generous of him. So I will leave you a generous tip."

The waiter smiled back. "No, sir, thank you. But that won't be necessary. As I said, your father called ahead. He takes very good care of the wait staff here. And I wouldn't offend him by taking your money. Why don't you buy your lovely wife a nice gift at one of our many boutiques?"

Now Charlotte was smiling. "I like that idea, honey." She turned to the waiter "You're a very wise man. Are you married?"

He showed her his ring. "I sure am. Happily married for many, many years."

"Not surprised," Charlotte winked at him.

Since the bill was taken care of and their waiter had made a brilliant suggestion as to what to do with what they would have spent, Charlotte and Bryan went for a walk around the quaint streets. Not many shops were open, so there wasn't much opportunity to buy Charlotte a gift. But she found herself riveted to the window display at the Ski and Sports Center.

"We need to buy new ski jackets for the boys this season. They have outgrown the ones they have now," she told Bryan, glancing at the stylish jacket in the window she would just love to have for herself.

"Yeah, well we won't be buying them here, look at those price tags!" Bryan joked. But he was watching her eyes and he took note of where they landed. With the money they had saved from what would have been a very expensive meal, he had the money to surprise her with the jacket, and he planned to go back the next day and get it for her.

"They likely put the nicest stuff on window display. We could maybe find something cheaper in the store," Charlotte was saying.

"We are NOT spending our last two days here stuffed up in a store, Charlotte. I'd rather do anything else," Bryan said, high-fiving himself on the inside because now Charlotte would never suspect he was going back there to get her the jacket she wanted. "Let's keep going, honey. It's a beautiful night."

As they walked on, Bryan's bright mood changed, and he grew more and more silent and pensive. Charlotte, always sensitive to her husband's moods, picked up on it right away.

"What is it Bry?" she asked. "Is something you're not telling me? Something about growing up?"

Bryan stopped walking and turned to face her.

"My parents, they were…well my mother was anyhow…violent. She would lash out at my Dad, lash out at me. I remember screaming once as a kid…what, maybe nine years old…after seeing my mother bloody up my dad's face with a spatula, frying pan, whatever her choice of weapon was at the time. I couldn't take it anymore…I screamed once *"Hit her the fuck back Dad!"*

Charlotte stood transfixed, silent, just listening. She was speechless with shock over this new revelation. But she also didn't want to speak. She just looked him straight in the eyes, oriented her torso toward him and nodded her head. She wanted Bryan to get this out. She knew it would be healing for him. Therapeutic.

"The next thing I knew, my mom had turned around and screamed at me 'Don't you ever use that foul language young man! Where did you learn that?! The gutter? We don't talk like truck drivers in this family!' She swung out with that metal pan and smacked me on the head so hard I was unconscious for hours. My dad had to call 911. He thought I might die. That happened so many times. I have scars not only all over my body, but also my heart."

Charlotte remembered the scars on Bryan's back and legs and cringed. She had always assumed they were a product of his days of crazy risk taking…rock climbing the steepest terrain without a harness, flying off the river rafts in waterfalls slapping against rocks.

It was as if Bryan could read her mind.

"The reason I took all those wild risks was I went through life feeling dead anyhow. Those were my ways of finding myself, trying to feel alive. My rich-boy abusive childhood messed me up something bad."

Charlotte felt tears coming. Suddenly she came back to the present moment.

"Oh my God Bryan! The kids are with your mother *now!*"

"Don't worry, honey. My mom would never hurt the boys. That was then. This is now. She would not hurt them Charlotte. I just know it. I can see the regret in her eyes each time she looks at me. That's why it's hard for her to spend time with me. She feels so guilty."

"Okay, honey," Charlotte grabbed him by the arm and started pulling him toward the limo. "You trust your mom now. But I don't. Let's go."

When they arrived at the house and the chauffeur had handed them out of the limo and driven away, they caught a glimpse of the scene in the living room as they walked up to the front door.

The boys were giving Grandma a lesson on how to complete Lego missions. The three of them were sitting close together on the floor in front of a roaring fire in the fireplace. Fresh mugs of steaming hot chocolate with a mountain of whipped cream on each were sitting on a tea tray on the coffee table. In front of them was a partially constructed King Arthur and The Round Table set.

Grandma was raptly listening to Kevin, who was demonstrating something with two of the pieces. Her face was unusually soft, and radiant in the firelight.

Charlotte squeezed Bryan's hand, and he squeezed back. They entered the house quietly and tiptoed up to their bedroom. It was Grandma Night. Their boys were in good hands, and Grandma was in good hands.

Time to continue their date in a more private way, in a more private place. With their own radiant firelight.

* * *

The next two days went by quickly, and as it turned out, it rained both days so they did not do much outside. Charlotte spent most of her time organizing and packing. It was helpful having the house maid do all their laundry.

Bryan used the opportunity to go back to the ski shop and buy Charlotte the jacket she loved. When she had finished packing the biggest suitcase and was otherwise occupied, he carefully slipped it in under everything else so that when she unpacked she'd find it. I'm a genius, he thought with glee. A total genius.

On the morning they were to return home, Clarence called them into his library for a chat.

"Bryan, I thought you and Charlotte…might accept a little gift from us. I know this doesn't make up for all the years…"

He choked up and couldn't speak.

"What kind of gift, Pops?" Bryan asked. He knew it would be a gift of money, and no small sum. *It always came to money.*

He didn't know when his family would see his parents again. But they could always come through with money. Bryan knew money can't buy you love, but he also knew, and finally accepted, that *this* might be the only way his parents knew how to show their love. And their love was genuine.

"Well…I…well you see," Clarence stammered and fidgeted with something in his hand. "There is something I haven't told you. Not that this has to do with the gift…oh…heck son. I have Parkinson's. My doctor says it's progressing quickly. I will rest much easier if I finally give to you what you deserved as my son long ago. That trust fund is still yours. Not as big as it was then, but still. Twenty-five million. I hope you will accept it, with my deepest most heartfelt apologies for how I failed you."

Clarence hadn't told Bryan why he was in the wheelchair. He would merely laugh and say "It sucks getting old, son." Bryan had thought...or hoped... it was some mean case of arthritis and that his dad simply preferred not to walk as much because of the pain.

But he had known deep inside it had to be more. The symptoms he saw but tried to ignore. Slight tremors and shaking, slower and more rigid movement. His dad's balance was off getting on and off the yacht. And he could barely do his golf swing—at times his arms just didn't move at all.

Bryan wanted to say "I don't want your money, Dad, just your love."

But then he thought of his boys. Of their future. College was expensive in this country without the free tuition other nations have. He didn't feel the need for a life of luxury. Quite the contrary. He was happier without it. At one time Charlotte had been obsessed with Prada, Gucci, Chanel, and Hermes, but she had changed. She wanted her boys to work hard at something they loved the way their dad did, and build confidence and pride in themselves that way. She wanted them to be happy.

But still... *Twenty five million dollars!*

Bryan suddenly realized he hadn't said anything. He'd just left his Dad hanging. He was about to say something, when Charlotte spoke up. It was as if she had read his mind.

"Wow Clarence," she said. "That's so generous of you. Twenty five million dollars is more money than we ever imagined having, or managing. But it sure would help to have plenty enough put away for the boys' college. Maybe put them into private school now. Pour some into Bryan's business. Put money into the house..." *Feed the hungry,* she thought to herself not knowing if Clarence is among the immoral rich that don't support the needy.

She wasn't so much talking to Clarence as she was thinking out loud. She knew Bryan would never want to stop the work he loved, the business he had worked so hard to build. *Regardless* of how much money they had now.

Charlotte realized the best part of this. She would not have to work and could spend *lots* of time with her boys. That's what was more important to her. Time with the boys. Not the big house or fancy cars. She just wanted to buy newer, safer vehicles running on clean energy to drive the kids around in... She had no desire for flashy status symbols.

But would she feel differently if this money had come to them through hard work? Earned rather than handed to them?

The sound of laughter interrupted Charlotte's thoughts. She glanced over to see Bryan and Clarence belly laughing about something. The only thing she had heard had something to do with taking up golf again, and being able to afford all the crazy golf bets now.

Father and son needed time alone. To reconnect. If it's mere money that brought them closer, that's better than nothing at all.

Then it struck her. It wasn't money that drew them together. It was Bryan's dad being faced with a horrible disease and possibly dying.

She quietly left the room, glancing back as she passed through the doorway. The two men were engrossed in each other, talking, laughing, touching. What a beautiful sight. What a beautiful, beautiful outcome. She silently blew them both a kiss, and sent up a thank-you to everything Divine.

She went back to the guest room she and Bryan had slept in that week. The eco-friendly fireplace was lit, a scented candle was burning, and something else smelled great. Then she realized the bath tub tap was running.

One of the many house maids came out of the bathroom. "I've run a bubble bath for you, Ms. Charlotte. I thought you'd like to relax a bit before you're taken to the airport."

Charlotte thanked her and stepped into the bathroom. What a delight! Candles were lit and the scent of lavender and jasmine filled the air. She threw off her clothes and slipped into the just right, hot scented bubbling water. Heaven! There was a cup of tea steaming off to her left, and she took a sip. It was a calming herb…maybe chamomile. Man, she would miss this!

Maybe not, she reminded herself. We have twenty five million dollars now! I can have as many bubble baths, hot teas, candles, and as much relaxation as I want. And in a mansion if I want, with servants. We could own several properties. Let's see, a Colorado ski house, a Tahoe ski house, heck, and a beach house in Hawaii.

This daydreaming was fun, especially since she knew all of these dreams were now well within her reach. Maybe she would never even work again. Or at least not for money.

Suddenly, Charlotte felt uneasy. She sat bolt upright in the bathtub. "But I don't *want* to change my lifestyle! I love my simple life as it is!" she said out loud. "I...I don't *want* to ever stop what I'm doing in ecology! I'm proud of my PhD. I worked hard for it! *Fuck!* I don't *want* to stop my efforts at saving the planet, the people! Our next generation!"

Bryan had come back to the bedroom to grab his cell phone and overheard Charlotte's bathtub ramblings. Curious, he stuck his head in the doorway. "Umm...honey, are you ok?"

She had teary eyes, bubbles on her head, mascara smudges. "I don't even care what I look like!"

"Oh, sweetie, you always look beautiful to me, even right now with your raccoon eyes!"

"No, no! That's not what I mean! I mean...as a rich woman now, am I not expected to turn shallow, get preoccupied with my looks? Wear Valentino, get the boob job, have Botox, the works? Oh...forget it! It's not even that. It's just that..." Charlotte thought about what she was trying to say.

After a moment, she continued. "I think about what makes me happy, and it's the simple things in life. You, our boys, my job, our modest home. I don't *want* a bigger house, I don't *want* expensive cars. And I *love* what I do—I feel so good about it. I feel like I am doing something to help our kids have a planet to live on! I help curb cancer, and a top problem in our nation, which is unsustainable environmental practices."

"Then *don't* change anything honey," Bryan said. "Coming into all this wealth all of a sudden doesn't mean our world needs to be turned upside down. We don't all of a sudden have to think of selfishness as a virtue. Just because we're rich now doesn't mean we have to start thinking like rich people. I don't want the boys to all of a sudden have so many changes either. Although I wouldn't mind switching them to a private school—our public schools are too crowded and chaotic."

Two hours later, they were in the limo on the way to La Guardia airport. The boys were busy playing with a Lego set in the back seat. Charlotte felt compelled to broach the subject again with Bryan.

"Hey Bry...like we were saying. Let's not change too much about our current lifestyle just because your dad is forking over that fortune of a trust fund to us."

"I told you already Charlotte, I agree," Bryan responded. "Why must you harp on this?"

"I'm not harping...just thinking. So how about we donate fifteen million or so to some of the top humanitarian charities? But not for 'developing' nations. Our own country has enough problems. I mean, half of our own people live in poverty. We are slowly becoming like a third world..."

Bryan cringed inside. *Fifteen million?* That would mean a big chunk of their trust fund. Perhaps that's too much of it to donate. But he surprised himself with his answer.

"You don't have to explain, honey. I get where you're coming from. And I agree. Let's give the majority of our inheritance to the disintegrating country our kids need to survive in—unless we move to another country to give them a better life the way our ancestors did!"

"Yes! Oh yes, honey!" Charlotte responded. "Oh I love this! We'll do our *real* duty to our country! Help our schools, healthcare, environmental disasters, our crumbling transportation and infrastructure, food..."

Bryan held up a hand. "Wait a minute, sweetie...hold on. That's a tall order! We can't fix everything! We need to set aside a little for ourselves! But yes, let's seek out foundations that nurture positive interactions between community, the environment, and the economy. We'll put our money where our children's future is concerned...to improve the world they live in.

"And, well, we don't have to think about this right now. And as I mentioned, we can switch the boys to private schools. Look at what seems to be happening with public education. It's all test and punish. And middle school years are frightening."

Charlotte looked over at her husband. She loved him so much, and she was so glad they were partners. She trusted his judgment and she knew he trusted hers.

Together they would make the best decisions about what to do with unimagined windfall.

And the world their boys would grow up in would be better because of their choices.

She reached over and took his hand in hers. Their fingers twined together.

The limo pulled up to the curb and the chauffeur said "We're here, folks. Mr. Gafferty has already cleared you through security and your bags will be expedited. Have a safe trip home."

Charlotte stepped out of the limo onto the curb. *I could so get used to this!* But first…?

Change the world.

* * *

In the end, Bryan and Charlotte did exactly what they planned, giving equal amounts of their windfall to each humanitarian cause.

Bryan invested a little in his struggling business, knowing there was only so much he could do to increase demand for landscaping services in an economy where people were losing their homes to dishonest banks. But he would never close shop, it was his pride and joy. What he had worked so hard for.

They found satisfaction giving back to our very own nation's communities first—being starved of resources while selling out our neighborhoods to developing worlds. In capitalism, money is the life blood of society. But charity is its soul.

Chapter Twenty

While Bryan and Charlotte were getting settled after their visit with Bryan's parents and grasp their vast change in fortunes, Caryssa was busy trying to figure out her next career steps.

She felt blessed to be surrounded by such progressive people. A recent coffee date with some of her mom friends who had left high-powered careers to raise their kids and were now finding ways to earn money working for a better future had deepened her resolve to find a way to shift into a career where she was making a difference.

She had written her next article for publication in the online magazine, *Serenity Media Inc*. It was titled "Responsible Investing: Share Price Not Only 'Value' that Counts."

Her message was that if we all made a conscious effort to divest in stocks not conducive to developing a positive society, and switch to clean energy, organic foods, *constructive areas* regardless of any short-sighted immediate returns now, we could help change the world for the better.

This morning as the sun streamed in her bedroom window she sat reading the paper over coffee in bed. She had one glorious hour to relax and read before getting ready for Sunday Mass, then taking Tyler to his weekly religious education classes.

He was scheduled to make his First Holy Communion in the spring, and the CCD classes were getting George, Caryssa, and Tyler off to church every Sunday. It was an especially spiritual journey to be taking during all this political upheaval—the Occupy movement had started and was making waves through every sector of global society.

As she sat there, her mind wandered from her article to her spiritual life. Was she closer to God now than when she had been caught up in her career and forgetting to pray or go to church? She thinks not…

The morality of God's true words seem half missing in the Church. A lack of social heart. Church-based spirituality seems, more and more to her, a Christian-themed performance on stage. Sensationalized dusty words. Someday, she may seek out a love-filled faith rather than the fire-and-brimstone of the Catholic rantings. She supposed they were going through the Holy Communion ritual more out of family tradition, than anything.

The sun was rising over the bay. She took a moment to appreciate the awe of the morning's beauty as it manifested out her window. And it got even more beautiful when her son walked into the room, with his stuffed pals, pillow, and blanket, to snuggle with Mommy.

It seemed almost a sacrilege to be reading about politically inspired financial upheaval with her little sweet pea snuggled up with her, so she put the paper aside and hugged Tyler, kissing his cheek ever so gently.

"Did you have a good breakfast sweetie? Daddy made pancakes? Yummy!" she whispered into his hair.

"Yup! With my favorite, Vermont maple syrup on top! Now I want some of your turkey bacon he's cooking for you!" Tyler said.

"Oh no! The turkey bacon monster stealing my breakfast again? I better watch out! Do I hear a magic word with that request?"

Tyler yelled "Daddy, may I *pleeeze* have some more turkey bacon?"

"What?! You already had your turkey bacon!" George called from the kitchen.

"Can I *pleeeze* be the turkey bacon monster and have Mommy's turkey bacon!" Tyler yelled back.

Caryssa told Tyler to hop out of her bed and go to the kitchen table for his…*her*…turkey bacon.

Tyler happily skipped out to the kitchen, hugging his stuffed Puffles to his chest, dragging his blanket and pillow behind him. He always carried nearly his entire bedroom around the house for comfort.

Caryssa smiled and picked up the Sunday paper again. She wanted to see how the Occupy movement was being covered. She knew how highly manipulated the mainstream media was, so she would also be researching for herself whatever was reported there. As she scanned the paper, she reflected on how frightening it was that so many believed the paper and the TV news, not even suspect of the media moguls seducing audiences and warping their views. The good news was, however the media twisted it, this movement was happening.

In over one thousand cities in eighty-five countries, people were protesting against corruption, big banks, and corporate greed. Hundreds of thousands were protesting against the Wall Street acts of fraudulently foreclosing on millions of homes, robbing college kids of more than double what they had borrowed to get through school, stealing from the middle class to fatten those corrupt coffers.

Caryssa suddenly realized she needed to get herself and Tyler ready for church. She put the paper down, called to him, and started scurrying to get him dressed, teeth brushed, hair combed.

The sermon that morning resonated well for Caryssa. It was about spiritual penitence versus mere physical needs. How we are not merely flesh and blood, but souls. The priest took his microphone to each child in Tyler's CCD class and asked "If you knew you were to die soon, what might you want to change about your attitude or behaviors?"

The kid's answers were so simple and sweet!

Caryssa couldn't help thinking that these innocent young children could not possibly have really *sinned*. Children mirror adult behavior, learn sin through what they see. Caryssa remembered as a young child trying to make up any sins she could tell the priest. She had always been so nervous about not having enough sins to confess.

Even the prayers these young kids were forced to memorize and get tested on, such as the Penitential Act "*Through my fault, through my fault, through my most grievous fault,*" while the children strike their chests twice to emphasize their "fault." It was emotional abuse, when you thought about it. Why put so much guilt onto their innocent souls?

Caryssa realized she was not alone in this thought, when she heard a woman sitting in the pew behind her say to her husband "The church should put our political leaders on the bench…in front of all the people, and have *them* confess their sins, not these innocent children."

Caryssa could not help but turn and smile at the woman: *how true!*

"Well, I'd listen to my mom and dad more, well, I might play baseball rather than computer games, oh, and I'd do really good in school. I wouldn't cry or whine as much."

Who told this precious child crying or "whining" is a sin?

Even so, the church and CCD classes every Sunday for the past nine months had been a spiritual rejuvenation for Caryssa. She was raised a *'good Catholic girl'*. What she wanted Tyler to get out of all this was a sense of right from wrong. And a spiritual connection. Not to any religion, but to a spiritual being, to God.

This morning as they left the church hand in hand, Tyler looked at Caryssa and asked "Mommy, if people all had God in the middle, would there be wars?"

"No sweetie," she replied. "If everybody had God in the middle, there would be no wars. Remember the Lord's commandment? 'You shall not kill'? People would have *that* in their hearts. People would have God's love in their hearts. War wouldn't be possible. Right now, people have *religion* too much in the middle, not God. But you have God in your middle, son. Keep God in there. And don't pay any attention to religion. You just keep God in your middle and you'll be fine."

"But my CCD class is religion, isn't it, Mommy? It's called Religious Education."

Tyler pronounced the words very carefully, as if he knew how important they were. *"Re-lig-ious. Ed-u-cation.* See, it says so right on my paper here." He pointed to the flyer he brought home from Sunday school each week. "See Mommy? It says 'You shall not lie.' That's religion, right?"

Caryssa glanced at the cover page and read the first question for the children to answer. "You don't have your homework finished. You A. Say, 'The dog ate my homework.' B. Say 'I didn't do my homework, I'm sorry.'"

"Yes, Tyler," she said. "You're right. It's Religious Education—based on Catholic teachings. But Mommy and Daddy will talk to you more about what we believe to be the truth in the eyes of God, and what we believe is not."

"Like what, Mommy?" Tyler asked.

"Well, the church claims that we need to confess our sins to a priest in order for God to forgive them. Your daddy and I believe that God will forgive our sins if we silently pray to him directly. We believe He knows if we really want to repent. The Lord knows more than a human priest could if we are truly sorry for our sins. Priests are human. They sin too, Tyler. Some of them are even very bad, and will not make it into heaven."

"Like, how bad?" Tyler asked.

"Do you remember the video you all had to watch during CCD class about what that soccer coach was doing to that young boy?" Caryssa cringed even bringing it up, but the church had made the kids watch, and now seemed the best time to talk about it with her little boy. And although the words "sexual abuse" or "molestation" were never mentioned, they were implied. And the handouts given to the parents spelled it out.

Tyler's eyes grew huge. "The soccer coach touched him in…well in…where he shouldn't have."

"Yes, he did…and some priests who are horrible sinners are doing that to kids, Tyler. So don't over trust what authority figures may say or do. Always question and always talk to Mom and Dad about *anything* that doesn't seem right to you."

"Okay, Mommy. I will," Tyler said, squeezing her hand.

"Good!" Caryssa said. "Now where's Daddy? Where's the car? We need to get home, change, and go out to the park to play!"

"Yeah!!!" Tyler laughed, skipping ahead. "Where's Daddy?!"

Chapter Twenty-One

Caryssa went to confession.

She, who had just told Tyler she didn't believe confessing to a priest grants God's forgiveness.

And what a relief that she got her favorite priest, the one with the clever sense of humor. The other priest—Father Thuong—had told the parents he had been given an extra sense of smell from God. He could tell when people had not repented for a long time because to him they smelled worse than leftover fish-bones.

While she was waiting for confession, Caryssa couldn't help laughing to herself, imagining how a confession to him might begin. *"Forgive me Father for I have sinned. It has been over twenty years since my last confession, and do I stink?"*

During the meeting when Father Thuong had professed his keen sense of smell for all those non-repenting sinners, people in the audience had looked around, as if trying to ferret out the sinners. The woman sitting next to Caryssa gave her a funny look.

"What?" Caryssa asked. "Do I smell? I haven't been to confession in over two decades!"

They had giggled together, and then Caryssa snapped back to attention hoping the priest didn't call out their mocking laughter.

After he had claimed to be able to smell sinners who held their sins all to themselves, Father Thuong mentioned that missing one Mass on any Sunday was a grave sin.

"Yes," he said, pounding the pulpit. "You throw leftover fish bones into the trash right away, right? Why would you hold on to your sins rather than throwing them away too?"

Caryssa snorted. Was this man really chosen to be the Lord's representative, with permission to lean on all these people like a bad cop? A primary example of how the Catholic Church lays guilt on the guiltless. By now, she was hoping she used a strong antiperspirant. It made her giggle just to think about it. Father Thuong turned and glared at her.

"Oops", she whispered. "Busted."

If it was a confession he was trying to get out of them, it worked. Off to confession she went, but not to this backward-thinking priest. Instead, she spoke with Father Bart, who was less radical.

On the way home from the meeting, Caryssa laughed some more. Father Bart had told her that her penance was one Hail Mary. She had stalled during her confession. *"I... didn't recycle a few items, let's see...I skied at a resort that had destroyed a sacred forest, ahhh...I get angry at our politicians declaring war."*

"That's all?" she had asked, astonished. *"One Hail Mary?* Are you sure you're not undervaluing my sins?"

"Yes, that simple" said the robed and solemn-looking priest. "You might want to say the Act of Contrition as well. But Caryssa, it is human, even *humanitarian* to get angry at unscrupulous politicians. The Lord had already forgiven you. And you mention you've spent a chunk of your life missing Sunday church services. That's not ideal, of course. But the Lord knows what is in your heart, and that's what matters. Church attendance is a ritual. It helps people to stay in touch with God and with the community of faith. But it's not a requirement, at least not in my view."

Later that night, after Tyler had fallen asleep and George was in the study catching up on some work, Caryssa took a hot bath with lavender bath salts and bubbles. She felt unclean from the inside out after having been bombarded with Father Thuong's...what was the right word? Hatred? Scorn? She sank into the water and let the feelings of the day melt away.

After a long time there was no more residue from the priest's assault, and she felt better. She put on a fresh nighty, pulled her spa robe on and knotted the belt around her waist, slipped into fuzzy slippers and padded out to the kitchen to make some chamomile tea. She carried the steaming tea to her bedroom and set it on her nightstand, fluffed her pillows against the headboard, took off her robe and hung it up. Then lit a candle and slipped into bed with a big sigh of contentment. For good measure, she pressed the button on her CD player for the relaxing nature sounds to play.

O-kay... What are we getting Tyler into, exposing him to this religion and having him adopt it? Dear Lord, please help me figure this out.

Was the other priest lying to make more money for the church? *It is a grave sin to miss one mass.* Too many missed collections? And what would our political leaders smell like to him? Surely with all the wars and backroom deals and financial fraud they are the ones smelling like the dead fish the priests use as guilt-bait! Religion has *always* been motivated by politics and power. In the name of God.

Caryssa took a sip of tea. The real sins are against humanity and nature. *Nature.* It's the way God communicates with us most clearly, more so than through organized religion.

So when we destroy large resources, when we cut off God's creation by putting oil pipes along river banks, polluting waters so people can't fish or enjoy nature, it's the moral equivalent of tearing pages out of the last Bible on earth.

George came into the bedroom and snuggled up next to her on the outside of the covers. The Bible was turned upside down on her lap.

"Whatcha doing, my little crusader? Brushing up on your Bible verses? Wow. One confession and they've turned you into a Saint!"

Caryssa laughed and poked him. "Hush!" This is serious. And you better not mean 'crusader' in the Middle Ages sense!"

George laughed and threw up his arms in pretended fear. "No! I'd never! You know how I mean it...I mean you are always on a crusade of some kind or other to improve the world!"

Caryssa sniffed. "That's better, mister!" she giggled. "No, but seriously, I'm applying my Caryssa analysis thingy to organized religion."

"Oh no. Tell me you're not! Organized religion? Look out! Now you're taking on the big guns! They will never survive your analysis. Goodbye religion! Western Civilization as we know it will dissolve. Only anarchy will be left!" George crowed.

Caryssa poked him with her elbow again, hard. "Shut UP!!!" I'm serious, honey! This is serious!!!"

Chastened, George settled back against the pillows, giving her all his attention. "Sorry honey. I can be serious." He reached over and kissed her on the cheek. "Here's me being serious" He put on a temporary frown mask. "Tell me about it."

Caryssa shot him a look that said "You better be good."

Then she began. "Well, I'm seeing the connection of the Roman Catholic Church to the murderous games of gladiatorial contest in ancient Rome. Today, the same shady political and religious forces that enable things like privatization of medical care and schools also enable the immoral sin of slapping a price tag on human lives for unbridled profits with our perpetual aggressive foreign policy—"

"Honey. Sweetheart. You know I love you. But seriously? You can't change the world. I wish you would stop over-analyzing everything. It will kill you one day. Or make you crazy. Or both. Besides, you need to get a little perspective here. It's not like America is the most politically corrupt nation in the world. Look at Somalia, Sudan, Chad, Iraq, and Afghanistan—"

Caryssa cut him off. "See? That's just it! Whenever we mention countries we consider to be more corrupt than us, we always mention third world countries. *We* sponsor the extremism in those places you mention. *We* pay for their weapons and training. And it's all about the Almighty Dollar! Which goes mainly to the 1%."

The soft music was playing sounds of waterfalls and the room smelled of fresh cut roses coming off the scented candle. Caryssa was amazed how zen-like they can be without being passive about politics. She lives for an attitude of appreciation and balance. Based in reality.

"Right now, there are hundreds of thousands of American kids in fatigues, obediently guarding the opium and oil fields in Afghanistan for shipments of heroin and oil. And those arms deals. Honey. Don't you get it?"

"What are you afraid of? You *know* I have a history of conscientious objection—"

She cut in again "Don't be so apathetic! It's all about poppies, pistols and pipelines! Remember Patrice? Remember that time she told us about her friend's nineteen-year-old daughter?"

George frowned. "Hmmmm....no. Refresh my memory?"

"We were in Boston having dinner at *Legal Sea Foods*? We were talking about war and family and kids?

"Oh! Sure. Yeah, yeah, I remember now. Her friend's daughter, a magazine model who had been attending Harvard Medical School. She was approached by the University's ROTC on campus. She signed up and was sent to Afghanistan. She was killed her first week out. The mass media didn't cover the story at all, even with '*if it bleeds it leads*' angles, blah blah blah."

"Yes, honey, our youth are cannon fodder. The system is designed that way. *Nobody* is immune. Something has to be done! Can't you see that?"

George was silent. He knew he was outmatched with his girl on fire like this. He threw his hands up as in surrender "So…are we to think of her as used and abused by the system more than others? Isn't this where the populace and president '*honor*' her? What are you getting at?"

"Honey," Caryssa rolled her eyes. "Of course not if she cheered on the *'freedom fighters'* and believed it's all about keeping America '*safe*'. If she was not against those human attack dogs called military recruiters on campus. That's not the point—"

George rolled over and blew out the candle. Then turned the music off.

"Are you trying to tell me something? Like shut up I want to sleep now?"

No…sorry, I just don't like the too rosy smell, and want to listen to you more than rain right now."

"Waterfalls…the nature sounds were birds and waterfalls. Look…I know I can't fix everything, and I love you for wanting to protect me from the burnout that comes from wanting to change the world. But our social structure is sick… Get this! A popular end-of-year ritual game the faculty administers in some high schools in New York City is called 'Killer' or 'Shoot-Out.' The school is considered the 'safety zone' and the kids strategically seek each other out, 'assassinate' each other until there is one man or one team standing. Granted they are using water pistols… but still. They have something called 'the pie chart of death' and the students get 'killing assignments.' The kids are even judged by teachers. Teachers are 'looking for some good massacres by the end of the year.'

They arrange things like 'boyfriend-girlfriend kills.' Just think about that."

George started to reach across the bed to touch Caryssa's arm, but had a sense the gesture would be unappreciated right now. He knew his wife well enough to know that she had to complete her rationale or there would be hell to pay. He didn't know what she was worried about.

"Well?" she went on. "Don't you find it a little disturbing? That we, as a society, could teach such violent interactions to our next generation? *Glorifying massacres!* Don't people see the direct correlation with the horrific shootings in schools or otherwise? Do *you* not see it?!"

George hesitated before he replied. He hadn't seen Caryssa this worked up in some time and he didn't want to hurt her. He stared out into the darkness of the room, searching for the right words…

"Well, of course. I don't like it one bit. But, Caryssa, I played war as a kid and I turned out okay. I mean, right? Look at me. Am I violent? Not all kids that play violent games will end up violent."

"I know, honey," Caryssa rolled over closer to him. The scent of roses and a just blown out candle lingered. She loved that smell, sort of like a campfire. "I know. You're a good man. Not violent at all. But…but this is bigger than playing war in the woods with sticks back in the fifties. I mean…it's *everywhere* now. It's everywhere we look. Everywhere Tyler looks. And when you factor in technology? Just in terms of video games targeting kids? *It scares the shit out of me.* It's like our kids are being trained from day one to be infected with killer voodoo for the power elite. Those who love money more than peace and beauty."

"Oh, I know," George replied, reaching for her hand. "But where's the girl I married? *I loved your happy dance!* Thing is, we'll never have everyone on board the peace train, Caryssa. We've built a pointless protective shield around our hearts and souls. Politicians build more hate walls. As you've said, our fake media is a powerful weapon. Not everyone is as positive and open as you are. And you have the courage to look at all sides of it, instead of burying your head in the sand. You're unique in that and I'm not suggesting you stop. I just…I just want to protect you when I see how upset you get sometimes."

"Our fake news *and* fake terrorism are what stops people from letting go!" Caryssa leaned over and kissed him on the forehead. "You are such a prince, honey. And I am *still* the girl with the happy dance! *That's just it.* I'm too happy to remain silent about the sickness."

"Then let it *completely* go."

"Our monetary *system* needs to let it go! For our kid's sake! Oh…I need another bubble bath, this time with a glass of sparkling wine. Wanna join me, or too tired?"

As soon as she got to the words "bubble bath," George had already read her mind and was heading out to the kitchen to pop some bubbly.

Caryssa smiled to herself, sighed, and leaned back onto the pillows. She knew her husband would take full charge of the evening's next experience, putting the Prosecco on ice, chilling the glasses. He'd maybe even find some rose petals somewhere to strew around the bedroom. All she had to do was relax and wait for him.

George walked in with two flute glasses of perfectly chilled Prosecco, and handed her one. "For you, my lady. How about a massage?"

Caryssa accepted the glass and put it to her nose. *Oh yes!* The fruity crisp scent and ambience! *Beautiful.* And massages always led to making love, just what the doctor ordered.

"Thank you, love," she smiled at him.

"No thanks necessary, my lady," he said, still in character. "You have had a rough day saving the world. It's time for your reward."

Chapter Twenty-Two

Anna knew something was wrong the second she stepped into her gallery. It was eerily quiet. Where was the music her overnight security guard typically played while manning the fort? Usually she walked into Black Eyed Peas or some kind of hip hop.

As she moved further into the lobby, something else startled her. A metallic scent. Was that...*blood?*

Then she saw him. His eyes were staring up at her, right through her. A pool of blood seeping from his head. Johnny, her security guard!

Anna panicked. She dropped her purse and ran to the ladies room. She rushed into the first stall and closed and locked the door. She pulled her cell phone out of her vest pocket and tried to dial 911. She couldn't make her fingers work. She kept on hitting the wrong numbers over and over.

Come on. Come *on!* She scolded herself as her panic grew.

Then she heard a sound outside the ladies room door. Oh my God, the murderer is after me! He can come in here any minute! She suddenly remembered the purse she had dropped. If the murderer didn't find her in here, he could find her at her home, since she had left her license within reach.

She held her breath, and made herself as still as she possibly could. Her heart was pounding so loudly she was afraid the killer would hear it and track her into the bathroom.

Then she heard the sound again. She heard someone calling her name. Johnny! He's alive!

She ran back out to the lobby. How could she have been such a coward to leave him? But he had looked dead, eyes open, still, and staring.

She bent down to him. He was still alive, and moaning softly. *So much blood!* There was a huge pool all around his head now, flowing towards the front door. She could see the head wound. Part of his skull was crushed.

He was trying to tell her something. Barely audible. She knelt beside him and put her ear near his mouth to try to make out his words. "The...they came and took...the Delacroix..."

Then he fainted. *Or died?* Trembling, Anna tried to feel for his pulse. But it seemed her own pulse was beating so hard she could not tell her own from his.

Oh my God, what am I doing? Anna grabbed her phone. This time her fingers worked. She pressed 911. She felt for Johnny's pulse again. *He's still alive!*

Barely.

Both the ambulance and police came within ten minutes. While the paramedics lifted Johnny onto a stretcher the police asked Anna a barrage of questions. She knew typically they would never talk to her during a crime scene investigation...but they knew her. *From her daughter's tragedy.*

"Mrs. Beauvais, do you know of any enemies Mr. Santos may have had?"

"No, God, he would not have hurt a fly!"

"Did he speak to you at all before becoming unconscious?"

"Yes, He had mentioned *'they'* came and took my prize painting!"

Police and crime scene investigators began taping off the area. The blood would not be cleaned up until all evidence had been fully collected.

"Excuse me, Mrs. Beauvais, did Mr. Santos say anything about what our boys looked like? Any description?"

Anna sensed something odd. An aroma, mixed with the scent of blood...a very subtle, but definitive scent. Perfume. Caron's *Poivre*. She had worn it when she and Pierre had been feeling rich. Back when her business was booming.

She turned to the policeman. "What makes you so sure it was men? I'm getting a strong indication here it just might not be."

"Why do you say that?" Sergeant Coral asked.

"Well, I just get this feeling. I'm sure it wasn't two guys in here." Although the French perfume scent lingering can be worn by men as well, she thought. Like an expensive version of CK One.

"Mrs. Beauvais, we can't use that as evidence. Women's intuition or not, we need something more concrete. You said Mr. Santos mentioned 'they,' so we know more than one person was involved, and we can safely assume he saw them. We can only hope he is well enough to speak to us."

One of the CSI agents pointed to something shiny on the floor. "Did you lose this, Ma'am?" he asked.

Anna walked over and looked at a lipstick case on the floor. Gold plated, covered with what looked like diamonds.

"No, that's not mine" She bent down to pick it up.

"No, don't touch it!" he shouted. "It's evidence. We need to drop it into this bag."

He reached with black nitrile gloves and picked up the lipstick, while Anna got a good look at it. Guerlain. Wow, she thought. Expensive perfume, expensive lipstick. What is going on here?

After they rushed Johnny to the hospital and the cops left her studio, Anna drove back to her home in a daze. She felt stressed out, so she ran a bath, lit candles, poured herself a glass of Bourgogne Rouge, and sank into the lavender-scented, hot bubbles. She could feel the tension seep out of her neck and back instantly.

After her bath she slipped into bed and fell into a fitful sleep.

The following morning, Anna was sitting at the kitchen table with Pierre, nursing a cup of coffee, when the phone rang. It was Sergeant Coral.

"We have a positive identification," he said. "It was two young women, age eighteen and nineteen. Both from Belvedere, both seniors in High School. From what I hear, they both excelled in school and sports, which may seem odd…"

Anna was suddenly wide awake and alarmed. Not merely because of what she is hearing, but that he would jeopardize the investigation by telling her all this. Is he telling her things he shouldn't due to trust built up during her own daughter's tragic investigation?

Girls, not much older than her oldest was at the time of...she chased the thought away, but was stunned and emotionally distraught by this information.

There was a prolonged silence on the other end of the phone.

Finally, Sergeant Coral said "I've been in this line of business for over thirty-five years, Mrs. Beauvais. I can assure you that I've seen it all. *Nothing* surprises me anymore. Anyhow, both their fingerprints and DNA have been found on the security desk, the weapon, and the lipstick case. It appears both the girls lifted the weapon used to bludgeon your security guard—"

"The weapon used, they lifted it...what are you talking about?" asked Anna, confused.

"It appears they bludgeoned Mr. Santos with another of your masterpieces. A very fine bronze statue. I am not an art expert, but what appears to be an expensively done sculpture of a woman was found in one of the girls' cars. They had carried it out, likely knowing it would be encrusted with his blood, but perhaps also for its value."

Anna slumped into her chair, stunned.

"Oh my God," she whispered. "How did I not notice it was missing? My, my..."

"I'm sorry, Mrs. Beauvais, I can barely hear you. Can you please speak up?"

"Oh, sorry," Anna said, louder this time. "Yes...that piece is very precious to me! My Jean-Jacques Pradier, an original nineteenth century Barbedienne casting. Yes, it's a very fine bronze, which was on a cherry wood piece of furniture as you walk into my gallery. How could I have not seen it was missing?"

She had not had the piece appraised in a while, because she meant never to sell it. The last time it had been valued at ten thousand dollars. Not nearly the half million her missing painting was worth. But to her, it was worth the world. It was her first gift from Pierre, as a token of honor for earning her art degree in Paris. Pierre had splurged big time for it... for her. Anna's heart sank.

But then she realized, the piece had been recovered. It was found in the girl's car. She breathed a sigh of relief. Until what she heard next.

"It appears your painting was not the only property destroyed, Mrs. Beauvais. The bronze sculpture was apparently scrubbed clean, with what smells like bleach. Again, I am no art expert, but it looks tarnished compared to bronze art pieces I've seen. I'm sure the girls did this knowing we could get DNA samples from it."

"Did you just say my painting was destroyed too?"

"Yes. It was. Sorry. I jumped ahead. Let me back up. Both girls are in police custody, both already admitted to breaking and entering, assaulting Mr. Santos, and stealing your property. Both pieces of art were picked up this morning…the bronze sculpture from one of the cars, the painting from one of their homes in Tiburon. The girls were hoping to sell your painting at their school fundraising auction… I know this sounds far-fetched but…"

"Wait a minute here," Anna interrupted. "Are you trying to tell me these girls bludgeoned my security guard and stole my art pieces to raise money for their school? I mean, no matter how bad the school budget cuts are, you don't *believe* that far-fetched story, do you?"

Anna suddenly remembered Johnny. She always vowed never to be so shallow as to put her livelihood ahead of any life itself, and here she was doing just that.

"Sergeant Coral, how…how is Johnny Santos doing? What have you heard so far?" she continued.

"I'm so sorry Mrs. Beauvais, but it doesn't sound promising. I'm afraid Mr. Santos took quite the blow to his head. He's still in surgery and will be for most of the day. Part of his skull was smashed and there was a significant amount of damaged brain tissue. His spinal cord may also have been injured and he suffered loss of cerebrospinal fluid and blood. Even if he makes it through this, he may have permanent brain damage. He also has a significant brain bleed, which they are trying to repair."

Anna couldn't speak, her heart heavy. But dam it she lost her parents as a kid, her girls before they finished puberty, her marriage---and now her business is being destroyed. She had to ask the question. "You said my bronze was not the only property destroyed…what happened to my Delacroix?"

There was a prolonged silence.

Then "How much was that painting worth? I'm hoping not too much, as I don't think it can be restored."

"Well, it's not one of the most valuable paintings in the world, but to me with my small business it was quite the investment. I paid a little over half a million for it about eleven years ago. I was hoping to sell it for more now. I loved it, so it was hard for me to let go of it even if a potential customer offered more than I expected."

"Wow. That's a lot of money. I'm so sorry to have to tell you this, but you would not even recognize the painting. It's been torn to shreds by two angry young ladies."

"But why would they damage the painting, if they wanted to make money from it?" Anna asked. "I don't understand!"

"It finally dawned on them they couldn't sell it at their school auction. It might be listed on the art loss registry and would easily be traced back to them. Apparently one of them became very agitated at all they had gone through to get the money for the school and went on a rampage, destroying the painting. She was screaming at us during questioning that the reason she wasn't accepted into Stanford was budget cuts for the district every year. How skills she needed to be competitive were cut."

Anna felt sick.

These girls had robbed her, may have killed an innocent man, and ruined her property...*all for their future*? Could this be their motive? It all sounded so implausible.

Sergeant Coral was still speaking "Then the other girl was shouting about how 'fucking expensive' college tuition is now and how even her successful, highly educated parents can't afford it with the cost skyrocketing." *Why was he telling her all this?*

"It wasn't money that stopped either of them getting into Stanford if they were stupid enough to think for a second they could sell stolen art at a school auction! They would have had to move those items on the black market!" Anna replied. "Sergeant Coral, I...I need to come see the art pieces, maybe I can salvage them with the help of an art restorer."

She was now seeing that the art insurance she invested in may pay off. But it won't bring the art masterpieces back. Just as it could not bring her girls back.

"Sure, come down to the station. We have to hold them as evidence until this case is formally closed," Sergeant Coral said. "The girls will have to stand trial. You can't touch anything, just look, and you'll need to be accompanied by an officer."

It was a few days before she could get to the police station, and was ushered into a back room. There she first saw her bronze. She could tell right away that whatever these girls had tried to clean it with had destroyed it, dissolving valuable patina. The natural green was reduced to a tarnished metal surface.

She looked up at the officer. "The Delacroix?" she asked.

He nodded and led her through another door to a smaller room. The painting was bad. Really bad. But not as horrible as she had imagined after hearing Sergeant Coral's description. It had two large rips and a few stab holes.

Anna thanked the officer, and made her way out of the station towards her car. While she was walking, she dialed the number of the best art restorer she knew. She got voice mail, and left a message asking him to return her call at the earliest possible moment.

Sergeant Coral called her name from across the parking lot. She walked back to the police station, where he met her on the steps.

"Anna...is it okay if I call you Anna?"

"Of course. I'd rather lose the formality. May I call you Jason?" she replied, smiling.

"Please do. There is something else I need to share with you...something weird."

"Okay," she said. "Let me have it. I've been through every weirdness that weirdness has to offer. How much weirder can it get?"

"Well, a really creepy strange," Coral replied. "Something was found behind your art gallery, between the dumpster and the back door. A dead dove. The odd thing...well there was more than one odd thing...but why was it left in back of your art gallery, for one thing? It was so obviously left there for someone to see, as some sort of message."

"Really?" Anna asked incredulously. "I mean, what makes you say 'obvious'? Couldn't the dove have gotten loose from a cage in a nearby house, and then a cat or a hawk got it?"

"Well, normally we would think so...but here's where the really strange part comes in. This dove had some things painted on it. *In blood.* Bloody teardrops under its eyes, and three blood drops on its breast. Our forensics team felt they were symbolic of something. So we made some calls."

"Jason…you're freaking me out. An emblematic bloody dove was left behind my art gallery? With symbolic messages? And what are those symbolic messages? What is this, The Da Vinci Code?"

Jason explained "In religious, military and pacifist groups, the white dove has historically symbolized love, peace or as messengers. The forensics team believe the bloody tear drops could symbolize being blinded so one cannot see an *'enemy'*. The three blood drops on the dove's breast could symbolize removal of the heart. Now here comes the most unusual part. We wondered if the bird had anything to do with the attack on your security guard and the robbery. It seemed too much of a coincidence not to be. So we talked with the girls' parents."

Anna braced herself.

"As it turns out, the white dove was one of the girls' pets.

Anna was shocked. *Did the girl kill her own pet?* If hearing two girls crushed her guards' skull was not enough of an infringement upon her bleeding heart after losing her *own* two girls, now the full horror of the situation really hit her.

Mercilessly, the police sergeant droned on. "We pulled the criminal psychologist into the investigation. This aspect is still being evaluated… but the psychologist's preliminary hit is that there is some societal message the girls were trying to convey. Something about violence, blind vengeance, lack of a social heart in our society, and robbing social services…in this case their education and by extension their futures."

Anna reflected on how these girls justified their action, mirroring what they're being imposed upon within society at large, by a global autocracy that wages war on small countries for profit and pretends to be "protecting freedoms at home."

It all came full circle. Peace in pieces.

She felt a shudder deep inside her. "The mass shootings in schools and communities.…I've read youth involved often blame society, take it out on local community. Tragic."

"Times of turmoil can develop troubled youth," responded the officer. Inside, he prayed for his own kids.

Then Anna shook Jason's hand and thanked him, started making her way back to the car. What the cop said next jolted her in place. "I know

I've told you too much already, but really Anna. We go way back with Bianca's trial. I trust you like no other civilian. I know what I say stays within these walls. The blood painted on the dove? It's Johnny's blood. Tests were run. Oh, and one of the girl's Dad is a former Google executive, now working for the CIA. He may be questioned as well."

How eerie. She couldn't wait to get home. Take another bath. She and Caryssa, with their calming baths. But first, one more call. And definitely one more stop.

She called the hospital to check on Johnny. The receptionist was shuffling papers, half speaking into her phone "Mr. Santos is still in a coma. We are allowing visitors now, because even in a near vegetative state some patients respond to loved ones---but family only." Anna paid no attention to that. She *had* to go see him. On the way she berated herself for having Johnny work the graveyard shift...when such robberies tend to happen.

Johnny's room was a cacophony of beeping noises and blinking lights. Then she looked at him. He appeared to be asleep. A tube was clamped to his mouth to keep him breathing. A hard plastic collar was around his neck, a blood-soaked gauze turban around his head. Wires snaked from both his arms, chest and skull.

*Images of Bianca flashed before her...*Bianca, her youngest who always wore a helmet, did not even make it to this state. But it was not a head injury that took her. Her spine and limbs were fractured, with fatal internal damage. Anna tried not to think of it all, as it always made her feel so depressed. But looking at Johnny, it was hard not to.

Stepping close to his side, she took one of his hands. She pulled the visitor chair closer and sat. She did not know if he would hear her, but she spoke softly to him.

"Johnny...its Anna. I'm here with you. I love you. Stay strong...think good thoughts. You'll pull though this." Guilt drove through her, thinking of how she had called him last minute to guard her art gallery. Because she saw signs of an attempted break in earlier that day...

And will he pull through this? Looking at him, one would think not. It will take nothing short of a miracle.

The nurse came in. "Excuse me, are you family?" a tad sternly.

Anna had told a little white lie at the reception desk, claiming she was Johnny's sister. This time she told the truth. "No, just a good friend. I will leave now. Thank you for letting me see him."

Before she left she spoke to him again. "I'll be back Johnny. Hang in there. We're praying for you."

She walked out of the room in despair, feeling in her heart that this just might be the last time she sees her employee of ten years—*alive*.

Two weeks later, Johnny died. He had never resurfaced from the coma.

* * *

Eight months after that awful tragedy at her art gallery, Anna was amazed. Though never the type to be self-congratulatory, it was herself she was amazed with.

The whole ordeal should leave her nerves frayed. But now, the emotions dulled. She had learned to be strong after all her losses, to find a calm wave and ride it. Her self-healing powers had grown exponentially.

She decided to walk away from her business. She loved her work and was proud of what she built. It had, in a sense, become her life. But as time passed and she healed, she realized that more than ever she wanted to focus now on—*life itself.*

It was as if the Universe was saying "Enough, Anna. Come home to yourself now." And slowly she came home.

She spent lots of time with her sweet grandson Jared, sold *Exotic Exposure* and started working part time again teaching children the love of art from her home studio. Back to where she had been before those life-changing tragedies. But this time, she won't shut the door on a child. *Ever.*

And there's at least one set of parent's whose child she never shut the door on. *The Garth's son.* For this action, she felt she had redeemed her mother's soul.

Chapter Twenty-Three

Caryssa had been job interviewing---*again*. She was pleasantly surprised, after taking a decade off her professional marketing career to have received so many bites.

She was offered a position heading up marketing efforts for a high tech startup, and told she could work from home, come into the office when needed, work whatever hours she wanted…as long as she brought value.

On the surface, this sounded great. Yet she had been with enough tech startups to realize it might be too intense for a mother in her fifties with a preteen. She didn't want to lose sight of Tyler's day-to-day struggles, what was going on with him in his hormone changing world.

After the final interview and verbal offer, she went home and then out for an invigorating walk in the San Francisco Bay hills. Then did Yoga stretches in her beautiful back garden. She needed to clear her mind.

She had recently attended a Spiritual Spa workshop with deep meditation, music, and healing techniques for inner peace. One thing the workshop stressed was in every decision you make in life, think in terms of "does it make me feel heavy, or light?"

And with the tech startup, she felt something heavy beyond the intense schedule. She knew right off what the problem was. It was their target market. Their product would serve massive military overreach. The servers, routers, robotics warfare, and computers to connect all the bases would make the company, and her, a pretty penny. *But at what social cost to society?* At what cost to her moral conscience?

She declined the offer, wanting to work for a business that would benefit communities and the planet. *Not destroy them.* An organization that made profit with a positive purpose. She needed some fresh perspective and some time away.

Her little family decided on a road trip along the scenic California coastline from San Francisco Bay to San Simeon. They took their time, stopping to see friends and filling the days with camping, hiking and biking..

The drive was breathtakingly beautiful. She had driven this coastline long ago when she first arrived in California, but in the company of her son and husband, it was even more magical. The sound of awe and laughter drifted from Tyler, filling the car with youthful wonder. The ocean cliffs, forests and highway hugging the coastline. The sea breeze wafting in her open window. The salt sea air and the sunshine. It all immersed her in an ocean of tranquility.

She had packed golf clubs so she and Tyler could play when they were in Monterey on 17-Mile Drive. George dropped them off at Pacific Grove Golf Course and then went exploring local shops for provisions, including a tasty bottle of wine. Caryssa was not sure Tyler was ready for playing holes, so they had just gone to the pro shop to get a couple buckets of balls to practice driving and putting.

While on the practice green with Tyler, Caryssa tipped her head back and gazed at the clear blue sky. A profound sense of her father's presence swept over her. They once stood at this exact spot. His presence wrapped around her, warm and strong—a fierce celestial hug. Caryssa reveled in the sensation, clinging to it as tears filled her eyes.

"Wow Mom, check that out!" Tyler had sunk a putt all the way from across the green, after meticulously sizing up the shot and taking his time with follow-through.

Caryssa was impressed. "Great, Tyler!" Then she gave her ball a tap and it slowly made its way towards the hole, stopping just short. She smiled at her boy. "Can you give Mommy some putting lessons?"

The sensation of her dad's nearness was still there a few minutes later as they made their way towards the driving range, buckets of balls in their hands, golf bags over their shoulders. Caryssa felt her father's presence often, but especially while doing something he had loved, like golf or playing cards or eating a good piece of fish.

As the trip continued, they enjoyed the rustic quaintness of Carmel, the Mexican-type charm of Santa Barbara and the splendid surreal beauty of Big Sur. The climax was seeing the grand opulence of William Randolph's Hearst Hilltop Castle. Tyler, a lover of history and medieval castles, seemed entranced, his voice echoing across the enchanting hill. "Wow, check it out! The coolest mansion ever!"

To Caryssa, Heart Castle is to California what the Eiffel Tower is to Paris. She glanced towards Tyler's adored mansion. Exquisite. The views to the ocean, breathtaking. They did the two-hour tour and watched the movie about the castle's history, then walked around the terraces and into the splendid gardens. Caryssa admired the magnificent pools and the Spanish-Italian-Moorish style architecture of the mansions and cottages.

At one point while dashing through the gardens, she and Tyler locked their hands and danced in circles, laughing with glee at the sheer beauty and splendor of it all. Caryssa was living in the moment, fully present, no other thoughts in her mind. The most beautiful and splendid thing of all, *her child.*

Together, she, Tyler, and George admired the roses, bright pink bougainvillea climbing terraces, and a myriad of flowers Caryssa could not name. Hundreds of butterflies flew from flower to flower as if to call attention to their own beauty. "Look at me! I am as pretty as that flower!" Hummingbirds buzzed all around them. Caryssa tried several times to capture one on camera, but they would flit away as quickly as they arrived, over beautiful Italian terra cotta and palms.

The sun was a great tranquilizer, and time passed in a haze of well-being, long, relaxed moments and almost torpid hours when it was so enjoyable to be alive that nothing else mattered.

As if such peaceful thoughts don't blend with our violent history, Caryssa's subconscious momentarily unlocked. It dawned on her the origins of this magnificent castle came from an unscrupulous bloodthirsty newspaper magnate. Hearst started the Spanish-American War to sell his newspapers and become powerful. It was our first "media war." He used his own twisted propaganda machine, purposely demonizing Spain to get the American people angry. Money, manipulation and power like today. She chased the thought away, back to Tyler and his happy place.

She sat on one of the benches thinking of the most recent parent-teacher meeting, and the beautiful writing Tyler's teacher had shown her. The children had been asked to write a piece about what makes them feel important. Tyler wrote "My mom and dad make me feel happy. They spend lots of time with me hiking, biking, skiing, and helping me do homework. They are always there for me, and make me feel safe and loved." He wrote that he feels like *"a person."* It had brought home that this was her most important job in the world, and she was doing it well.

Shortly after they returned from this fabulous road trip, Caryssa started packing for another upcoming trip across the continent to her beloved home city of Boston. And that's when it happened—or the media frenzied version of what happened. The modern propaganda machine will forever refer to it as the "*Boston Bombing.*" History repeats.

While some let this rather suspicious tragedy deepen their misplaced anger, the serenity that Caryssa felt did not dissipate. Likely another shadow government op to keep our profitable war games alive.

When she saw her sweet-natured, beautiful son running back and forth in the sunshine laughing with one of his buddies, throwing water balloons at each other, her heart wrenched. This beautiful child, who has flown to and from Boston twice a year since he was three weeks old to visit family.

To Caryssa, the response of some—more shocking than the event itself—spoke volumes about the state of American culture, of the American soul. A tinder-box of boxed up bitterness. Her heart will always remain in Boston. Yet her conscience has expanded

People remain locked into localized beliefs, our culture of extreme 'patriotism,' the sense of American exceptionalism, and can't look beyond that. And our soldiers are propaganda pawns, the *biggest* victims of all. Why not think beyond our superficial conditioning?

When she mentioned to George later that afternoon how she had tried to create awareness about this for a *long time*, he simply said "Yes, Caryssa. But remember the quote from the Arcturians? 'Your work is not to drag the world kicking and screaming into new awareness. Your job is to simply do your work, sacredly, secretly, silently…and those with eyes to see and ears to hear will respond.' It's good to keep that in mind if you can."

"While millions more die? *Come on George!*"

She glanced at one of the many inspirational quotes she had hanging in her home, and reminded herself of the one that read "Let go, or be dragged." She'd had that fridge magnet for over a decade, and strived to live by it. Specifically, she wouldn't let herself be dragged through our politically incorrect system itself.

That night she slept deeply, calmly. But not without one of those recurring dreams of trying to help people…trying to mold the intersection of people, planet, and profits into a better form. In those dreams, she went from school to school, city to city, spreading peace and love and sharing her heart. She picked up trash, helped the small farmers use organic seed.

She always awakened, as she did again at five the next morning, to find herself in her own bed.

Her first thought that morning was Yes George, your wife is even trying to save the world in her dreams.

"Am I the intense one George? Is there something wrong with me? Or those sliding through the madness without noticing? Embracing it as the norm? When half the American people support our horrific drone strikes to *stop terrorism,* we should suspect a sociopathic culture." George just shook his head, escaping reality.

Just yesterday volunteering in the school library, Caryssa came across a book teaching young kids to draw military tanks. How horrifying to see this on the library shelf in her sweet child's elementary school! A glaring example of the violent values instilling cruel "norms" within innocent, fragile, developing minds. Did nobody else notice this? Did nobody else object? How could that be?

It was Saturday. Caryssa strolled out to the kitchen, where George was making coffee. She gave him a hug, and then slumped into a chair at the table.

"Rough night, honey?" George placed homemade muffins on the table. "Coffee will be ready soon."

Caryssa breathed in the homey aromas of Peet's and pumpkin spice "Thanks hon…I swear, I work so hard to save the world in my dreams I wake up exhausted some days. And this whole Boston Bomber thing just has me…aaaaagggghh. People don't understand they're living in a military dictatorship and nothing is as it seems! They just open their mouths like baby birds waiting for the predigested worms of corporate media sanitized information and then they swallow it without a second thought."

"Honey, it's seven in the morning." Focused on his fingers, George tore a napkin until a paper mountain stood between them. "Must we start with the conspiracy theories before coffee?! And as you know…I don't totally agree with you that America is a military dictatorship."

"Come on honey, don't *you* of all people go into denial as well! We have a weapons transfer program militarizing our police forces, and people have been brainwashed into believing it's for their *'protection'*. Unless they're people of color and live in the inner cities. Those folks aren't fooled, because they're getting mowed down almost every day!" Caryssa snapped.

"We *are* global police, and it's not right." George poured two big mugs of steaming coffee and set one in front of her. "More like global exploiters. You're preaching to the choir here. But I don't consider America the dictatorship you say."

"Oh come on George, we have high school kids being hunted down by military punks! Who is number one in selling deadly weapons to all sorts of governments around the world? USA! *We* are number one! What is this doing for anyone? It endangers all of us is what it does. Arming the world to the teeth is not the path to world peace!"

"Drink your coffee, honey. I'm going out to the patio to read the paper."

"You mean the propaganda," Caryssa picked up her mug. "Watch out you don't get brainwashed! And check out the militarized police violence 'protecting' all our citizens!"

George laughed and blew her a kiss. "I'll do my best," disappearing around the corner.

Caryssa sat there nursing her cup of coffee. *Sometimes I wish I could be like George.* A recent conversation came to mind. Some parents and teachers were standing outside the school, talking about our increasingly oppressive police state surveillance. She heard them going back in forth.

One parent said it all. "With this overdone 'If you see something say something' thing, I'd like to say something myself! I see an orchestrated twenty-four-hour propaganda machine spinning our minds until we are too dizzy to think for ourselves. I see current events in a dazed maze of pop infotainment and fatuous opinion sold as fair and balanced objectivity. I see our federal prisons gorged with nonviolent drug offenders while war criminals walk. I see a system privatizing everything from education to water. I see media-manipulated false panic and paranoia turning people against each other!"

Caryssa had wanted to high-five the guy as she walked past. He had laid it all out perfectly. *No denial there…*

One mom simply smiled, her light-hearted bounce of a step in tune with the beautiful child beside her, while balancing another beautiful child on her hip. "We are an Orwellian Society!" she laughed in passing.

This community, living in modest houses they own, with good jobs, great immediate family situations---happy, productive citizens. No direct experience of oppression. Yet, they can discuss this openly, out of healthy awareness and concern for our next generation.

What the next parent said struck a chord with Cayrssa's concern about New England's overly patriotic stance. "It's easily explained why so many people on the East Coast hold on to the radical military perspective. Massachusetts alone has twenty of the nation's top defense contractors. It's a *'way of life'* there, how they make a living."

The next afternoon, Caryssa was sitting out by the bay in a quaint little café with some girlfriends, drinking espresso and eating paté, grapes, brie and crackers, and the topic came up again. Michelle—who had been a coworker in Silicon Valley and made similar life decisions after starting her family—said "Hey Caryssa, what an awful thing happening in your hometown Boston! Wow! How are you doing with all that?"

Carrysa took a sip of vanilla latte. She had just finished Jazzercise class, then did Yoga and felt fabulous. "What shocks me more than it actually happening, however it *'happened'* we will never know, is how people *responded* to it. With unwarranted anger, unable to look at our own violent culture coming back to haunt us—"

Michelle interjected "*Wow!* I am amazed a person from Boston could say such a thing! I mean…I mean this in a good way. As someone from Italy who has traveled around the world twice, I was thinking the same thing. But I was afraid to say so in case you took offense—"

"Come on Michelle, you've known me for over twenty years!" Cayrssa blurted. "You *know* I don't get offended easily! I just think it shows how desensitized to violence we have become as a people, to not even be able to think *rationally* about the ordeal."

They sat staring out at the beauty around them. The winter sun setting over the bay, sailboats still gliding across the water in the late afternoon breeze. Gladys, from Argentina added "How humble for you to see this, Caryssa. Does this mean you won't be wearing one of those 'Boston Strong' T-shirts?"

"Oh no, I already bought one of those. I wear it, and so does Tyler. I consider it a motto for healing as a people, and coming together for support. I'm just a big picture thinker."

"Oh yeah?" Gladys asked. "And what does the big picture look like to you?"

Caryssa took another sip of her latte. "You sure you want to know?"

Her friends both nodded, a bit wearily.

"Okay," Caryssa put her latte down, spreading her hands into a globe like arch. "Here's the big picture as I see it. The Wall Street banking cartel controls Capitol Hill. Capitol Hill controls the world, holding it hostage with the American dollar. Big banksters lower the American dollar to the dark side through conspiracy, fraud, and manipulation of interest rates around the world. *Clang Clang Clang!!* Wall Street's opening bell. There's that hero again, *cash.* Every dollar, euro, peso, yen, and whatever coinage is called elsewhere in the world goes on a lightning speed pilgrimage to downtown Manhattan…driving the war capital of the world. That's the big picture. Aren't you glad you asked?"

The sound of a foghorn blew in from the bay, causing them all to glance out at the beauty of the sky, landscape, and water. The fog was starting to roll in over the Golden Gate and Bay bridges. The sun was setting in its majestic bright orange streaks across the misty sky and the rains were finally predicted after a long drought. Nobody spoke for a few minutes.

Caryssa wondered if her big picture analysis shocked them. "Michelle…do you remember way back when…when I first moved to California to work in the Silicon Valley office with you?"

"Well of course I remember, Caryssa, how could I ever forget? In walks this leggy blond bombshell and all the guys drooled. But when you started showing how much technical knowledge you had, *watch out!* This was no dumb blond here! No wonder you were among the first in the department to get promoted!"

"Well, I was good at faking my knowledge, ha! That's what marketing people do! We talk all techy on paper! Anyway, a couple years before that, before I moved to California, the Gulf War was going on, remember? *And I didn't give a shit.* I was too busy getting ahead to even think about it, much less *care* about what was going on in that far, far away land."

"Of course you didn't, me either. We were young. We were ambitious. We were single. We didn't have *kids* to think about. It didn't affect us in that safe little dotcom bubble we floated in." Michelle's cell phone rang, but she merely glanced at it and let it ring. "And we didn't see then how we are selling our neighborhoods to Wall Street."

A light breeze swept over the women, and Caryssa took a deep cleansing breath of the fresh bay air. Everything enchanted her. The sun hanging like a ball behind the Golden Gate Bridge, its light glistening off the water in sparkles like brilliant diamonds. The simple and sheer beauty of it all. And the people surrounding her, with social grace and calm, able to churn through this topic with ease and eloquence.

"I know you're right, gf," "It was a different time for us. But…just… I'd love people to stop enabling what our corporate media and special interest lobbyists are selling to their souls—their ideas, their version of history, their wars, their weapons, and their notion of inevitability. I've got to believe another world is not only possible but on the way."

"Amen, sister," Michelle intoned. "Amen to that. People remain docile, because…well, the bombs aren't dropping here."

"Yet they *are*. Our financial weapons of mass destruction, while America's youth are in the arena." Caryssa rolled her neck, taking a deep breath of the fresh bay air.

Michelle leaned inward, eyes locked with Caryssa's. "Well Caryss, you and I both worked our cherished Silicon Valley circuit, seeing firsthand how at least a handful of those multinational tech corporations are an invention of DARPA. This so called defense agency on the dark side. The internet, and certain tech giants deep into futuristic robotic sci-fi inventions addicted to military contracts."

"How were we to know then that merely four years later, we would be holding newborn babies, frightened for their future mainly *due* to this?"

Caryssa was adjusting the bistro umbrella, as the sun was in her eyes. "How disheartening to know even the multinational internetworking tech giant we worked for blended good with evil."

"At least neither of us worked directly with *those* contracts" Michelle reasoned.

"No, but plenty of them passed my path while I supported the sales force." Caryssa slathered lavender scented sunscreen on her face and neck. She couldn't believe the sun was still as strong after starting to set an hour ago. "My life outside work back then was magical. Snow skiing, water skiing, golfing, rollerblading, biking, running the calming palm-lined streets. Concerts in Saratoga, parties in Palo Alto, wining and dining in Los Gatos, nights in The City. I traveled to and from New England, throughout California, to Hawaii, business trips around the country and abroad"

"And your life now?" Michelle would be surprised if Caryssa thought her life was any better then.

"Oh...now, at least as wonderful, but in a different way." I guess...a more...I don't know. A more caring, humane way?"

Michelle nodded, all ears.

"While I was nursing Tyler, everything clicked. My eyes popped opened to the political, social, environmental, and economic woes of the world—along with Corporate America's pivotal role in it all. This was the world, I realized, that my child would inherit. The more I read, the more news reports I saw, the more horrified I became about what it might be by the time he was grown."

Michelle merely nodded, her sincere eye contact validating these emotions. Gladys, who had walked closer to the water's edge to feed the ducks, came back to the table. She glanced towards Caryssa "I am really surprised you can be this open minded, knowing your parents were on an early morning flight out of Boston the day of the attack on the World Trade Center."

"And if they were not grounded safely? I'd *still* be saying this--- NYC and Boston happened due to our own historic political doings. *Not* because anyone hates us for our freedom!"

The conversation turned to ski trips, family golf and camping outings, fun stuff at their children's schools. After a while, the group paid their bill and departed to move on to picking up the kids, supervising homework, getting to sports activities. This wonderful thing called life.

When Caryssa got home, Tyler was still at his twice a week daycare to give her extra time and him social interaction. She saw an intriguing job posting. A startup focused on building a new stock exchange paradigm —to value natural and societal assets, rather than destructive. Things like clean water, clean air, and human potential. She checked the time. She had an hour left before she had to pick Tyler up. Time enough to get her application in. She went into her home office, fired up the computer, and began.

Yet, two weeks later the new stock exchange paradigm the young moral tech geeks tried to start, was attempted to be crushed by the money monsters on Wall Street.

Chapter Twenty-Four

Two years passed. One summer evening Caryssa, George, and Tyler took a catamaran cruise on the bay. As the cat sailed into the sunset towards the Golden Gate Bridge, a group of twenty-somethings sitting near them began discussing the Santa Barbara and UCLA mass shootings.

Subtle fingers of fog began to creep over the headland. The air was full of the aromas of cruise delicacies—barbecue and Mediterranean finger foods— and the fresh bay breeze. Despite the topic in the group behind her, Caryssa was deeply at peace.

In the background she heard, in her point of view, a rather elementary and clichéd response to the University tragedies. It came from a lively, well-dressed man about seventy. He and his wife had brought caviar and champagne with them, and were sipping and snacking. "Well, we can't blame society. Individuals need to take ownership of their actions."

Caryssa chimed in "Yes, in a perfect world that makes perfect sense. But guess what? America is hardly 'society'…there is a big wide world out there. We need to address *American culture*. Our Capitol needs to take responsibility. What kind of human goodness is being represented by the violence in our media and pop culture? The vice we call virtue of our foreign policy? How are our young people supposed to learn right from wrong in a context like that?"

Mr. Caviar washed down his pink salmon eggs with a sip of exquisitely expensive champagne, his Jaeger-LeCoultre watch glistening in the sunshine, and glanced out at the bay. They sailed on in silence for a few minutes, each enjoying the fresh air and beauty surrounding them.

One of the college students behind Caryssa turned to her and said "I know, right? What is causing all this violence? How about an emotional disconnect between human beings due to being ruled by an oligarchy? How about a subjugated set of people losing any sense of moral conscience due to a culture of bullying the world at gunpoint, and seeing the fallout of bullying here?"

"*Exactly*!" Caryssa breathed a sigh of relief.

The young woman reached a hand over the seat back. "My name's Lori."

"Great to meet you," Caryssa responded, taking her hand and shaking it. "Caryssa."

Lori continued her rationale about our common violence "A disenfranchised people so hell bent on revenge, angry and full of hate for all those 'bad guys.' A zombie apocalypse of smart bomb obsession, with this echo chamber of twisted ideas and perpetual glory of violence!"

"Yes!" Caryssa said loud enough so Mr. Caviar heard her. "No other modern country endures mass shootings so frequently. We can't just change the laws and do criminal background checks. These kids have *no* criminal backgrounds. The criminal background check needs to be done with respect to the global military system *itself*. We need a cultural health reform."

Lori nodded. "Damn straight."

George interrupted. "Honey…If you are going to be having this conversation? I'm taking Tyler somewhere else. He doesn't need to hear this doom and gloom stuff about the world he's growing up in."

Caryssa waved her hand in assent and George took Tyler's hand and led him away from the conversation. "Come on buddy, let's see if we can see any harbor seals out there. Or better yet, dolphins!"

She turned back to Lori. "It's the darkening of the soul. We have effectively commoditized everything—land, air, water, people, and animals. All shackled with price tags, enslaved within what we call 'civilization'. Much of the violence in this country is happening due to a culture, *ours*, that mindlessly consumes all that is near and dear to each and every one of us, right down to our beautiful families that love us the most, finding fault with each other, rather than seeing the cultural culprits tearing people apart."

"Violence sells," agreed Lori. "That dystopian future we as students might be asked to write about in a creative essay on a future America where certain technological advances and climate change lead to something evil? *It's happening.* It's no sci-fi novel. It's reality! We are not the ones talking 'doom and gloom', it's those that think violence is necessary because...well, the world sucks!"

Both women glanced over at Mr. Caviar, oblivious in his overdressed-for-a-sail white Armani shorts and polished shoes. Likely thinking they were misfits living on the edge of society. Then one of Lori's companions got her attention, and she turned back to her group.

Caryssa was glad for the break. She was loving the sail. They were passing by Alcatraz, and she captured a picture. The gorgeous palm trees swaying against the rolling hills, the Golden Gate Bridge with the mystic lines of fog intertwined in its fiery orange structure, Alcatraz with its harsh history and astounding beauty. *Just like America*, she thought. The California sunshine glistened off the water like diamonds, against the dramatic shapes of the Marin headlands.

She sipped a glass of Pinot Grigio, while tasting the hors d'oeuvres, and enjoying the sunshine. Wow! Twenty-one years I've lived in California. And the breathtaking beauty of San Francisco Bay still utterly amazes me.

As the catamaran soared under full sail, she thought how she had journeyed full sail from corporate professional to advocating corporate accountability for social abuse. Twenty-one-plus years ago she played the corporate game that had brought her here. How much had changed, and how beautifully. She knew she would never go back, but will always treasure it in her heart. And she would never again regret her decision or beat herself up because she was a "tech dinosaur."

As she sat on the catamaran speeding across the waters of the bay, she was at home in her own soul. Her new livelihood would come to her, and it would be in line with her values and all that she had learned in the past twenty years. She felt a kind of closure.

Soon the catamaran docked at the Embarcadero in San Francisco, and everybody disembarked. George, Caryssa, and Tyler joined hands and wandered the city streets. At the harbor there were booths set up with jewelry, paintings, and delicious foods. Quintessential San Francisco sights and smells.

Caryssa was surprised to bump into a group of girlfriends and hung out with them at a tiny French bistro, while Tyler and George played the games set up on the street. She sat and chatted over escargot, a warm goat cheese salad with arugula and some muscles with leeks, paired with a glass of wine.

"So has anyone seen Stan lately?" It was Carla asking this, one of Caryssa's ski pals who met Stan at a rocking happy hour at her house.

Caryssa answered "Not in a while, our play-dates seem to have ceased with the kids getting older. But heard he finished studying Environmental Law and works bringing social responsibility into the corporate world. Each legal campaign he works on involves human rights around toxic chemicals used in the workplace or schools."

* * *

It was great getting Tyler out of the house and away from a computer, socializing with real people rather than some digital Pokémon.

The next day, she signed up for a writer's conference in the city about becoming a change agent through writing a book— *"Changing the World through Words."* What convinced her to sign up was the blurb on the brochure: "A book that changes the United States will change the world, because America is leading the world into the future."

When she read that, something clicked on inside her. *This was it.* This was the final piece in her puzzle. She knew it. And she had to follow that inspiration.

All those words on paper! Her tech writing had made a huge impact on the networked world before. Now she is trying her hand at being a novelist while doing marketing for the greater good. Her voice on paper could be amplified to the world through technology. A Mom's heart with a voice…"mum's the word!"

She didn't have to be a digital marketing guru for any company, a puppet master to corporacy. She could do digital-age e-books. Sell her words online and offline. This can be her *"online presence."*

"This is who I am," she thought, with deep satisfaction. "It's all good!"

With this new goal…she may not be sipping the finest champagne in a first class cabin on her way to climb the high tech corporate ladder of Silicon Valley, yet she felt was sipping from a sustainable soul.

As she shared her excitement about the conference with girlfriends, one of them asked "Can a book really change the world? There seems so many that have tried. Yet the games go on."

"I know, girlfriend," Caryssa said. "I know. But we have to at least try. Anyway I do. It's who I am."

She had reached a place of final acceptance. The digital craze that brought her to California was at least in part—the same thing keeping her high-tech career at a standstill today.

Tech Marketing had gone to the robots, buried under too much technology. Until she realized she could set her words on fire globally over that world of big data…*words* to try to shift culture and transform society. While at it, she found more fun part-time marketing outreach gigs connecting and building communities. Utilizing the digital marketing trend after all.

And those annoying "Breaking News" headlines flashing on TV screens playing out the deceiving shrill of our Capital's blind vengeance? She had learned to not only see through their debauched masks, but laugh at them.

The world is a beautiful place. Despite the monster lurking behind the masks.

The End … for now.
Thank you for reading.
T.L Mumley

ENJOY THE SEQUEL!

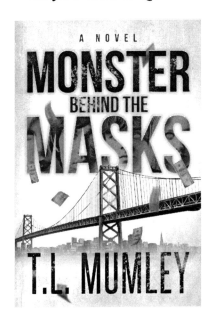

American politics is a crazy beast, performing in a three-ring circus that never goes out of style. It's been fifteen years since Caryssa left her fast-track Silicon Valley career; twelve since the tragic loss of Anna's daughters and subsequent murder of her art gallery security guard. But all efforts to let go of hidden political powers wreaking havoc on precious memories of their tender past, come back to haunt them—Leading directly into the path of the monster lurking in the shadows.

What is driving the monster behind the masks? A trail of clues is hidden within bloody symbolic messages on a dead dove found outside Anna's art gallery. Clues uncovering a secret society visible for all to see yet ingeniously disguised by ruling elites.

. . . And another dead dove was just found.

The story continues in Book #2
For Release Summer 2018

Excerpt from *MONSTER BEHIND THE MASKS*:

Chapter One,

January 2017

They all came. Pretend queens, kings, rooks and crooks—claiming to be selflessly fundraising. The place was packed, everyone dressed as either royalty or villains. Yet, there was no way to differentiate them, since the elite were criminals.

Everyone was attired in splendid, custom-made masks paired with extravagant costumes. The masks changed into menacing shapes and spoke in robotic voices. I couldn't understand a word. My thoughts zoomed in and out in a hazy netherworld of consciousness, spiraling in my psyche.

Coal black masks looking like Darth Vader, I half expected them to whip out lightsabers. In with the intergalactic masks were heavily gilded Venetian disguises passing by. People undercover for faceless multinational corporations and shady government operations. Hiding accountability and a violent brand image.

I wandered invisible myself behind mysterious black lace, through the elegant ballroom near the White House. The combination of fresh cut tobacco, leather and perfume cast off a sensual scent. I was not afraid, as I hid my own identity. I floated by the boldest of bankers, most prominent politicians, and ruthless leaders of the world.

I shouldn't be here. But who will know? I mingled like an unseen spy, a private eye. The good people came to enjoy the masked political theatre. Fools duped by the masquerade.

I strode with intent up to the most sinister of masks, and ripped it off. Down came the plaster and paint, the cardboard box covering the face. What I saw beneath the veneer shocked me. I couldn't help but gasp. What scared me most was— he knew my name.

"Hello Caryssa."

I awoke with a jerk, heart thundering in my chest. George lay beside me, sipping coffee. He sat the coffee cup on the nightstand before wrapping his arms around me. "Saving the world again in your dreams, babe?" I was drenched in perspiration, shaking out the dream, shedding the unpleasant feeling.

We snuggled. "Man, these dreams are happening more the older Tyler gets." I glanced outside our bedroom window at the blue-green bay and sparkling city. A light fog twined around the magnificent Golden Gate Bridge, compromising its visibility. God, I live surrounded with such beauty and peace.

George rolled his eyes. "Let me guess . . . killer robots and the human race forced to go live on a spaceship, fleeing the Mother Earth it destroyed?" He gave me a side glance, one eyebrow raised with the other curled down.

"Something along those lines. Only I was in D.C. at a masquerade fundraiser for 'the people.' Masks were blurring, cracking and talking in mechanical voices. I pulled off the darkest mask, an Emperor Palpatine look-alike—and saw my former boss's face."

**Visit my website at tlmumleybooks.com
to find out when second installment is available.**

About the Author

T.L. Mumley (born Teresa Lynn Sullivan) is a former senior marketing analyst in Silicon Valley, a mother, wife and happy homebody. She holds an A.S. in Fashion Merchandising from Lasell, a B.S. in Marketing from MCLA and studied towards an MBA from Northeastern. She is currently a Writer Coach for middle school students.

Fueled by dark chocolate and good red wine, she can be found skiing and hiking mountains, walking, writing or doing a downward facing dog while gardening.

Although she will always be a Bostonian at heart, she lives in the San Francisco Bay Area with her husband and son.

Visit her website at:
tlmumleybooks.com

CPSIA information can be obtained
at www.ICGtesting.com
Printed in the USA
LVOW11s2338110318
569497LV00002B/28/P